丛书总主编 / 白庚胜

顾问 / 喻遂生

主编 / 李晓亮

副主编 / 李真真

本书编委 / 和力民　曾小鹏　赵庆莲　付　梅　张江梅　韩　超

境外东巴经释义丛书

第一辑 · 海外馆藏洛克收录东巴经典释义

挽 歌

总主编 / 白庚胜　　编译 / 李晓亮

云南大学出版社

● 国家“十三五”少数民族语言文字出版规划项目 ●
● 民族文字出版专项资金资助项目 ●

图书在版编目（CIP）数据

挽歌 / 李晓亮编译. -- 昆明：云南大学出版社,2021
（境外东巴经释义丛书 / 白庚胜总主编. 第一辑.海外馆藏洛克收录东巴经典释义）
ISBN 978-7-5482-4188-1

Ⅰ. ①挽… Ⅱ. ①李… Ⅲ. ①纳西族－叙事诗－中国
Ⅳ. ①I222.7

中国版本图书馆CIP数据核字(2020)第218515号

策划编辑　蔡红华
　　　　　段　然
责任编辑　石　可
装帧设计　高　伟

境外东巴经释义丛书

第一辑 · 海外馆藏洛克收录东巴经典释义

挽　歌

WANGE

总主编 / 白庚胜　　编译 / 李晓亮

出版发行　云南大学出版社
印装　昆明理煜印务有限公司
开本　787mm×1092mm　1/16
印张　14
字数　320千字
版次　2021年5月第1版
印次　2021年5月第1次印刷
书号　ISBN 978-7-5482-4188-1
定价　115.00元

社址　云南省昆明市一二一大街182号
（云南大学东陆校区英华园内）
邮编　650091
电话　（0871）65033244　65033307
网址　http://www. ynup. com
E-mail　market@ynup. com

若发现本书有印装质量问题，请与印厂调换，联系电话：0871-64167045。

总 序

由我主编的“境外东巴经释义丛书·第一辑·海外馆藏洛克收录东巴经典释义”近日起就要由云南大学出版社陆续出版。

丛书第一辑四种的选目由西南大学汉语言文献研究所的李晓亮博士确定、整理、翻译，并经国内知名的东巴文研究专家喻遂生教授审定。我以为，以洛克收录东巴经典作为丛书发端，无论从任何一个角度讲，都是合适的。因为约瑟夫·洛克是当之无愧的国际东巴文化研究先驱者、旗手、权威、集大成者，已被尊之为“西方纳西学之父”。

这意味着，自此伊始，除了成规模的编著、译著、论著之外，大量散见于国际报纸杂志的纳西学、尤其是东巴文化研究的文章、手稿、论文，将会源源不断被收集、整理、翻译、汇编成册出版，以有助于“他山之石，可以攻玉”，进一步丰富、壮大纳西学资料的积累，促进一百多年来国际纳西文化研究成果的共享，强化纳西学研究的国际交流，不断完善纳西学学科体系，使之真正发展成为对中华文明、人类进步具有重要意义的国际显学。

与之相呼应的是，云南社科院东巴文化研究院早于多年前主持翻译出版了6卷本《哈佛燕京学社藏纳西东巴经书》；国家社科基金项目“世界记忆遗产东巴经典传承体系数字化国际共享平台建设研究”课题组，亦已完成对全球馆藏东巴经典的初步摸底、编目、数字化；贵州民族出版社经与美国国会图书馆多方联系，正在计划编目、提要出版该馆所藏3000多卷东巴经典文本。

对国内的有关资料及文献，从北京到纳西文化的故乡，相关工作亦迈开坚实的步伐。继云南人民出版社出版100卷本《纳西东巴古籍译注全籍》之后，我主编的“纳西学丛书”“纳西博士论文丛书”“纳西学历史文化资料丛书”“现当代纳西族作家作品选集丛书”等多种先后问世。另有杨林军先生等已经启动对国家档案馆中有关纳西族档案的全面清理；学苑出版社则已清点整理完国家图书馆收藏的数万件纳西族文物，并将很快推出首批成果。

立足于这些丰厚的学术基础之上，承接着各界朋友的援手，一个波澜壮阔的纳西学建设景象不再是海市蜃楼：纳西学研究院正式成立；《纳西学集刊》正式创刊；国际纳西学论坛正式诞生；丽江国际母系研究会正式建立；国际母系文化论坛行将举办；纳西学人才培养从本科生到研究生教育体制一应详备；每年数以百计的有关论文、论著、重大课题蜚声学苑，成为中华人文科学发展的有生力量。这一切都证明，自国际纳西学学会成立以来，坚持纳西学建设的基本方向、基本方针、基本方法、基本方略是正确的：立足本土、放眼世界，走纳西学建设的中国化道路；坚持国内外、族内外联合攻坚、共享成果；坚持田野作业为第一、资料积累为根本；坚持队伍育成、精英培养；坚持学科整体观照与分支析理相结合；坚持组织、教学、研究、出版、活动、交流共协进；坚持形而上与形而下的相映照；等等，永远是我始终不变的初心。

作为以上七大坚持的必然结果是，纳西学何其有幸，我们一次次沐浴在来自国家新闻出版署的阳光，尤其是将本丛书列为重大民族文化出版资助项目的关爱中；我们更感受到云南大学出版社的坚强助力——为了扶持滇云本土的地方文化、民族文化，他们不惜血本、积沙成塔，决定长期作战，与我们一起共筑文化长城，共创学术辉煌。

让我坚信不疑的是，随着全球性的开放日益扩大，我国的物质与精神实力不断强大，以及为适应中华文明伟大复兴的迫切需要，云南大学出版社承担起学术使命，他们有远大的建设精神家园的理想、他们有一支像殷永林总编辑和段然、石可编辑这样高质量的出版队伍，以这套丛书为代表的、高品位高质量的滇云文化出版大业将更前景无限。在此，我和我的民族、同仁对他们表示由衷的敬意、谢意，并充满热情的期待。

是为序。

白庚胜

2020 年 11 月于北京

序

纳西学研究，特别是纳西东巴文化研究，肇始于19世纪中晚期到我国西南地区探险、传教的西方人士，这决定了纳西学研究从一开始就是一门国际性的学问。我国的纳西学研究，一开始就受到西方学者的启发和影响。如方国瑜先生研究东巴文，就缘于1932年夏刘半农先生以法国人巴克《么些研究》相质询(《纳西象形文字谱·弁言》)；李霖灿先生1939年在昆明于古琴国手郑颖荪先生家中第一次看到东巴经，随后在沈从文先生家中见到一本洛克的东巴经译著，更提振了他研究东巴文的兴趣和决心（李霖灿《么些研究论文集》，第285页）。几十年过去了，国内外纳西学研究都取得了长足的进展和巨大的成绩。国内的纳西学研究，还后来居上，成为了研究的主体，其中一个重要的原因，就是认真学习和吸收了西方学者的理论、方法和成果。回顾纳西学发展的历史，我们对西方学者筚路蓝缕，开创奠基的功绩，怀有深深的敬意。

国内学者对学习和引进国外纳西学研究的成果是比较重视的，重要的译介成果有：白庚胜、杨福泉编译《国际东巴文化研究集萃》，刘宗岳等译洛克《中国西南古纳西王国》，和匠宇译洛克《纳西语英语百科辞典》上册，刘永青等译《纳西、摩梭民族志》，白庚胜译《日本纳西学论集》，白羲等编译《西方纳西学论集》，宋军、木艳娟译巴克《么些研究》，等等。白庚胜先生还有宏大的计划，由他和黄乃镇主编的《国际纳西学译丛》将陆续出版。尽管如此，也得承认，我们在这方面的工作还是做得很不够的。其表现一是翻译的数量仍然较少，如洛克的纳西学论著有19种，大部分都没有翻译，连《纳西语英语百科辞典》也只译了上册。二是对西方纳西学论著研究和使用得很不够。如我们现在做东巴文献字释，一般只追溯到傅懋勣先生的《丽江么些象形文“古事记”研究》(1948年)，但实际上洛克19世纪30年代译注东巴经时就采用了类似于字释的方式，而他的这些做法很少有人提及。三是对国外纳西学资料，包括经书、档案等，还缺乏全面的调查和清理，底数不清，情况不明，无法有效发挥其效用。如巴克在《么些研究》中刊布了几种东巴经的选页，并说“我们字典的一部分来自这份手稿”（中译本 74 页）。李晓亮通过法国学者米可博士从法国巴黎东方语言学院图书馆收藏的东巴经中找到了这几册经书，通过比勘，对巴克《么些研究》字表的材料来源，时间地域、取材方式、讹误原因等，就有了更深刻细致的认识。

纳西东巴文化虽然现在仍然以活态留存于世，理论上讲文化的基因会继续传承，但变异也是铁定的规律，现在的东巴文化肯定不会完全等同于历史上的东巴文化，西方学者记录东巴文化比国内学者早，这就凸显出早期西方纳西学论著的可贵。我曾见过一张洛克拍摄的马帮的照片，几十匹马一字排开，气势非凡。据记载，洛克出行时，除了有助手、保镖、厨师，连折叠桌椅和浴缸都是带上的。在那个年代，以西方人的财力和权势（很多是得到了官方、企业、宗教或学术团体的支持和资助的），再加上他们的敬业刻苦和科学精神，再加上那个时代东巴文化还没有受到政治的冲击而保留了较自然的生态，那个时候采集记录的东巴文化，自非中华人民共和国成立以后、改革开放以后的所见所闻可以相比。洛克说他收集了 8000 多册东巴经，他能把和华亭东巴带到昆明一住数年（和华亭日记说 53 个月）从容整理，能带着一众东巴到美国表演；看看网上哈佛所藏东巴经的照片，大多品相完好，书写精美，类别完整；其中的原因，不言自明。杨福泉先生在《西方纳西东巴文化研究述评》中说：“他（引按：洛克）在丽江进行研究工作期间，很多知识渊博的大东巴仍健在，他对帮助自己工作的东巴的筛选也很慎重，经反复考察后才任用，因此，他对东巴教仪式和经书的翻译和解释中保留了很多珍贵的资料，有许多是后世年青的东巴已解释不清楚的……洛克的论著中还有多种关于纳西族社会历史、宗教活动的调查报告，积累了大量现在已很难获得的民族学资料。”不同时期的调查材料都有它的价值，但我们得承认，前人“老照片”所记录的东西，很多事过境迁，不可再得，已是唯一的存在，值得我们特别珍视。新时代高水平的纳西学研究，应立足于对中西纳西学历史成果的总结和吸收，加大翻译引进的力度，认真学习鉴别，取其所长，用到研究中去，是势在必行的事情。

云南大学出版社策划的“境外东巴经释义丛书 第一辑 · 海外馆藏洛克收录东巴经典释义”，是“十三五”国家重点图书出版项目，是很有学术价值和社会意义的项目。现在李晓亮博士承担的洛克东巴经译注4种的中译本即将出版，可喜可贺！晓亮博士本科学习英语专业，硕士和博士从我学习东巴文，也许是专业出身和学识特长的缘故，对西方纳西学研究情有独钟。硕士论文为《洛克〈纳西语英语百科辞典〉研究》，博士论文为《西方纳西学史研究（1867—1972）》，近年又到美国做访问学者，多次访问哈佛燕京图书馆、阿诺德植物园档案馆、怀德纳图书馆，披阅收集洛克的日记、书信、手稿等档案材料。事须得人，由晓亮来做洛克著作的翻译，是非常合适的。粗粗看了一下译稿，晓亮在尊重原著的基础上也有一些创新，如在洛克音标下加注通行的国际音标，在音标下加注汉语对译，以便于读者阅读。在《鲁般鲁饶》下卷，补出了哈佛所藏经书原本的彩图，与洛克摹本相得益彰，可增加读者对经书的感性认识。对原文中出现的讹误或者某些观点性的错误，也以按语的形式加以纠正等。

感谢晓亮博士为纳西学做出的贡献和付出的辛劳！任重道远，希望晓亮再接再厉，译出更多的论著，特别是涉及纳西学研究基础的关于东巴文献、东巴文字词研究的论著，包括洛克《纳西语英语百科辞典》下册。

是为序。

喻遂生

2020年10月于重庆

目 录

前　言

《挽歌》又名《梦咨》（纳西语音译）。纳西族老人去世后，要举行开丧（洛克译作日美仪式）仪式，仪式要举行三天，在第一、二天晚上唱挽歌，由东巴在死者灵前领唱，村里的长辈则与东巴相应和。据和志武先生的《东巴经典选译·梦咨（挽歌）》①介绍：《挽歌》分为三大部分，即送丧挽歌、养马卖马（又名女贵族衰老记）和买卖寿岁（又名男贵族衰老记）。送丧挽歌又分为出处来历、治办丧礼、说老议事、送丧之歌、丧舞之词和迎受福泽六个部分。养马卖马只限于妇女死时唱，买卖寿岁只限于男人死时唱。这里翻译的经书只有送丧挽歌和买卖寿岁的内容，因此是在男死者的葬礼上使用的。

洛克使用的底本是自己搜集的，现藏在美国哈佛大学燕京图书馆，洛克编号为2760朱宝田编号为K37。经书一共20页，本色构皮纸线订册页装，墨书页面10×31cm，无封面首页残损，抄写者不明。洛克在《中国西南纳西族的日美丧仪》中所使用的是重抄本，与原文基本相同。下图是洛克的书签。

① 和志武:《东巴经典选译》，云南人民出版社 1994 年版第 234—246 页。

二、关于洛克的译本

洛克的译本一共分为四个部分：1.经书重抄本；2.经文的标音；3.句译；4.对于经文字词的说解。以下是洛克译本的样张。

1.经书重抄本

^{3}MUN̲ ^{2}NDZĔR ^{3}Ä ^{1}LÄ ^{2}DZHU

First Page:

Rubr. 1: Ō! ^{1}Ä-^{1}ssĭ ^{3}dta ^{1}lä ^{2}dzhu
Rubr. 2: ^{2}Wùa-^{1}ssĭ ^{3}dta ^{1}lä ^{2}dzhu
Rubr. 3: ^{2}Dzhu ^{2}t'u ^{2}gkv ^{2}muàn̲ ^{3}shou, ^{2}Dzhu ^{1}dzo ^{3}shou ^{2}muàn̲ ^{2}nyi
Rubr. 4: ^{2}Dzhu ^{3}bbŭe ^{2}gkv ^{2}muàn̲ ^{3}shou
Rubr. 5: ^{2}Dzhu ^{1}dzo ^{2}bä ^{2}muàn̲ ^{2}nyi
Rubr. 6: ^{2}Ä-^{1}ts'ä ^{2}dzī ^{2}muàn̲ ^{2}dzhu
Rubr. 7: ^{2}Dzhu ^{2}t'u ^{2}Mùan̲-^{3}llü-^{1}ssu-^{1}lo-^{2}k'o ^{2}nnü ^{2}t'u
Rubr. 8: ^{2}Dzhu ^{3}bbŭe ^{2}Mùan̲-^{3}llü-^{1}ssu-^{1}lo-^{2}k'o ^{2}nnü ^{3}bbŭe
Rubr. 9: ^{2}Mùan̲-^{3}llü-^{1}ssu-^{1}lo-^{2}k'o, ^{2}zo ^{2}nnü ^{2}gkv ^{3}ssu ^{1}ssä
Rubr. 10: ^{2}Ä-^{1}khi ^{2}Ndaw-^{1}ssu ^{2}dzhu, ^{2}Dzhu ^{3}bbŭe ^{2}gkv ^{1}lä ^{2}bä.

2.经文的标音

First Page:

1) Ō! The bitterness (experienced) by the father we will relate
2) The father's bitterness we will again relate
3) If one does not relate of the origin of bitterness then one cannot speak about it
4) One must relate of the origin of bitterness
5) Or about bitterness one must not speak
6) In the beginning of things man knew no bitterness
7) Bitterness originated at ^{2}Mùan̲-^{3}llü-^{1}ssu-^{1}lo-^{2}k'o
8) At ^{2}Mùan̲-^{3}llü-^{1}ssu-^{1}lo-^{2}k'o it was that bitterness first came forth
9) From ^{2}Mùan̲-^{3}llü-^{1}ssu-^{1}lo-^{2}k'o it was that the son first led bitterness
10) At ^{2}Ndaw-^{1}ssu-^{2}dzhu of ^{2}Ä-^{1}khi bitterness first originated.

3.句译

Explanation of text

Page 1

Rubr. 1: The first symbol is that of the ^{2}dto-^{1}mba in charge of the funeral; he is called ^{2}Lo-^{1}ch'ung-^{2}ndaw-^{1}khü, the name is not translatable, it is the official designation of such a ^{2}dto-^{1}mba, he holds in his hand the funeral wand called ^{3}Müen̲-^{1}t'u or bamboo staff, the upper part of which is of especial design (1).

4.字词的解说

三、洛克音标

洛克音标是洛克在记录纳西语时发明的一套标音系统，绝大部分符号源自拉丁字母。洛克不是语音学家，我们在他的论著中没有发现他归纳的纳西语音系。洛克在《纳西语英语百科辞典》中对他记录的纳西语方言做了简单说明。

辞典中所使用的方言是丽江地区居民所说的方言，不是丽江城里（译者按，即大研镇）的方言，因为城里人发不出纳西语的某些复合音，而且丽江城居民的语言中已掺杂了汉语，就像生活在西藏与丽江交界地区的纳西族说话时掺杂了藏语一样。辞典所选择的方言是金沙江河谷中丽江北部和西部村子中所说的纳西语。①

关于东巴文记录的纳西语方言，和志武先生曾指出："东巴经语言的音位系统，基本上与西部方言口语一致，各地东巴诵经时均按各自操土语读音，所不同的是：大研镇土语只有一套浊辅音，其他土语，如维西、香格里拉的白地、丽江的塔城、鲁甸、宝山等广大地区，则分为纯浊辅音和鼻冠浊辅音两套；再者，宝山土语少 zz、rh、f 三个辅音音位。"② 根据洛克的描述，我们基本可以判断洛克音标记录的是纳西族西部方言，并且带有鼻冠浊辅音。

洛克在《纳西语英语百科辞典》中对他使用的音标也作了说明。

辞典中并没有使用国际音标记录纳西语，但是有一个我的音标与国际音标的对照表。我们认为国际语音学会所采用的符号并不能完全准确地记录纳西语中的某些复合音，所以必须发明一些新的符号。另外，对于其他语种的人来说，纳西语中的某些音是很难发的，而且仅根据国际语音学会所用的字母把纳西语

① Rock J . A Na-khi-English encyclopedic dictionary. Istituto italiano per il Medio ed Estremo Oriente, 1963, ppXXVI.

② 和志武：《纳西东巴文化》，吉林教育出版社，1989 年，第 151 页。

音完全正确地标出来是不可能的。[1]。

洛克认为，国际音标的符号不足以记录纳西语，所以发明了一些新的符号。虽然洛克自己制定了《纳西语洛克音标与国际语音学会音标对照表》，但是对于一般读者来说，认读洛克音标难度依然很大。在洛克的论著《纳西族的纳迦崇拜及其相关仪式》（简称《纳》）第 21 页、《东巴教教主东巴什罗的来历》（简称《东》）第 50 页都有《纳西语单词的发音说明》。下面我们结合洛克的说明解读一下洛克音标的实际读音。

（一）元音

1. 单元音

a,《纳》: a，后低元音。例词，father。《东》: a，发音与英语中的 father 相同。

按: father 中的 a 发 [ɑ:]，后低不圆唇长元音。与《对照表》中的 [ɑ] 发音部位和方法相同，区别在于长短音。

ă,《纳》: ă,（发音部位）同 a，短促。例词,（德语）hat。《东》: ă，音很短，像英语中的 harbour。

按: 根据《纳》的描述，ă 应发 [ɑ]，后低不圆唇元音。比 a 短促。但是例词 hat 中 a 发 [æ]，前中低不圆唇元音。ɑ 在中 harbour 发 [ɑ:]。[ɑ:] 是长音，与描述不符。《对照表》中 ă 对应的是 [a]，前低不圆唇元音。这三者的描述不统一。

‘a,《纳》: ‘a，低后元音，伴随着挤喉，像阿拉伯语中的 ‘asin。《东》: ‘a，相当于阿拉伯语的 ‘Ain，一个喉音，当发 a 的时候，下颚猛然向下。

---

① Rock J . A Na-khi-English encyclopedic dictionary. Istituto italiano per il Medio ed Estremo Oriente, 1963, ppXXV.

按：根据描述，ʻa 应发 [ʕa]。ʻasin 中 ʻa 发 [ʕ]，低后挤喉元音。《对照表》中 ʻa 也对应 [ʕ]。

ä，《纳》：ä，前中元音。例词，（德语）Häfen。《东》：ä 像德语元音 ä。

按：根据《纳》的描述，ä 应该发 [ɜ]，不圆唇中元音。Häfen 中的 ä 发 [ɛ]，前中低不圆唇元音。又 ä 在德语中发 [ɛ]。《对照表》中 ä 对应 [ɛ]。我们认为，ä 应该介于 [ɜ] 和 [ɛ] 之间。

aw，《纳》：aw，半低后圆唇元音。例词，awe。《东》：aw 的读音像 law 中的 aw。

按：根据描述，aw 发 [ɔ]。aw 在 awe 中发 [ɔː]，在 law 中发 [ɔː]。《对照表》中 aw 对应 [ɔ]。因此，aw 发 [ɔ] 或 [ɔː]。

e，《纳》：e，前半高元音。例词，egg。

按：根据描述，e 发 [e]，前半高不圆唇元音。e 在 egg 中读 [e]。《对照表》中 e 对应 [e]。

ĕr，卷舌，中元音，带轻微喉阻碍。

按：根据描述，ĕr 发 [ʕɚ]，卷舌，央元音，挤喉音。《对照表》中 ĕr 对应 [eɹ]。[ɹ] 发音方法是：舌尖向上微触上齿龈，一般听不见摩擦。

erh，《纳》：erh，用于拼写与 ĕr 同音的汉语借词。

按：《对照表》中 erh 对应汉语中同音的音节。根据描述，erh 与 ĕr 相同，发 [ʕɚ]。

i，《纳》：i，高前元音。例词，police。

按：根据描述，i 发 [i]，前高不圆唇元音。i 在 police 中读 [i]。《东》：像德语中 i 的发音。德语中 i 发 [i] 或 [iː]。《对照表》中 i 对应 [i]。

ī，《纳》：ī，高前长元音。

按：根据描述，ī 发 [iː]，高前长元音。《对照表》中 ī 对应 [iː]。

ĭ，《纳》：ĭ，前高元音，稍集中。ˇ 表示声调。

按：根据描述，ĭ 发 [ĭ]，前高元音。《对照表》中 ĭ 对应 [ĭ]。

ō，《纳》：ō，半高后圆唇元音。例词，德语 sohn。《东》：ō，音从深喉发出，圆唇。

按：根据描述，ō 发 [o]，半高后圆唇元音。oh 在 sohn 中读 [oː]。《对照表》中 ō 对应 [oː]。

ŏ，《纳》：ŏ，后元音，短促。

按：根据描述，ŏ 可能发 [o] 或者 [ɔ]。《对照表》中 ŏ 对应 [ɔ]。

ö，《纳》：ö，半高前元音。例词，德语 söhne。《东》：ö，音同德语中的元音 ö。

按：根据描述，ö 发 [ø]，中高前圆唇元音。德语中 ö 发 [œ]，中低前圆唇元音。ö 在 söhne 中也发 [œ]。《对照表》中 ö 对应 [œ]。

u，《纳》：u，后高圆唇元音。例词，rude。《东》：u，像 oo 在英语 food 的发音。

按：根据描述，u 发 [u]，后高圆唇元音。u 在 rude 中读 [uː]。oo 在 food 中读 [uː]。《对照表》中 u 对应 [uː]。

ŭ，《纳》：ŭ，跟 u 一样，唇稍微不圆，短促。

按：根据描述，ŭ 发 [ɯ]，后高不圆唇元音。《对照表》中 ŭ 对应 [ʌ]，中低不圆唇元音。

ü，《纳》：ü，高前元音，但是在 gh，kh，ḳh，ndd，ll，gg 和 ngg 之后，后不圆唇元音。例词，德语 Lüge。

按：根据描述，ü 一般发 [y]，前高圆唇元音。在 gh，kh，ḳh，ndd，ll，

gg，和 ngg 之后发 [ɯ]，后高不圆唇元音。ü 在 Lüge 中发 [y]。《对照表》中 ü 对应 [y]。

y，《纳》：y，腭音，浊，持续。例词，yes。《东》：y，像 y 在 yard 中的发音。

按：根据描述，y 发 [j]，舌面中，浊，半元音。y 在 yard 中读 [j]。《对照表》中 y 对应 [j]。

w，《纳》：w，双唇，浊，持续。例词，way。《东》：w，像英语中的 w。

按：根据描述，w 发 [w]，双唇，浊，半元音。w 在 way 中读 [w]。《对照表》中 w 对应 [w]。

2. 复合元音

oa，《纳》：oa，前半低复合元音，短促。例词，board。

按：根据描述，oa 发 [o͡a]，复合元音。oa 在 board 中读 [o]。《对照表》中 oa 对应 [o͡a]。

ou，《纳》：ou，后圆唇复合元音。例词，no。

按：根据描述，ou 发 [o͡u]。o 在 no 中读 [əu]。《对照表》中 ou 对应 [o͡u]。

ùan，《纳》：ùan，（在 m 后）突出 u，并参看 n 的描述。

按：《对照表》中 ùan 对应 [ũaṉ]。

uàn，《纳》：uàn，与 ùan 同，突出 a，并参看 n 的描述。

按：《对照表》中 ùan 对应 [uàṉ]。

ŭe，《纳》：ŭe，（在唇音后）复合音包括后高元音，不圆唇，跟在中高元音后（鼻唇音后相同，参看 n 的描述）。

按：《对照表》中 ŭe 对应 [u͡e̪]。

wùa，《纳》：wùa，特殊的音节，突出 u，集中在 a。《东》：wua，ua 快速的拼读在一起，听起来像一个音。

（二）辅音

b，《纳》：b，双唇，浊塞音。例词，be。

按：根据描述，b 发 [b]，双唇，浊塞音。b 在 be 中发 [b]。《对照表》中 b 对应 [b]。

bb，《纳》：bb，双唇，浊塞音，强长音，例如 bbū 是长音，bb，dd，ff，gg，ll，nn 都是长音，可以与单个的 b，d 比较。

按：根据描述，bb 发 [bb]，双唇，浊塞长音。《东》：bb 是一个强化的 b，闭唇，然后发爆破音。《对照表》中 bb 对应 [bb]。

bp，《纳》：bp，双唇，清，不送气，强塞音。《东》：bp 既不是发软音的 b，也不是发硬音的 p，而是介于两者之间。

按：根据《纳》的描述，bp 发 [p]，双唇，清塞音。《对照表》中 bp 对应 [p]。

p'，《纳》：p'，双唇，送气，清塞强音。

按：根据描述，p' 发 [ph]，双唇，送气，清塞音。《对照表》中 p' 对应 [p']。

ff，《纳》：ff，用在词的开头，唇齿，清擦音，强长音。

按：根据描述，ff 发 [ff]，唇齿，清擦音，长音。《对照表》中 ff 对应 [ff]。

v，《纳》：v，唇齿，浊，摩擦音，位置在 g，gk，k'，dd，nd，dt，l 之后。

按：根据描述，v 发 [v]，唇齿，浊擦音。《对照表》中 v 对应 [v]。

d，《纳》：d，齿阻碍，浊塞音。例词，day。

按：根据描述，d 发 [d]，舌尖中，不送气，浊塞音。d 在 day 中发 [d]。《对照表》中 d 对应 [d]。

dd，《纳》：dd，齿阻碍，浊塞强长音。《东》：dd，就像在 ddü 中的读音。

口闭合或者接近闭合，舌头抵住上齿。

按：根据《纳》的描述，dd 发 [dd]，舌尖中，不送气，浊塞长音。根据《东》的描述，dd 发 [ɖ]。《对照表》中 d 对应 [ɖ]，卷舌，不送气，浊塞音。

dt，《纳》：dt，齿音，清塞强音。《东》：dt，就像在 dtü 中的读音。dt 既不是一个 d 也不是一个 t。但也不完全是介于 d 和 t 之间。口稍微张开，舌头抵住上齿。这里的 ü 像德语中的元音 ü，而 ü 在 dd 之后声音发不清楚。

按：根据描述，dt 发 [ʈ]，卷舌，不送气，清塞音。《对照表》中 dt 对应 [ʈ]。

t'，《纳》：t'，齿，送气，清塞强音。

按：根据描述，t' 发 [th]，舌尖中，送气，清塞音。《对照表》中 t' 对应 [t']。

l，《纳》：l，浊，后持续。例词，low。

按：根据描述，l 发 [l]，舌尖中，浊边音。l 在 low 读 [l]。《对照表》中 l 对应 [l]。

ll，《纳》：ll，浊，侧持续，强长音。《东》：ll，闭口，舌头稍抵住上齿，它只在元音 ü 之前，后面的元音短且模糊。

按：根据描述，ll 发 [ll]，舌尖中，浊边长音。《对照表》中 ll 比 l 厚。

lv，《纳》：lv，前面的 l 加上音节 v。《东》：lv，常发 lu 的音，其中 l 很短，所以用 v。

m，《纳》：m，双唇，鼻音，可以独立使用，也可以跟 b 或 bb 结合构成 mb，mbb。例词，mother。

按：根据描述，m 发 [m]，双唇，清鼻音。也可以与 b 结合，表示鼻冠音 [mb]。m 在 mother 读 [m]。《对照表》中 m 对应 [m]。

n，《纳》：n，齿，鼻音，可以独立使用，也可以跟 d 或 dd 结合构成 nd，ndd。例词，no。

按：根据描述，n 发 [n]，舌尖中，浊鼻音。也可以与 b 结合，表示鼻冠音 [nd]。n 在 no 读 [n]。《对照表》中 n 对应 [n]。

n̠，《纳》：n̠，放在词尾，鼻化前面的元音。《东》：n̠，经常出现在词尾，鼻化前面的元音。口几乎闭合，音从鼻腔发出，舌头在上唇下面。国际音标中用 ˜ 表示鼻化。

按：《对照表》中 n̠ 不发音，鼻化元音。

ng，《纳》：ng，软腭，鼻音，本来是独立的，例如在 ng'a 中，n 和 g 的发音是分开的；在 n͡go 中，它们的发音又是合在一起的。或者再加上 g 构成复合音 ngg；ng 如果放在词尾，表示鼻化，如 chung。例词，long。

按：根据描述，ng 在词头发 [ŋg]，在词尾发 [ŋ]。ng 在 long 中读 [ŋ]。《对照表》中 n͡g 在音节开头，发音像 nasal。ng 对应 [ŋ]，在音节的最前或最后面。

nn，《纳》：nn，齿，鼻音，强长音。《东》：nn，就像德语中的两个 n 发的音。口几乎闭合，舌尖抵住上齿，然后通过鼻腔发音。

按：根据描述，nn 在词头发 [nn]，舌尖中，浊鼻音，长音。《对照表》中 nn 对应 [nn]。

nv，《纳》：nv，鼻化前面的音节 v。《东》：nv，n 鼻音化严重，几乎发不出来，v 在元音中是很软的，好像 v 后面跟着另一个 n。

按：根据描述，nv 发 [ṽ]。《对照表》中 nv 对应 [nv]，此符号与国际音标中的鼻化符号不符。

ch，《纳》：ch，齿龈，清，不送气，破擦音。《东》：ch 像英语中的字母组合 ch 的发音。英语中 ch 发 [ʧ]。

按：根据描述，ch 发 [ʧ]，舌叶，清塞擦音。《对照表》中 ch 对应 [ʧ]。

ch'，《纳》：ch'，齿龈，清，送气，破擦音。

按：根据描述，ch’发 [ʧ]，舌叶，送气，清塞擦音。《对照表》中 ch’对应 [ʧ]。

ds’，《纳》：ds’，齿音，送气，清破擦音。

按：根据描述，ds’发 [dsh]。[d] 是浊塞音，[s] 是清擦音。两者是不能相拼的。《对照表》中 ds’对应 [ds’]。

dz，《纳》：dz，齿音，浊破擦音。例词，adze。

按：根据描述，dz 读 [ʣ]，舌尖前，浊塞擦音。dz 在 adze 读 [ʣ]。《对照表》中 dz 对应 [ʔ]。

dsh，按：《对照表》中 dsh 对应 [dʃ]。[d] 是浊塞音，[ʃ] 是清擦音。一清一浊不能组合在一起。因此 dsh 发 [tʂ] 或 [dʐ]。

g，《纳》：g，软腭，浊塞音。例词，go。

按：根据描述，g 发 [g]，舌根，浊塞音。g 在 go 中读 [g]。《对照表》中 g 对应 [g]。

gg，《纳》：gg，软腭，浊强长塞音。

按：根据描述，gg 发 [gg]，舌根，浊塞音。《对照表》中 gg 对应 [gg]。

gh，《纳》：gh，小舌（或喉）摩擦，浊辅音，像法语的小舌颤音或阿拉伯语 ghain。《东》：gh，是阿拉伯语 Ghain 中 gh 的发音，软元音，被称为用小舌颤音发 r。

按：根据描述，gh 发 [ʀ]，小舌颤音。gh 在 Ghain 中读 [ɣ]，舌面后浊擦音。《对照表》中 gh 对应 [ʁ]，舌根浊擦音。

gk，《纳》：gk，软腭，清强塞音。《东》：gk 既不是软音 g，也不是硬音 k，而是介于两者之间。

按：根据描述，gk 发 [k]，只是该音比 [k] 要强，偏浊。《对照表》中 gk 对

应 [k]。

gkv,《东》: gkv, 口闭合, 舌头抵住下齿。v 像在 vow 中的发音。

h,《纳》: h, 喉, 清擦音。

按: 根据描述, h 发 [h], 喉, 清擦音。《对照表》中 h 对应 [h]。

k’,《纳》: k’, 软腭, 送气, 清塞音, 强音。

按: 根据描述, k’ 发 [kh], 舌面后, 送气, 清塞音。《东》: k’, 送气的 k。《对照表》中 k’ 对应 [k’]。

ḳh,《纳》: kh, 软腭, 清摩擦音。例词, 德语 ach。《东》: kh, 德语中字母组合 ch 的音, 如同在 ich 中发的音。德语中 ach 发 [x]。

按: 根据的描述, kh 发 [x], 舌面后, 清擦音。ch 在 ach 中读 [x]。《对照表》中 kh 对应 [x]。

kh,《纳》: kh, 腭音, 清摩擦音。例词, 德语 ich。

按: 根据描述, kh 发 [ç], 舌面中, 清擦音。ch 在 ich 读 [ç]。《对照表》kh 对应 [ç]。

r,《纳》: r, 参见 ĕr。《东》: r, 像英语中的 r, 放在词尾的辅音, 比如 her。r 在 her 中是弱摩擦。

按: 根据描述, r 不出现在词头, 只出现在词尾, 发 [ɹ], 发音方法是: 舌尖向上微触上齿龈, 一般听不见摩擦。

s,《纳》: s, 齿音, 清, 摩擦强音。例词, sister。

按: 根据描述, s 发 [s], 舌尖前, 清擦音。s 在 sister 中也读 [s]。

ss,《纳》: ss, 齿音, 清, 摩擦, 强长音。例词, 德语 β。《东》: ss, 像德语中的 β 或者 ss。

按: 根据描述, ss 比 s 音长, 应发 [ss]。德语中的 ss 和 β 都读 [s]。《对照表》中 ss 对应 [s]。

sh,《纳》: sh，齿槽，清摩擦音。例词，shou。《东》: sh，就像 shelf 中 sh 的发音。

按: 根据描述，sh 发 [ʃ]，舌叶，清擦音。sh 在 shelf 和 she 中读 [ʃ]。《对照表》中 sh 对应 [ʃ]。

ts,《纳》: ts，齿，不送气，清塞擦音。

按: 根据描述，ts 发 [ts]，舌尖前，不送气，清塞擦音。《对照表》中 ts 对应的国际音标符号不识。

ts',《纳》: 齿，送气，清塞擦强音。

按: 根据描述，ts' 发 [tsh]，舌尖前，不送气，清塞擦音。《对照表》中 ts' 对应的国际音标符号不识。

sz,《纳》: sz，齿，摩擦，强长音（或者后面跟着 ĕr）。《东》: sz，像蜜蜂嗡嗡的声音。sz（er），er 几乎是听不到的。就像是 ir 在 sir 中的发音。

按: 根据描述，sz 与 [z] 相近，舌尖前，浊擦音。《对照表》sz 对应 [z]。

z,《纳》: z，如同 z 在英语中的发音。z 在英语中读 [z]，舌尖前，浊擦音。

zh,《纳》: zh，齿槽，浊，摩擦音。例词，法语 je。《东》: zh，像法语中的 je。

按: 根据描述，zh 发 [ʒ]，舌叶，浊擦音。j 在 je 读 [ʒ]。《对照表》中 zh 对应 [ʒ]，舌叶，浊擦音。

以上是洛克对他使用音标的发音说明，这应该比较准确地描写出洛克所记录的纳西语音，但是在洛克所译的东巴经中，洛克经常把同一个词用不同的音标记录，标准前后不统一。如果我们按照上述标准将洛克音标转写成国际音标，读者依然很难读懂。我们在研究中发现，洛克音标与方国瑜先生在《纳西象形文字谱》中使用的音标是可以相互转换的，只是两者记录的纳西语方言土语不同。考虑到《纳西象形文字谱》中的音系一般读者比较容易理解，于是我们以《纳西象形文字谱》的音系为基础，将洛克音标转写成国际音标，但又考虑到洛克记录的纳西语音是带鼻冠音的，在该加鼻冠音的地方加上鼻冠音。需要说明的是，这种转写并不太严谨，只是为了方便读者阅读。关于洛克音标的研究也可以参考法国学者麦沛德、米可和中国学者和学光等人合著的《骆克的纳西语英语百科辞典拼音系统对照国际音标》[①]。本书的具体转写如下。

表 1 韵母转写表

<table>
<tr><th>洛克音标</th><th>《纳西象形文字谱》</th><th>本书音标</th></tr>
<tr><td>a</td><td>ɑ/æ</td><td>a/æ</td></tr>
<tr><td>aw</td><td>ɑ</td><td>ɑ</td></tr>
<tr><td>‘a</td><td>æ</td><td rowspan="2">æ</td></tr>
<tr><td>aṉ</td><td>æ</td></tr>
<tr><td>ä</td><td>ɑ/ə</td><td>ɑ/ə</td></tr>
<tr><td>ā</td><td>ə</td><td>ə</td></tr>
<tr><td>er</td><td>ər</td><td rowspan="4">ər</td></tr>
<tr><td>ĕr</td><td>ər</td></tr>
<tr><td>ĕrh</td><td>ər</td></tr>
<tr><td>ăr</td><td>ər</td></tr>
<tr><td>oa</td><td>ə</td><td>ə/ua</td></tr>
<tr><td>ou</td><td>ə</td><td>ə</td></tr>
<tr><td>i</td><td>i/ʅ/</td><td>i/ʅ/ʅ</td></tr>
<tr><td>yi</td><td>i</td><td>i</td></tr>
</table>

① Michailovsky, B. and A. Michaud. “Syllabic inventory of a Western Naxi dialect, and correspondence with Joseph F. Rock’s transcriptions.” Cahiers de linguistique - Asie Orientale, 2006, 35(1): 3-21.

续上表：

<table>
<tr><th>洛克音标</th><th>《纳西象形文字谱》</th><th>本书音标</th></tr>
<tr><td>ĭ</td><td>ʅ</td><td>ʅ</td></tr>
<tr><td>ī</td><td>i</td><td>i</td></tr>
<tr><td>iu</td><td>iə</td><td>iə</td></tr>
<tr><td>o</td><td>o</td><td rowspan="3">o</td></tr>
<tr><td>ō</td><td>o</td></tr>
<tr><td>ŏ</td><td>o</td></tr>
<tr><td>ö</td><td>y/ɯ</td><td>y/ɯ</td></tr>
<tr><td>u</td><td>u/i/ʅ</td><td rowspan="2">u/v</td></tr>
<tr><td>ung</td><td>u</td></tr>
<tr><td>ü</td><td>ɯ/y</td><td>ɯ/y</td></tr>
<tr><td>e</td><td>e</td><td>e</td></tr>
<tr><td>v</td><td>v</td><td rowspan="3">v</td></tr>
<tr><td>vu</td><td>v</td></tr>
<tr><td>ŭ</td><td>v</td></tr>
<tr><td>un̠</td><td>u</td><td>u/o</td></tr>
<tr><td>ùen̠</td><td>ɯ</td><td rowspan="2">ɯ/ə</td></tr>
<tr><td>ùan̠</td><td>ɯ/ə</td></tr>
<tr><td>wuo</td><td>uo</td><td>uo</td></tr>
<tr><td>wua</td><td>uɑ</td><td>ua</td></tr>
<tr><td>wu</td><td>u</td><td>u</td></tr>
<tr><td>yu</td><td>iə</td><td>iə</td></tr>
<tr><td>yü</td><td>y</td><td>y</td></tr>
<tr><td>ŭe</td><td>ɯ/y</td><td>ɯ/y</td></tr>
<tr><td>ghügh</td><td>ɯ</td><td>ɯ</td></tr>
</table>

表 1　声母转写表

洛克音标	《纳西象形文字谱》	声母
b	b	b
bb	b/p	b/p
bp	p	p/b
mb	b	mb
mbb	b	
p’	p’	ph
pp’	p’	
m	m	m
f	f	f
ff	f	
ds	ʦ	ʦ
dz	ʦ/ʥ	ʦ/ʥ
ts’	ʦ’	ʦh
dz	ʥ	ʥ
ndz	ʥ	nʥ
ss	s	s
sz	z/s	z/s
z	z	z
d	d	d
dd	d	
nd	d	nd
ndd	d	

续上表：

<table>
<tr><th>洛克音标</th><th>《纳西象形文字谱》</th><th>声母</th></tr>
<tr><td>t’</td><td>t’</td><td>th</td></tr>
<tr><td>dt</td><td>t</td><td>t</td></tr>
<tr><td>n</td><td>n/ŋ</td><td>n/ŋ</td></tr>
<tr><td>nn</td><td>n</td><td>n</td></tr>
<tr><td>l</td><td>l</td><td rowspan="2">l</td></tr>
<tr><td>ll</td><td>l</td></tr>
<tr><td>dsh</td><td>tʂ</td><td rowspan="2">tʂ</td></tr>
<tr><td>ch</td><td>tʂ</td></tr>
<tr><td>ch’</td><td>tʂ’</td><td>tʂh</td></tr>
<tr><td>dzh</td><td>dʐ</td><td>dʐ</td></tr>
<tr><td>nds</td><td>dʑ</td><td>ndʑ</td></tr>
<tr><td>ndsh</td><td>dʐ</td><td rowspan="2">ndʐ</td></tr>
<tr><td>ndzh</td><td>dʐ</td></tr>
<tr><td>sh</td><td>ʂ</td><td>ʂ</td></tr>
<tr><td>zh</td><td>ʐ</td><td>ʐ</td></tr>
<tr><td>ny</td><td>ȵ</td><td>ȵ</td></tr>
<tr><td>t’gkh</td><td>tɕ’</td><td>tɕh</td></tr>
<tr><td>tgk</td><td>tɕ</td><td rowspan="2">tɕ</td></tr>
<tr><td>dgk</td><td>tɕ</td></tr>
<tr><td>gy</td><td>dʑ</td><td>dʑ</td></tr>
<tr><td>dgy</td><td>dʑ/tɕ</td><td>dʑ/tɕ</td></tr>
</table>

续上表：

洛克音标	《纳西象形文字谱》	声母
kh	ɕ	ɕ
ndgy	dʑ	ndʑ
gg	g	g
gk	k	k
k’	k’	kh
ng	g	ŋg
h	h	h
ḳh	h	

纳西语的声调共有四声，洛克用数字 1、2、3、4 标在词的左上方。第一声为低降调，第二声为平调，第三声为高短调，使用这三个声调的词是纯粹的纳西语词。第四声为低升调。《纳西象形文字谱》采用的是五度标音法：21（低调）、33（中调）、55（高调）、24（低升调）。《纳西象形文字谱》与洛克音标所使用的声调一致，所以本书将洛克的声调转化为五度标音法的调值。

表 3　声调转写表

洛克音标	《纳西象形文字谱》	本书声调
1	21	21
2	33	33
3	55	55
4	24	24

洛克音标声韵配合表

韵 / 声	a	ā	ă	ʻa	ăr	an̲	aw	ä	e	ĕr	erh	i	ı	ī	ĭ	o	ō	ŏ	ö	oa	ou	on̲	iu	u	ŭ	ū	ü	ŭe	un̲	yu	yo	yi	ye	yü	wua	wue	wuo	ung	uàn̲	ùan̲	ŭe	ùen̲	uèn̲	v	vu	0
b	√			√			√	√				√							√	√			√	√		√																				
bb										√															√	√															√					
mb	√			√			√	√	√	√		√							√					√																						
mbb																									√																√					
bp	√							√				√				√			√				√		√																					
p’	√							√		√		√							√					√			√	√																		
pp’																												√																		
m	√					√		√				√											√				√		√						√				√	√		√	√			
ch										√																									√			√								
ch’										√		√									√			√											√			√								
d	√			√								√												√			√																			
dd							√									√											√																	√		
dg																														√				√												
dgk																																		√												
dt	√					√			√	√		√				√											√																	√		
dty																								√																						

续上表：

韵 声	a	ā	ă	‘a	ăr	aṉ	aw	ä	e	ĕr	erh	i	ɪ	ī	ĭ	o	ō	ŏ	ö	oa	ou	oṉ	iu	u	ŭ	ū	ü	ŭe	uṉ	yu	yo	yi	ye	yü	wua	wue	wuo	ung	uàṉ	ùaṉ	ŭe	ùeṉ	uèṉ	v	vu	0
dtg																								√																						
dsh												√					√							√																						
ds						√	√	√						√	√	√								√																						√
ds’															√																															
dz				√					√					√	√	√								√			√																			√
dzh												√												√																						
f	√																																													
ff																									√																					
g																								√						√		√			√		√							√		
gg																		√									√																			
gk	√			√		√	√					√				√								√			√					√	√		√									√		
ghügh																																														√
h	√				√		√	√								√	√		√	√				√			√																			
k																																					√									
k’	√						√									√			√					√											√		√							√		

续上表:

韵/声	a	ā	ǎ	‘a	ǎr	aṉ	aw	ä	e	ěr	erh	i	ɪ	ī	ǐ	o	ō	ǒ	ö	oa	ou	oṉ	iu	u	ǔ	ū	ü	ǔe	uṉ	yu	yo	yi	ye	yü	wua	wue	wuo	ung	uàṉ	ùaṉ	ǔe	ùeṉ	uèṉ	v	vu	0
kh												√												√						√				√												
ḳh																											√																			
l	√					√	√	√		√		√				√								√			√																	√		
ll																											√																			
n	√					√		√		√												√	√						√	√		√		√										√		
nn																											√																			
nd				√			√		√	√		√				√								√			√																	√		
nds	√						√									√								√	√																					
ndsh										√		√												√																						
ndz	√			√			√			√				√										√																						
ndzh										√				√																					√											
ng	√			√			√									√								√						√		√	√											√		
ngg																		√									√																			
n͡g	√			√												√																														
ss	√					√	√	√						√	√	√								√			√																			√

续上表：

韵 声	a	ā	ă	‘a	ăr	an̠	aw	ä	e	ĕr	erh	i	ɪ	ī	ĭ	o	ō	ŏ	ö	oa	ou	on̠	iu	u	ŭ	ū	ü	ŭe	un̠	yu	yo	yi	ye	yü	wua	wue	wuo	ung	uàn̠	ùan̠	ŭe	ùen̠	uèn̠	v	vu	0
sh										√		√									√			√											√											
sz										√		√			√												√																			
t												√																																		
t’	√					√		√				√				√									√		√																	√		
t’kh												√																					√													
tgk																																	√													
ts	√					√																																								
ts’	√					√	√	√		√		√				√								√			√																			√
w						√																		√															√							
z				√			√	√								√											√																			
zh										√		√									√			√											√											
0	√	ε	√	√		√	√				√						√													√		√		√	√											
	a	ā	ă	‘a	ăr	an̠	aw	ä	e	ĕr	erh	i	ɪ	ī	ĭ	o	ō	ŏ	ö	oa	ou	on̠	iu	u	ŭ	ū	ü	ŭe	un̠	yu	yo	yi	ye	yü	wua	wue	wuo	ung	uàn̠	ùan̠	ŭe	ùen̠	uèn̠	v	vu	0

STUDIA INSTITUTI ANTHROPOS

VOL. 9

JOSEPH F. ROCK

Research Fellow, Harvard-Yenching Institute,
Cambridge, Mass.

The ^{2}Zhi ^{3}mä Funeral Ceremony of the ^{1}Na-^{2}khi of Southwest China

Described and translated from ^{1}Na-^{2}khi manuscripts

PUBLISHED BY ST. GABRIEL'S MISSION PRESS VIENNA-MÖDLING

1955

^{3}MUN̲ ^{2}NDZĔR ^{3}Ă ^{1}LĂ ^{2}DZHU or SONG OF THE DEAD, RELATING THE ORIGIN OF BITTERNESS

Slow *(ad libitum)* ^{2}ZĂ-^{1}ZĂ ^{2}TS'O

Tune to which ^{3}Mun̲ ^{2}ndzĕr ^{3}ä ^{1}lä ^{2}dzhu is sung.

This song I found recorded in a very ancient manuscript which I acquired by purchase from a peasant from north of Li-chiang in the commune of La-pao within the Yangtze loop. Manuscripts of this type are very rare indeed. The transcription and translation of this song was made from the above mentioned manuscript which bore the number 2760. However this book was lost with other ^{1}Na-^{2}khi material when the S. S. Richard Hovey was sunk by the Japanese in 1944, in the Arabian Sea, *en route* to the States from Calcutta. I had however found two other manuscripts bearing that title, one of which, no 1091, is no more in my possession, but a photostat copy is in my library; the negative is preserved in the Library of Congress in Washington D. C.

Only the first page and first rubric of page 2 are different from *ms.*, no 2760. The actual song commences with the second rubric of page 2. The second *ms.*, I was fortunate to acquire in 1947, is practically identical with no 2760. It is no 7020 and is in my private library.

The *ms.* from which the translation was made in 1940 was very old and nearly fell to pieces, but the text was still very clear. It consisted of nine folios (18 pages), 11 inches long, and 3$^{1}/_{2}$ inches wide, with each page divided into three lines.

On the cover of *ms.*, no 7020 is an oblong frame with double line margins crowned by a ^{1}lĕr-^{2}mbbŭ-^{1}ch'i = love knot, the Tibetan dpal-gyi-beu, the Sanscrit Srīvatsa. Within the frame on the left, is depicted a ^{2}dto-^{1}mba sitting on a bench holding the ^{3}Mùen̲-^{1}t'u or funeral wand. On each side is a figure with legs astride, the left one holding a trident in one hand and the head of a ^{1}Dv demon with the other. The right hand one is brandishing a sword with one hand, arm raised, and in the other he also holds a ^{1}Ddv demon's head by the hair.

Explanation of symbols in the title

The first symbol represents a large horse fly, such as occur on the high alpine meadows in the summer, they emerge only when the sun shines, and hide when overcast, they are blood suckers and a plague to both man and beast; the ^{1}Na-^{2}khi call them ^{3}mun̲, here the symbol stands for ^{3}mun̲ = dead, it has also the meaning of old. ^{3}Mun̲ is a refined term for dead, the colloquial for dead is ^{2}shi. Below is the symbol for tree ^{1}ndzěr, here its phonetic value is borrowed for ^{2}ndzěr = to sing, it is often written thus:

a tree which stands for the phonetic and to it attached a mouth with sound issuing, hence ^{2}ndzěr = to sing. Another way of writing

it is: a man walking along with his mouth open and on his tongue the phonetic ^{1}ndzěr, here ^{2}ndzěr = to sing. The ^{1}Na-^{2}khi when traveling with companions over the mountains usually sing impromtu songs, one man will improvise a line and the others will sing an appropriate verse in reply. Ballads or ditties are called in ^{1}Na-^{2}khi ^{1}na-^{1}bbŭe, the first syllable stands for ^{1}Na-^{2}khi and ^{1}bbŭe is a ballad or ditty, or lyric song. ^{2}Ä means the first in time, long ago, in the dim past, here for euphony's sake read in the third tone, it has reference to the origin of the subject of the song bitterness, sorrow = ^{2}dzhu the first to experience sorrow. Below is the symbol for musk deer = ^{2}lä, here ^{1}lä means "again". The last symbol represents an ancient rifle, called ^{1}dzhu in ^{2}dto-^{1}mba books, ^{2}dzhu also means to empty; here it stands for ^{2}dzhu = bitterness, sorrow.

³MUN̲ ²NDZĚR ³Ä ¹LÄ ²DZHU

First Page:

Rubr. 1: Ō! ¹Ä-¹ssĭ ³dta ¹lä ²dzhu
Rubr. 2: ²Wùa-¹ssĭ ³dta ¹lä ²dzhu
Rubr. 3: ²Dzhu ²t'u ²gkv ²muàn̲ ³shou, ²Dzhu ¹dzo ³shou ²muàn̲ ²nyi
Rubr. 4: ²Dzhu ³bbŭe ²gkv ²muàn̲ ³shou
Rubr. 5: ²Dzhu ¹dzo ²bä ²muàn̲ ²nyi
Rubr. 6: ²Ä-¹ts'ä ²dzī ²muàn̲ ²dzhu
Rubr. 7: ²Dzhu ²t'u ²Mùan̲-³llü-¹ssu-¹lo-²k'o ²nnü ²t'u
Rubr. 8: ²Dzhu ³bbŭe ²Mùan̲-³llü-¹ssu-¹lo-²k'o ²nnü ³bbŭe
Rubr. 9: ²Mùan̲-³llü-¹ssu-¹lo-²k'o, ²zo ²nnü ²gkv ³ssu ¹ssä
Rubr. 10: ²Ä-¹khi ²Ndaw-¹ssu ²dzhu, ²Dzhu ³bbŭe ²gkv ¹lä ²bä.

First Page:

1) Ō! The bitterness (experienced) by the father we will relate
2) The father's bitterness we will again relate
3) If one does not relate of the origin of bitterness then one cannot speak about it
4) One must relate of the origin of bitterness
5) Or about bitterness one must not speak
6) In the beginning of things man knew no bitterness
7) Bitterness originated at ²Mùan̲-³llü-¹ssu-¹lo-²k'o
8) At ²Mùan̲-³llü-¹ssu-¹lo-²k'o it was that bitterness first came forth
9) From ²Mùan̲-³llü-¹ssu-¹lo-²k'o it was that the son first led bitterness
10) At ²Ndaw-¹ssu-²dzhu of ²Ä-¹khi bitterness first originated.

Explanation of text

Page 1

Rubr. 1: The first symbol is that of the ²dto-¹mba in charge of the funeral; he is called ²Lo-¹ch'ung-²ndaw-¹khü, the name is not translatable, it is the official designation of such a ²dto-¹mba, he holds in his hand the funeral wand called ³Mùen̲-¹t'u or bamboo staff, the upper part of which is of especial design (1).

Below his staff is the symbol for grain ^{3}ō, here it stands for the first syllable of a ^{2}dto-^{1}mba chant beginning with *Ō Ō Ō Ō!* The next two symbols are read ^{1}ä-^{1}ssĭ, the first upper represents a mouth with voice issuing from it, it means first, the beginning as of sound, here it is the first syllable in the name for father, the latter is indicated by the figure of a man with the symbol for wood ^{2}ss on the top of his head; it is here actually read ^{1}ssĭ the second syllable in the word; father is always written that way and usually without the phonetic ^{1}ä. ^{3}Dta is the phonetic value of the third symbol, it actually represents a box with a cover, here its phonetic has been borrowed for ^{3}dta = to tell, to relate. The animal head is that of a musk deer with fangs, it is called ^{2}lä, it is used for the adverb ^{2}lä = again, but for euphony's sake read in the first tone. The last symbol is a picture of an ancient gun, of the flint-lock type or muzzle-loader with three bullets, as such it is read ^{2}dzhu, it means to empty, and the symbol seems to indicate that three bullets were being emptied from the gun. Its phonetic value has here been borrowed for ^{2}dzhu = sorrow, Bitterness, misery.

Rubr. 2: This is a repetition of rubric one with the exception that the syllable ^{2}wùa = house is used instead of ^{1}ä in the term for father, as a variation, as he is the lord of the house or home. The meaning is the same.

Rubr. 3: The first syllable has been explained; below is the symbol for trough ^{1}t'u, here used for ^{2}t'u = to come forth in conjunction with ^{2}gkv = head, the third syllable here meaning first, for the head comes first, hence first come forth. Below it is the negation ^{2}muàn̲ = not, it represents an empty trap hence nothing. Other ^{2}dto-^{1}mbas explain the symbol as the lightless moon or the new moon which is invisible hence *no* light, *not*. Below it is a ^{2}ggŏ-^{1}baw letter which appears to be of Chinese origin but with a totally different phonetic value and meaning, the ^{1}Na-^{2}khi reading is ^{3}shou = to speak, talk, while the Chinese reading is shang = above, etc. This is followed again by the symbol ^{2}dzhu = bitterness, and below it the symbol for a manger with fodder in it, indicated by the dots or short lines, a manger is called ^{1}dzo, here it stands for ^{1}dzo the adverb about, *i.e.* about bitterness, in ^{1}Na-^{2}khi the adverb follows the noun, (one) must not talk. We have again the ^{2}ggŏ-^{1}baw letter ^{3}shou = to talk, speak, the negation ^{2}muàn̲ and the numeral ^{1}nyi = two, here it stands for ^{2}nyi in conjunction with ^{2}muàn̲ = not, *i.e.* should not, ought not to, is not needed; ^{2}nyi also means to want, wish.

Rubr. 4: The meaning is the same as of the first sentence of rubric 3, the only word that is different is ^{3}bbŭe, ^{3}bbŭe and ^{2}t'u have the same meaning and often occur together ^{2}t'u-^{3}bbŭe = origin, it is the second symbol of the first row and represents a twig of a weed (Artemisia) of which two species occur in waste places around villages and ditches, one has white roots and has green leaves, and one has black roots and grayish tomentose leaves. The first one is always used in the purification ceremony; as representing the Artemisia it is read in the second tone. ^{3}Bbŭe has actually the meaning moving, in the sense of a nestling making its first flight, its first attempt to leave the nest.

Rubr. 5: This has again the same meaning as the second sentence of rubric 3, only here the word ^{2}bä = do occurs, it is the lower third symbol and represents a hoe, the dots below are clots of earth, actually digging, working with a hoe, hence doing.

Rubr. 6: The first symbol ^{1}ä has been explained in rubric one, ^{2}ts'ä is the symbol below ^{1}ä, it represents a lump of salt = ^{2}ts'ä, here read in the first tone in conjunction with ^{2}ä it has the meaning in the beginning of things, of life. The animal head is that of a jackal = ^{2}dzī, strange to say this symbol, unless otherwise indicated always stands for people, it is used phonetically; the pre-flood ancestors of man are meant *i. e.* of the ^{1}Na-^{2}khi, the post-flood ancestors are indicated by ^{1}ts'o an elephant. The last of the pre-flood ancestors was ^{2}Dzī-^{2}zä-^{1}ts'o-^{2}zä and the first post-flood ancestor, he that alone survived the flood, was ^{1}Ts'o-^{2}zä-^{3}llü-^{2}ghügh, the word ^{2}ss = to know is not written nor is it read, but is understood. In the beginning man (knew) no bitterness.

Rubr. 7: The first two symbols have been explained, the third is a demon with a tail, he is called ^{2}Mùan̲-^{3}llü-^{1}ssu-^{2}ndzǐ, he was the enemy of the father of the human race ^{2}Mùan̲-^{3}llü-^{1}ddu-^{2}ndzǐ; the origin of bitterness may have originated with him but in another *ms.*, we read: ^{2}Dzhu ^{2}t'u ^{2}Mùan-^{3}llü-^{1}ssu-^{1}lo-^{2}k'o ^{2}nnü ^{2}t'u, here it is the name of a place and the third syllable in the demon's name = ^{1}ssu is used phonetically and the other syllables are not written. In *ms.* no. 1091 the phrase is written thus:

Now ^{2}Mùan̲-^{3}llü-^{1}ssu-^{1}lo-^{2}k'o is a place in Mu-li [18] to the north of the Mu-li lamasery in Hsi-k'ang [19] on the banks of the Shu-gyi or Iron River; it is not the Wu-liang Ho [20] but a river which has its source in Na-wu and which river I baptized the T'ieh-ho [21], a Chinese translation of the ^{1}Na-^{2}khi name = Iron River; for discussion as to the source etc., of that river *see* my *The Ancient Na-khi Kingdom*, etc., Vol. I, p. 110, n. 60; Vol. II, pp. 384–385, n. 5. The symbol above that for trough = ^{1}t'u, represents a human heart called ^{2}nnü, here it stands for ^{2}nnü = it, *i. e.* bitterness.

Rubr. 8: This is identical with rubric 7 except that the word ^{3}bbŭe is used instead of ^{2}t'u; *see rubric 4.*

Rubr. 9: This reads ^{2}Mùan̲-^{3}llü-^{1}ssu-^{1}lo-^{2}k'o, ^{2}dzhu ^{2}t'u ^{2}gkv ^{1}lä ^{2}bä (it was from) ^{2}Mùan̲ ^{3}llü-^{1}ssu-^{1}lo-^{1}k'o that all bitterness first came forth, (it was) the son (of that place) who first led bitterness. Instead of writing the symbol for son = ^{2}zo, the phonetic of ^{2}zo = jar has been used as the figur of a man can be read in several ways besides ^{2}zo. The last symbol in the rubric represents a die = ^{1}ssu, here its phonetic value has been borrowed for ^{3}ssu = to lead. Literally: son he bitterness first led. Below the ^{1}ssu symbol is a syllabic character or ^{2}ggŏ-^{1}baw letter read ^{2}ssä, added to a verb it denotes the past tense. Some times instead of the ^{2}ggŏ-^{1}baw letter the pictograph ^{1}ssä = goral is used for the same purpose.

Rubr. 10: The first symbol ^{2}ä, already described, is the first syllable in the name of a hsiang [22] or commune on the western branch of the Yangtze loop and west of the snow range, namely ^{2}Ä-^{1}khi, the symbol ^{1}khi is the second one, it represents an ear of paddy, polished rice is called ^{2}ch'wua. ^{2}Ndaw-^{1}ssu-^{2}dzhu is the name of a village in ^{2}Ä-^{1}khi, it is situated on the east bank of the Yangtze between Shih-ku [23] and A-hsi [24] the Chinese transcription of ^{2}Ä-^{1}khi or ^{2}A-^{1}khi as it is also called. The symbols whose phonetic values spell the name of the village are ^{3}Ndaw a sword or knife with a line through it meaning to cut, then the numeral 3 = ^{1}ssu, composed of three short lines, and ^{2}dzhu already explained; perhaps this village has been selected as being one place where bitterness originated, because of the last syllable ^{2}dzhu in its name. The other symbols have already been explained.

Second Page:

Rubr. 1: ^{1}Ō ^{2}dzhu ^{2}t'ä ^{1}sso ^{3}k'ö
Rubr. 2: ^{1}Ssu-^{1}lo ^{3}Ssu-^{2}ssä-^{2}zo
Rubr. 3: ^{2}Nyu ^{3}mun̲ ^{2}nyu ^{2}muàn̲ ^{2}non̲
Rubr. 4: ^{2}Ss ^{1}shi ^{2}lo-^{1}bpä ^{3}ndaw
Rubr. 5: ^{1}Ha ^{1}szŭ ^{2}lä ^{1}wu ^{3}k'ö
Rubr. 6: ^{2}Nyu ^{1}ō ^{1}gyi ^{2}nyu ^{3}k'a
Rubr. 7: ^{1}Gyi ^{1}ō ^{2}nyu ^{2}lä ^{1}ddo
Rubr. 8: ^{2}Nnü ^{1}ō ^{2}nyu
Rubr. 9: ^{2}lä ^{1}ddo
Rubr. 10: ^{2}Nyu ^{3}mun̲ ^{2}nyu ^{2}lä ^{2}non̲
Rubr. 11: ^{2}Mùan̲-^{2}bä ^{1}gkyi ^{1}p'ĕr ^{3}chung, ^{2}gko ^{3}mun̲ ^{2}gko ^{2}muàn̲ ^{2}non̲.

Second Page:

1) To learn to make things (learn a profession) here is bitterness
2) ^{3}Ssŭ-^{2}ssä-^{2}zo (of) ^{1}Shu-^{1}lo
3) When he was old he did not know it
4) he made a yellow wooden ^{2}Lo-^{1}bpä
5) and went again to wash gold
6) his shadow was projected on the water
7) he saw his shadow reflected on the water
8) his own shadow
9) he saw (reflected)
10) he was old and he then knew it;
11) on the horizon where the clouds adjoin heaven, the old crane did not know (was not aware of) he was old.

Explanation of text

Page 2

Rubr. 1: The first symbol read ^{1}ō represents turquoise, more probably a silver charm box worn around the neck and studded with turquoise, or a brooch worn by ^{1}Na-^{2}khi women, hence also an object, a thing, the second symbol ^{2}dzhu stands for bitterness. ^{2}T'ä represents a flag, here ^{2}t'ä = to provide, to make,

^{1}sso is said to be a picture of a scale such as is used in China, others say it represents a fallen tree with dead branches, hence ^{2}sso = dry, here read ^{1}sso = to learn. The last symbol read ^{2}k'ö = foot stands here for ^{3}k'ö = to go, it is so used in conjunction with ^{1}sso and is a colloquialism, *see* rubric 7, of page 9.

Rubr. 2: The first symbol has been explained, below it is that for valley = ^{1}lo, here it is the fourth syllable in the name of the place. The next two are ^{3}ssu = a species of grass, and ^{1}ssä = the goral *(Naemorhedus griseus)* and the figure of a boy = ^{2}zo, all three serve phonetically in the name ^{3}Ssu-^{2}ssä-^{2}zo a boy from ^{1}Ssu-^{1}lo, this latter is called also ^{1}Shu-^{1}lo and is a place in Mu-li, the valley of the ^{2}Shu-^{1}gyi or Iron River is also called ^{1}Shu-^{1}lo or Iron valley, hence it need not stand for the long name ^{2}Mùan̲-^{3}llü-^{1}ssu-^{1}lo-^{2}k'o, but ^{2}Mùan̲-^{3}llü may be an ancient transcription of Mu-li.

Rubr. 3: We see two figures wiggling and with hair standing on end on their bodies, these symbols are actually read ^{1}ndshĕr = fright, afraid, frightened, there is a symbol like it but without the hair, and that is read ^{2}nyu = to sway, to wiggle, to shake, it stands for the personal pronoun I, also for he, ^{3}mun̲ = old, he not know, or I (was) old (and) I (did) not know (it). The symbol ^{3}mun̲ represents the large horse-fly so common on the high alpine meadows and in the grass lands, it is phonetically used for ^{3}mun̲ = old, also to die. The symbol ^{2}non̲ under the second ^{2}nyu symbol is composed of two, the upper part is ^{1}p'ĕr  white, below the curved line with dots represents liquid, hence white liquid or milk, here ^{2}non̲ = to know or to learn a news, to acquire knowledge, *i. e.*, he learned that he was old.

Rubr. 4: The first symbol is that of a tree = ^{1}ndzĕr, it can also be read ^{2}t'o = pine tree, and ^{2}ss = wood, and as such it is here intended; below it is the symbol for meat = ^{2}shi, employed phonetically for ^{1}shi = yellow, hence yellow wood, the adjective qualifying a noun always follows it with the exception when the adjective can have another meaning and is used as a verb as in ^{1}ha ^{2}zaw = golden shoes or golden yellow shoes, for ^{1}ha also means to buy and to say ^{2}zaw ^{1}ha could thus have two meanings, so in this case the adjective preceedes the noun.

The third symbol is a picture of a square or oblong, flat, wooden bowl which the ^{1}Na-^{2}khi use to chop things in, they are crudely made by hand of a yellow wood and are called ^{2}lo-^{1}bpä, and are about 1½ to 2 feet square or oblong, various sizes are made but not smaller than one foot square; the symbol below it is read ^{1}bpä and is the second syllable in the name, it represents steamed rice dried and pressed into a cake called ^{3}bpä. The last symbol ^{3}ndaw = to cut has been explained, *i. e.*, he cut from yellow wood a ^{2}lo-^{1}bpä, the larger ones are also used in gold washing for scooping up sand from the river bed or bank, and for such he employed it as we learn in the next verse.

Rubr. 5: The first symbol is read ^{1}ha = gold, the leaf symbol read ^{2}szŭ represents a willow leaf, here it stands for ^{1}szŭ = wash, actually washing is ^{1}dsä,

^{2}lä = again, ^{1}wu = a slave represented by an empty dish, indicative of the treatment of slaves, ^{2}k'ö = dog, here ^{1}wu-^{3}k'ö = went, although he was old and following a habit of his youth, he went again to wash gold. ^{3}Wu has the meaning of far; ^{2}lä ^{1}wu ^{3}k'ö (he) returned, *i. e.* to his old habit; ^{2}wu also means himself, a reflexive pronoun.

Rubr. 6: The syllable and symbol ^{2}nyu have been explained in rubric 3, ^{1}ö = a turquoise ornament, here ^{1}ō = shadow, ^{1}gyi = water, below the water symbol a pair of eyes = ^{1}miu, ^{1}nyu, here it is read ^{1}nyu = on, ^{3}k'a = to shoot off an arrow, here ^{3}k'a = reflection, the word ^{1}ddo = see is in the next line; literally his shadow water on reflected,

Rubr. 7: water shadow his again ^{1}ddo = see. Notice the difference between the eyes symbol and the last symbol in the rubric, with the lines protruding from the eyes, indicating to see.

Rubr. 8: ^{2}Nnü = heart, here ^{2}nnü his own, reflexive pronoun, ^{1}ō = shadow,

Rubr. 9: again see, these symbols have been explained.

Rubr. 10: These symbols have been explained in rubric 3.

Rubr. 11: ^{2}Mùan̲-^{2}bä = Horizon, the vault of heaven with the symbol for the verb ^{2}bä = to do, by itself it has also the meaning of "side"; below is the symbol for cloud = ^{1}gkyi, a little above it the symbol ^{1}p'ĕr = white, and to the right the symbol ^{3}chung = awl, here used for ^{3}chung = to join on, adjoin. ^{2}Gko = crane, ^{3}mun̲ = old, crane, not, aware of.

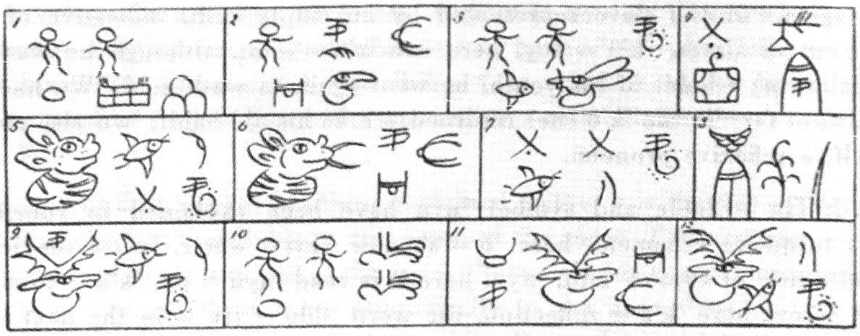

Third Page:

Rubr. 1: ^{2}Nyu ^{2}gv ^{2}nyu ^{3}p'u-^{3}lv
Rubr. 2: ^{1}Non̲ ^{1}p'ĕr ^{2}gko ^{2}gkan̲ ^{2}ggü
Rubr. 3: ^{2}Nyu ^{3}mun̲ ^{2}nyu ^{2}lä ^{2}non̲
Rubr. 4: ^{2}La-^{2}gyu-^{3}sso-^{2}gkv-^{1}p'ĕr
Rubr. 5: ^{2}La ^{3}mun̲ ^{2}la ^{2}muàn̲ ^{2}non̲
Rubr. 6: ^{1}Nds'a ^{1}p'ĕr ^{2}la ^{2}gkan̲ ^{2}ggü
Rubr. 7: ^{2}La ^{3}mun̲ ^{2}la ^{2}lä ^{2}non̲
Rubr. 8: ^{2}Nv-^{2}lv-^{1}nddü-^{3}t'khi-^{2}ghügh
Rubr. 9: ^{3}Ch'wua ^{1}p'ĕr ^{3}mun̲ ^{2}muàn̲ ^{2}non̲
Rubr. 10: ^{2}Nyu ^{2}gv ^{2}nyu ^{3}dshi-^{2}dshi
Rubr. 11: ^{2}K'o ^{1}p'ĕr ^{3}ch'wua ^{2}gkan̲ ^{2}ggü
Rubr. 12: ^{3}Ch'wua ^{3}mun̲ ^{3}ch'wua ^{2}lä ^{2}non̲.

Third Page:

1) His own body he shook
2) His own white down feathers dropped in front of him
3) He knew now that he was old
4) The old tiger of ^{2}La-^{2}yu-^{3}sso-^{2}gkv-^{1}p'ĕr
5) he knew not that he was old
6) his long white fangs (canines) fell in front of him
7) and he knew that he was old.
8) At ^{2}Nv-^{2}lv-^{1}nddü-^{3}t'khi-^{3}ghügh
9) the white stag did not know that he was old
10) his own body he shook
11) and his white antlers fell in front of him
12) he knew then that he was old.

Explanation of text

Page 1

Rubr. 1: The words ^{2}nyu for personal pronoun have already been explained; below the first ^{2}nyu is the symbol for egg = ^{1}gv, here used for ^{2}gv = body, ^{3}p'u-^{3}lv = to shake, here composed of two symbols, the first ^{3}p'u the Tibetan woolen cloth (p'u-lu, written in Chinese [25]), the second is ^{2}lv = rock, both are phonetically used.

Rubr. 2: ^{1}Non ^{1}p'ĕr = feather(s) white, crane, ^{2}nyu is again the personal pronoun but is not read, it amplifies the symbol ^{2}gko = crane. ^{2}Gkan is a children's swing such as is used at Chinese New Year, it is colloquially called ^{2}tgkye-^{1}lĕr, here ^{2}gkan stands for "in front". The last symbol is read ^{2}ggü it represents a mouth, if the symbol is doubled it stands for satiated, full, here it is phonetically used for ^{2}ggü = to drop, fall down.

Rubr. 3: This is the same as in rubric 9 of page 2.

Rubr. 4: ^{2}La-(^{2}gyu)-^{2}yu-^{3}sso-^{2}gkv-^{1}p'ĕr is a place name, it is a high mountain usually called ^{2}ngyu-^{1}shwua = mountain high; the word ^{2}sso in conjunction with ^{1}ngyu = mountain always stands for a high range. The first is a character or ^{2}ggŏ-^{1}baw letter read ^{2}la, below it the symbol ^{1}gyu, it is a mould for casting silver and gold ingots, here it is phonetically used. The last symbols are ^{1}sso = an upturned dry tree showing the roots, hence it stands for ^{1}sso = dry, here it represents a high mountain, the symbol for the latter is written but not read. Within the ^{1}ngyu = mountain symbol is that for white = ^{1}p'ĕr, ^{2}gkv = head is not written, a high snow-covered mountain is indicated.

Rubr. 5: The first symbol is ^{2}la = tiger, the phonetic symbol for ^{2}la is below that of ^{3}mun which stands for old, all these symbols have already been explained.

Rubr. 6: All symbols in this rubric have been explained, except ^{1}nds'a = fangs, canines, these are attached to the tigers mouth.

Rubr. 7: All the symbols in this rubric have been explained except the fourth which is a ^{2}ggŏ-^{1}baw letter read ^{2}lä and is used instead of the ^{2}lä = musk-deer symbol as in rubric 5 of page 2, it stands for ^{2}lä = again.

Rubr. 8: ^{2}Nv-^{2}lv-^{1}nddü-^{3}t'khi-^{2}ghügh is the term for a high mountain on which the mist or fog settles, it is the habitat of the stags; ^{1}nddü means to sink, settle, ^{3}t'khi = cold, also mist, the word ^{2}ghügh stands for embrace. The first upper symbol is ^{1}nv = silver, below it that for mountain = ^{1}ngyu, together they are read ^{2}nv-^{2}lv = silver rocks indicating any mountain covered with perpetual snow. The second symbol is read ^{1}ndi and represents a fern *(Pteridium aquilinum)*; this fern is the great stand-by of the ^{1}Na-^{2}khi in the spring, during those months there is little food and the ^{1}Na-^{2}khi dig out the young fronds and eat them. The last symbol represents a spine = ^{2}t'khi, here it stands for ^{3}t'khi = mist, fog. ^{2}Ghügh is not written it means embrace.

Rubr. 9: The first symbol represents a stag with the symbol ^{1}p'ĕr = white between the antlers, hence a white stag, the other symbols have already been explained.

Rubr. 10: Here remain to be explained the last two symbols read ^{3}dshi-^{1}dshi; both represent the feet and claws of an eagle = ^{1}dshi, here they stand for

^{3}dshi-^{1}dshi = to shake but the shaking done by an animal, as when a dog shakes his body. It also stands for the rotating motion when winnowing grain.

Rubr. 11: The first symbol is a conventional symbol for horns = ^{2}k'o, the circle represents the head, the upward curved lines the horns, the symbol white = ^{1}p'ĕr is below, hence the white horns or antlers; the remaining symbols have been explained.

Rubr. 12: These symbols have already been explained.

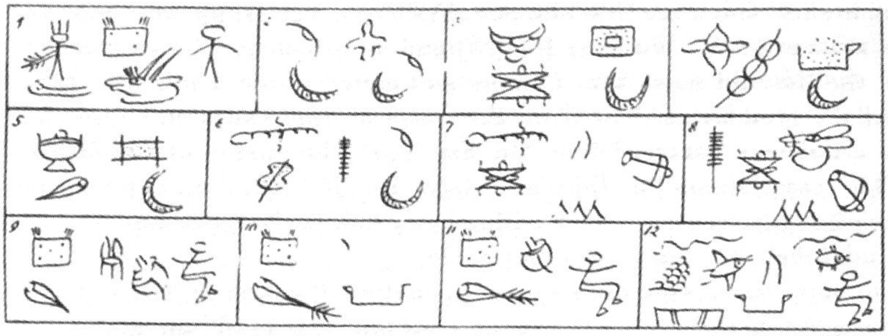

Fourth Page:

Rubr. 1: ¹Ssu-¹lo ³Ssu-²ssä-²zo
Rubr. 2: ²Muàn̲ ²dgyu ¹ssü ²muàn̲ ²dgyu
Rubr. 3: ¹Nv ¹ha ³dta ³shĕr ²dgyu
Rubr. 4: ¹Ō ¹ch'ung ²bpö ³shĕr ²dgyu
Rubr. 5: ²Haw-¹gyi ²ngu ³shĕr ²dgyu
Rubr. 6: ³K'v ¹nä ²szĭ ²muàn̲ ²dgyu
Rubr. 7: ³K'v ¹ha ¹mùen̲ ²lä ¹ds'i
Rubr. 8: ²Szĭ ¹ha ¹mùen̲ ²lä ¹ds'i
Rubr. 9: ²Ssu-¹gyi-²gkv ²nnü ¹dtü
Rubr. 10: ²Ssu-¹gyi-²man̲ ²lä ²t'u
Rubr. 11: ²Ssu-¹gyi-²man̲ ²nnü ¹dtü
Rubr. 12: ²Bbĕr-²ddĕr ²llü ²lä ²t'u, ²Bbĕr-²ddĕr ²llü ²nnü ¹dtü.

Fourth Page:

1) ³Ssu-²ssä-²zo of ¹Shu-¹lo
2) possessed everything
3) his chest was full of silver and gold
4) he had one measure full of turquoise and carnelian
5) his grain chest was full of grain
6) years and long life he had not;
7) to buy years he went south,
8) long life he came south to buy.
9) From ²Ssu-¹gyi-²gkv he rose
10) and at ²Ssu-¹gyi-²man̲ he arrived
11) from ²Ssu-¹gyi-²man̲ he rose
12) and arrived in the land of ²Bbĕr-²ddĕr, from ²Bbĕr-²ddĕr he then rose.

Explanation of text

Page 4

Rubr. 1: ¹Ssu-¹lo is the name of a valley = ¹lo, and is the ¹Na-²khi ¹Shu-¹lo = Iron valley in Mu-li [26] territory, in this valley flows the ²Shu-¹gyi or Iron river, the Tibetan lChags Chhu [27]. The aborigines of Mu-li call the river Zho-chhü. It is inhabited by a tribe called the Shu-khin̲ who speak a language of their own. It seems to be however a mixture of Ch'ra-me, ¹Na-²khi and Tibetan. They are only to be found above the cantilever bridge at Shen-dzong;

below toward ^{1}Ō-^{2}yü are ^{1}Na-^{2}khi. *See ANKSWC*, Vol. II, pp. 384–385. The river is an affluent of the Wu-liang Ho [28] and as it had no Chinese name I translated the ^{1}Na-^{2}khi name into Chinese and called it the T'ieh Ho [29] or Iron River; the symbols used to write the name of this valley are ^{1}Ssu the name of an archdemon namely ^{2}Mùa<u>n</u>-^{3}llü ^{1}Ssu-^{2}ndzĭ, the enemy of the father of the ^{1}Na-^{2}khi race ^{2}Mùa<u>n</u>-^{3}llü ^{1}Ddu-^{2}ndzĭ (*see* the *NNCRC*, Vol. I, p. 79, note 10). The symbol represents a demon with a hairy tail, it always stands for ^{2}Mùan-^{3}llü ^{1}Ssu-^{2}ndzĭ, below is that for valley = ^{1}lo.

The next three symbols serve as phonetics, the first is ^{1}ssu = a die (dice) but with the three lines on the corners on top, it is read ^{3}ssu and is the name of a species of grass from which the ^{1}Na-^{2}khi make their straw sandals, below is the head of a Goral = ^{1}ssä, and the figure of a man or boy = ^{2}zo, it is a male person called ^{3}Ssu-^{2}ssä, the two first symbols are phonetics and the third one is an ideograph. Nothing is of course known now of this individual called ^{3}Ssu-^{2}ssä who lived at ^{1}Ssu-^{1}lo. There is also a river which forms the border between Mu-li and Ch'ien-so [30] a Mo-so inhabited territory, called ^{1}Shu-^{1}lo-^{2}k'o, *q. v. l. c.* pp. 407, 420.

Rubr. 2: The first symbol is the negation ^{2}mùa<u>n</u> = not, below it the symbol ^{1}dgyu representing a silver bracelet, here it stands for ^{2}dgyu, have, exist, possess, there is; the cross-like symbol is read ^{1}ssü and is said to represent the metal lead, here it stands for ^{1}ssü = kind, in the sense of thing; the sentence actually reads not have kind not exist, in other words he had everything, the ^{1}Na-^{2}khi always express an affirmative by two negations.

Rubr. 3: The first two symbols represent ^{1}nv = silver, ^{1}ha = gold, the third is a box = ^{3}dta, the word ^{3}shĕr = full is expressed by the many dots within the box symbol; ^{2}dgyu means again to have, possess.

Rubr. 4: The first two symbols stand for ^{1}ō = turquoise, ^{1}ch'ung = beads of carnelian, the Tibetan mchhong [31] = carnelian; ^{2}bpö is a dry measure, such as the ^{1}Na-^{2}khi use for measuring grain, the Chinese sheng [32] box; the many dots in the symbol indicate again ^{3}shĕr = full (of).

Rubr. 5: The first two symbols are read ^{2}haw-^{1}gyi, ^{2}haw = food is indicated by a covered dish, ^{1}gyi = water, these two words stand for all the different grain cultivated, for without water no (grain) food can be grown. ^{2}Ngü is a wooden chest with movable boards, the box or chest can thus be hightened and increased in size. The ^{1}Na-^{2}khi store their grain in such boxes; the dots in the symbol again indicate ^{3}shĕr = full (of), and ^{2}dgyu = to have, possess.

Rubr. 6: The first symbol represents the ^{1}Na-^{2}khi sickle which is called ^{1}ndaw, it is not round like a foreign sickle but elongate with a curved point, its edge is serrated, hence it is also called ^{2}shu-^{1}p'ĕr = white iron (steel) ^{1}ndaw = sickle, ^{1}dzu = born with or having teeth or serrations, the latter is omitted; its present day colloquial name is ^{3}ssu-^{2}gkv. The vertical line through the center of the symbol causes it to be read ^{3}ts'ĕr or ^{3}ts' = to cut, but it can also be read ^{2}k'v = to reap, to harvest grain, here its phonetic value has been borrowed for ^{3}k'v = year an abstract term which cannot be written with a pictograph. The symbol below is read ^{1}nä = millet, here it stands for the conjunction ^{1}nä = and. The third symbol represents grass = ^{2}szĭ, here its phonetic value has been borrowed for ^{2}szĭ = longevity, long life. The other symbols have been explained.

Rubr. 7: Under the symbol ^{3}k'v = years, is the symbol for gold = ^{1}ha, this symbol does duty here for the verb ^{1}ha = to buy. The three triangles reduced in hight are read ^{1}mùen = below, actually south; the symbol, were the triangles longer, would have to be read ^{2}mi = fire, apparently a dying down fire, or low flames are used to indicate down below, *i.e.* in the south, ^{2}Yi-^{1}ch'i-^{1}mùen means the ancient city of Ya-ch'ih [33] the name the Mongols gave to the present day K'un-ming [34], ^{1}mùen indicates that the city is south of Li-chiang. The ^{2}ggŏ-^{1}baw letter ^{2}lä = stands here for "then", "thereupon" the Chinese tsai [35]. The last symbol represents a shoulder blade of a sheep and as such it is read ^{1}p'i, it has also another phonetic value *viz.*, ^{1}ds'i, it is here read ^{1}ds'i = to come, the past tense is not written nor is it read yet it must be so understood, hence he "went" or he came south.

Rubr. 8: The phrase is the same as the foregoing but ^{2}szĭ = longevity is the first symbol instead of ^{3}k'v = year(s). Instead of the phonetic character for ^{2}lä, the pictograph ^{2}lä = musk-deer is used.

Rubr. 9: ^{2}Ssu-^{1}gyi stands here for the waters of ^{3}Ssu-^{1}lo-^{2}k'o, it can be seen that the symbol for the particular grass = ^{3}ssu is used instead of the symbol for the demon ^{1}Ssu. The third symbol is read ^{2}gkv = head, here the meaning is he starts his journey at the headwaters of the ^{3}Ssu-^{1}lo-^{2}k'o in Mu-li. The fourth symbol is a picture of a heart = ^{2}nnü colloquially called ^{3}nun-^{2}mä, here it stands for ^{2}nnü = the personal pronoun "he". The last symbol is read ^{1}dtü = to rise to start, and the symbol depicts a man rising as from a chair.

Rubr. 10: We see here again the first two symbols *viz.* ^{2}Ssu-^{1}gyi = the waters of ^{1}Ssu, however the end of the symbol for water is prolonged with lines to both sides indicating a hairy tail = ^{2}man, hence the tail-end of the waters of ^{3}Ssu-(^{1}lo-^{2}k'o); ^{2}lä = then; the last syllable is read ^{1}t'u = a trough, here it is used for ^{2}t'u = to arrive.

Rubr. 11: All the symbols in this rubric have been explained in the foregoing rubrics.

Rubr. 12: The wavy line in the left upper part of the rubric represents a rope = ^{1}bbĕr, the colloquial for which is ^{1}erh; below it is a symbol representing foam = ^{1}ddĕr, both these symbols are used phonetically for the name of the district of ^{2}Bbĕr-^{2}ddĕr in Chung-tien [36]. Below them is the symbol for land = ^{1}dü it is not read, but ellucidates the words ^{2}Bbĕr-^{2}ddĕr, it is the Chinese Pei-ti [37], *see l.c.* pp. 262–268. Below the symbol for rope is that of ^{3}llü = a tick, cattle or sheep tick, here it is used phonetically in conjunction with ^{1}dü = land, *v.s.*, for ^{2}llü = fields, he arrived at the land or fields of ^{2}Bbĕr-^{2}ddĕr, and from there he rose again; the last phrase is only written with three symbols.

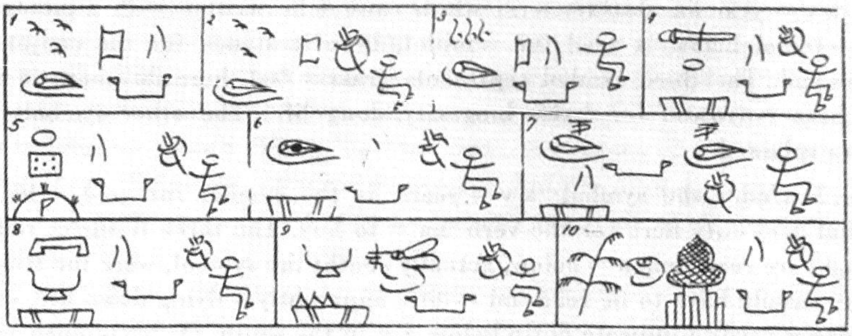

Fifth Page:

Rubr. 1: ²Ts'u ²gu ²k'u ²lä ²t'u

Rubr. 2: ²Ts'u ²gu ²k'u ²nnü ¹dtü

Rubr. 3: ¹Zhu ²gu ²k'u ²lä ²t'u, ¹zhu ²gu ²k'u ²nnü ¹dtü

Rubr. 4: ²Ndaw-²gv ¹dü ²lä ²t'u, ²Ndaw-²gv ¹dü ²nnü ¹dtü

Rubr. 5: ²Gv-²ssu-¹gko ²lä ²t'u, ²Gv-²ssu-¹gko ²nnü ¹dtü

Rubr. 6: ¹Gyi-¹na-¹lo ²lä ²t'u, ¹Gyi-¹na-¹lo ²nnü ¹dtü

Rubr. 7: ¹Gyi-¹p'ĕr-¹lo ²lä ²t'u, ¹Gyi-¹pĕr-¹lo ²nnü ¹dtü

Rubr. 8: ¹Ggŏ ²Nga-¹ba ²lä ²t'u, ¹Ggŏ ²Nga-¹ba ²nnü ¹dtü

Rubr. 9: ¹Mùe͟n ²Nga-¹ba ²lä ²t'u, ¹Mùe͟n ²Nga-¹ba ²nnü ¹dtü

Rubr. 10: ³Llü-¹gko-²gyi ²lä ²t'u, ³Llü-¹gko-²gyi ²nnü ¹dtü

Fifth Page:

1) and arrived where the Yangtze is crossed in the winter
2) from there he again rose
3) and arrived where the Yangtze is crossed in the summer, from there he again rose
4) and arrived in the land of ²Ndaw-²gv, from ²Ndaw-²gv land he rose
5) and arrived on the alpine meadow of ²Gv-²ssu-¹gko, from ²Gv-²ssu-¹gko he rose
6) and arrived again at ¹Gyi-¹na-¹lo, from ¹Gyi-¹na-¹lo he rose
7) and arrived at ¹Gyi-¹p'ĕr-¹lo, from ¹Gyi-¹p'ĕr-¹lo he rose
8) and arrived at upper ²Nga-¹ba, from there he rose again
9) and arrived in lower ²Nga-¹ba, from lower ²Nga-¹ba he rose again
10) and arrived at ³Llü-¹gko-²gyi, from ³Llü-¹gko-²gyi he rose

Explanation of text

Page 5

Rubr. 1: The three small curved crosses form one symbol and represent snow-flakes, hence ²mbe = snow, it is however also employed for the three winter months ²ts'u ³ssu ²hä; ²gu ²k'u is a ford where a stream can be crossed, ²gu is not written, instead the water symbol ¹gyi in a valley is written but here not read, a big stream or river is meant, here the ^{2}Yi-^{1}bi or Yangtze; the third symbol is read ^{2}k'u and represents a door or gate, here it stands for ^{2}k'u = river bank and with the symbol ^{1}gyi it means a ford. At ^{2}Ndaw-^{2}gv a village on the Yangtze to the north of Li-chiang there are two places where the river can be crossed, one in the winter when the water is low, and one in the summer when the river is in flood.

The other two symbols have already been explained.

Rubr. 2: See previous rubrics.

Rubr. 3: The only symbol to be explained here is the first one read ^{1}ḳhü = rain, as the summer months are the rainy season, the symbol for ^{1}ḳhü = rain is used for ^{1}zhu = summer; all the other symbols have been explained previously.

Rubr. 4: The first two symbols are read ^{2}ndaw-^{2}gv, below them is the symbol for earth, ^{1}dü = land, the first represents a sword with a line through it, hence the meaning is ^{3}ndaw = to cut, to chop, similar to the symbol ^{2}k'v = to reap, *see* page 4, rubric 6; below it is the symbol ^{2}gkv = egg, here read ^{2}gv, both are phonetically used for ^{2}Ndaw-^{2}gv, a town on the Yangtze, known in Chinese as Ta-ku [38], it is north of Li-chiang at the exit of the Yangtze through the ^{3}'A-^{2}ts'aṉ-^{3}gko gorge through the Li-chiang Snow range; *see l. c.* Vol. I, pp. 227–228. The other symbols have already been explained.

Rubr. 5: The first three symbols, reading from the top down are ^{2}gv, ^{2}ssu, and ^{1}gko, the first one has been explained in the previous rubric; the second is ^{1}ssu = a die, and the third ^{1}gko = alpine meadow. It is the name of the alpine meadow ^{2}Gv-^{2}ssu-^{1}gko; the latter is situated at the foot of the third highest snow-peak of the Yü-lung Shan namely ^{1}Gyi-^{1}na ^{2}nv-^{2}lv, which adjoins the highest one Shan-tzu-tou [39], *see l. c.*, Vol. I, pp. 187–191, 224–227, Plate 91. The ^{1}Gko = alpine meadow – symbol, has another symbol within it, namely ^{1}gko = needle, it acts as phonetic. The short lines on the rounded part of the symbol represent grass. The other symbols have been explained.

Rubr. 6: The upper symbol is a compound one, without the black dot in the center it would read ^{1}gyi-^{1}lo = a valley, the black dot is read ^{1}na = black, it modifies the noun ^{1}gyi = water, ^{1}Gyi-^{1}na-^{1}lo is a stream which descends from the eastern slopes of (Mt.) ^{1}Gyi-^{1}na ^{2}nv-^{2}lv and flows parallel to the glacier stream ^{1}Gyi-^{1}p'ĕr-^{1}lo or the white water stream (valley); they unite beyond Nga-tza and debouch into the eastern part of the Yangtze loop. The word ^{1}dü = land below the upper symbol indicates that a place (name) is meant. The other symbols have been explained, they also occur in the other rubrics of this page.

Rubr. 7: ^{1}Gyi-^{1}pĕr-^{1}lo or the valley of the white water is a glacier stream of a bluish white colour, while the ^{1}Gyi-^{1}na-^{1}lo is not a glacier stream and as it flows over darker rocks the water looks blackish in comparison. It has its source in a glacier on the eastern flanks of Shan-tzu-tou, *v. s.*; the symbol ^{1}p'ĕr = white is above the water symbol ^{1}gyi. *See l. c.*, Vol. I, p. 223, Plate 83.

Rubr. 8: Of the first three symbols the upper two need to be explained, the top one represents a bench and as such is read ^{1}ggŏ, here it stands for ^{1}ggŏ = the upper, also northern, it can also be read "on high", below is the symbol for cup ^{3}k'wua = cup, of which it is a picture. It has here however the meaning of mountain pass = ^{1}k'wua hence "the upper pass", or the northern pass which leads from Pai-shui [40], the ^{1}Na-^{2}khi ^{1}Gyi-^{1}p'ĕr-^{1}lo, to ^{2}Nga-^{1}ba an ancient ice lake the word ^{1}k'wua is not read, but as upper ^{2}Nga-^{1}ba is known by that name in the ancient ^{2}dto-^{1}mba books it is thus read. *See l. c.*, Vol. I, p. 221–224, Plates 79, 80.

Rubr. 9: The only symbol that needs explanation is the second one at the bottom of the rubric. It is the symbol ^{1}dü = land with the symbol ^{1}mùen = below superimposed, hence "he arrived at lower ^{2}Nga-^{1}ba" (at the lower or southern pass of ^{2}Nga-^{1}ba).

Rubr. 10: There are three symbols in this rubric which have not yet been encountered in previous rubrics. The first two serve as phonetics, they are read ^{3}Llü-^{1}gko, the ^{3}llü is a conifer, it is a fir or Abies and known as ^{3}llü-^{1}ndzĕr = fir tree; ^{3}gko is a hawk or eagle but it is here read in the first tone, while the fir-symbol is read in the third tone; these two syllables ^{3}Llü-^{1}gko are the name of a guard house which stood in ancient days, during the Ming dynasty (1368–1644) at the lower pass which leads to ^{2}Nga-^{1}ba. The guard house existed during the reign of the ^{1}Na-^{2}khi Chief Mu Tseng [41] better known as Mu Sheng-pai [42], he ruled from 1600 to 1646 A. D. This speaks for the age of the song. The third symbol is read ^{2}gyi = a house, it stands for the guard house at ^{3}Llü-^{1}gko.

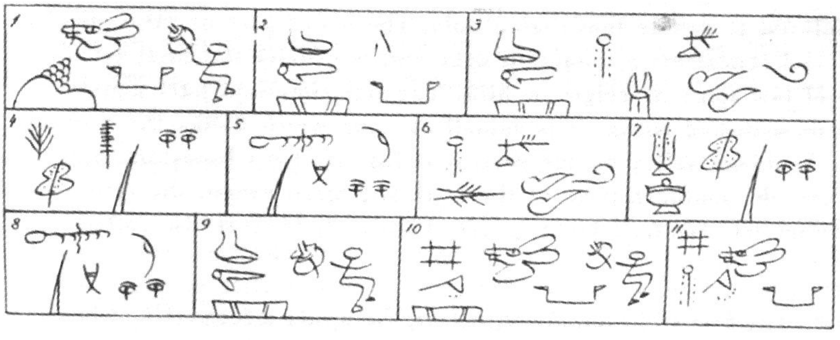

Sixth Page:

Rubr. 1: ^{1}Dz'a-^{2}dz'a-^{1}mbu ^{2}lä ^{2}t'u, ^{1}Dz'a-^{2}dz'a-^{1}mbu ^{2}nnü ^{1}dtü
Rubr. 2: ^{2}Boa-^{2}shi ^{1}dü ^{2}lä ^{2}t'u
Rubr. 3: ^{2}Boa-^{2}shi ^{2}dzhi ^{2}gkv ^{1}sso ^{3}ḳhü-^{2}ḳhü
Rubr. 4: ^{2}Ss ^{1}nä ^{2}szĭ ^{2}t'khi ^{1}ddo
Rubr. 5: ^{3}K'v ^{2}t'khi ^{2}mä ^{2}muàṉ ^{1}ddo
Rubr. 6: ^{2}Dzhi ^{2}maṉ ^{1}sso ^{3}ḳhü-^{2}ḳhü
Rubr. 7: ^{2}Zhi ^{1}nä ^{2}haw ^{2}t'khi ^{1}ddo
Rubr. 8: ^{3}K'v ^{2}t'khi ^{2}mä ^{2}muàṉ ^{1}ddo
Rubr. 9: ^{2}Boa-^{2}shi ^{1}dü ^{2}nnü ^{1}dtü
Rubr. 10: ^{1}Ngu-^{2}bä ^{1}dü ^{2}lä ^{2}t'u, ^{1}Ngu-^{2}bä ^{1}dü ^{2}nnü ^{1}dtü
Rubr. 11: ^{1}Ngu-^{2}bä ^{2}dzhi ^{1}lä ^{2}t'u.

Sixth Page:

1) and he arrived at ^{1}Dz'a-^{2}dz'a-^{1}mbu, from there he rose again
2) and he arrived in the land of ^{2}Boa-^{2}shi.
3) At ^{2}Boa-^{2}shi he went around the top of the market three times
4) there he saw them sell wood and grass
5) but people selling years he did not see;
6) at the tail-end of the market he went around three times
7) he saw people sell wine and food
8) but years he saw no one sell.
9) He then rose again from ^{2}Boa-^{2}shi land
10) and arrived again in the land of ^{1}Ngu-^{2}bä, from the land of ^{1}Ngu-^{2}bä he rose,
11) and arrived on the ^{1}Ngu-^{2}bä market.

Explanation of text

Page 6

Rubr. 1: All that concerns us here is the first symbol, it is a compound one, but actually cannot be separated, it represents a spur covered with loose rocks and stands for the region called ^{1}Dz'a-^{2}dz'a-^{1}mbu, the symbol has no other use and is employed to denote that region only. The lower part of the symbol is read ¹mbu and represents a mountain spur and is usually the final syllable in the name of low spurs or ridges or hills. The superimposed part denotes piles of rocks or scattered rocks. It is actually a spur which flanks the northern end of the Li-chiang valley on the east, it is full of sharp limestone outcroppings and faces the southern peak of the Li-chiang Snow range; the spur is covered with scrub oak. *See l. c.*, Vol. I, p. 220, Plates 77, 78. It is also called ¹Dza-²dza-¹mbu.

Rubr. 2: The first two symbols represent, the upper a foot or boot in which the sole has been exagerated, hence ²boa = sole, below ²shi = meat, a conventional symbol, both stand for the name ²Boa-²shi the Chinese Pai-sha [43], a commune or hsiang [22] north of Li-chiang, half way up to the foot of the snow range. *See l. c.*, Vol. I, p. 173, Plates 52, 54, 66.

The symbol ¹dü = land indicates a place name.

Rubr. 3: The first three symbols have been explained in rubric 2, the fourth is read ²dzhi = market, the dots along the main line representing the stalls; to the right of it is the symbol ²gkv = head, here meant at the head of the market. The symbol ¹sso has been explained in rubric 4, of page three; here it stands for the numeral three, which is actually ³ssu in ¹Na-²khi, it is borrowed from the Tibetan gsum = three; below it are two identical symbols representing each a lake = ³ḳhü, here they are used for ³ḳhü-²ḳhü = to go around, to circumambulate, the last symbol is not read but illucidates the meaning of ³ḳhü-²ḳhü.

Rubr. 4: The first symbol represents a pine tree called ²t'o, it can also be read ¹ndzĕr = tree, and ²ss = wood, here it has the latter meaning; the symbol ¹nä = and has been explained also the symbol ²szĭ which here stands for grass. The spine-like symbol read ²t'khi = spine, is used phonetically for ²t'khi = to sell; the last symbol a pair of eyes with protruding lines is read ¹ddo = to see. The literal reading is wood and grass sell see.

Rubr. 5: ³K'v = years (*see* page 4, rubr. 6), ²t'khi = sell, ²muàn̤ = not, ¹ddo = see.

Rubr. 6: The second symbol is ²man̤ = tail (end), here the tail-end of the market is meant in juxtaposition to ²gkv = the head of the market, *q. v.*

Rubr. 7: The upper symbol is read ²zhi = wine, spirits, this symbol tells a story and relates of the way the ¹Na-²khi used to drink wine. A large container as here depicted was used, and when filled with strong spirits, a bamboo tube was inserted, men used to sit around the vessel and each used to take a sip through the bamboo tube; as much as had been consumed was substituted with an equal amount of water. When nothing more than water was left, the party broke up, drunkeness was thus avoided; below is the symbol ²haw = food, the remaining symbols have been explained.

Rubr. 8: The symbols in this rubric have been explained in Rubr. 5; there is however the third symbol which needs explanation, it is read ²mä and represents the vagina, and stands for mother, here its phonetic value has been borrowed for ²mä = indeed.

Rubr. 9: These symbols have already been explained.

Rubr. 10: The first two symbols are read ¹ngu = a chest in which the ¹Na-²khi keep or store grain, see rubric 5, of page four, and ²bä = to do, to make, it shows a hoe with the clots of earth flying; both are used phonetically for the ¹Na-²khi name of Li-chiang which is ¹Ngu-²bä, *see l.c.*, Vol. I, p. 172; the symbol ¹dü = land again indicates that the foregoing symbols denote a place name. The other symbols have been explained.

Rubr. 11: For explanation of symbols see previous rubrics.

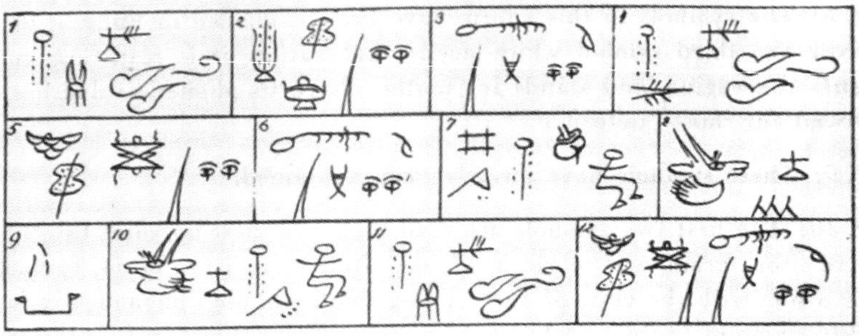

Seventh Page:

Rubr. 1: ^{2}Dzhi ^{2}gkv ^{1}sso ^{3}ḳhü-^{2}ḳhü
Rubr. 2: ^{2}Zhi ^{1}nä ^{2}haw ^{2}t'khi ^{1}ddo
Rubr. 3: ^{3}K'v ^{2}t'khi ^{2}mä ^{2}muàn̲ ^{1}ddo
Rubr. 4: ^{2}Dzhi ^{2}man̲ ^{1}sso ^{3}ḳhü-^{2}ḳhü
Rubr. 5: ^{1}Nv ^{1}nä ^{1}ha ^{2}t'khi ^{1}ddo
Rubr. 6: ^{3}K'v ^{2}t'khi ^{2}mä ^{2}muàn̲ ^{1}ddo
Rubr. 7: ^{1}Ngu-^{2}bä ^{2}dzhi ^{2}nnü ^{1}dtü
Rubr. 8: ^{2}Yi-^{2}ch'i-^{1}mùen̲
Rubr. 9: ^{2}lä ^{2}t'u
Rubr. 10: ^{2}Yi-^{2}ch'i ^{2}dzhi ^{2}bä ^{1}dtü
Rubr. 11: ^{2}Dzhi ^{2}gkv ^{1}sso ^{3}ḳhü-^{2}ḳhü
Rubr. 12: ^{1}Nv ^{1}nä ^{1}ha ^{2}t'khi ^{1}ddo, ^{3}k'v ^{2}t'khi ^{2}mä ^{2}muàn̲ ^{1}ddo.

Seventh Page:

1) He encircled the market head three times
2) he saw them sell wine and food
3) but years he saw no one sell.
4) He went around three times the tail end of the market
5) he saw them sell silver and gold
6) but people selling years he did not see.
7) From the market of ^{1}Ngu-^{2}bä he rose
8) and at ^{2}Yi-^{2}ch'i-^{1}mùen̲
9) he arrived
10) he rose from the market of ^{2}Yi-^{2}ch'i
11) and went around three times the head of the market
12) he saw them sell silver and gold, but years he saw no one sell.

Explanation of text

Page 7

Rubr. 1–7: The symbols in these rubrics have already been explained.

Rubr. 8: The three symbols in this rubric spell the ^{1}Na-^{2}khi name of the present day K'un-ming [34] the provincial capital of Yün-nan [3]. The ^{1}Na-^{2}khi call K'un-ming ²Yi-²ch'i-¹mùe<u>n</u>, ²Yi-²ch'i is the Chinese Ya-ch'ih [47] or Ya-ch'ih ch'eng, the capital of the Wu-man [48] or Black barbarians, the Mongol Kara-jang or Lo-lo tribes, the ancient Ts'uan [49] tribes, in contradistinction to the ¹Na-²khi who were known to the Mongols as the White barbarians or Chaγan jang. The first symbol is a Serow = ²Yi, the second ²ch'i represents the weight of a Chinese balance, the weight tied to a string being moved along a graduated rod. ¹Mùe<u>n</u> means below, south of ¹Na-²khi land.

Rubr. 9–12: All the symbols in these rubrics have been explained in the foregoing pages.

Eighth Page:

Rubr. 1: ^{2}Dzhi ^{2}maṉ ^{1}sso ^{3}ḳhü-^{2}ḳhü
Rubr. 2: ^{2}T'o-^{3}bpŭ ^{1}ssaw-^{2}sso ^{2}t'khi
Rubr. 3: ^{1}Yi-^{2}bbū ^{2}khi-^{2}bbū ^{2}t'khi ^{1}nä ^{1}ddo
Rubr. 4: ^{3}K'v ^{2}t'khi ^{2}mä ^{2}muàṉ ^{1}ddo
Rubr. 5: ^{2}Szĭ ^{2}t'khi ^{2}mä ^{2}muàṉ ^{1}ddo
Rubr. 6: ^{1}Ng'a ^{2}mä ^{1}nv ^{2}nnü ^{1}nv
Rubr. 7: ^{1}Nv ^{2}lä ^{2}lä ^{1}dgyu-^{1}ds'i
Rubr. 8: ^{2}Yi-^{2}ch'i ^{2}dzhi ^{1}ddü ^{2}lä
Rubr. 9: ^{2}Muàṉ ^{2}lü ^{2}muàṉ ^{3}t'a ^{2}t'a
Rubr. 10: ^{2}Lä ^{1}dgyu ^{2}ddü ^{1}lü ^{1}nä
Rubr. 11: ^{2}Yi-^{2}ch'i ^{2}dzhi ^{2}t'ü ^{2}dzhi.

Eighth Page:

1) He encircled three times the tail end of the market
2) a miscellany of cloth he saw them sell
3) also satin and brocade
4) but years he saw no one sell
5) neither did he see them sell long life.
6) There is a silver plated sword
7) and weeping he turned back again
8) the ^{2}Yi-^{2}ch'i market is so large,
9) not to look again will not do
10) so he went around once more to see
11) on the ^{2}Yi-^{2}ch'i market, on that market.

Explanation of text

Page 8

Rubr. 1: These symbols have already been explained.

Rubr. 2: The two first symbols are read from top down ^{2}T'o-^{3}bpŭ = cotton cloth; the first symbol represents either a shield or a sword-guard, very likely the latter, its original meaning has been lost only its phonetic value is still known; the second represents a colander, a vessel with steam escaping, and as such it is read ^{3}bpŭ, both are used phonetically. The next two symbols are read ^{2}ssaw-^{1}sso, the first represents ^{3}ssaw = breath, the second ^{1}sso has already been explained, both phonetically stand for miscellaneous, here a variety of cloth is meant, ^{2}t'khi = sell.

Rubr. 3: The first is a ^{2}ggŏ-^{1}baw character read ^{1}yi, below it a symbol representing a man holding an object, to hold is ^{3}bbū; to present, offer, give is ^{1}bbū, both are used phonetically for ^{1}yi-^{2}bbū = satin; the next two are read ^{2}khi-^{2}bbū and stand for brocade, the first is the symbol for ^{2}khi = paddy, the second for to hold, as before; their phonetic values have been used.

Rubr. 4–5: The symbols in these rubrics have already been explained.

Rubr. 6: The first symbol represents an ancient ^{1}Na-^{2}khi or perhaps Mo-so [50] sword such as was used during the Nan chao kingdom (740 A.D.), the sword was suspended from narrow leather straps which on the outer surface were studded with beads cut from the white conchshell. The straps were long and hung from behind the neck over the shoulders. It was a type of sword only in use by the ^{1}Na-^{2}khi or perhaps Mo-so, probably the former. A few of such swords still exist, I personally possess two, with complete armor and iron helmet, *see l. c.*, Vol. I, Plate 82: They are or were until some ten years ago still used in Yung-ning [5] by the ^{2}Lü-^{2}khi tribe, who call themselves Hli-khin̲, but are known as Mo-so to the Chinese. The Yung-ning chiefs had in their possession 3 or 4 armors complete with sword and helmet, these were used at the funeral ceremonies of chiefs when three or four men dressed in armor, carrying flags and swords danced rhythmically in front of the funeral procession to clear the way for the deceased. Such swords were known as ^{1}Ng'a, the symbol in our manuscript is an identic picture of such a sword as figured on Plate 82 in my book on the *Ancient Na-khi Kingdom*, etc. *See* Plate II, this book.

The word ^{2}mä here is an affirmative with the meaning "there is, there exists", ^{1}nv = silver, ^{2}nnü = it, ^{1}nv = silver, actually silver-plated is meant. This phrase has been introduced because of the next phrase, ^{1}nv = silver is a play on the word ^{1}nv = to weep in the next sentence. This is often done when ^{1}Na-^{2}khi improvise stanzas when traveling and singing.

Rubr. 7: The first is a compound symbol, a man in the act of walking, the enlarged eyes with the curved lines protruding is read ^{1}nv = to weep, the syllable ^{2}lä is read twice but only written once; below the muskdeer symbol is that of a cock crowing = ^{1}dgyu, here used phonetically in ^{1}dgyu-^{1}ds'i = to return, run back; the symbol ^{1}ds'i has been explained in rubric 7 of page four.

Rubr. 8: The only symbol that needs explaining is the fourth next to last one, it is read ^{1}ddü = large, it is said to represent the fruit of *Machilus bournei* or ^{1}Ddü-^{1}ndzĕr, its phonetic value has been borrowed here. The word ^{2}lä is a postfix which cannot be translated, I translated it with the word "so", *i.e.* so large.

Rubr. 9: The first symbol is read ^{2}lü, it represents a spear with a long round point, here it stands for ^{2}lü = to look, compare the word ^{2}lü of the next sentence; next to it is the negation ^{2}muàn̲ = not, it is written twice, the second negation belongs to he second half of the phrase; the last two symbols represent pagodas, the Chinese t'a [52], from which the word has apparently been borrowed, for the ^{1}Na-^{2}khi also use the word ^{3}t'a for pagoda, here ^{3}t'a ^{2}t'a preceded by the negation not, means "will not do", *i. e.* it must be done.

Rubr. 10: ^{2}Lä-^{1}dgyu = he again went, ran back, to see once more, ^{2}ddü = once, ^{1}lü = to see, ^{1}nä is a postfix.

Rubr. 11: Of this rubric all the symbols have been explained except the one before last, it shows a man drinking from a wine jug in the way described under rubric 2 of page 7, this symbol is read ^{1}t'ü = to drink, here it is used for ^{2}t'ü = that, it also stands for 3d person, personal pronoun, but is then read in the second tone as here.

Ninth Page:

Rubr. 1: ^{2}Dzhi ^{2}llü ^{1}ng'a ^{1}ssä ^{2}yu
Rubr. 2: ^{2}Yi-^{2}ch'i ^{3}ḳhü ^{2}t'ü ^{3}ḳhü
Rubr. 3: ^{3}Ḳhü ^{2}llü ^{3}gko ^{1}ssä ^{2}yu
Rubr. 4: ^{2}Yi-^{2}ch'i ^{2}Lv-^{2}mä-^{1}na
Rubr. 5: ^{2}Lv ^{2}llü ^{2}nggü ^{1}ssä ^{2}yu
Rubr. 6: ^{2}Yi-^{2}ch'i ^{3}Mùen̲-^{3}llü-^{1}ndzĕr
Rubr. 7: ^{3}K'ö ^{1}dgyu ^{1}hăr ^{2}lĕr-^{1}lĕr
Rubr. 8: ^{2}Lä ^{1}ts'i ^{1}shi ^{3}p'u-^{2}p'u
Rubr. 9: ^{1}Ndzĕr ^{2}llü ^{3}mun̲ ^{2}ndu ^{2}yu
Rubr. 10: ^{3}Gko ^{2}llü ^{1}lä ^{2}ndu ^{2}yu
Rubr. 11: ^{3}Mun̲ ^{2}mä ^{2}dgyu ^{2}yu ^{1}shu.

Ninth Page:

1) the market people were all dispersed
2) and the ^{2}Yi-^{2}ch'i lake
3) that lake was dry.
4) The black rocks of ^{2}Yi-^{2}ch'i
5) even these rocks were split
6) and of the ^{3}Mùen̲-^{3}llü-^{1}ndzĕr (bamboo) of ^{2}Yi-^{2}ch'i
7) the leaves were a rich green when he first came
8) but when he was leaving they were a deep yellow.
9) So trees must also die, it is the custom,
10) the leafy branches of the trees turn yellow
11) there is after all death, is there?

Explanation of text

Page 9

Rubr. 1: The first symbol has been explained the second ^{3}llü = tick read here ^{2}llü is a postfix difficult to explain but it is said to denote surprise and is equivalent to the Chinese particles or so-called "empty words" which are untranslatable. The third symbol read ^{1}ng'a represents an armour such as is figured on Plate II, here its phonetic value is borrowed for ^{1}ng'a = to disperse, to scatter in confusion. The ^{1}ng'a is actually not the outside armour, but a kind of shirt of mail to protect the body, while an armour with sleeves such as is depicted on Plate II, is called ^{1}ng'a-^{2}gyi, also known as ^{3}k'wua. The character before last is a ^{2}ggŏ-^{1}baw letter and not a symbol and is read ^{1}ssä, it stands for the past tense, to this is added the auxiliary verb ^{2}yu = is, been, hence ^{1}ng'a ^{1}ssä ^{2}yu = had dispersed, had scattered. The first word ^{2}dzhi = market is followed by ^{2}llü, this has also another meaning, and can stand for "people", for the people are the descendents of ^{3}Llü-^{2}ghügh the post-flood ancestor of the ^{1}Na-^{2}khi.

Rubr. 2: The first character is read ^{2}yi it is a ^{2}ggŏ-^{1}baw or syllabic character, below is the symbol ^{2}ch'i already explained both stand for ^{2}Yi-^{2}ch'i = K'un-ming as described previously, this is followed by the symbol ^{3}ḳhü = lake, the K'un-ming lake, known in Chinese as the Tien-ch'ih [53] K'un-ming Ch'ih or K'un-ming Lake is meant. *See l. c.*, Vol. I, Plates 1, 2. The next to last symbol represents a man drinking wine or liquor in the manner previously described, to drink is ^{1}t'ü, here it stands for ^{2}t'ü the demonstrative pronoun "that"; the last symbol is again ^{3}ḳhü = lake.

Rubr. 3: We have again the symbols ^{3}ḳhü = lake, and ^{2}llü with the first meaning as explained in rubric 1; the third symbol represents a needle showing the eye, as such it is read ^{1}gko, here it is used phonetically for ^{3}gko = dry. The words ^{1}ssä ^{2}yu have already been explained.

Rubr. 4: For ^{2}Yi-^{2}ch'i see rubric 2; the third symbol read ^{2}lv = rock has three black dots indicating ^{1}na = black, a large rock is called ^{2}lv-^{2}mä, in addition to the black dots within the rock symbol we have the phonetic ^{1}na, a letter borrowed from the Tibetan, black in Tibetan is nag [54].

Rubr. 5: We have again the rock symbol ^{2}lv but without the black dots, then ^{2}llü as previously explained in the first rubric. The third symbol is an ideograph and is read ^{2}nggü = to split, it represents two boards being split. There is another rock symbol in the upper right hand corner of the rubric, this is not read, but indicates the splitting of the rock, the past tense expressed by ^{1}ssä ^{2}yu has already been explained.

Rubr. 6: Here in ^{2}Yi-^{2}ch'i the first syllable is written with the serow's head = ^{2}yi instead of the syllabic character ^{2}yi; the next three symbols represent the name of a bamboo growing on the mountains of K'un-ming. ^{3}Müeṉ = bamboo, the symbol represents a bamboo, showing the joints with leaves, the latter are indicated by short lines, ^{3}llü = tick is a phonetic here, and the last syllable is ^{1}ndzĕr = tree, it represents actually a pine tree; the bamboo is a large one or the word ^{1}ndzĕr would not be used.

Rubr. 7: The first symbol represents a dog = ^{2}k'ö, here it has been borrowed for the Chinese expression ch'ü [55], pronounced k'ö or k'e in Yünnan, meaning to go, to leave, ^{1}dgyu = there is, there were, or they were, the symbol ^{2}ō-^{1}hăr

= turquoise is here read ¹hăr = green, below are two men calling, each is read ¹lĕr = to call, here used for ²lĕr-¹lĕr a deep rich color, with ¹hăr a deep rich green. The word ²k'ö is ill chosen, but in order not to use the ¹Na-²khi word ¹ts'i twice, as it occurs in the next rubric, ²k'ö has been used.

Rubr. 8: The first two symbols have been explained; the third uppermost one is read ²shi = meat, here it stands for ¹shi = yellow, the symbols ³p'u-²p'u = mean a deep yellow color, ²p'u is a bubble as previously explained.

Thus when he came to K'un-ming the leaves were a rich green and when he left, returned, they were deep yellow.

Rubr. 9: Here only the word ¹Ndu has to be explained. ¹Ndu is the equivalent of the male active principale of the Chinese, Yang [56]. The ¹Na²khi have personified it, *see NNCRC*, p. 158, note 211, here it stands for ²ndu – custom, hence ²Ndu ²yu = (such) custom there is? the word ²llü again expresses surprise as explained in the first rubric.

Rubr. 10: The first symbol represents an eagle = ³gko, here it stands for ³gko = a branch of a tree, a leafy branch is understood, the symbol ³llü, is again used for ²llü as in the previous rubric. Now the third symbol representing a musk deer = ²lä, stands here for ¹lä = to turn yellow, it seems that the ¹Na-²khi are the only people in Western China who have a word for such a condition; ²ndu ²yu (such) custom there is, is the same as in the foregoing rubric.

Rubr. 11: These symbols have been explained in rubric 1 of page ten, with the exception of the use of the symbol ²mä instead of ²llü, the former is an affirmative particle, "yes there is".

Tenth Page:

Rubr. 1: ^{3}Mun̲ ^{2}llü ^{2}dgyu ^{2}yu ^{1}shu
Rubr. 2: ^{1}Ng'a ^{2}mä ^{1}ha ^{2}nnü ^{2}z'a
Rubr. 3: ^{1}Z'a ^{2}lä ^{2}lä ^{1}dgyu ^{1}ts'i
Rubr. 4: ^{1}Ggŏ ^{1}yü ^{3}Dto-^{2}k'ö-^{1}pĕr ^{2}Gv-^{1}dzu ^{1}ä-^{1}ssĭ ^{3}mun̲
Rubr. 5: ^{1}Bpŭ-^{1}shwua ^{1}bbŭ ^{2}nnü ^{3}mun̲
Rubr. 6: ^{2}Dzhu ^{2}ggŏ ^{2}zo ^{1}ddü-^{3}hoa
Rubr. 7: ^{1}Bpŭ-^{1}shwua ^{1}bbŭ ^{2}nnü ^{2}dzhu
Rubr. 8: ^{2}Bbŭ-^{3}lv-^{2}zhi-^{1}zaw-^{2}man̲, ^{2}Lä-^{2}bbŭ ^{1}ä-^{1}ssĭ ^{3}mun̲, ^{2}wuà-^{1}gyi ^{1}bbŭ ^{2}nnü ^{3}mun̲.

Tenth Page:

1) To become old and die is after all true?
2) The sword is plated with gold
3) After he had laughed he again turned back.
4) Born in the north, the father of the Tibetan died at ^{3}Dto-^{2}k'ö-^{1}p'ĕr
5) he died under an earth (tamped) roof,
6) all the sons of bitterness
7) below the earth-tamped roof there is bitterness.
8) At ^{2}Bbŭ-^{3}lv-^{2}zhi-^{1}zaw-^{2}man̲ the father of the ^{2}Lä-^{2}bbŭ died, he died under the tiled roof house.

Explanation of text

Page 10

Rubr. 1: Below the symbol ^{3}mun̲ = die is the pictograph ^{3}llü = tick, here read in the second tone is an interrogative particle, perhaps equivalent to the Chinese adverb fu [57], as an initial particle, now, then; the symbol ^{2}dgyu = is, there is, has been explained. The fourth symbol is read ^{1}yu, it represent wilted leaves, and stands for decay, rotten, here read in the second tone but with the same meaning, *i. e.* that one must die and decay. The last symbol ^{1}shu represents an axe and hence stands for iron, here its phonetic has been borrowed for ^{1}shu = true, correct, that is unchangeable as iron. ^{1}Shu-^{1}mun̲ = custom.

Rubr. 2: The symbols ^{1}ng'a ^{2}mä have been explained in rubric 6 of page eight. The next two symbols are ^{1}ha = gold and ^{2}nnü = heart here it stands for the third person personal pronoun he, she, it; the last symbol is read ^{1}z'a = to laugh, here it stands for ^{2}z'a = glittering, that is plated here with gold. This phrase has been introduced similarly as the phrase of rubric 6, of page eight, ^{2}z'a is used in juxtaposition of the ^{1}z'a in the next rubric, it is a play on words.

Rubr. 3: Here the same symbol is read in the first tone ^{1}z'a = to laugh. The symbol ^{2}lä has already been explained, ^{1}dgyu means the first, the beginning, in the beginning, because the cock is the first to stir, hence this symbol has been selected, here it stands for ^{1}dgyu = to return, turn back, the next and last symbol is read ^{2}ts'u = a suicide by hanging here it is read ^{1}ts'i = to return, hence ^{1}dgyu-^{1}ts'i = returned or turned back.

Rubr. 4: The symbol ^{1}ggŏ has been explained and so has the symbol ^{1}yü; the third is that of a mountain ^{1}ngyu, with the symbol ^{2}dto = board, plank inside, ^{1}dto is actually a hill and the symbol's phonetic value has been borrowed, and ^{1}ngyu is not read, but without the symbol for mountain it would not be understood that a hill is meant, the hill's name is ^{3}Dto-^{2}k'ö-^{1}p'ĕr, in other *mss.*, the name is preceded by the words ^{2}La-^{1}ssaw which stand for Lhasa, the capital of Tibet. Next to the mountain symbol we have the pictograph ^{2}k'ö = foot, and the symbol ^{1}p'ĕr = white, both parts of the name. The next figure represents a Tibetan with long hair and a big felt hat, such as the nomads wear west of the Yellow River near the Amnye Ma-chhen Range. The ^{1}Na-^{2}khi call a Tibetan ^{2}Gv-^{1}dzu and in Yün-nan the Chinese call a Tibetan Ku-tsung [58] which is a transcription of the ^{1}Na-^{2}khi name for a Tibetan. The other symbols have been explained.

Rubr. 5: The first symbol represents a house = ^{1}gyi, it is not read, but without the next two symbols would not be understood, ^{3}bpŭ = colander, and ^{1}shwua = high, are here used for ^{1}bpŭ-^{1}shwua under which an earth (tamped) flat roof is understood. Most Tibetan houses have flat roofs, they put rhododendron branches from the shrubby species, also willow branches in layers a foot or more thick, fill the whole with mud and then fine earth, all this is rolled in the spring and autumn with a stone roller to pack the earth well as otherwise the roof would leak; such a roof the ^{1}Na-^{2}khi call ^{1}bpŭ-^{1}shwua, ^{1}bpŭ is also a tamped dirt wall, a wooden frame is first erected, filled with dry earth and then tamped, the same process being used for a roof, the word ^{1}shwua is added, as it is high up on the house. The remaining symbols have been explained.

Rubrs. 6–7: The symbols in these rubrics have already been explained.

Rubr. 8: The first six symbols stand here for five syllables, one symbol the man with a stick usually read ^{3}nddü = to drive out, is not read. All are used phonetically but the actual phonetic value of two, the afore mentioned, and that of the sheep symbol are not read, yet they express the action of herding sheep and that is called ^{2}bbŭ-^{3}lv, to be sure that the symbols are understood correctly, the symbol for stone, rock = ^{2}lv, three piled up rocks are added to illucidate the phonetic; ^{2}zhi = road is not written, but ^{1}zaw = a planet, and ^{2}man = tail, all employed phonetically, the whole meaning of the sentence is Shepherd road, ^{1}zaw = descend, ^{2}man = tail-end, *i. e.*, the road where the herding of sheep ends, south of Li-chiang where Min-chia [59] land begins; the ^{2}Lä-^{2}bbŭ or Min-chia land is only about 40 li about 12 miles south of Li-chiang, and the boundary is known to the ^{1}Na-^{2}khi as ^{2}Bbŭ-^{3}lv-^{2}zhi-^{1}zaw-^{2}man. The semi-prostrate figure represents a Min-chia or ^{2}Lä-^{2}bbŭ, the phonetic ^{2}ss = wood is attached to his head, it stands for ^{1}ä-^{1}ssĭ = father as explained previously, all the remaining symbols have already been dealt with except ^{2}wuà-^{1}gyi = tiled house, the symbol represents a house with the numeral 5, indicated by five lines, the word ^{2}wuà is a loan-word from the Chinese wa = a tile; ^{1}gyi = house; the words ^{1}bbŭ ^{2}nnü ^{3}mun mean below he died.

Eleventh Page:

Rubr. 1: ^{2}Dzhu ^{2}zo ^{2}ch'i-^{1}ddü-^{3}hoa
Rubr. 2: ^{2}Wuà-^{1}gyi ^{1}bbŭ ^{2}nnü ^{2}dzhu
Rubr. 3: ^{2}Dzī ^{1}yü ^{3}lü-^{2}gv ^{1}ō
Rubr. 4: ^{1}Na-^{2}khi ^{1}ä-^{1}ssĭ ^{3}mun̲
Rubr. 5: ^{1}Nggü-^{1}gyi ^{1}bbŭ ^{2}nnü ^{3}mun̲
Rubr. 6: ^{2}Dzhu ^{2}zo ^{2}ch'i-^{1}ddü-^{3}hoa
Rubr. 7: ^{1}Nggü-^{1}gyi ^{1}bbŭ ^{2}nnü ^{2}dzhu
Rubr. 8: ^{2}Muàn̲ ^{3}mun̲ ^{2}mùan̲ ^{2}muàn̲ ^{3}mun̲
Rubr. 9: ^{2}Mùan̲ ^{3}llü ^{1}ä-^{1}ssĭ ^{3}mun̲
Rubr. 10: ^{2}Mùan̲ ^{1}tgkye ^{1}ssu-^{2}ndzĕr ^{3}mun̲
Rubr. 11: ^{2}K'wua-^{1}dtv-^{1}mbĕr-^{2}ddv ^{3}mun̲, ^{2}Dzī-^{1}la-^{1}ä-^{2}p'u ^{3}mun̲, ^{2}Mùan̲-^{2}zo-^{3}bpä-^{2}dsä ^{3}mun̲.

Eleventh Page:

1) All the sons of bitterness
2) beneath the tiled roof house there is bitterness
3) The man born in the centre
4) the father of the ^{1}Na-^{2}khi died
5) he died under the shingle roof house
6) all the sons of bitterness
7) beneath the shingle roof house there is bitterness.
8) Who does not die? Heaven does not die
9) but the father of heaven died
10) in heaven there died three venerable ones
11) ^{2}K'wua-^{1}dtv-^{1}mbĕr-^{2}ddv died, ^{2}Dzī-^{1}la-^{1}ä-^{2}p'u died, and ^{2}Mùan̲-^{2}zo-^{3}bpä-^{2}dsä died.

Explanation of text

Page 11

Rubr. 1: The first symbol is ^{2}dzhu = bitterness, it has been explained in the title; the next is read ^{2}zo = boy, man, son, ^{2}ch'i-^{1}ddü-^{3}hoa = all, everyone, ^{2}ch'i has been explained in rubric 8 of page 7, and so has the symbol ^{1}ddü in rubric 8 of page 8, the last symbol represents the ^{3}hoa-^{1}p'ěr the Tibetan eared-pheasant *(Crossoptilon Crossoptilon Crossoptilon)*, it is a large bird which goes in flocks in the high alpine regions at 13,000–14,000 ft; the top of its head and the legs are red, the body feathers are a whitish gray and the broad tail is black. The three curved lines attached to the head represent the large tail feathers (*see BODMSL*, Plate XII) ^{2}ch'i-^{1}ddü-^{3}hoa = all; literally this, ^{1}ddü = large, ^{3}hoa = a crowd, hence all, another expression for all is ^{2}ch'i-^{1}wuà.

Rubr. 2: All these symbols have been explained previously.

Rubr. 3: The first symbol represents a jackal = ^{2}dzī, colloquially called ^{1}p'a, ^{2}dzī stands for "people", as in ^{2}dzī ^{1}nä ^{1}ts'o *i. e.*, the descendants of the daughter of ^{2}Dzī-^{1}la-^{1}ä-^{2}p'u and ^{1}Ts'o-^{2}zä-^{3}llü-^{2}ghügh, *see MBC*, pp. 71–88. It is also possible that the word ^{2}dzī for people is derived from the name of the pre-flood ancestor of the ^{1}Na-^{2}khi ^{2}Dzī-^{2}zä-^{1}t'so-^{2}zä, or actually ^{1}Dgyu-^{2}zä ^{2}Dzī-^{2}zä, the father's name always precedes that of the son, so ^{1}Ts'o-^{2}zä ^{3}Llü-^{2}ghügh is the grandson of the former, *see also ANKSWC*, Vol. I, p. 82. The symbol ^{1}yü = born has been explained. The next is a compound symbol consisting of ^{2}Mùan̲ = heaven, ^{3}lü = a spear, ^{1}dü = land, and the four circles representing the four quarters of the compass, it is read ^{2}Mùan̲ ^{1}nä ^{1}dü ^{3}lü ^{2}gv = heaven and earth centre, hence the centre between heaven and earth, here it is only read ^{3}lü-^{2}gv = centre, that is between the Tibetans and the Min-chia (tribes), live the ^{1}Na-^{2}khi. The last symbols represents a turquoise-studded charm box, hence it is used for ^{1}ō-^{1}hăr = turquoise, also for the color blue or green, here it stands for ^{1}ō = there.

Rubr. 4: The first is a character read ^{1}na = black, it is the twelfth letter of the Tibetan alphabet; the second symbol is read ^{2}khi = paddy both are used phonetically for ^{1}Na-^{2}khi, but it does not mean black man, for that would be ^{2}khi-^{1}na, the adjective modifying a noun follows it as in Tibetan. The symbols for ^{1}ä-^{1}ssĭ = father and ^{3}mun̲ = to die, dead, have already been explained.

Rubr. 5: The first symbol represents a house = ^{1}gyi, on the top are to be seen two boards (shingles) and a stone, ^{1}nggü = shingles, hence a ^{1}nggü-^{1}gyi is a shingle-roofed house, in contradistinction to a tamped-earth roof such as the Tibetans build in certain areas, and the tile-covered roofs of the Min-chia houses. *See l. c.*, Vol. I, Plate 132. The symbol ^{3}mun̲ = to die, dead, is written within the house symbol. The others have already been explained.

Rubr. 6 and 7: The symbols in these two rubrics have already been explained.

Rubr. 8: It needs only to remark about the syntax, the sentence is an interrogative one, the word "who" is not written and must be supplied, who did not die? Heaven did not die, notice the difference between ^{2}muàn̲ = not and ^{2}mùan̲ = heaven, on the former the prominence is on à, and on the latter on ù, both are read in the second tone.

Rubr. 9: All the symbols of this rubric have been explained.

Rubr. 10: The first symbol is ^{2}mùan̲ = heaven, below the pictograph ^{2}tgkye = an oil lamp or butter lamp, here it is used phonetically for ^{1}tgkye = in, on, in heaven; the next is the symbol for three = ^{1}ssu, followed by that for tree = (pine tree) ^{1}ndzĕr, here it is used for ^{2}ndzĕr an honorific term, and may be translated "venerable".

Rubr. 11: We see three beings in a more or less prostrate position, two have animal heads, the first has a ^{1}mbĕr = yak head, the second a ^{2}la = tiger head, above his head the syllable or symbol ^{2}p'u; the third figure has the helmet of a ^{1}Dsä demon; all three act as phonetics only and do not indicate that they possess such heads. The names of the two first are not written, but that of the third is fully written out with pictographs representing the phonetic values as in the name. ^{2}Mùan̲ = heaven, below, ^{2}bpä = residue of distilled liquor, the drained mash, ^{1}zo = an earthen jar, and ^{1}dsä = the head and helmet of a ^{1}Dsä demon. The ^{2}p'u above the head of the second figure is the last syllable in the name. These three are considered to have died first in heaven. They are mentioned in a *ms.*, called ^{2}Ts'u ^{1}yi, no. 1078, of the ^{2}Zhi ^{3}mä funeral ceremony, *q. v.*

Twelfth Page:

Rubr. 1: ²Mùan̲ ²ggŏ ¹t'o ²nnü ³mun̲
Rubr. 2: ²Mùan̲ ²zo ²ngv ²bä-²gu
Rubr. 3: ²Mùan̲ ²ggŏ ¹t'o ²nnü ²dzhu
Rubr. 4: ²Muàn̲ ³mun̲ ¹dü ²muàn̲ ³mun̲
Rubr. 5: ¹Dü ³llü ¹ä-²mä ³mun̲
Rubr. 6: ¹Dü ¹tgkye ¹ssu-²ndzĕr ³mun̲
Rubr. 7: ²La-²lĕr-¹dü-²ndzĭ ³mun̲, ¹Dü-³mi-³ts'ä-¹ts'u ³mun̲, ¹Dü-³mi-²yu-¹lu ³mun̲
Rubr. 8: ¹Dü ²ggŏ ¹t'o ²nnü ³mun̲
Rubr. 9: ¹Dü ²zo ²shĕr ²bä-²gu
Rubr. 10: ¹Dü ²ggŏ ¹t'o ²nnü ²dzhu.

Twelfth Page:

1) They died far behind the heavens
2) Their nine celestial sons (experienced bitterness);
3) Even in heaven there is bitterness.
4) Who did not die? the Earth did not die
5) but the mother of the earth died,
6) on the earth there died three venerable ones
7) ²La-²lĕr-¹dü-²ndzĭ died, ¹Dü-³mi-³ts'ä-¹ts'u died, and ¹Dü-³mi-²yu-¹lu died,
8) they died behind the horizon;
9) the seven terrestrial sons
10) they experienced bitterness.

Explanation of text

Page 12

Rubr. 1: The symbols ²mùan̲ = heaven, and ²ggŏ = of, the genetive case, have been explained, below them is the symbol ¹t'o, it has been explained in rubric 2, of page eight, here it stands for the adverb ¹t'o = behind, back of, hence behind or back of the heavens, ²nnü ³mun̲ = they died, has been explained.

Rubr. 2: ²Mùan̲ ²zo = heaven's sons ²ngv = nine, ²bä-²gu, actually brothers, ²bä = to do, and ¹gu = to carry a load, ¹bä has reference to having been (made) conceived, and born, the offspring is then carried, older brothers carry their younger brothers, or older persons carry the children. The numeral 9 is indicated by the nine short lines, three in each of three rows.

Rubr. 3: For the word ¹t'o = behind, back of, another symbol is used instead of the one in the first rubric, here the symbol for pine = ¹t'o is used; the other symbols have already been explained.

Rubr. 4: The symbols and their use are identical with those of rubric 8, of page eleven, except that the symbol ¹dü = earth, is substituted for that of ²mùan̲ = heaven.

Rubr. 5: The symbols of this rubric are similar to those of rubric 9 of page eleven, except that ¹ä-²mä = mother is substituted for ¹ä-¹ssĭ = father. Heaven is considered male and the earth = ¹dü female. The symbol ¹dü = land, earth, is the second in the rubric, and ¹ä-²mä are the third and fourth symbols, ¹ä = represents a mouth open, as if saying "ä", ²mä represents the vagina.

Rubr. 6: These symbols are identical with those in rubric 10, of page eleven, only the symbol ¹dü earth is substituted for that of ²mùan̲ = heaven.

Rubr. 7: These are three females who were the first to die on earth, they are apparently the wives of those who died in heaven. The first one has a tiger's head, this does not indicate that she has a tiger's head, but the symbol for tiger = ²la acts as phonetic; the ¹Na-²khi have the rule to use animal heads on figures as phonetics, only when demons, Nāgas, certain gods etc., actually are figured as having animals' heads then the particular animal head is mentioned with the additional syllables ²gkv ¹dzu = head born (with). She sits on the symbol for land on which grass is seen growing, as such the symbol is always read ²Dzī-¹gyu-²la-²lĕr-¹dü which stands for the inhabited world, literally the people running (about on) the vast land. This tiger-headed female sitting on that symbol is always read ²La-²lĕr-¹dü-²ndzĭ (³mi = female), hence no other identifying phonetic symbol occurs. The syllable ³mun̲ = to die (it also stands for old in years) has been explained.

The second female stands on the symbol ¹dü = land, she has the typical headdress of a ¹Na-²khi woman, at her feet is the symbol ²mi = fire, here it acts phonetically for ³mi = female, ¹dü-³mi = terrestrial female; her actual name is ³ts'ä-¹ts'u, ²ts'ä = salt, the symbol represents that article, a rectangle with diagonally crossed lines, below it is the syllabic ²ggŏ-¹baw letter ¹ts'u, it is the phonetic equivalent for ¹ts'u = demon, and rather than write the symbol for demon, its phonetic ²ggŏ-¹baw counterpart has been used. The third terrestrial female's name is ²yu-¹lu, both act as phonetics, the first is a symbol already explained, the second is a ²ggŏ-¹baw phonetic. The last is again ³mun̲ = die. Like the three celestial males in rubric 11, of page eleven, whose counterparts they are, they are also mentioned in *ms.*, ²Ts'u ¹yi of the ²Zhi ³mä funeral ceremony, *see* rubric 11, of page eleven.

Rubr. 8: This is the same as in rubrics 1 and 2 (in part) of this page, only the symbol ¹dü = earth is substituted for that of ²mùan̲ = heaven.

Rubr. 9: We see here a male figure standing on the symbol ¹dü = earth, the next is the numeral 7, seven short lines, the remaining symbols are the same as in rubric 2 of this page. It should not read seven sons of the earth, for the earth as well as the numeral seven are always associated with the female sex, however girls or daughters are not considered mourners at a funeral of a parent, but only sons are, for daughters are sold or given away in marriage and hence belong to someone else (they have from childhood already been spoken for) and thus they cannot be considered mourners.

Should a daughter after having been given in marriage return to her home for a visit, and be seriously taken ill preventing her returning to her husband's home, she is put outside the house of her parents and left to die under the grain rack. It is no more her home, she does not belong to it, and hence cannot die in her parent's house.

Rubr. 10: For explanation see rubric 3, of this page, but ¹dü = land is substituted for ²mùan̲ = heaven.

After the 12th page has been chanted the song is continued outside as explained in the introduction.

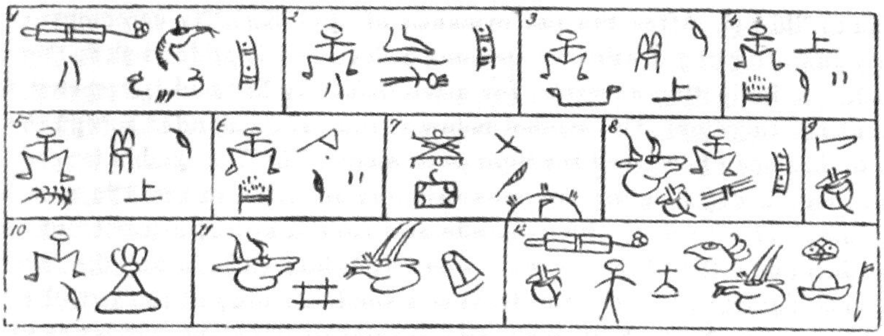

Thirteenth Page:

Rubr. 1: ^{2}Dzhu ^{2}lä ^{1}zhi ^{3}bpŭ ^{2}bbŭe
Rubr. 2: ^{2}Ts'o ^{2}lä ^{1}ts'u ^{1}szĕr ^{2}bbŭe
Rubr. 3: ^{2}Ts'o ^{2}t'u ^{2}gkv ^{2}muàn̲ ^{3}shou
Rubr. 4: ^{2}Ts'o ^{1}dzo ^{3}shou ^{2}muàn̲ ^{2}nyi
Rubr. 5: ^{2}Ts'o ^{3}bbŭe ^{2}gkv ^{2}muàn̲ ^{3}shou
Rubr. 6: ^{2}Ts'o ^{1}dzo ^{2}bä ^{2}muàn̲ ^{2}nyi
Rubr. 7: ^{1}Ha-^{2}gyu-^{2}la-^{3}ts'ü ^{1}gko
Rubr. 8: ^{1}Mbĕr ^{2}nnü ^{2}ts'o ^{2}bbŭe ^{3}dzĭ
Rubr. 9: ^{1}Mbĕr ^{2}nnü
Rubr. 10: ^{2}Ts'o ^{2}muàn̲ ^{2}ndu
Rubr. 11: ^{1}Mbĕr ^{1}ngu ^{3}ds'ĭ ^{1}ds'i ^{3}ds'ĭ
Rubr. 12: ^{2}Dzhu ^{2}nnü ^{2}zo ^{2}ch'i-^{3}hoa, ^{3}Ds'ĭ-^{2}bpa ^{2}gu-^{1}mun̲ ^{2}t'an̲.

Thirteenth Page:

1) Now we will escort the deceased and again experience bitterness;
2) we will again dance and suppress the demons.
3) If it is not told whence the dance originated
4) one must not speak about it.
5) Unless one knows the origin of the dance
6) one cannot dance.
7) On ^{1}Ha-^{2}gyu-^{2}la-^{3}ts'ü ^{1}gko
8) the yak said he would like to dance
9) the yak he
10) for him there is no such custom to dance,
11) after the yak came the goat,
12) all the sons of bitterness, they wear a ^{3}Ds'ĭ-^{2}bpa ^{2}gu-^{1}mun̲.

Explanation of text

Page 13

Rubr. 1: The first two symbols have been explained ^{2}dzhu-^{2}lä = bitterness again (experience). The third symbol is that of a snake = ^{1}zhi; on the death of a person it is believed that the deceased is changed into a snake and he is addressed as

^{1}Zhi-^{3}mun̲-^{2}llü-^{2}ssĭ. After the performance of the ^{2}Khi ^{3}Nv ceremony (within three years after the death of a person) a deceased is addressed as ^{1}Yü-^{3}mun̲-^{2}llü-^{2}ssĭ, ^{1}yü indicating ancestor, for after ^{2}Khi ^{3}Nv his soul is escorted to the realm of his ancestors. The symbol below is that of a colander = ^{3}bpŭ, here its phonetic has been borrowed for ^{3}bpŭ = to escort. The last symbol is read ^{1}bbŭe it represents a dry measure for measuring grain, it is no more in use, it was in the shape of a pitcher with a handle and carved out of a tree trunk in one single piece; now the Chinese square sheng [32] boxes are in use, the four sides of the box slant towards the top leaving a small opening at the top; the ^{1}bbŭe was still in use in Mu-li, Yung-ning, (the former in Hsi-k'ang, the latter in Yün-nan) and in western Kan-su some twenty five years ago when I explored there. Here the ^{1}bbŭe symbol is used for ^{2}bbŭe to go (and do a thing) actually "will do", it expresses the future at the end of a verb.

Rubr. 2: The first symbol is read ^{2}ts'o = to dance, it shows a person in the act of dancing, below is the phonetic character ^{2}lä = again; the next is a compound one, it depicts a foot stepping on a prostrate demon = ^{1}ts'u, it is read ^{1}ts'u = demon ^{1}szĕr = suppress. The symbol ^{2}bbŭe again expresses the future or "will do".

Rubrics 3–6: All the symbols in these rubrics have been explained under rubrics 3–5 of page one, only the symbol ^{2}ts'o = to dance is substituted for ^{2}dzhu bitterness.

Rubr. 7: ^{1}Ha-^{2}gyu-^{2}la-^{3}ts'ü is the name of an alpine meadow = ^{1}gko. All the symbols used as phonetics have been explained previously, except the one before last, ^{3}ts'ü = millet.

Rubr. 8: The first symbol is ^{1}mbĕr = yak, ^{2}nnü = he, ^{2}ts'o = dance ^{2}bbŭe ^{3}dzĭ, ^{2}bbŭe = to go; the symbol ^{2}dzĭ = to tie, a knot, it is the picture of a knot; here read ^{3}dzĭ, it serves as an interrogative particle at the end of a sentence, with the meaning of "is it so"?

Rubr. 9: The first is a ^{2}ggŏ-^{1}baw character read ^{1}mbĕr, it stands for ^{1}mbĕr = yak; ^{2}nnü = he, the meaning is "the yak (for) him".

Rubr. 10: ^{2}ts'o = to dance, ^{2}muàn̲ = not, ^{2}ndu = custom, these symbols have been explained.

Rubr. 11: We have again the ^{2}ggŏ-^{1}baw letter ^{1}mbĕr = yak, then ^{1}ngu = a grain chest, here it stands for ^{1}ngu = behind, or after, as ^{3}ds'ĭ = goat of which the symbol is a picture; after the yak, ^{1}ds'ĭ = to come, the symbol represents a mutton shoulder blade, it has two readings ^{1}p'i and ^{1}ds'i, here it stands for ^{1}ds'i = to come; as the song is in the meter of five syllables the word goat = ^{3}ds'ĭ is again repeated.

Rubr. 12: The first five symbols have been explained in rubric 6, of page eleven, the syllable ^{2}nnü = they is here written and ^{1}ddü has been omitted. The next two symbols are ^{3}ds'ĭ = goat, ^{2}bpa = frog, here they stand for the name of a hat = ^{2}gu-^{1}mun̲ of which the symbol next to the last is a picture. The hat is actually called ^{3}ds'ĭ-^{2}bpa-^{1}na as it was made of "^{1}na = black" goat's hair, it could also be made of ^{1}Mbĕr = yak hair, it was then called ^{1}Mbĕr-^{2}ssu (yak-wool) ^{3}ds'ĭ-^{2}bpa-^{1}na, this shows that the actual name of such a hat was ^{3}ds'ĭ-^{2}bpa; the hat was worn by mourners during the funeral dances, no such hats are now in existence. The last symbol is read ^{2}t'an̲ it represents a wooden stick or branch of an oak, all branchlets are cut off except one or two at the end and these are cut a few inches from the stem; these ^{2}t'an̲ are used to pick up thorny branches for the making of fences around fields, here the symbol's phonetic value has been borrowed for ^{2}t'an̲ = to wear. *See SNL*, Plate XXV, p. 80. This stick usually of oak wood is colloquially called ^{3}gku-^{2}t'an̲.

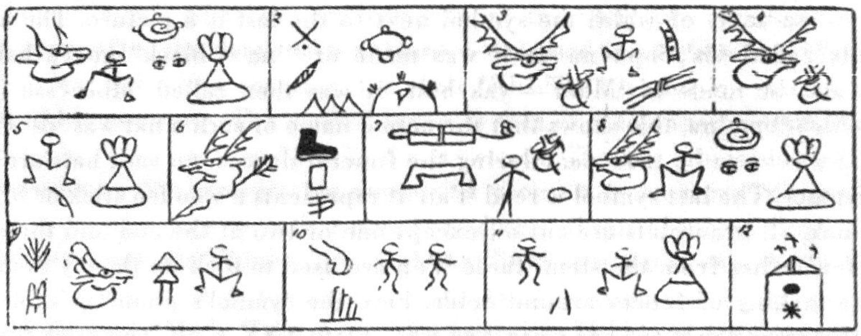

Fourteenth Page:

Rubr. 1: ¹Mbĕr ²ts'o ³ch'ou-¹nyu ²ndu
Rubr. 2: ²La-³ts'ü-¹hö-¹ddü ¹gko
Rubr. 3: ³Ch'wua ²nnü ²ts'o ²bbŭe ³dzĭ
Rubr. 4: ³Ch'wua ²nnü
Rubr. 5: ²Ts'o ²muàn̲ ²ndu
Rubr. 6: ³Ch'wua ²khi ²zaw ³dto ¹p'ĕr
Rubr. 7: ²Dzhu ²ggŏ ²zo ²nnü ³gkü
Rubr. 8: ³Ch'wua ²ts'o ³ch'ou-¹nyu ²ndu
Rubr. 9: ²T'o ²gkv ¹t'khi ³t'a ²ts'o
Rubr. 10: ²K'wua ¹dzu ²kw'ua ³nyu-²nyu
Rubr. 11: ³Nyu ²lä ²ddü ²ts'o ²ndu
Rubr. 12: ¹Na-²mun̲-²mbe-³dtv-²ddü.

Fourteenth Page:

1) The yak he dances there it is the custom
2) on ²La-³ts'ü-¹hö¹ddü ¹gko
3) the stag said he would like to dance there.
4) For the stag
5) to dance is not the custom,
6) the elkskin shoes with the white front
7) the sons of bitterness wear;
8) the stag he dances there it is the custom.
9) Where the pines are the young deer wanted to dance,
10) the cloven-hoofed they sway in rhythm,
11) they sway and dance as is the custom.
12) All the people of the village.

Explanation of text

Page 14

Rubr. 1: The first two symbols have been explained. The third symbol is ³ch'ou = foul, evil smelling, impure, it is the picture of human excrement, other ²dto-¹mbas said it represented a human embryo, hence unclean; below it are two eyes = [1]miu, also read [1]nyu, both stand for [2]ch'ou-[1]nyu = here, [2]ndu = custom. The meaning of this phrase is that while from the goat and yak hair a hat is made and worn by the mourners, it is not the goat and yak who dance, but the wearers of the goat and yak hair hat, thus these animals dance indirectly.

Rubr. 2: Four of the five symbols have been previously explained, the third while discussed elsewhere, is here differently used, it is the symbol [2]mi = fire, here it is read [1]hö = red, all of the first four symbols are phonetically used and spell the name of the [1]gko or alpine meadow.

Rubr. 3: The symbols in this rubric have been explained, the first is that of a stag = [3]ch'wua, it is the stag who wants to dance.

Rubrics 4–5: The symbols in these rubrics have already been explained.

Rubr. 6: The first symbol is a compound one, it shows a stag to whose upper body a front leg is attached, below it is the symbol [2]khi = paddy, here it stands for [2]khi = a cured skin, hence a cured, tanned, stag or elkskin; an uncured skin is called [2]ghügh. The next symbol is [2]zaw = shoe, [2]dto = a board, is below the [2]zaw symbol, here it is used phonetically for [3]dto = the front, forehead, [1]p'ĕr = white, hence an elkskin shoe with a white front (toe).

Rubr. 7: The symbols read: bitterness of sons they, [3]gkü = wear, [3]gkü is the last symbol in the rubric, it represents a star = [1]gkü, and its phonetic has been borrowed for [3]gkü = wear.

Rubr. 8: The symbols in this rubric have already been explained, *see* rubric 1, of this page; only the stag is substituted for the yak.

Rubr. 9: The first symbol is read [2]t'o and represents a pine, below it is the symbol [2]gkv = head, it serves here for [2]gkv = there, a demonstrative pronoun in regard to a place, hence there where the pines (grow) the [1]t'khi [3]t'a = deer young, (wishes) to dance; the symbol [3]t'a between the deer and the dancing figure, represents a pagoda, here it stands for [3]t'a-([2]mä) = a young deer two or three years old. Here young people are meant and their friends or companions of the next page.

Rubr. 10: The first symbol represents a cloven-hoofed front leg, below is the symbol [2]dzu representing a wall here it stands for [1]dzu = born (with), hence those born with cloven hoofs; the next two symbols are read [3]nyu-[2]nyu = to sway, to wiggle, hence to sway with rhythm while dancing.

Rubr. 11: [3]Nyu = to sway, [2]lä = again, [2]ts'o = dance, [2]ndu = (as is the) custom.

Rubr. 12: All these syllables stand for = all the [1]Na-[2]khi villages, the main symbol is a house, above it the symbol for snow = [2]mbe, and within the main symbol we find [1]na = black, the [1]Na-[2]khi are here meant, and [1]dtv = 1000, all serve as phonetics; it can mean all the village people, also all the villages or people of the neighboring villages, it is a phrase which cannot be defined word for word.

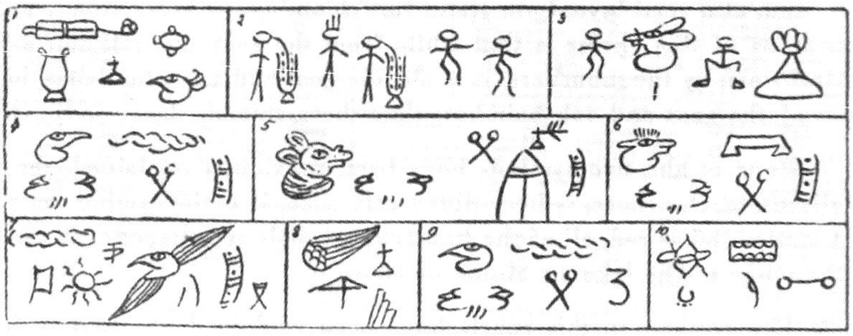

Fifteenth Page:

Rubr. 1: ^{2}Dzhu ^{2}zo ^{2}ch'i-^{1}ddü-^{3}hoa
Rubr. 2: ^{3}T'ü-^{1}ts'u ^{2}t'ü ^{3}nyu-^{2}nyu
Rubr. 3: ^{3}Nyu ^{2}lä ^{2}ddü ^{2}ts'o ^{2}ndu
Rubr. 4: ^{2}Gko ^{3}bpŭ ^{1}gkyi ^{2}gkyi ^{2}bbŭe
Rubr. 5: ^{2}La ^{3}bpŭ ^{2}sso ^{2}gkyi ^{2}bbŭe
Rubr. 6: ^{1}Yü ^{3}bpŭ ^{1}ggŏ ^{2}gkyi ^{2}bbŭe
Rubr. 7: ^{1}Gkyi ^{2}k'u ^{1}p'ĕr ^{3}lv-^{2}la, ^{2}gko ^{1}ndzī ^{2}lä ^{2}bbŭe ^{2}mä
Rubr. 8: ^{2}Ndŭ ^{2}mun̲ ^{2}ndŭ ^{2}ch'i ^{1}dzu
Rubr. 9: ^{2}Gko ^{3}bpŭ ^{1}gkyi ^{2}gkyi ^{1}ssä
Rubr. 10: ^{2}Non̲-^{1}ō ^{2}ḳhü ^{2}muàn̲ ^{1}chĕr.

Fifteenth Page:

1) All the sons of bitterness
2) with their slim waists they sway in rhythm,
3) they sway and dance again as is the custom.
4) We will escort the crane to his clouds,
5) and will escort the tiger to his high mountain,
6) we will escort our ancestor on high.
7) To the dazzling white gate of the clouds the crane wants to fly,
8) all those born with wings
9) have escorted the crane to the clouds
10) but his ability (we) do not allow to pass.

Explanation of text

Page 15

Rubr. 1: All these symbols have been explained.

Rubr. 2: The first two symbols are read ^{1}t'ü = to drink, and ^{1}ts'u = demon respectively, their phonetic value has been borrowed for ^{3}t'ü-^{1}ts'u = waist slim, a narrow, slim waist; the second ^{1}t'ü is read in the second tone and stands for the personal pronoun they. ^{3}Nyu-^{2}nyu = sway as the symbols indicate.

Rubr. 3: This is identical with rubric 11, of page fourteen.

Rubr. 4: ²Gko = crane, ³bpŭ = escort, the third symbol is read ¹gkyi = cloud, it is a picture of clouds, below it is a pair of shears = ³gkyi, such as are used in shearing sheep, here it stands for ²gkyi = to place, to put, and the last syllable ²bbŭe = the future tense.

Rubr. 5: ²La ³bpŭ = tiger escort, the remaining symbols have been explained, ²sso is a high mountain *see* rubric 4 of page three, the tiger is always associated with a high mountain, the word ²gkyi = to put, to place is added with the meaning that the tiger is escorted till he has arrived, *i. e.*, till he has been placed where he belongs.

Rubr. 6: The only symbol that needs explaining is the first, it represents a monkey = ¹yü, here it stands for ¹yü = ancestor, it is interesting to note that while the Tibetans believe their ancestor to have been a monkey, the ¹Na-²khi make no such claim, they do use however the monkey symbol, it may be because the two phonetics are the same. Yet in the story of ¹Ts'o-²zä-³llü-²ghügh it is related that in his union with a demoness one of his offsprings was a monkey, but he was done away with.

Although the symbol ¹ggŏ = bench, which can stand for the genitive particle "of", also for above, upper, north, is here used in the sense of "on high", that is he is escorted on high, to the realm of the gods.

Rubr. 7: In this rubric there are two symbols which have not appeared before, they are the fourth and fifth. ¹Gkyi ²ku = cloud gate or the gate of the clouds the symbol ¹p'ĕr = white is next to the clouds, below the latter is a circle with wavy lines extending from it, it is read ³lv-²la = brilliant, dazzling, scintillating, a brilliant object. The next symbol is a bird in flying attitude, above the bird's head is the symbol ¹p'ĕr, it is not read but it indicates that the white crane ²gko-¹p'ĕr is meant, ¹ndzī means to fly, and the crane is here shown in a flying attitude, hence ²gko ¹ndzī = crane fly. The word ²mä is a final particle at the end of a sentence denoting the affirmative.

Rubr. 8: We meet here with two symbols previously not explained, the first is read ²ndŭ, it is a picture of a wing, below it is the symbol ²mun̠ it is another pictograph for ²mùan̠ = heaven, here it stands for ²mun̠ = a being, a creature, the symbol ²ndŭ is here read twice, ²ch'i = all an abbreviation of ²ch'i-¹wuà = all, the last symbol ¹dzu = born (with), literally winged creatures, wings all born (with); the next part of the sentence is in rubric 9.

Rubr. 9: ²Gko ³bpŭ = crane escort, ¹gkyi = clouds, ²gkyi place, ¹ssä is a ²ggŏ-¹baw letter and denotes the past tense.

Rubr. 10: The first is a compound symbol, the upper is read ¹ō, the lower ²non̠ and represents milk, the first ¹ō is different from the symbol ¹ō which stands for turquoise, the wavy lines above and below indicate that ¹ō = soul is meant; actually ²non̠-¹ō, it must be read reversed, stands for = qualities, the ability, efficiency, accomplishments, etc., all this is embraced in the words ²nōn̠-¹ō, the word ²non̠ = milk, a derivative from a creature, is used to express this,

this is however only a conjecture, all the good qualities of the deceased, as well as his belongings are meant, for a deceased's perspiration-impregnated clothing is also called ²non̲-¹ō, the things that he left behind to be divided after the funeral ceremony. There is a regular book called ²Non̲-¹ō ³ssaw = invite the ²non̲-¹ō of a deceased, it is chanted at funerals, for instance at the funeral of a ²dto-¹mba or priest, the book is chanted when the ²dto-¹mba's requisites of office, as his ²ds-¹lĕr, five-lobed crown = ²k'o, sword, etc., are handed to his son by officiating ²dto-¹mbas. The next symbol represents a mouth with teeth, hence teeth = ²k̦hü, here it stands for the verb ²k̦hü = to pass, let go; next is the negation ²muàn̲ = not, and the last symbol is read ³chĕr = a joint, a bone joint, it is also read ²ō = bone of which it is a picture, here it is read ¹chĕr = permit, allow, hence the ²non̲-¹ō = qualities, etc., pass not permit.

Sixteenth Page:

Rubr. 1: ^{1}Noṉ ^{1}p'ĕr ^{2}t'ä ^{2}nyi ^{2}mä
Rubr. 2: ^{2}Noṉ-^{1}ō ^{2}ssu ^{1}mùeṉ ^{2}lä ^{3}ssaw
Rubr. 3: ^{2}Sso ^{2}k'u ^{1}shi ^{3}ghügh-^{2}ghügh ^{2}la ^{2}ts'o ^{2}lä ^{2}bbüe ^{2}mä
Rubr. 4: ^{1}Dshi ^{2}muṉ ^{2}ch'i ^{1}dzu ^{2}la ^{3}bpŭ ^{2}sso ^{2}lä ^{2}gkyi
Rubr. 5: ^{2}Noṉ-^{1}ō ^{2}ķhü ^{2}muàṉ ^{1}chĕr
Rubr. 6: ^{1}Yü ^{3}bpŭ ^{1}hä ^{1}dü ^{2}t'u
Rubr. 7: ^{2}Ssu-^{2}bbŭ ^{2}ngv ^{1}mbu ^{3}lo
Rubr. 8: ^{2}Noṉ-^{1}ō ^{1}mbu ^{3}lo ^{2}ķhü ^{2}muàṉ ^{1}chĕr
Rubr. 9: ^{1}P'ä-^{1}gyi ^{2}shĕr ^{1}ho ^{2}ndĕr
Rubr. 10: ^{2}Noṉ,^{1}ō ^{1}gyi ^{2}ndĕr ^{2}ķhü ^{2}muàṉ ^{1}chĕr.

Sixteenth Page:

1) Like the white down-feathers of the crane.
2) the power (ability) of the departed we invite down to us below.
3) To the brilliant yellow gate of the high mountain, the tiger wants to dance and return;
4) all animals born with claws escort the tiger to his high mountain,
5) but let not his power depart with him.
6) Let us escort the departed that he may arrive in the land of the gods,
7) the departed must cross the nine spurs,
8) but his power (ability) must not cross the spurs.
9) He must cross the seven waters of ^{1}P'ä
10) but let not the power of his personality cross with him.

Explanation of text

Page 16

Rubr. 1: The first symbol is ^{1}p'ĕr = white, the second ^{1}noṉ = down-feather, of which it is a picture; the white down-feathers of the crane are considered his ^{2}noṉ-^{1}ō, here is a play on words. The third symbol is ^{2}t'ä = flag, the fourth is the numeral 2 = ^{2}nyi, here ^{2}t'ä-^{2}nyi means 'like the' (^{1}noṉ = down feathers of the crane); often the phrase ^{2}t'ä-^{2}nyi ^{2}gv is encountered in ^{2}Dto-^{1}mba *mss.*, the actual meaning of the phrase is ^{2}t'ä = that, ^{2}nyi = two, ^{2}gv = body, *i. e.* of two things that, hence similar to that. ^{2}Mä is again the affirmative.

Rubr. 2: The first symbol is ^{2}non-^{1}ō, the second ^{2}ssu = wool, here it stands for part of the name given to ancestors = ^{2}ssu-^{2}bbŭ-^{1}yü, this is often written with the symbol for wood = ^{2}ss, or with that of a wool felt ^{2}ssu, and always ending up with ^{1}yü = monkey, ^{2}bbŭ is written with the symbol for pot = ^{2}bbŭ. Below it is the symbol for ^{2}mi = fire, it has the same meaning here as in the rubric 7, of page four *q. v.*, *viz.*, ^{1}müen = down below, ^{2}lä = again, ^{3}ssaw = invite, the symbol represents ^{3}ssaw = breath, used here phonetically.

Rubr. 3: ^{2}Sso = high mountain, *see* rubric 5, of page fifteen; ^{2}k'u = gate, ^{2}shi = meat, here ^{1}shi = yellow, = the yellow gate of the high mountain; these symbols are followed by Swastikas of the Bön, with a right to left direction, the phonetic value is ^{2}ghügh, here ^{3}ghügh-^{2}ghügh = brilliant, bright. The remainder has already been explained.

Rubr. 4: Te first symbol is a front leg of a predatory clawed animal, it is read ^{1}dshi = claws, with the symbol ^{2}mun = clawed creatures; the next two symbols ^{2}ch'i ^{1}dzu = all born, or all creatures born with claws, ^{2}la ^{3}bpŭ = tiger escort, ^{2}sso = high mountain, ^{2}lä = then, ^{2}gkyi = place.

Rubr. 5: *See* rubric 10, of page fifteen.

Rubr. 6: The first symbol is here read ^{1}yü = ancestor, actually the symbol's full name or reading is ^{1}Yü-^{3}mun-^{2}llü-^{2}ssĭ = a deceased changed into an ancestor in contradistinction of ^{1}Zhi-^{3}mun-^{2}llü-^{2}ssĭ = a deceased changed into a snake. The vertical line with the many latteral ones represents a pine branch, superimposed by the symbol ^{1}yü = monkey. At the ^{2}Khi ^{3}nv funerary ceremony which is performed during the eleventh moon within three years after the death of a person, a whole village will perform it at one time for all the deceased men of the village; each family who takes part brings a sheep as offering. The ceremony is performed on a meadow, small paper houses are erected, one for each deceased, these are in double rows and face each other, in each house is a ^{2}nv = a pine branch which represents the deceased. A book is chanted at the ^{2}Khi ^{3}nv ceremony called ^{2}Nv ^{3}hăr = the ^{2}nv cut *i. e.*, while the book is chanted the ^{2}dto-^{1}mba takes a pine branch with two latteral short branches representing the arms, the top leaves represent the hair, and with a knife he cuts, eyes, ears, mouth, nose, etc., into the wood of the branch, this pine branch becomes a ^{2}nv, a substitute or image of the deceased. After the sheep have been killed and offerings have been made, each family takes its particular ^{2}nv out of the paper house, and places it on a large white felt, the son of the family who leads in the ^{2}Khi ^{3}nv ceremony and whose paper house is at the head of, and between the two rows of paper houses, wraps up all the ^{2}nv in the felt, and mounting a horse, but reversed, that is he sits on the horse facing backward, rides to the funerary caves called ^{2}Nv-^{1}t'khi-^{2}k'o-^{1}ndv also ^{2}Nv-^{1}gkyi-^{2}k'o-^{1}ndv and ^{2}Nv-^{1}gkyi-^{1}'a-^{2}k'o. There used to be a caretaker in olden times at that cave, but now, since ^{2}Khi ^{3}nv is no more performed in the Li-chiang district, there is no caretaker and ^{2}nv are no more deposited in these small caves. They are situated in a limestone shelf, facing east, between the last village on the Li-chiang valley plain, and lower ^{2}Nga-^{1}ba, *see* Plate IV.

The chief is called ^{2}Ts'u-^{1}bpö-^{2}swue-^{2}p'ä-^{3}haw the meaning of which is = ^{2}swue-^{2}p'ä = chief, ^{1}ts'u = demon, ^{1}bpö = ceremony, ^{3}haw = sleep; before the ^{2}Khi ^{3}nv ceremony has been performed a deceased is still considered a demon, the chief is the leader of the ceremony = ^{1}bpö, and as such supplies the food = ^{2}haw for all those who participate in the affair. As they also sleep in house the word ^{3}haw is added. The place where the ^{2}Khi ^{3}nv ceremony is performed is called ^{2}Ts'u-^{1}bpö-^{2}lü-^{2}k'u-^{2}dtü, the general term is ^{2}Khi ^{3}nv ^{1}d'a = the place of the ^{2}Khi ^{3}nv. The officiating ^{2}dto-^{1}mba at a funeral ceremony is called ^{2}Lo-^{1}ch'ung-^{2}ndaw-^{1}ḵhü, he wears a huge black felt hat and carries the ^{3}Mùen̲-^{1}t'u or funeral wand. ^{3}Bpŭ = escort; the next symbol represents a deity, gods are termed ^{1}hä, below it is the symbol for ^{1}dü = land, and the last symbol is ^{2}t'u = arrive.

Rubr. 7: The first two symbols are read ^{2}ss-^{2}bbŭ, it stands for ^{2}ssu-^{2}bbŭ = ancestor, *v. s.*, then follows the numeral 9 = ^{2}ngv, and ^{1}mbu = a spur or ridge, above it is the phonetic character read ^{3}lo = to cross.

Rubr. 8: ^{2}Non̲-^{1}ō spur crossed not permitted (*see* rubric 5 and previous rubric). The nine spurs are called ^{1}P'ä-^{1}mbu ^{2}ngv-^{1}mbu, *see* next rubric.

Rubr. 9: The first symbol is usually read ^{1}ddaw = weaver's loom, it has another phonetic value, namely ^{1}p'ä = hemp cloth, it is here read ^{1}p'ä and with the symbol for water = ^{1}gyi, ^{1}p'ä-^{1}gyi, the word ^{1}p'ä has reference to the place ^{1}P'ä-^{1}mbe-^{3}lo-^{1}nddü. With the numeral 7 = ^{2}shĕr and the symbol ^{1}ho = ribs, here read ^{1}ho = to cross (a stream), the seven ^{1}P'ä-^{1}gyi-^{2}shĕr ^{1}ho = to cross the seven waters of ^{1}P'ä, the word ^{1}ho actually means to drive across, as men drive animals into a stream, which they are urged to swim. The last symbol represents a semi-dried-up pond, the dots indicate the visible bottom, it is read ^{2}ndĕr, here it stands for ^{2}ndĕr = must.

Rubr. 10: These symbols have already been explained; ^{2}non̲-^{1}ō water crossed not permit.

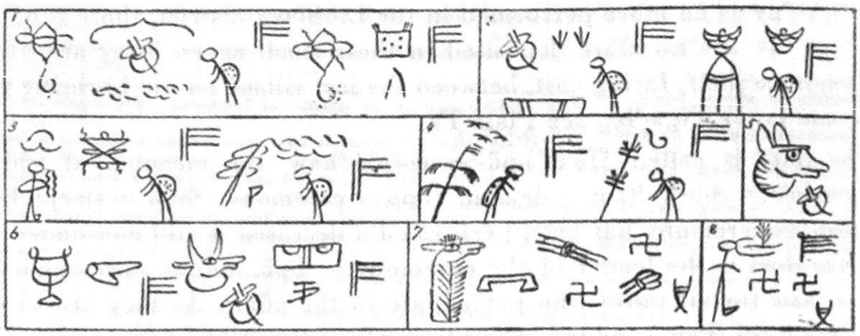

Seventeenth Page:

Rubr. 1: ^{2}Non̲-^{1}ō ^{2}mùan̲ ^{2}nnü ^{1}gkyi ^{2}gu ^{3}ssaw, ^{2}non̲-^{1}ō ^{3}ssu ^{2}lä ^{3}ssaw

Rubr. 2: ^{1}Dü ^{2}nnü ^{1}zhou ^{2}gu ^{3}ssaw, ^{2}Nv-^{2}lv ^{1}nv ^{1}gu ^{3}ssaw

Rubr. 3: ^{2}Yi-^{1}bi ^{1}ha ^{2}gu ^{3}ssaw, ^{3}khyü ^{3}gko ^{1}gkyi ^{1}gu ^{3}ssaw

Rubr. 4: ^{2}Llü ^{3}gko ^{2}mbe ^{1}gu ^{3}ssaw, ^{3}mùen̲-^{2}ts'ä ^{2}ndzhĕr ^{1}gu ^{3}ssaw

Rubr. 5: ^{1}Ngu ^{2}nnü

Rubr. 6: ^{3}gkyi ^{1}shi ^{3}ssaw, ^{1}mun̲ ^{2}nnü ^{1}lo ^{1}p'ĕr ^{3}ssaw,

Rubr. 7: ^{1}Yü-^{3}mun̲-^{2}llü-^{2}ssĭ ^{2}ggŏ ^{1}dzĭ ^{2}ghügh ^{3}gku ^{2}ghügh ^{2}mä

Rubr. 8: ^{2}Ndzĕr ^{2}ghügh ^{1}ho ^{2}ghügh ^{2}mä.

Seventeenth Page:

1) Let us invite his power as if it were a load of celestial clouds, such let us invite to return to us.
2) Like a load of grass of the land, and like a load of silver of the snow mountain, such let us invite
3) Like a load of gold from the Yangtze such let us invite, and like a load of clouds resting on the juniper branches such let us invite
4) like a load of snow on the branches of the fir trees, and like a load of dew on the bamboo, such let us invite;
5) like the horse's
6) yellow saddle let us invite the power of the deceased, and like the white yoke of an ox one retains, so
7) let us retain all the good qualities of the deceased, like his ability to count and to record,
8) and his ability to sing and follow suit in singing.

Explanation of text

Page 17

Rubr. 1: Practically all the symbols in this rubric have been explained, the first is ^{2}non̲-^{1}ō = the deceased's power, ability, etc., this is followed by ^{2}mùan̲ = heaven, ^{2}nnü = heart, here it forms the possessive = heaven's, ^{1}gkyi = clouds;

the next symbol read [1]gu shows a man carrying a load on his back, hence to carry a burden, a load, here it stands for [1]gu a load and also for [2]gu = "like, as", [3]ssaw = invite; the sentences are very ters, the verbs are all in the present tens, the singular or plural is not expressed. The second half of the sentence reads [2]non̲-[1]ō [3]ssu = bring, take, pick up, collect, [2]lä = again, [3]ssaw = invite.

Rubr. 2: The sentence construction is the same, [1]dü = earth, [2]nnü = possessive case, the two small symbols next to [2]nnü = heart are read [1]zhou and stand for grass, hence the earth's grass, [1]gu = load (like, as) invite; [2]Nv-[2]lv = snow mountain actually the symbol [1]ngyu = mountain with the symbol [1]nv = silver superimposed, can also stand for the Li-chiang snow range which is thus called, [1]nv = silver, [1]gu = load, [3]ssaw = invite.

Rubr. 3: The first two symbols or rather the phonetic [2]ggŏ-[1]baw letter [2]yi and the symbol [1]bi = to twist (it shows a man twisting rope with his hands) are both used phonetically for [2]yi-[1]bi = the Yangtze, or a river in general; the Yangtze which encircles the Li-chiang district at a height of from 6,000 to 5,000 feet to the west and east respectively, is rich in gold, hence it is called by the [1]Na-[2]khi [2]La-[2]lĕr-[1]ha-[2]yi-[1]bi = Vast gold stream, and by the Chinese Chin-sha Chiang [60] = River of the golden sand. The next symbol is [1]ha = gold, [1]gu = load, [3]ssaw invite. The second half shows the following symbols: [3]khyü = a juniper tree to the top of which the symbol [1]gkyi = cloud is attached, below the juniper symbol is that for needle = [1]gko, here it stands for [3]gko = branch, the branches of the juniper, [1]gu = load, [3]ssaw = invite.

Rubr. 4: The first symbol is read [2]llü = fir tree *(Abies Forresti)*, on the top of it is the symbol [2]mbe = snow, the word [3]gko = branch is not written but read, [1]gu = load, [3]ssaw = invite. The second half reads [3]mùen̲-[2]ts'ä = the cane-brake a slender species of bamboo which grows in clumps among the fir trees at 11,000 to 12,000 ft elevation, the common form is *Arundinaria Faberi*, here only the symbol [3]mùen̲ = bamboo is written and not the syllable [2]ts'ä; the curved line on the top indicating a dew drop is read [2]ndshĕr = dew, [1]gu = a load, [3]ssaw = invite.

Rubr. 5: There are just two symbols in this rubric, [1]ngu = horse and [2]nnü = heart, here again read [2]nnü = its, the possessive form. The [1]Na-[2]khi have several names for horse, the literary term is [1]ngu, colloquially it is called [2]zhwua, and often we find in [2]Dto-[1]mba *mss.*, the word [2]dta, this is a Tibetan loan word from rta = horse.

Rubr. 6: The first symbol is read [3]gkyi = saddle, it can also mean a horse-load, here it stands for saddle, next to it is the symbol [1]shi = yellow, already explained, then [3]ssaw = invite. The second half of the phrase reads [2]ghügh = ox, cow, it has another phonetic value namely [2]mun̲ = ox, cow, it is not so frequent as [2]ghügh, the latter is the colloquial; [2]nnü = its, the possessive form, then [1]lo = the yoke of which it is a picture, and [1]p'ĕr = white; then again [3]ssaw = invite.

The ^{2}dto-^{1}mba first read the passage horse its saddle dead invite, the symbol ^{2}shi = meat, can be read ^{1}shi = yellow and ^{2}shi = dead, but as it follows the noun ^{3}gkyi = saddle and as the adjective follows the noun, I translate it ^{1}shi = yellow, for in the second phrase the word ^{1}p'ĕr = white follows the noun ^{1}lo = yoke, these two are in juxtaposition, hence ^{1}shi cannot mean dead but yellow; he explained that the power, ability. etc. of the deceased is to be retained below, as one takes off the saddle from a dead horse. It is true the word ^{1}mun can also mean a dead ox, an ox that has been offered, ^{2}mun = ox, cattle is read in the second tone, while a ^{1}mun or sacrified ox is read in the first tone. It is possible that the ^{2}Dto-^{1}mba was right. *See* rubric 8 of page fifteen but here the word ^{2}mun stands for creature, a being.

Rubr. 7: The first symbol should have a snake head instead of that of a monkey = ^{1}yü = ancestor, as only after the ^{2}Khi ^{3}nv ceremony a deceased is addressed as ^{1}Yü-^{3}mun-^{2}llü-^{2}ssĭ, and this is chanted at the actual funeral. The second symbol is ^{2}ggŏ = of, the genetive case, ^{1}dzĭ = to count, the symbol represents a knot, this is indicative of ancient days before the invention of writing when people used knots; the Swastika symbols read ^{2}ghügh have here the meaning of good, fine (quality). Between the two Swastikas is the symbol ^{1}gku it represents the roots of the ginger plant, hence ginger, here it stands for ^{3}gku = to record. ^{2}Mä is again the affirmative.

Rubr. 8: The first symbol represents a man walking along singing, for detailed description of the same see introduction to the song, it stands for singing, while the symbol ^{1}ho = rib, ribs, stands for ^{1}ho = to chant, (in a deep voice), it also has the meaning to follow suit in singing. The words ^{2}ghügh again stand for "good", it represents to the ^{1}Na-^{2}khi the heart of a god, hence goodness, the quality good. ^{2}Mä is again the affirmative.

Eighteenth Page:

Rubr. 1: ¹Gkwua ²ghügh ³t'khi ²ghügh ²mä, ³gkv ²ssĭ ²ndzĭ ¹nddü ²mä
Rubr. 2: ²Gkv ¹p'ĕr ¹nds'a ¹shĕr ²mä
Rubr. 3: ²P'u ¹ddo ³llü ¹ddo ²mä
Rubr. 4: ²T'ä-²nyi ²non̲-¹ō ²ssu ³yu ¹mùen̲ ²lä ³ssaw
Rubr. 5: ²Non̲-¹ō ¹ssĭ ²nnü ²zo ¹nyu ³ssaw
Rubr. 6: ¹Ssĭ ²dto ²zo ²dto ³ddü-²ddü ³hu
Rubr. 7: ²Mä
Rubr. 8: ²nnü ³mi ¹nyu ³ssaw
Rubr. 9: ²Mä ¹hö ³mi ¹hö ²shwua-²shwua ³hu
Rubr. 10: ²Non̲-¹ō ³bpŭ ²nnü ²mbe ¹nyu ³ssaw
Rubr. 11: ³Bpŭ ¹ddü ²mbe ¹la ³hu.

Eighteenth Page:

1) His ability to sing the ¹Gkwua and ³T'khi and like the ability and knowledge of the chief and headman
2) let us have white hair and long teeth as the deceased
3) let there be seen grandfather and grandchildren (under one roof)
4) All these like the ²non̲-¹ō of the ancestors let these be given us (let us invite them back)
5) Let us invite these powers of the father unto the son
6) Let the abilities and powers of the father be equal in the son
7) and those of the mother
8) imparted to the daughter.
9) May the stature of the mother be even with the daughter
10) may these powers be imparted to the neighbors and the villages
11) May there be increase in the villages and among the neighbors.

Explanation of text

Page 18

Rubr. 1: The first symbol ³gkwua is a carpenter's tool to scoop out a dish from a piece of wood; it is a curved blade with a handle at each end, it was used in olden days for the making of wooden bowls and the ²lo-¹bpä, it was also used like a carpenter's plane before that tool was introduced. Here it stands for ^{1}gkwua a type of song sung at wedding ceremonies by old men, who remained sitting while they sang. The song is colloquially known as ^{3}Ssu-^{3}wùa-^{1}wùa-^{1}gkwua. The ^{3}Ssu is the life god, *see NNCRC*, p. 250, note 527. It contained historical matter and references to their tribal ancestors; ^{2}ghügh = the good (quality, ability). The third symbol represents a spine = ^{2}t'khi, it can mean, pain, and is then read in the first tone, ^{2}t'khi = to sell, ^{3}t'khi = cold, ^{1}t'khi = sweet, for all of which the symbol ^{2}t'khi = spine is used. Here it stands for ^{3}t'khi a type of song, sung on the mountains either by several travellers, or by young men alone. It begins with *Eh eh eh eh* which is continued till the man's wind is almost exhausted and then ends in a phrase; the ^{3}t'khi is sung in a high pitched voice and relates usually of the bitterness of life hence ^{3}t'khi = cold. When boys and girls sing these songs, and as the end phrase is impromptu, they are apt to become suggestive. The other symbols of this half of the phrase have been explained. Of the second half we have the symbol ^{2}gkv = head, here it stands for ^{3}gkv = able, ability, next to it is a pine tree read either ^{1}ndzĕr = tree, ^{2}t'o = pine, or ^{2}ss = wood, here it stands for ^{2}ss or ^{2}ssĭ = wisdom, knowledge. The next symbol is that of a chief = ^{2}ndzĭ.

The origin of this symbol has been lost, the lower body is that of a deity, this shows the veneration in which the chief was held. He wears a peculiar coiffure with upturned hair. The next to last symbol represents the ^{1}ndi or frond of a fern, it is the young shoot of the Eagle or Bracken fern *(Pteridium aquilinum)*, here it is read ^{1}ndü or ^{1}nddü = a minor official, as a headman of a village, the symbol is also written

^{1}ndü. The word ^{2}mä is again the affirmative, it also stands for our colon.

Rubr. 2: Among the symbols of this rubric, there is none, that represents a verb nor the sentence "let us have" usually expressed by = ^{2}gv ^{2}bä ^{3}hu, but only ^{1}p'ĕr = white, ^{2}gkv = head, ^{1}nds'a = fangs, it shows the mouth of a predatory animal, it is followed by the numeral ^{1}shĕr = seven, here it stands for ^{1}shĕr = long, hence white head and long teeth, the meaning is a ripe old age let us have, indicated by white hair and teeth from which the gums have receded, a sign of old age.

Rubr. 3: The first symbol is read ^{2}P'u and represents a grandfather with long hair; ^{3}p'u-^{2}p'u is great grandfather, next is the symbol ^{1}ddo = to see, and below it a small male child on the symbol for tick = ^{3}llü, this compound symbol of which the lower serves as phonetic is read ^{3}llü = grandchildren, hence grandfather see, grandchild see, the meaning being let there be visible three generations under one roof. In the colloquial grandchild is ^{2}lv-^{2}bbŭ, while great grandchild is ^{3}lv-^{2}bbŭ, the two terms are only differentiated by the tone.

Rubr. 4: The first two symbols and their equivalent sound complexes ^{2}t'ä-^{2}nyi, have already been explained. The symbol for pine appears again, here it stands for ^{2}ssu = ancestor, the symbol ^{1}yu under that of tree, wood, is here read ^{3}yu and means to give, this is followed by the words ^{1}mùen̲ ^{2}lä ^{3}ssaw = below again invite.

Rubr. 5: These symbols have been explained, ^{2}non̲-^{1}ō = abilities, etc., ^{1}ä-^{1}ssĭ = father, ^{2}nnü = his, ^{2}zo = son, ^{1}nyu = on, unto, ^{3}ssaw = invite. The pair of eyes can be read ^{1}miu and ^{1}nyu, here it stands for ^{1}nyu = on.

Rubr. 6: ^{1}Ä-^{1}ssĭ = father, ^{2}dto = in, ^{2}zo = son, ^{2}dto = in, ^{3}ddü-^{2}ddü = equal; the last symbol represents a gate = ^{2}k'u, here it is read ^{3}hu, and is part of the phrase usually found towards the end in ^{2}dto-^{1}mba books ^{2}gv ^{2}bä ^{3}hu = let that be so!

Rubr. 7: ^{2}Mä = mother.

Rubr. 8: ^{2}Nnü = her, ^{3}mi = daughter, ^{1}nyu = on, ^{3}ssaw = invite, that is her abilities etc., *see* rubric 5.

Rubr. 9: ^{2}Mä = mother, this is followed by the symbol ^{2}mi = fire, here it is read ^{1}hö = standing, the latter is actually read ^{3}hö, but for euphony's sake is read ^{1}hö. There is a symbol for this expression namely a man with spread out limbs firmly standing: = ^{3}hö, here the idea of height is intended, or stature, hence may the stature of the mother be ^{2}shwua-^{2}shwua = even (in height) with that of the daughter ^{3}hu = may that be so!

Rubr. 10: ^{2}Non̲-^{1}ō = ability, power, etc., ^{3}bpŭ = neighbors, it is written with the symbol for house and the symbol ^{3}bpŭ = colander is added, it acts as a phonetic for ^{3}bpŭ neighbor, the symbol for house illucidates the phonetic; ^{2}nnü is here a conjunction; ^{2}mbe = village(s), it is also figured with the symbol for house, and that of ^{2}mbe = snow inside it, it acts as phonetic for ^{2}mbe = village(s). The last symbols are ^{1}nyu = on, unto, impart, ^{3}ssaw = invite. Sometimes both symbols ^{3}bpŭ and ^{2}mbe are written in the symbol for house, and that single compound is then read ^{3}bpŭ ^{2}mbe = neighbors (and) villages.

Rubr. 11: ^{3}Bpŭ = neighbors, ^{1}ddü = large, ^{2}mbe = village(s) ^{1}la = thick, ^{3}hu = let that be so. The meaning is let the neighbors increase and the villages prosper.

*

After the singing is finished, the descendant kneels before the ^{2}Dto-^{1}mba who gives the son of the deceased sweetened water from a bowl to drink, this symbolizes the imparting of the ^{2}non̲-^{1}ō or all the good qualities of the deceased.

译　文

书名详解

^{3}mu̱n ^{2}ndzĕr ^{3}ä ^{1}lä ^{2}dzhu[mu^{55}ndʑər^{33}ə^{55}le^{21}dzu̜^{33}]

挽歌，悲伤的来历

缓慢、即兴的 ^{1}ZÄ-^{1}ZÄ ^{2}TS'O[ze^{21}ze^{21}tsho^{33}]

这首歌词保存在一本非常古老的经书中，它是我在扬子江大峡谷中丽江北部的刺宝乡从一个农民手中买来的。这种类型的经书十分罕见。以下这本经书的翻译是根据编号为2760的这本经书。1944年，这本经书和我的其他纳西资料拟通过美国的理查德·霍维号邮船运回美国，这艘船从加尔各答到美国，但是在阿拉伯海附近被日本军舰击沉，该经书与其他纳西资料一同沉入大海。①

我后来又发现另外两本同名的经书，一本编号为1091，已经不在我这里了，但是我还保存着该书的照片，底片保存在华盛顿的美国国会图书馆。

这本经书只有第1页和第2页的第1节与编号2760的经书不同。实际上，这首歌从第2页的第2节开始。第二个版本是我在1947年获得的，它跟编号2760的经书一模一样，编号为7020，现在我还收藏着这本经书。

这个译本我是在1940年完成的，原本已经非常破旧，但是文字仍然十分清

①译者按，译者在哈佛燕京图书馆藏的东巴经中找一本洛克编号为2760的经书，经过对比发现，这本经书与洛克的摹写本基本一致。我们认为，可能是洛克记错了。

晰。经书一共 9 张（18 页），长 11 英寸，宽 3.5 英寸，每一页都分为三栏。

编号 7020 的经书的封面是一个长方形的标题栏，用如意结做双线边栏。“如意结”纳西语作^{1}lěr-^{2}mbbǔ-^{1}ch'i[lər^{21}mbɯ^{33}tʂhʅ^{21}]，藏语叫 dpal-gyi-beu，梵语叫 Srivatsa。边框的里面，左边是一个东巴坐在长凳上，手里拿着一根丧棒（^{3}mùen-^{1}t'u[mɯ^{55}thu^{21}]）。左右两边各画一个双腿叉开的人形，左边的那个人一手拿着一杆三叉戟，另一只手拿着一个毒鬼的头。右边那个人一手挥舞着宝剑，另一只手也拿着一个毒鬼的头。

第一个字像马蝇，它一般出现在夏天的高原松树林中，它们只在有阳光的时候才出来，阴天就躲起来。马蝇吸人和动物的血。纳西语作^{3}mun[mu^{55}]，这里作标音符，借用它的读音作“死”，也有“老”的意思。下面一个字像树，读作^{1}ndzěr[ndʑər^{21}]，这里也作标音符，借音作^{2}ndzěr[ndʑər^{33}]，意为“唱”。经常写作

，“树”作声符，“树”上画了一张嘴，嘴张开像在唱歌。另外一种写法是

，像一个正在走路的人，嘴巴张开，舌头上有一个标音符^{2}ndzěr[ndʑər^{33}]，该字也是“唱歌”的意思。因此，该字读作^{2}ndzěr[ndʑər^{33}]，意为“唱歌”。纳西人与同伴一起爬山的时候通常会即兴演唱。通常一个人会先即兴唱一段，另一个人再唱一段作为回应。民谣在纳西语中叫^{1}na-^{1}bbǔe[na^{21}bɯ^{21}]，第一个音节表示纳西人，^{1}bbǔe[bɯ^{21}]是“民谣或情歌”。^{3}ä[ə^{55}]意为“很久以前，最初的时候”，这里由于押韵读作第三声，它与悲伤之歌的起源有关（纳西语“悲伤”作^{2}dzhu[dʐu^{33}]）。下面一个字像獐子，读作^{1}lä[le^{21}]，这里借音作“又”。最后一个字像一把古代的火枪，在东巴经中读作^{1}dzhu[dʐu^{21}]，借音作^{2}dzhu[dʐu^{33}]，意为“空白、掏空”，这里的意思是“悲伤、痛苦”。

经卷第一页释义

一、全页标音及直译

第一节	Ō!	^{1}Ä-^{1}ssĭ	^{3}dta	^{1}lä	^{2}dzhu
	o！	ə^{21}sʅ^{21}	ta^{55}	le^{21}	dzʯ^{33}
	喔	父亲	说	又	丧事

第二节	^{2}Wùa-^{1}ssĭ	^{3}dta	^{1}lä	^{2}dzhu
	ua^{33}sʅ^{21}	ta^{55}	le^{21}	dzʯ^{33}
	父亲	说	又	丧事

第三节	^{2}Dzhu	^{2}t'u	^{2}gkv	^{2}muàn̠	^{3}shou,
	dzʯ^{33}	thu^{33}	kv^{33}	mə^{33}	ʂə^{55}
	丧事	出现	处	不	说

^{2}Dzhu	^{1}dzo	^{3}shou	^{2}muàn̠	^{2}nyi
dzʯ^{33}	ʥo^{21}	ʂə^{55}	mə^{33}	ȵi^{33}
丧事	有关	说	不	要

第四节	^{2}Dzhu	^{3}bbŭe	^{2}gkv	^{2}muàn̠	^{3}shou
	dzʯ^{33}	pɯ^{55}	kv^{33}	mə^{33}	ʂə^{55}
	丧事	来历	处	不	说

第五节	^{2}Dzhu	^{1}dzo	^{2}bä	^{2}muàn̠	^{2}nyi
	dzʯ^{33}	ʥo^{21}	be^{33}	mə^{33}	ȵi^{33}
	丧事	有关	做	不	要

第六节	^{2}Ä-^{1}ts'ä	^{2}dzī	^{2}muàn̠	^{2}dzhu
	ə^{33}tshe^{21}	dzi^{33}	mə^{33}	dzʯ^{33}
	起初	人类	没有	丧事

第七节	^{2}Dzhu	^{2}t'u	^{2}Mùan̠-^{3}llü-^{1}ssu-^{1}lo-^{2}k'o
	dzʯ^{33}	thu^{33}	mɯ^{33}lɯ^{55}su^{21}lo^{21}kho^{33}
	丧事	出现	美利署罗科

nɯ^{33}	thu^{33}
^{2}nnü	^{2}t'u
它	出现

第八节	^{2}Dzhu	^{3}bbŭe	^{2}Mùa̠n-^{3}llü-^{1}ssu-^{1}lo-^{2}k'o
	dz̥u^{33}	pɯ^{55}	mɯ^{33}lɯ^{55}su^{21}lo^{21}kho^{33}
	丧事	来历	美利署罗科

^{2}nnü	^{3}bbŭe
nɯ^{33}	pɯ^{55}
它	来历

第九节	^{2}Mùa̠n-^{3}llü-^{1}ssu-^{1}lo-^{2}k'o,	^{2}zo	^{2}nnü	^{2}gkv
	mɯ^{33}lɯ^{55}su^{21}lo^{21}kho^{33}	zo^{33}	nɯ^{33}	kv^{33}
	美利署罗科	儿子	他	头

^{3}ssu	^{1}ssä.
su^{55}	se^{21}
带领	了

第十节	^{2}Ä–^{1}khi	^{2}Ndaw–^{1}ssu–^{2}dzhu,	^{2}Dzhu	^{3}bbŭe
	ə^{33}ɕi^{21}	ndɑ^{33}su^{21}dz̥u^{33}	dz̥u^{33}	pɯ^{55}
	阿喜	达苏主	丧事	来历

^{2}gkv	^{1}lä	^{2}bä.
kv^{33}	le^{21}	be^{33}
头	又	做

二、句译

第一节：喔！我们将要讲述父亲经历的丧事①。

---

①译者按，洛克本译作悲伤，但是译文不通，我们根据和志武《东巴经选译·挽歌》译作丧事或丧仪。

第二节：我们将再次讲述父亲的丧事。

第三节：如果不知道丧事的来历，那么就不要谈论丧事。

第四节：如果不知道丧事的来历，

第五节：就不要办丧事

第六节：万物开端之时，人类还没有丧事。

第七节：丧事源自美利署罗科。

第八节：在美利署罗科，第一次办了丧事。

第九节：美利署罗科的儿子在灵前带领，

第十节：在阿喜的达苏主，丧事第一次产生。

三、字词详解

第一节：第一个字像东巴在主持丧葬仪式。这个东巴的名字叫^{2}Lo-^{1}ch'ung-^{2}ndaw-^{1}khü，名字的具体含义无法翻译，这是东巴的官方称号。他手里拿着的丧棒叫^{3}Mùen-^{1}t'u（竹竿），丧棒的上半部分是经过特殊设计的。“竹竿”下面那个字像谷物之形，读作^{3}ō，这里表示东巴吟唱的第一个音节 ō ō ō ō！下两个字读作^{1}ä-^{1}ssĭ，上面那个字像张开的嘴，意为“最开始出现的声音”，这里作“父亲”的第一个音节。下面那个字像一个男人头上有一根木头，“木”本读作^{1}ssĭ。这个字在此处读作^{1}ssĭ，作“父亲”的第二个音节。“父亲”这个字经常写作下面这个形式

，没有第一个音节^{1}ä。第三个字读作^{3}dta，字形像一只有盖的箱子，这里借音作“说，告诉”。下一个字像一个长着尖牙的獐子的头，它读作^{2}lä，这里用作副词“又”，但是由于押韵

的原因读第一声，即^{1}lä。最后一个字像一把古代的火枪，即燧石枪或者可装三颗子弹的前膛枪，读作^{2}dzhu，意为“空白、掏空”，这个字看上去像三颗子弹都被发射出去的状态，这里借音作“悲伤、痛苦”。

第二节：这一节的与第一节中的意思相同，不同的是人上面的那个字，像一座房子，读作^{2}wùa，以此代替第一节^{1}ä-^{1}ssĭ中的^{1}ä这个音节。是“父亲”这个字的变体，指父亲是一座房子或一块土地的主人。^{1}Ä-^{1}ssĭ和^{2}Wùa-^{1}ssĭ的意思是一样的。

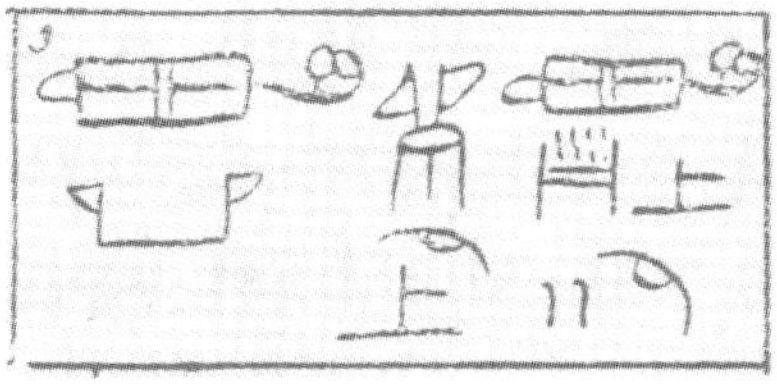

第三节：第一个字已经解释过了。下一个字像水桶，读作^{1}t'u，这里借音读作^{2}t'u，意思是“出现”。第三个字读作^{2}gkv，意思是“人头、第一”，因为头是人体之首，因此^{2}t'u ^{2}gkv的意思是“出处”。下一个字是否定词^{2}muàṉ，像一个空的陷阱，表示什么猎物都没有捕到。其他东巴解释说，该字像新月，月初很难见到月亮，所以表示“没有”之意。下一个字是哥巴文，借自汉字“上”，但是它跟汉字“上”的读音和意思都不同，这里读作^{3}shou，意为“告诉，说”，汉字读作 shang，意为“上面”。下一个字在这一节第二次出现，读作^{2}dzhu，意为“悲伤”。下一个字像装满了饲料的马槽，其中的点和短线表示饲料，读作^{1}dzo，这里借音作副词“关于”，^{2}dzhu ^{1}dzo 即关于悲伤，纳西语中副词在名词之后。接下来“说”这个字第二次出现。再往下是否定词“不”和数词“二”，两字连读作^{2}muàṉ ^{2}nyi，意为“不应该，不能够”。^{2}nyi 意为“想，希望”。

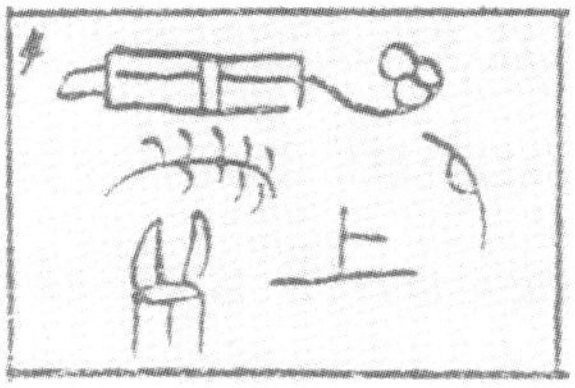

第四节：这一节的内容与第三节的第一句相同，只有一个词不同，那就是^{3}bbŭe。^{3}bbŭe 和^{2}t'u 的意思一样，^{3}bbŭe-^{2}t'u 意为“来历”，第一纵列的第二个字像艾蒿（拉丁学名作 *Artemisia*）的细枝。艾蒿有两个品种，一种是白色的根和绿色的叶子，另一种是黑色的根和浅灰色的叶子，它们生长在村庄周围的荒地沟渠中。第一种艾蒿常用在除秽仪式中，“艾蒿”读作^{2}bbŭe。^{3}bbŭe 实际的意思是“移动”，最初的意思是雏鸟第一次离开鸟巢尝试飞行。

第五节：这一节跟第三节后半部分意思相同，只是这里把^{3}shou（说）换成了^{2}bä（做）。^{2}bä（做）由这一节的第三个字表示，该字像一把锄头，点表示土块，实际表示“挖”，用锄头劳作，因此译作“做”。

第六节：第一个字读作^{1}ä，已经在第一节解释过了。^{1}ä下面那个字读作^{1}ts'ä，字形像盐块，这里读第一声。^{1}ä ^{1}ts'ä意为“万物之始或生命之初”。下一个字像豺狼的头，读作^{2}dzī，这个字很少作“豺狼”讲，通常作标音符代表人类，指“洪水之前的人类祖先”。洪水之后人类的祖先用大象（大象读作^{1}ts'o）表示。①洪水之前的最后一个人类祖先叫作^{2}dzī-^{2}zä-^{1}ts'o-^{1}zä，洪水之后的人类祖先叫作^{1}ts'o-^{2}zä-^{3}llü-^{2}ghügh 崇则利恩，崇则利恩是洪水之后人类唯一的幸存者。^{2}ss 意为“知道”，既没有写出来，也没有读出来，但是阅读经文时要这样理解。整句对译为：开始的时候/人类/（知道）/没有/丧事。

①译者按，^{1}ts'o 是^{1}ts'o-^{2}zä-^{3}llü-^{2}ghügh 崇则利恩的简称。

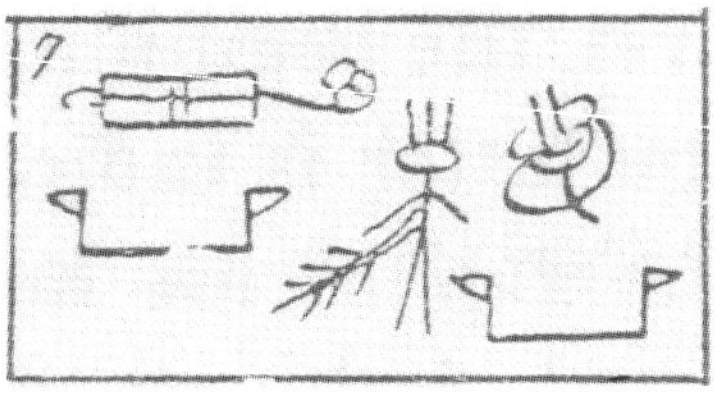

第七节：前两个字已经解释过了。第三个字像带尾巴的魔鬼，他的名字叫作美利苏主（^{2}Mùaṉ-^{3}llü-^{1}ssu-^{2}ndzǐ），他是人类祖先美利董主（^{2}Mùaṉ-^{3}llü-^{1}ddu-^{2}ndzǐ）的敌人，丧事可能就是从他这里开始的。在另外一册名为^{2}Dzhu ^{2}ťu ^{2}Mùaṉ-^{3}llü-^{1}ssu-^{1}lo-^{2}k'o ^{2}nnü ^{2}ťu的经书中，美利署罗科（^{2}Mùaṉ-^{3}llü-^{1}ssu-^{1}lo-^{2}k'o）是一个地名；在那册经书中只写出鬼名美利苏主（^{2}Mùaṉ-^{3}llü-^{1}ssu-^{2}ndzǐ）的第三个音节^{1}ssu，该字用作标音符，其他音节都没有写出来。在编号 1091 的经书中，这段话被完整地记录下来，见下图：

美利署罗科（^{2}Mùaṉ-^{3}llü-^{1}ssu-^{1}lo-^{2}k'o）是木里县的一个地名，位于西康的木里县北部，鼠河（铁河）岸边。它不是无量河，这条河发源于纳武。用汉语翻译这条河纳西语的名作“铁河”。关于它的源头的讨论见《中国西南古纳西王国》第 1 卷的第 110 页，注释 60，以及第二卷的第 384—385 页，注释 5。像水桶之形的那个字读作^{1}ťu，像人的心脏的那个字读作^{2}nnü，这里借音作“它”，即丧事。

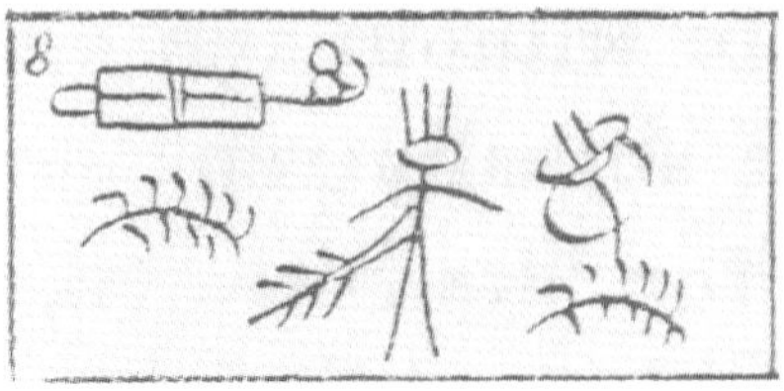

第八节：这一节跟第七节内容相似，这里用^{3}bbǔe 替换了^{2}ťu。（关于^{3}bbǔe 的解释参见本页第四节）

第九节：这一节读作^{2}Mùaṉ-^{3}llü-^{1}ssu-^{1}lo-^{2}k'o，^{2}dzhu ^{2}t'u ^{2}kv ^{1}lä ^{2}bä（它来自）^{2}Mùaṉ-^{3}llü-^{1}ssu-^{1}lo-^{2}k'o，那是所有丧事产生的地方。在那个地方出生的儿子第一次办了丧事。^{2}zo 是“儿子”，这里借用像罐子的那个字记录^{2}zo 这个音节，一般借用像人之形的字①记录^{2}zo 这个音节，但是像人形的字可以记录几个不同的音节。最后一个字像骰子，读作^{1}ssu，这里借音作“领、率领”。对译作：儿子/他/丧事/第一/领。^{1}ssu 字下面的那个字是一个音节文字，即哥巴文，读作^{1}ssä，它在动词后面表示过去式。有时候用像“野羊”（读作^{1}ssä）的那个字来代替这个哥巴文，表达的意思是相同的。

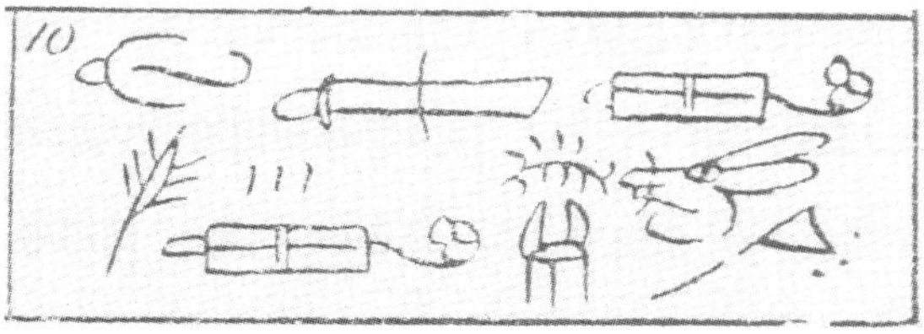

第十节：第一个字^{2}ä已经解释过了，这里作一个乡名的第一个音节，这个乡位于扬子江拐弯处的西边，玉龙雪山以西，名字叫阿喜（^{2}Ä－^{1}khi）。^{1}khi 字像稻穗之形，抛光的米纳西语作^{2}ch'wua。达苏主（^{2}Ndaw-^{1}ssu-^{2}dzhu）是阿喜乡的一个村子，在扬子江的东岸，石鼓和阿喜之间。字形像一把剑或者刀的那个字，剑或刀上的线表示“砍”，读作^{2}ndaw，这里借音作一个村庄名。“三”读作^{1}ssu，像三条短线。^{2}dzhu 已经解释过了，可能这个村子被选作丧事的发源地，因为村庄名里有^{2}dzhu 这个音节。其余的字已经解释过了。

---

①译者按，即。

经卷第二页释义

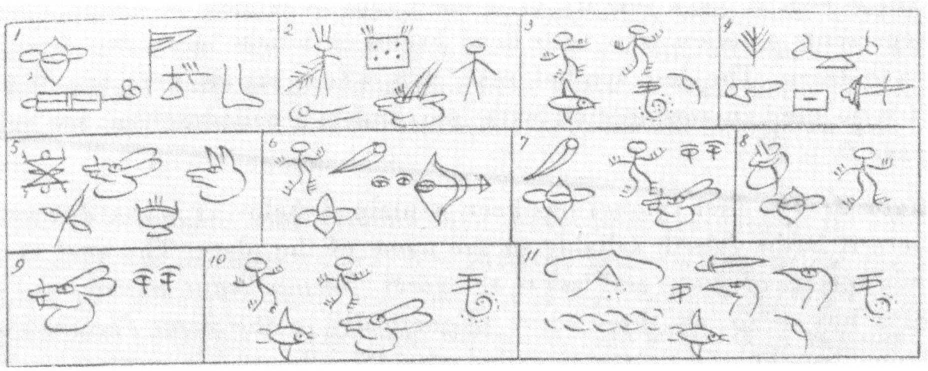

一、全页标音及直译

第一节	^{1} Ō	^{2}dzhu	^{2}t'ä	^{2}sso	^{3}k'ö
	o^{21}	dzʮ^{33}	the^{33}	so^{33}	khɯ^{55}
	事情	丧事	做	学	去
第二节	^{2}Ssu–^{1}lo	^{3}Ssu–^{2}ssä–^{2}zo			
	su^{33}lo^{21}	su^{55}se^{33}zo^{33}			
	鼠罗	鼠赛若			
第三节	^{2}Nyu	^{3}mun̠	^{2}nyu	^{2}muàn̠	^{2}non̠
	ȵy^{33}	mu^{55}	ȵy^{33}	mə^{33}	no^{33}
	他	老	他	不	觉
第四节	^{2}Ss	^{1}shi	^{2}lo-^{1}bpä	^{3}ndaw	
	sɿ^{33}	ʂʅ^{21}	lo^{33}pe^{21}	ndɑ^{55}	
	木	黄	木盆	砍	
第五节	^{1}Ha	^{1}szŭ	^{2}lä	^{1}wu	^{3}k'ö
	hæ^{21}	zv^{21}	le^{33}	u^{21}	khɯ^{55}
	金	淘	又	自己	去
第六节	^{2}Nyu	^{1}ō	^{1}gyi	^{2}nyu	^{3}k'a
	ȵy^{33}	o^{21}	ʥi^{21}	ȵy^{33}	khæ^{55}
	他	影	水	里	射
第七节	^{1}Gyi	^{1}ō	^{1}gyi	^{2}nyu	^{1}ddo
	ʥi^{21}	o^{21}	ʥi^{21}	ȵy^{33}	do^{21}
	水	影	水	我	见
第八节	^{2}Nnü	^{1}ō	^{2}nyu		
	nɯ^{33}	o^{21}	ȵy^{33}		
	你	影	他		

第九节	^{2}lä	^{1}ddo
	le^{33}	do^{21}
	又	见

第十节	^{2}Nyu	^{2}muṉ	^{2}nyu	^{2}lä	^{2}noṉ
	ȵy^{33}	mu^{33}	ȵy^{33}	le^{33}	no^{33}
	他	老	他	又	觉

第十一节	^{2}Mùaṉ-^{2}bä	^{1}gkyi	^{1}p'ĕr	^{3}chung,	^{2}gko
	mɯ^{33}be^{33}	tɕi^{21}	phər^{21}	tʂu^{55}	ko^{33}
	地平线	云	白	接	鹤

^{3}muṉ	^{2}gko	^{2}muàṉ	^{2}noṉ.
mu^{55}	ko^{33}	mə^{33}	no^{33}
老	鹤	不	觉

二、句译

第一节：去学习做丧事的礼仪。

第二节：鼠罗河边的鼠赛男，

第三节：他老了，但是他也不觉得。

第四节：他做了一个黄色的木盆，

第五节：然后去淘金。

第六节：他的影子倒映在水里，

第七节：他看见了自己的影子映在水里。

第八、九节：他看见自己的影子，

第十节：他才觉得自己老了；

第十一节：在云和天相接的地方，有一只老鹤不觉得自己老了。

三、字词详解

第一节：第一个字读作^{1}ō，字形像绿松石，可能实指镶嵌了绿松石的银项链，或者是纳西妇女戴的领针，因此这里作“一样东西，一件事情”。第二个字读作^{2}dzhu，意为“悲伤”。^{2}t’ä像一面旗，这里作“做”。^{1}sso 字据说像汉人使用的秤，也有人认为它像树上落下的腐朽树枝，本义是“干燥”，读作^{2}sso，这里作^{1}sso“学习”。最后一个字读作^{2}k’ö，像人的脚，这里读作^{3}k’ö，意为“去”。^{3}k’ö与^{1}sso 连用，常用在口语中。关于^{3}k’ö的解释参见本书第九页第七节的字词详解。

第二节：第一个字已经解释过了。下面那个像山谷的字读作^{1}lo，这里作地名的第四个音节。接下来两个字一个读作^{3}ssu，字形像一种草。另一个读作^{2}ssä，字形像一只喜马拉雅斑羚（拉丁学名作 *Naemorhedus griseus*），最后一个字像一个男孩，读作^{2}zo。这三个字作一个人名^{3}ssu–^{2}ssä–^{2}zo，意为“来自鼠罗河的男孩”。^{2}ssu–^{1}lo 也可以读作^{1}shu-^{1}lo，是木里的一个地名，可以译作铁河（^{2}shu-^{1}gyi）的河谷或铁谷。^{2}ssu–^{1}lo 是^{2}Mùan̲-^{3}llü-^{1}ssu-^{1}lo-^{2}k’o 的简称。^{2}Mùan̲-^{3}llü可能是“木里”的古称。

第三节：我们看到两个身体扭曲，身上汗毛竖立的人形，这两个字实际读作^{1}ndshĕr，意为“害怕、惊吓”。另一个字跟这个字很像，但是身上没有汗毛，那个字读作^{2}nyu，本义为“摇摆、颤抖”，它作人称代词“我”或“他”。^{3}mun̲是“老”，他不知道他老了或者我不知道我老了。

^{3}muṉ字像一只马蝇，它在高原地区和草地中很常见。第二个^{2}nyu 字下面那个字读^{2}noṉ，这个字实际上由两个部分构成，上半部分是

，读作 p'ĕr，意为“白”；下半部分带点的曲线表示液体。因此，该字表示白色的液体或者牛奶。^{2}noṉ意为“去学习新知识”，即，他知道他已经老了。

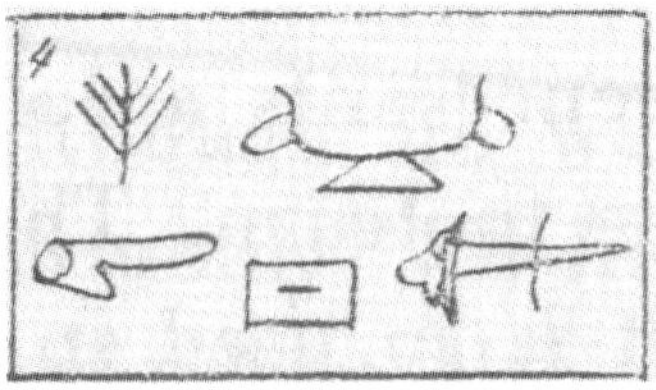

第四节：第一个字像一棵树，“树”读作^{1}ndzĕr，该字又可以读作^{2}t'o，意为“松树”，又可以读作^{2}ss，意为“木”。根据经文，它在这里读作^{2}ss。下面一个字读作^{2}shi，意为“肉”，借音读作^{1}shi，意为“黄色”。因此，^{2}ss ^{1}shi 意为“黄木”，形容词修饰名词时一般放在名词的后面。形容词可以变作动词，比如^{1}ha ^{2}zaw，意为“金色的鞋子或金黄色的鞋子”；但^{1}ha 也有“买”的意思，所以^{2}zaw ^{1}ha 有“金鞋”和“买鞋”两个意思，所以在这种情况下，形容词放在名词前面。①

第三个字像正方形或长方形，扁平状，像纳西人用来盛东西的木盆，读作^{2}lo-^{1}bpä，意为“木盆”，它是用天然的黄木制作而成的，大小一般在 1.2 到 2 平方英尺之间，各种尺寸都有，但不小于 1 平方英尺。这个字下面那个字像酒糟，读作^{3}bpä，这里作^{2}lo-^{1}bpä的第二个音节。最后一个字读作^{3}ndaw，意为“砍”，之前已经解释过了。也就是他用砍来的黄木做成一个^{2}lo-^{1}bpä，用大木盆从河床或河岸上挖沙淘金，我们在下一节中知道，他就用它来淘金。

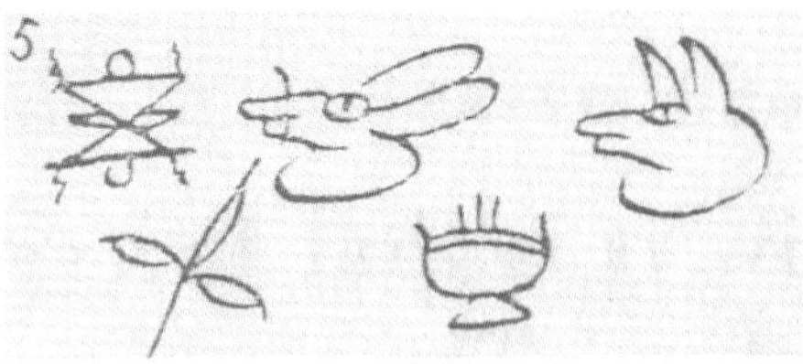

第五节：第一个字读作^{1}ha，意为“金”。像叶子之形那个字读作^{2}szŭ，实际像一片柳叶，这里借音读^{1}szŭ，意为

①译者按，这里的“金”是名词不是形容词，所以，洛克的说法不对。

“洗”。实际上在口语中“洗”读作^{1}dsä。^{2}lä是“又”。^{1}wu 是“奴隶”，字形像一只空盘子，表示用空盘子来招待奴隶。像狗之形的那个字读作^{2}k’ö，本义为“狗”，这里作^{1}wu-^{2}k’ö“去”的第二个音节。尽管他已经老了，但是还想像年轻时一样去淘金。^{1}wu 还有“远”的意思，^{2}lä ^{1}wu ^{3}k’ö的意思是“返回”，即回到他的旧习惯。^{1}wu 也有“他自己”的意思，作反身代词。

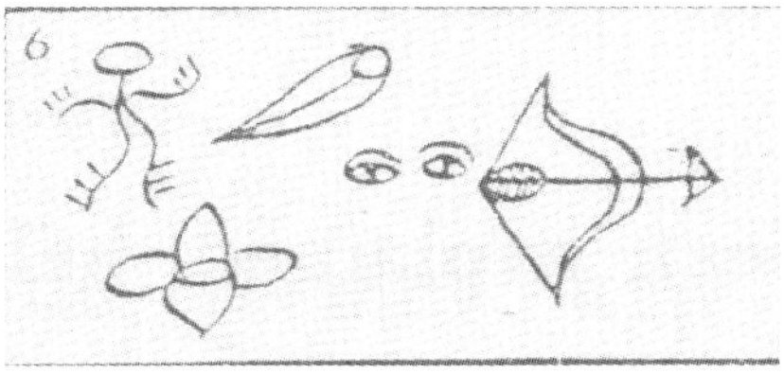

第六节：^{2}nyu 这个字在本页第三节已经解释过了。^{1}ō字像一件绿松石的首饰，这里借音作“影子”。^{1}gyi 是“水”，“水”字下面像一双眼睛，读作^{1}miu 或^{1}nyu，这里应该读作^{1}nyu，意为“在……之上”。^{3}k’a 意为“射箭”，这里作“反射”。^{1}ddo 意为“见”，字在下一节。这一节经文对译作“他/影子/水/中/射”。

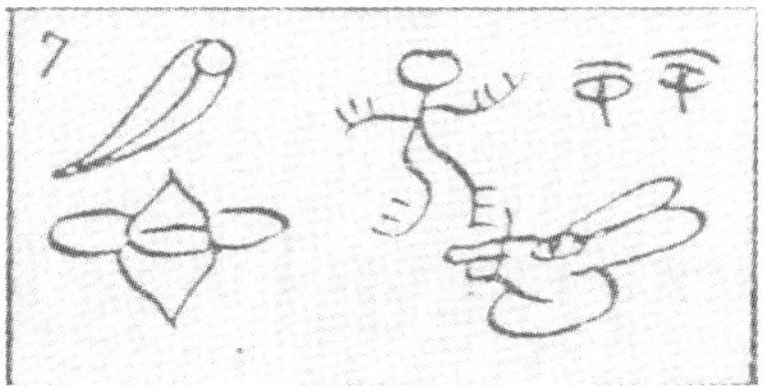

第七节：这一节对译为“水/影子/他/又/见”。注意“眼睛”这个字与本节最后一个字不同。从眼睛中延伸出来的线表示“看见”。

第八节：^{2}Nnü字本义是“心”，这里表示他自己，作反身代词。^{1}ō是“影子”。

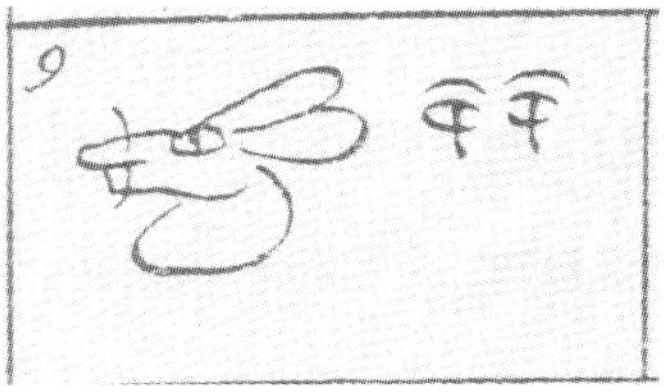

第九节：这一节译为“又见”，这些字已经解说过了。

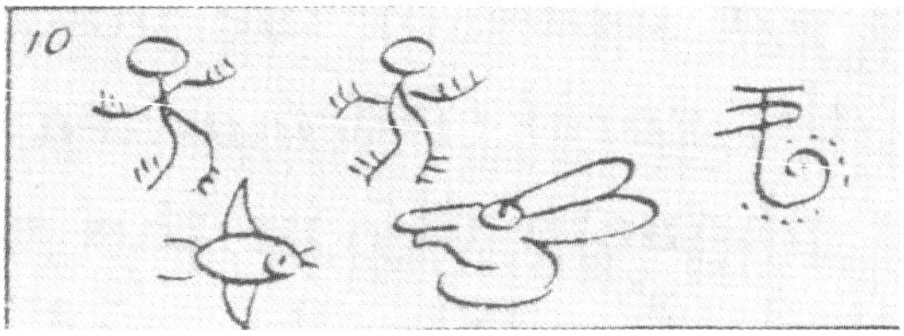

第十节：这些字在第三节已经解释过了。

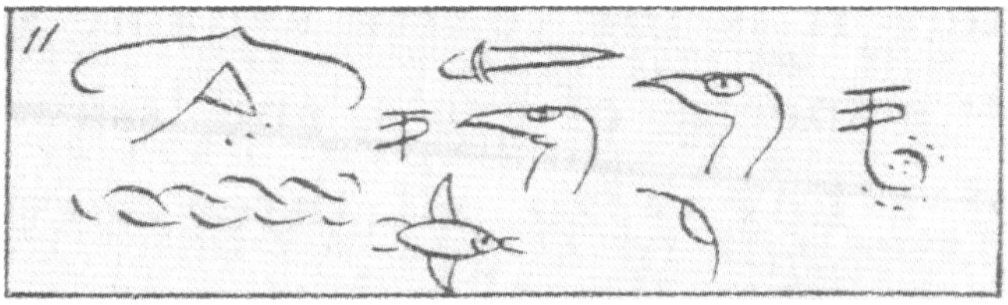

第十一节：²Mùaṉ-²bä意为“地平线天边”，一个弧形的“天”加一个动词“做”。²bä单独也有“边”的意思。“做”下面那个字是“云”，读作¹gkyi。“马蝇”上面那个字读作¹p'ĕr，意为“白”。“白”右边那个字读作³chung，本义为“锥子”，这里借音作“连接”。这一节经文对译作“鹤（²gko）/老（³muṉ）/鹤/不/觉”。

经卷第三页释义

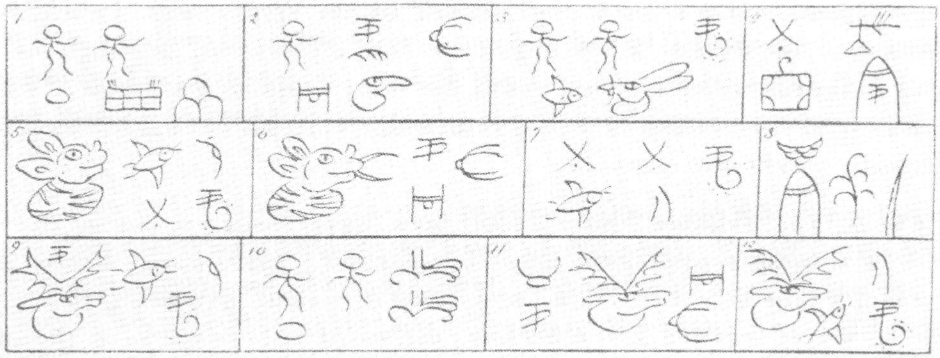

一、全页标音及直译

第一节	^{2}Nyu	^{2}gv	^{2}nyu	^{3}p’u-^{3}lv	
	ȵy^{33}	gv^{33}	ȵy^{33}	phu^{55} lv^{55}	
	他	身	他	发抖	

第二节	^{1}Non̠	^{1}p’ĕr	^{2}gko	^{2}gkan̠	^{2}ggü
	no^{21}	phər^{21}	ko^{33}	kæ^{33}	gɯ^{33}
	羽毛	白	鹤	前	落

第三节	^{2}Nyu	^{3}mun̠	^{2}nyu	^{1}lä	^{2}non̠
	ȵy^{33}	mu^{55}	ȵy^{33}	le^{21}	no^{33}
	他	老	他	又	觉

第四节 ^{2}La-^{2}gyu-^{3}sso-^{2}gkv-^{1}p’ĕr

la^{33}ʥə^{33}so^{55}kv^{33}phər^{21}

拉久梭古盘

第五节	^{2}La	^{3}mun̠	^{2}la	^{2}muàn̠	^{2}non̠
	la^{33}	mu^{55}	la^{33}	mə^{33}	no^{33}
	虎	老	虎	不	觉

第六节	^{1}Nds‘a	^{1}p’ĕr	^{2}la	^{2}gkan̠	^{2}ggü
	nʥæ^{21}	phər^{21}	la^{33}	kæ^{33}	gɯ^{33}
	獠牙	白	虎	前	落

第七节	^{2}La	^{3}mun	^{2}la	^{2}lä	^{2}non̠
	la^{33}	mu^{55}	la^{33}	le^{33}	no^{33}
	虎	老	虎	又	觉

第八节 ^{2}Nv-^{2}lv-^{1}nddü-^{3}t’khi-^{2}ghügh

ŋv^{33} lv^{33}ndɯ^{21}tɕhi^{55}ɯ^{33}

乌璐得其恶

第九节	^{3}Ch'wua	^{1}p'ĕr	^{3}mun̠	^{2}muàn̠	^{2}non̠
	tʂ̥hua^{55}	phər^{21}	mu^{55}	mə^{33}	no^{33}
	鹿	白	老	不	觉

第十节	^{2}Nyu	^{2}gv	^{2}nyu	^{3}dshi-^{2}dshi
	ȵy^{33}	gv^{33}	ȵy^{33}	tʂ̥ʅ^{55}tʂ̥ʅ^{33}
	他	身体	他	抖一抖

第十一节	^{2}K'o	^{1}p'ĕr	^{3}ch'wua	^{2}gkan̠	^{2}ggü
	kho^{33}	phər^{21}	tʂ̥hua^{55}	kæ^{33}	gɯ^{33}
	角	白	雄鹿	前	落

第十二节	^{3}Ch'wua	^{3}mun̠	^{3}ch'wua	^{2}lä	^{2}non̠
	tʂ̥hua^{55}	mu^{55}	tʂ̥hua^{55}	le^{33}	no^{33}
	雄鹿	老	雄鹿	又	觉

二、句译

第一节：他的身体抖一抖。

第二节：白色的羽毛掉落在鹤的面前。

第三节：他现在知道自己老了。

第四节：老虎在拉久梭古盘。

第五节：他不觉得自己老了。

第六节：长长的尖牙掉落在虎的面前。

第七节： 他才知道自己老了。

第八节：在乌璐得其恶，

第九节：白色的雄鹿不觉得自己老了。

第十节：他的身体抖一抖，

第十一节：白色鹿角掉落在鹿的面前。

第十二节：他才知道自己老了。

三、字词详解

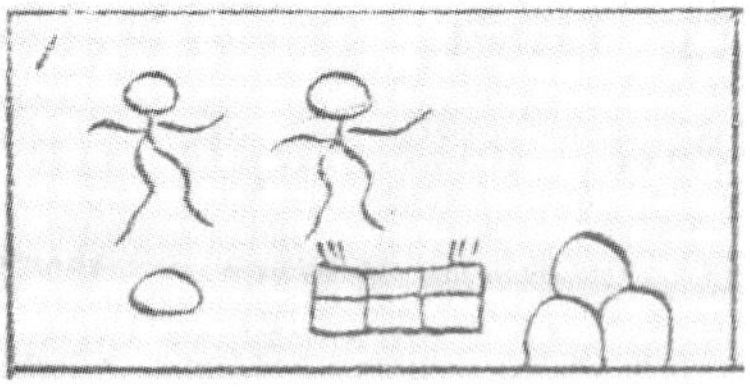

第一节：^{2}nyu 是代词，已经解释过了。第一个^{2}nyu 字下面像鸡蛋之形，读作^{2}gv，这里意为“身体”。^{3}p’u-^{3}lv 意为“颤抖”，这个词由两个字组成，第一个读作^{3}p’u，像藏人制作的一种布料，汉语叫“氆氇”，读作 p’u-lu；第二个字像石头，读作^{2}lv，本义为“石头”，这两个字在这里用作标音符。

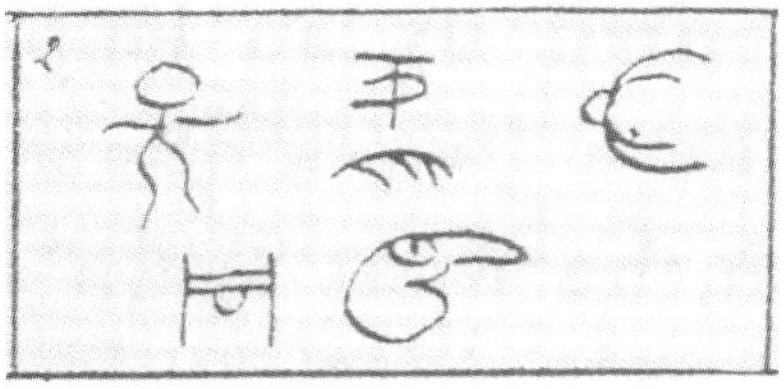

第二节：^{1}Noṉ ^{1}p’ĕr 是“白羽毛”，^{2}nyu 是人称代词，但是没读出来。^{2}gko 是“鹤”，^{2}Gkaṉ 是“在中国新年时孩子玩的一种玩具”，口语作^{2}tgkye-^{1}lĕr，这里借音作“前面”。最后一个字像一张嘴，读作^{2}ggü，如果两字连读作^{2}ggü ^{2}ggü，意为“满足，饱了”，这里作标音符，意为“落下”。

第三节：这一节与第二页的第九节相同。

第四节：^{2}la-(^{2}gyu)-^{2}yu-^{3}sso-^{2}gkv-^{1}p'ĕr 是一个地名。高山通常叫作^{2}ngyu-^{1}shwua（对译作山高），^{3}sso经常与^{2}ngyu 连读表示高山。第一个字是哥巴文，读作^{2}la。下一个字像铸造金锭和银锭的模具，读作^{2}gyu，这里用作标音符。下一个字像一棵树的树干倒在地上，树根外露，读作^{1}sso，本义为“干燥”，这里借音作^{3}sso，意为“高山、山巅”，最后一个字写了，但是没有读出来。在“山”字的里面有个“白”字。^{2}gkv 是“头”的意思，字没有写出来。^{2}la-(^{2}gyu)-^{2}yu-^{3}sso-^{2}gkv-^{1}p'ĕr 指一座被雪覆盖的高山。

第五节：第一个字读作^{2}la，意为“老虎”，下一个字读作^{3}mu̱n，意为“老”。这一节的所有字都已经解释过了。

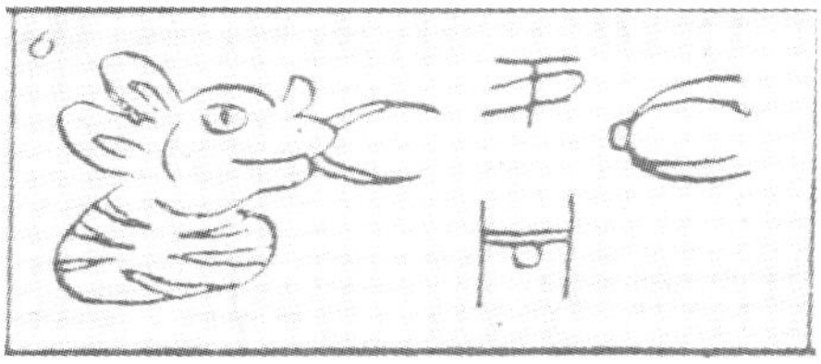

第六节：这一节除了^{1}nds'a 之外，其他字已经解释过了。^{1}nds'a 的意思是“獠牙”，这个字附着在虎嘴上。

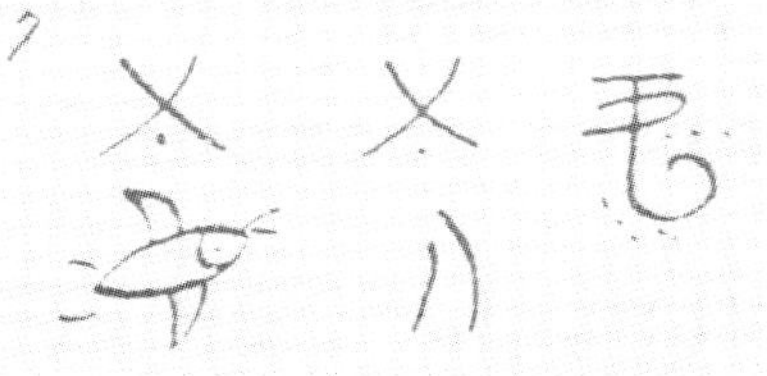

第七节：除了第四个哥巴文，其他字已经解释过了。第四个字读作^{2}lä，在本书的第二页第五节用“獐子”代替，这里作“又”。

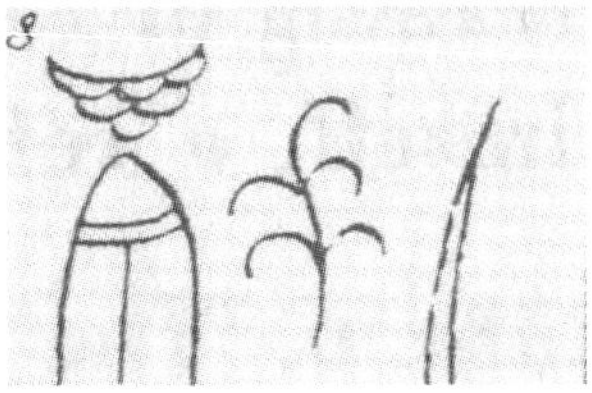

第八节：^{2}Nv-^{2}lv-^{1}nddü-^{3}t'khi-^{2}ghügh 是一座高山的名字，山上云雾缭绕，是雄鹿的栖息地。^{1}nddü意为“降、定居”，^{3}t'khi 意为“冷，也有“雾”的意思，^{2}ghügh 意为“怀抱”。第一个字读作^{1}nv，意为“银”。下面那个字是“山”，读作^{2}ngyu，两字连读作^{2}nv-^{2}lv，直译为：银色的石头，指山上终年被积雪覆盖，看起来像银色的。第二个字读作^{1}ndi，意思是“一种蕨类植物”，这种蕨类在纳西地区春天时很多，嫩蕨叶可以食用。最后一个字像一根刺，读作^{3}t'khi，这里借音作“迷雾”。^{2}ghügh 字没写出来，意思是“怀抱”。

第九节：第一个字像鹿头，鹿角上的那个字读作^{1}p'ěr，意为“白色”。因此，^{3}ch'wua ^{1}p'ěr 就是“白鹿”。其他字已经解释过了。

第十节：这里除了最后两个字外，其他字都已经解释过了。它们读作^{3}dshi-^{2}dshi，字形像鹰爪，读作^{1}dshi，这里^{3}dshi-^{1}dshi 表示颤抖，只用于动物的身体颤抖，比如狗颤抖。它也可以表示扬谷或者给谷物脱粒的时候抖动手中的簸箕。

第十一节：第一个字是常见字，读作[2]k'o，字形像动物的角，圆圈表示“头”，上面的曲线表示角。下面一个字读作[1]p'ĕr，意为“白”，所以，合起来意为“白色的角”，其他字已经解释过了。

第十二节：这些字已经解释过了。

经卷第四页释义

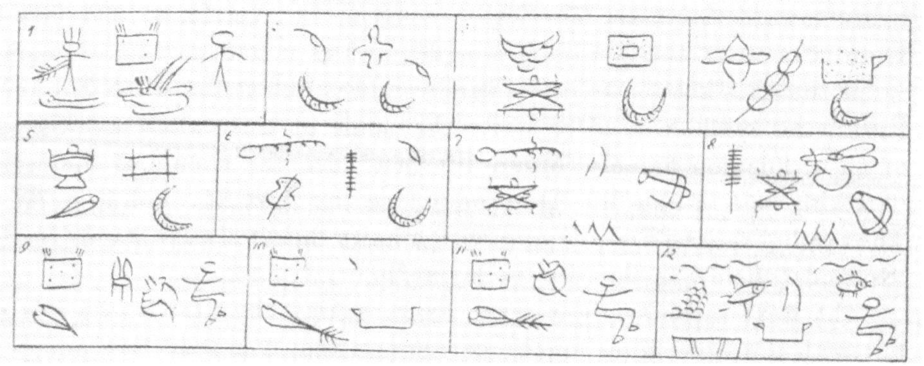

一、全页标音及直译

第一节	^{1}Ssu-^{1}lo	^{3}Ssu-^{2}ssä-^{2}zo			
	su^{21}lo^{21}	su^{55}se^{33}zo^{33}			
	鼠罗	鼠塞男			
第二节	^{2}Muàn̠	^{2}dgyu	^{1}ssü	^{2}muàn̠	^{2}dgyu
	mə^{33}	dʑy^{33}	sy^{21}	mə^{33}	dʑy^{33}
	没	有	东西	没	有
第三节	^{1}Nv	^{1}ha	^{3}dta	^{3}shĕr	^{2}dgyu
	ŋv^{21}	hæ^{21}	ta^{55}	ʂər^{55}	dʑy^{33}
	银	金	柜子	满	有
第四节	^{1}Ō	^{1}ch’ung	^{2}bpö	^{3}shĕr	^{2}dgyu
	o^{21}	tʂhu^{21}	py^{33}	ʂər^{55}	dʑy^{33}
	绿松石	玛瑙	升	满	有
第五节	^{2}Haw-^{1}gyi	^{2}ngu	^{3}shĕr	^{2}dgyu	
	hɑ^{33}dʑi^{21}	ŋgu^{33}	ʂər^{55}	dʑy^{33}	
	谷子	仓	满	有	
第六节	^{3}K’v	^{1}nä	^{2}szĭ	^{2}muàn̠	^{2}dgyu
	khv^{55}	ne^{21}	zɿ^{33}	mə^{33}	dʑy^{33}
	岁	和	寿	没	有
第七节	^{3}K’v	^{1}ha	^{1}mùen̠	^{2}lä	^{1}ds’ĭ
	khv^{55}	hæ^{21}	mɯ^{21}	le^{33}	tshɿ^{21}
	岁	买	南	又	来
第八节	^{2}szĭ	^{1}ha	^{1}mùen̠	^{2}lä	^{1}ds’ĭ
	zɿ^{33}	hæ^{21}	mɯ^{21}	le^{33}	tshɿ^{21}
	寿	买	南	又	来

第九节　^{2}Ssu-^{1}gyi-^{2}gkv　^{2}nnü　^{1}dtü
su^{33}ʥi^{21}kv^{33}　nɯ^{33}　tɯ^{21}
鼠河头　他　启程

第十节　^{2}Ssu-^{1}gyi-^{2}maṉ　^{1}lä　^{2}t'u
su^{33}ʥi^{21}mæ^{33}　le^{21}　thu^{33}
鼠河尾　又　到

第十一节　^{2}Ssu-^{1}gyi-^{2}maṉ　^{2}nnü　^{1}dtü
su^{33} ʥi^{21} mæ^{33}　nɯ^{33}　tɯ^{21}
鼠河尾　他　启程

第十二节　^{2}Bbĕr-^{2}ddĕr　^{2}llü　^{2}lä　^{2}t'u,
bər^{33} dər^{33}　lɯ^{33}　le^{33}　thu^{33}
北地　地　又　到

^{2}Bbĕr-^{2}ddĕr　^{2}llü　^{2}nnü　^{1}dtü.
bər^{33} dər^{33}　lɯ^{33}　nɯ^{33}　tɯ^{21}
北地　地　他　启程

二、句译

第一节：鼠罗河的鼠塞男，

第二节：什么东西都不缺。

第三节：他的柜子里装满了银和金。

第四节：箱子里装满了绿松石和玛瑙。

第五节：粮仓装满了粮食。

第六节：但是他没有了寿岁。

第七节：他到南边买岁。

第八节：他到南边买寿。

第九节：他从鼠河头启程，

第十节：到鼠河尾。

第十一节：他从鼠河尾启程，

第十二节：到北地，然后从北地又启程。

三、字词详解

第一节：^{1}Ssu-^{1}lo 是一个山谷的名字，^{1}lo 是山谷。^{1}Na-^{2}khi ^{1}shu-^{1}lo 是指铁山谷，在木里境内。在这个山谷中鼠河或铁河流过，藏语叫 lChags Chhu，藏文作 ལྕགས་ཆུ 。木里当地人把这条河叫 Zho-chhü。那里居住着纳西人的一个支系，叫 Shu-khin̠，他们有自己的语言。他们外表看起来像甲迷人（Ch'ra-me）、纳西人和藏人的混血。他们只生活在 shen-dzong 的伸臂桥上边，俄亚（^{1}ō-^{2}yü）的下边，他们属于纳西。（参见《中国西南古纳西王国》第 2 卷，第 384—385 页）这条河是无量河的支流，它没有汉语名字，我把纳西语翻译成汉语叫铁河。这个字用于记录山谷的名字，^{1}Ssu 是指美利苏主（^{2}Mùan̠-^{3}llü ^{1}Ssu-^{2}ndzĭ），鬼名，它是纳西人的祖先美利董主（^{2}Mùan̠-^{3}llü ^{1}Ddu-^{2}ndzĭ）的敌人。（参见《纳西族的纳迦崇拜及其相关仪式》第 1 卷，第 79 页，注释 10）这个字像一个长尾巴的鬼，它通常指美利苏主，下面是“山谷”这个字。

下面三个字作标音符，第一个读作^{1}ssu，意为“骰子”，该字上面再加三条短线，这里读^{3}ssu，意为“一种茅草”，纳西人用它来编草鞋。下面那个字像一只野羊的头，“野羊”读作^{2}ssä。最后一个字像男人或男孩，“男人或男孩”读作^{2}zo，这个男人的名字叫^{3}Ssu ^{2}ssä。前两个字是标音符，第三个字是表意字。居住在鼠罗河边的人被称为^{3}ssu ^{2}ssä，我们对他们一无所知。有一条河从木里和左所之间穿过，这里是摩梭人居住区，叫作^{1}Shu-^{1}lo-^{2}k’o。（参见《中国西南古纳西王国》第 2 卷，第 407 和 420 页）

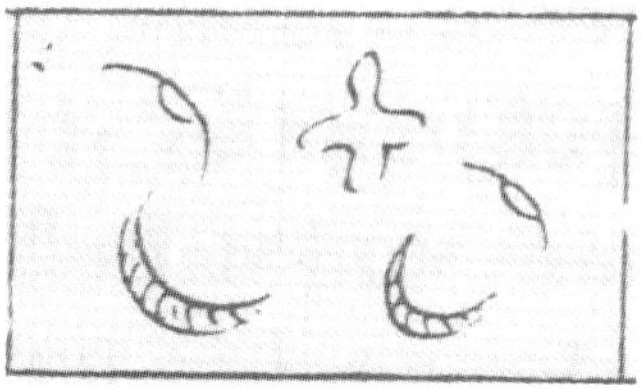

第二节：第一个字是否定词^{2}muàn̲，下面一个字读作^{1}dgyu，字形像手镯，这里借音读作^{2}dgyu，意为“有，存在”。像“十”的字读作^{1}ssü，据说字形像铅块，这里借音作“东西”。这句话实际意思是，没有东西没有，换句话说，就是他拥有所有东西，纳西语中经常用两个否定来表示肯定。

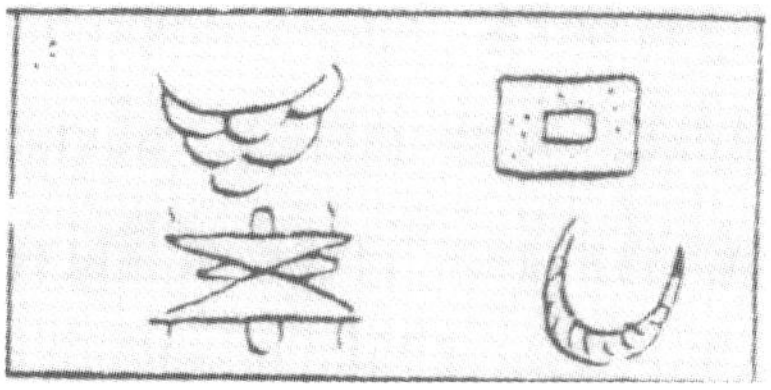

第三节：前两个字是^{1}nv 和^{1}ha，^{1}nv 意为“银”，^{1}ha 意为“金”。第三个字像一个箱子，读作^{3}dta，^{3}shĕr 意为“满”，箱子里有很多点，表示数量多。^{2}dgyu 又是“有”的意思。

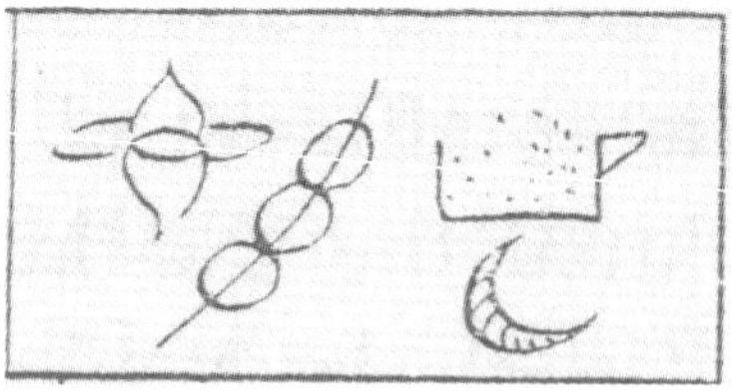

第四节：前两个字是^{1}ō 和^{1}ch’ung，^{1}ō 是绿松石，^{1}ch’ung 是玛瑙珠，藏语叫 mchhong，藏文写作

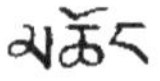

。^{2}bpö是“量器”，纳西人用来量粮食，汉语叫“升”。该字上的点表示数量多，读作^{3}shĕr，意为“满”。

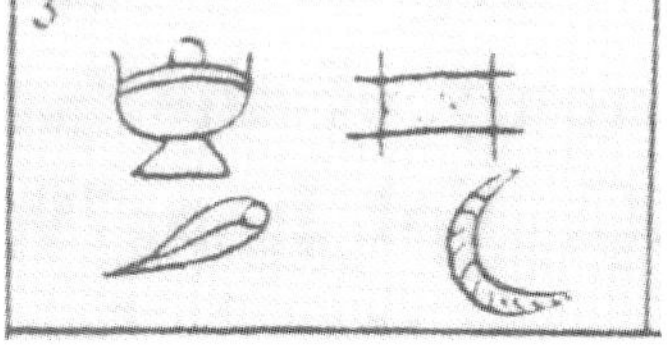

第五节：前两个字读作^{2}haw-^{1}gyi，^{2}haw 是“食物”，由一个带盖子的盘子表示。^{1}gyi 是“水”，这两个词表示所有不同的谷物，谷物生长需要浇水。

^{2}Ngu（意为“谷仓”）这个字像一个木头箱子，这个箱子四周的木板是可拆卸的，可以增加四周木板的高度来增加箱子的容积。纳西人把粮食储存在这种箱子里。这个字上的点表示“满”，读作^{3}shĕr。^{2}dgyu 是“有”的意思。

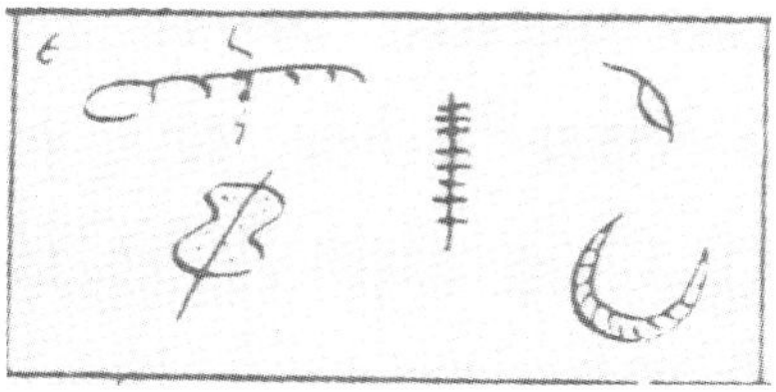

第六节：第一个字像纳西人用的镰刀，叫作^{1}ndaw，它不是圆形的，像外来的镰刀，前端还有一个弯钩。它的边缘是锯齿状的，因此它又被叫作^{2}shu-^{1}p'ĕr ^{1}ndaw ^{1}dzu，意为“带锯齿白铁镰刀”，其中^{1}dzu 常会被省略掉。现在口语“镰刀”叫作^{3}ssu-^{2}gkv。穿过这个字中间的直线读作^{3}ts'ĕr 或者^{3}ts'，意为“切或砍”，也可以读作^{2}k'v，意为“收获或者收割谷物”，这里借音作^{3}k'v，意为“年”，“年”是一个抽象名词，不能用象形字来表现。“镰刀”下面的那个字读作 nä，本义是“小米或籼米”，这里作连词“和”。第三个字像草，读作^{2}szĭ，这里借音作“寿”。其他字都已经解释过了。

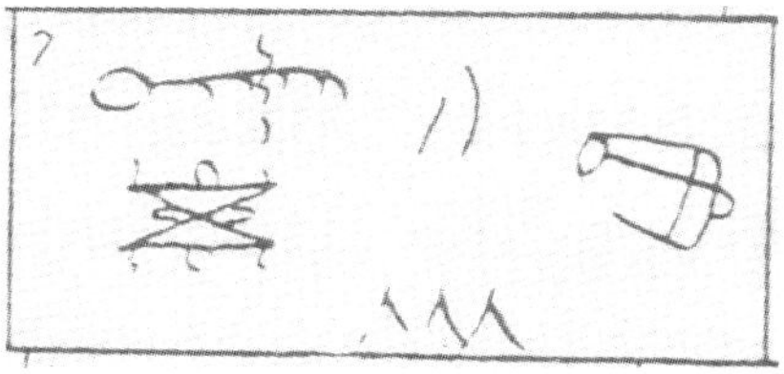

第七节：在^{3}k'v 字下面的是“金”字，读作^{1}ha，这里作动词“买”。像三个三角形的字读作^{1}mùen̲，意为“下面”，实际上指“南方”。如果三角形比较高，这个字读作^{2}mi，意为“火”。用快要熄灭的火或者火苗比较低的火表示“低”。“南方”作^{2}yi-^{1}ch'i ^{1}mùen̲，即古代的押赤城，这是蒙古人对现在昆明的称呼。^{1}mùen̲指昆明在丽江的南面。哥巴文^{2}lä这里意为“又”。因此相当于汉语的“才”。最后一个字像羊的肩胛骨，读作^{1}p'i，还可以读作^{1}ds'i，这里读作^{1}ds'i，意为“来”。过去时没有写出来，也不读，但是要理解成过去。因此是他已经去了或者去过南方。

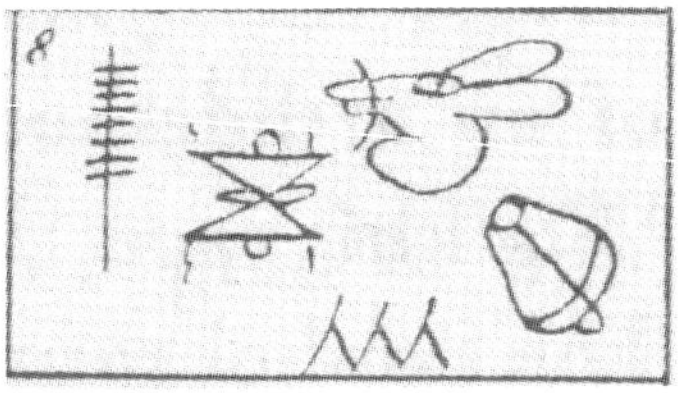

第八节：这个句式跟上一节相同，除了用^{2}szǐ（寿）替换了^{3}k’v（岁）。把哥巴文^{2}lä换成了象形字，字形像獐子的头部。

第九节：^{2}Ssu-^{1}gyi 这里指名为^{3}Ssu-^{1}lo-^{2}k’o 的河，这个字像一种特殊的草，这种草叫^{3}ssu，以此替换字形像署鬼的那个字，那个字也读作^{1}Ssu。第三个字读作^{2}gkv，意为“头”，这里指从木里^{3}Ssu-^{1}lo-^{2}k’o 的上游出发开启旅程。第四个字像心脏，读作^{2}nnü，口语作^{2}nuṉ-^{2}mä，这里借音作^{2}nnü，作代词“他”。最后一个字读作^{1}dtü，意为“启程”，这个字像一个人正从椅子上起来。

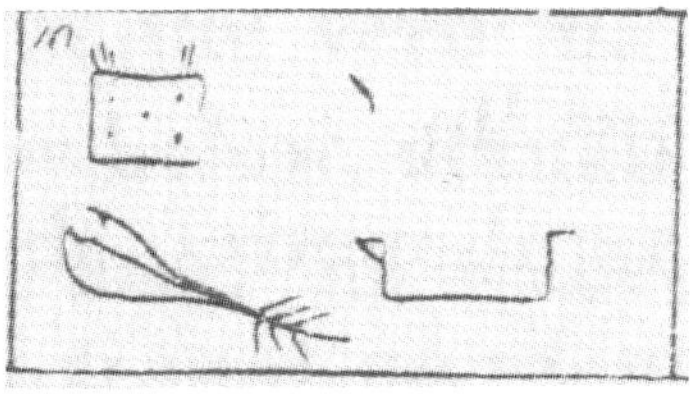

第十节：这一节又出现上一节出现的两个字，它们读作^{2}Ssu-^{1}gyi，意为“鼠水”，不同的是，这里的“水”字的末尾像尾巴之形。“尾巴”读作^{2}maṉ，因此这里指^{3}Ssu-^{1}lo-^{2}k’o 的下游。^{2}lä是“又”，最后一个字读作^{2}t’u，字形像一只水桶，这里借音作“到”。

第十一节：这一节的所有字在前面已经解释过了。

第十二节：这一节的左上角那个字像一根绳子，读作^{2}bbĕr，口语作^{1}erh。绳子下面那个字像泡沫，读作^{2}ddĕr。以上两字都借音作地名^{2}Bbĕr-^{2}ddĕr 北地注音。北地位于中甸县。下面那个像大地的那个字读作^{1}dü，这里不读出来，用来说明^{2}Bbĕr-^{2}ddĕr 这个地名，汉语叫 Pei-ti，即“北地”。①（参见《中国西南古纳西王国》第 1 卷，第 262—268 页）在“绳子”下面的那个字是“虱子”，读作^{3}llü，这里作标音符，意思是“田地”。^{1}dü与^{3}llü意思相近，但它意思是“地”。整句译为：他到达北地，又从那里启程。后一句只写出三个字。

①译者按，泡沫右边那个字读作^{3}muṉ，意为“牛蝇”。此字本应写作

，与第二个绳子下面那个字一样，读作^{3}llü，本义为“虱子”，这里借音作^{2}llü“地”。

经卷第五页释义

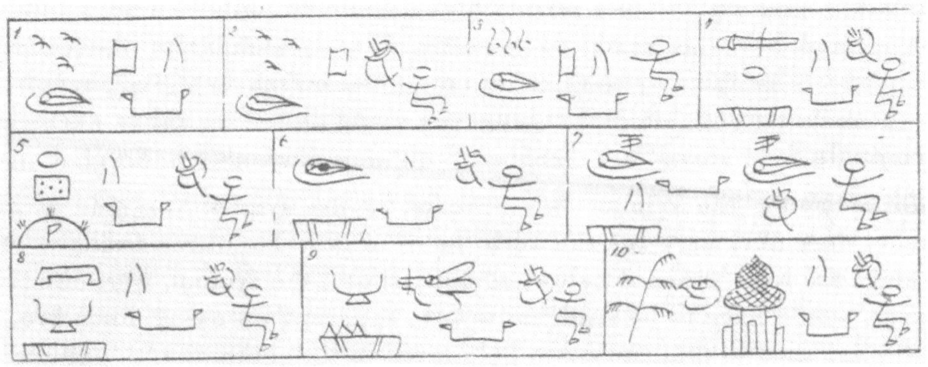

一、全页标音及直译

第一节	^{2}Ts'u	^{2}gu^{2}k'u	^{2}lä	^{2}t'u
	tshu^{33}	gu^{33}khu^{33}	le^{33}	thu^{33}
	冬天	渡口	又	到

第二节	^{2}Ts'u	^{2}gu^{2}k'u	^{2}nnü	^{1}dtü
	tshu^{33}	gu^{33}khu^{33}	nɯ^{33}	tɯ^{21}
	冬天	渡口	他	启程

第三节	^{1}Zhu	^{2}gu^{2}k'u	^{2}lä	^{2}t'u,	^{1}zhu	^{2}gu^{2}k'u
	zu̜^{21}	gu^{33}khu^{33}	le^{33}	thu^{33}	zu̜^{21}	gu^{33}khu^{33}
	夏天	渡口	又	到	夏天	渡口

^{2}nnü	^{1}dtü.
nɯ^{33}	tɯ^{21}
他	启程

第四节	^{2}Ndaw-^{2}gv	^{1}dü	^{2}lä	^{2}t'u,	^{2}Ndaw-^{2}gv	^{1}dü
	ndɑ^{33}gv^{33}	dy^{21}	le^{33}	thu^{33}	ndɑ^{33}gv^{33}	dy^{21}
	打鼓	地	又	到	打鼓	地

^{2}nnü	^{1}dtü
nɯ^{33}	tɯ^{21}
他	启程

第五节	^{2}Gv-^{2}ssu-^{1}gko	^{2}lä	^{2}t'u,	^{2}Gv-^{2}ssu-^{1}gko
	gv^{33}su^{33}ko^{21}	le^{33}	thu^{33}	gv^{33}su^{33}ko^{21}
	古署郭	又	到	古署郭

^{2}nnü	^{1}dtü
nɯ^{33}	tɯ^{21}
他	启程

第六节　^{1}Gyi-^{1}na-^{1}lo　^{2}lä　^{2}t'u,　^{1}Gyi-^{1}na-^{1}lo
dʑi^{21}na^{21}lo^{21}　le^{33}　thu^{33}　dʑi^{21}na^{21}lo^{21}
吉纳罗　又　到　吉纳罗

^{2}nnü　^{1}dtü
nɯ^{33}　tɯ^{21}
他　启程

第七节　^{1}Gyi-^{1}p'ĕr-^{1}lo　^{2}lä　^{2}t'u,　^{1}Gyi-^{1}p'ĕr-^{1}lo
dʑi^{21}phər^{21}lo^{21}　le^{33}　thu^{33}　dʑi^{21}phər^{21}lo^{21}
吉佩罗　又　到　吉佩罗

^{2}nnü　^{1}dtü
nɯ^{33}　tɯ^{21}
他　启程

第八节　^{1}Ggŏ　^{2}Nga-^{1}ba　^{2}lä　^{2}t'u,　^{1}Ggŏ　^{2}Nga-^{1}ba
go^{21}　ŋga^{33}ba^{21}　le^{33}　thu^{33}　go^{21}　ŋga^{33}ba^{21}
上面　嘎巴　又　到　上面　嘎巴

^{2}nnü　^{1}dtü
nɯ^{33}　tɯ^{21}
他　启程

第九节　^{1}Mùeṉ　^{2}Nga-^{1}ba　^{2}lä　^{2}t'u,　^{1}Mùeṉ　^{2}Nga-^{1}ba
mɯ^{21}　ŋga^{33}ba^{21}　le^{33}　thu^{33}　mɯ^{21}　ŋga^{33}ba^{21}
下面　嘎巴　又　到　下面　嘎巴

^{2}nnü　^{1}dtü
nɯ^{33}　tɯ^{21}
他　启程

第十节	^{3}Llü-^{1}gko-^{2}gyi	^{2}lä	^{2}t'u,	^{3}Llü-^{1}gko-^{2}gyi
	lɯ^{55}ko^{21}dʑi^{33}	le^{33}	thu^{33}	lɯ^{55}ko^{21}dʑi^{33}
	勒各吉	又	到	勒各吉

^{2}nnü	^{1}dtü
nɯ^{33}	tɯ^{21}
他	启程

二、句译

第一节：到冬季扬子江的渡口，

第二节：从那里又启程了。

第三节：到夏季达扬子江的渡口，从那里又启程。

第四节：到打鼓，从那里又启程。

第五节：到古署郭的松树林，从那里又启程。

第六节：到吉纳罗，从那里又启程。

第七节：到吉佩罗，从那里又启程。

第八节：到高地嘎巴，从那里又启程。

第九节：到低地嘎巴，从那里又启程。

第十节：到勒各吉，从那里又启程。

三、字词详解

第一节：第一个字像三个变形的小叉号，它们代表雪花，“雪”读作^{2}mbe，但是这里该字读作^{2}ts'u ^{3}ssu ^{2}hä，意为“冬三月”。^{2}gu ^{2}k'u 意为“渡口”，可以从那里涉水过河。^{2}gu 这个词没有写出来，取而代之的是“山谷”这个字，这个字由“水”字加一条曲线构成，但是这个字并不读出来，在这里只是表示一条较大的小溪或河流，可能是^{2}yi-^{1}bi，即扬子江。第三个字读作^{2}k'u，本义为“门”，这里表示“河岸”，跟“水”字一起表示“渡口”。这个渡口在打鼓（^{2}Ndaw-^{2}gv）村，打鼓村位于扬子江上，丽江的北面，有两个渡口可以过江，一个是冬天江水的水位很低的时候；一个是夏天洪水来的时候。

其他的字都已经解释过了。

第二节：参见前面段落的解释。

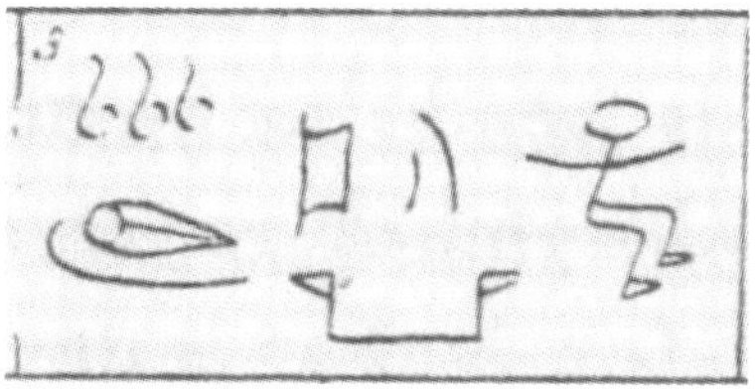

第三节：这一节唯一需要解释的是第一个字，读作^{1}ḳhü，意为“雨水”，由于夏季属于雨季，所以，这个字还可以表示“夏天”，读作^{1}zhu。其他所有字都已经解释过了。

第四节：前两个字读作^{2}ndaw-^{2}gv，它们下面那个字是“地”，读作^{1}dü。第一个字的由一把剑和一条线组成，意为“砍”，跟“砍”字类似的是^{2}k'v，意为“收获”。（参见本书的第四页第六节的字词详解）“砍”下面的那个字读作^{2}gkv，本义为“蛋”，这里读作^{2}gv，两个字作标音符，读作^{2}ndaw-^{2}gv，地名，是扬子江上的一座城，汉语叫“打鼓①”，在

①译者按，即现在的大具。

丽江的北面，在穿过虎跳峡（^{3}A-^{2}ts'an̠-^{3}gko）和玉龙雪山的扬子江的出口处。（参见《中国西南古纳西王国》第 1 卷，第 227—228 页）其他字已经解释过了。

第五节：前三个字从上到下依次读作 ^{2}gv、^{2}ssu 和 ^{1}gko。第一个字在前面已经解释过了。第二个字的本义是“骰子”，第三个字的本义是“高原”。这个高原的名字叫 ^{2}gv-^{2}ssu-^{1}gko，它位于玉龙雪山的海拔第三的山峰 ^{1}gyi-^{1}na ^{2}nv-^{2}lv 的山脚下。^{1}gyi-^{1}na ^{2}nv-^{2}lv 与第一高峰扇子陡相邻。（参见《中国西南古纳西王国》第 1 卷，第 187—191 页和第 224—227 页，图 91）^{1}gko 这个字的里面还有一个字，它也读作 ^{1}gko，意为“针”，这里作标音符。在半圆形上的短线表示“草”。其他字已经解释过了。

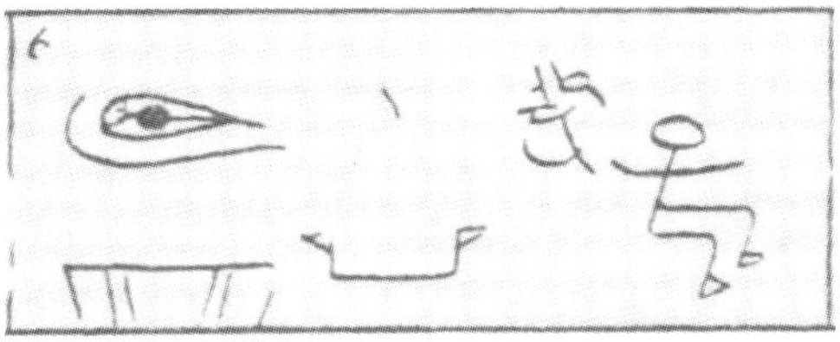

第六节：最上面那个字是个复合字。如果中间没有黑点，这个字读作 ^{1}gyi-^{1}lo，意为“山谷”，黑点读作 ^{1}na，意为“黑色”。它用来修饰名词 ^{1}gyi。黑水谷（^{1}Gyi-^{1}na-^{1}lo）指一条小溪，发源于东边的黑水雪峰（^{1}Gyi-^{1}na ^{2}nv-^{2}lv）。黑水雪峰的冰川融化汇入黑水谷。它又汇聚了上面的 Nga-tza 一起流入扬子江大峡谷。^{1}dü是“地”，上面的字表示一个地名。其他的字都已经解释过了，它们都在这一页的其他节。

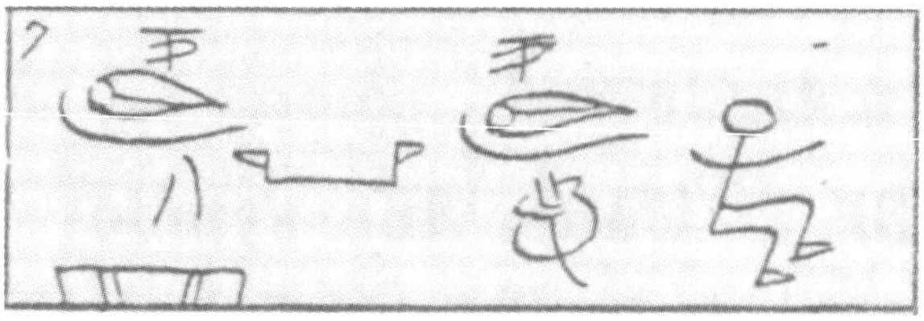

第七节：¹Gyi-¹p'ěr-¹lo（白水谷）是一条冰川融化后汇成的河流，是白色的。白水谷不属于一条冰川河流，它流过一片黑石地区，相比之下，它的水就是黑色的。白水谷的源头在扇子陡的一处冰川。¹p'ěr 是“白色”，上面那个字是“水”。（参见《中国西南古纳西王国》第 1 卷，第 223 页，图 83）

第八节：这一节的前三个字是需要解释的。最上面一个字像一个板凳，读作¹ggŏ，这里借音作“高”，也就是指北边，意为“在高处”。“高”下面那个字像一只杯子，“杯子”读作³k'wua，这里借音读作¹k'wua，意为“山口”。¹ggŏ ¹k'wua 意为“上面的山口”，即北方的山口，通过这里可以从白水（纳西语读作¹Gyi-¹p'ěr-¹lo）到嘎巴（²Nga-¹ba）①。嘎巴过去是一个冰川湖的河床。¹k'wua 这个字没读出来。高地嘎巴（²Nga-¹ba）是很有名的，在很多古老的东巴经中都出现过这个名字。（参见《中国西南古纳西王国》第 1 卷，第 222—224 页，图 78、80）

第九节：只有一个字需要解释，就是在这一节最下面的第二个字。¹dü是“地”，¹mueṉ是“低”，因此，他离开位于下面的嘎巴（²Nga-¹ba），也就

①译者按，嘎巴即干海子。

是离开低地嘎巴（^{2}Nga-^{1}ba）。

第十节：这一节有三个字之前没有解释过。前两个字作标音符，读作^{3}llü-^{1}gko，^{3}llü字像一棵杉树，一般读作^{3}llü-ndzĕr。^{1}gko 字的本义是“鹤”，这里读第一声。^{3}llü-^{1}gko 的第一个音节读第三声。^{3}llü-^{1}gko 是古代关吏的名字，他守护明代（公元 1368—1644 年）通往低地嘎巴（^{2}Nga-^{1}ba）的道路。^{3}llü-^{1}gko 出现在木增（他的另一个名字木增白更为人们熟知）统治纳西人的时期，他在公元 1600—1646 年统治丽江，也就是这首歌产生的时代。第三个字读作^{2}gyi，意为“房子”，它表示^{3}llü-^{1}gko 守护的房子。

经卷第六页释义

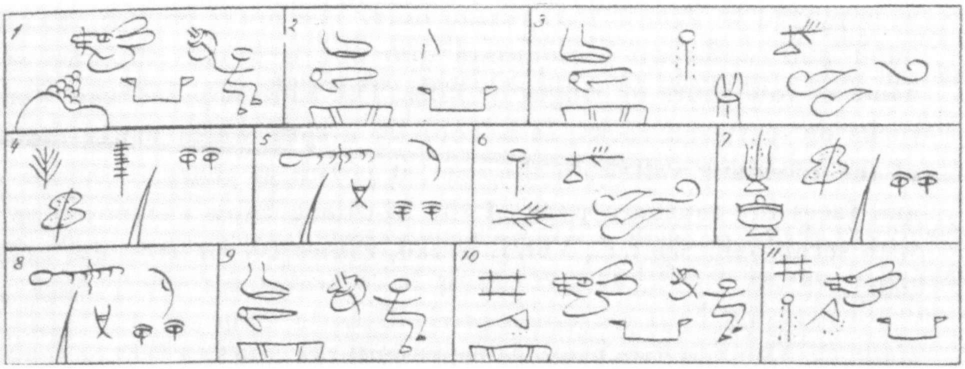

一、全页标音及直译

第一节	^{1}Dz‘a-^{2}dz‘a-^{1}mbu	^{2}lä	^{2}t’u,	^{1}Dz‘a-^{2}dz‘a-^{1}mbu	^{2}nnü	^{1}dtü
	ʥæ^{21}ʥæ^{33} mbu^{21}	le^{33}	thu^{33}	^{1}ʥæ^{21}ʥæ^{33}mbu^{2}	nɯ^{33}	tɯ^{21}
	章章坡	又	到	章章坡	他	启程

第二节	^{2}Boa-^{2}shi	^{1}dü	^{2}lä	^{2}t’u
	bə^{33}ʂʅ^{33}	dy^{21}	le^{33}	thu^{33}
	白沙	地	又	到

第三节	^{2}Boa-^{2}shi	^{2}dzhi	^{2}gkv	^{1}sso	^{3}k̦hü-^{2}khü
	bə^{33}ʂʅ^{33}	dʐʅ^{33}	kv^{33}	so^{21}	hɯ^{55} hɯ^{33}
	白沙	集市	头	三	围绕

第四节	^{2}Ss	^{1}nä	^{2}szĭ	^{2}t’khi	^{1}ddo
	sʅ^{33}	ne^{21}	zʅ^{33}	ʨhi^{33}	do^{21}
	柴	和	草	卖	见

第五节	^{2}K’v	^{2}t’khi	^{2}mä	^{2}muàn̠	^{1}ddo
	khv^{33}	ʨhi^{33}	me^{33}	mə^{33}	do^{21}
	年	卖	的	不	见

第六节	^{2}dzhi	^{2}man̠	^{1}sso	^{3}k̦hü-^{2}k̦hü
	dʐʅ^{33}	mæ^{33}	so^{21}	hɯ^{55}hɯ^{33}
	集市	尾	三	围绕

第七节	^{2}zhi	^{1}nä	^{2}haw	^{2}t’khi	^{1}ddo
	ʐʅ^{33}	ne^{21}	hɑ^{33}	ʨhi^{33}	do^{21}
	酒	和	饭	卖	见

第八节	^{3}K'v	^{2}t'khi	^{2}mä	^{2}muàn̠	^{1}ddo
	khv^{55}	tɕhi^{33}	me^{33}	mə^{33}	do^{21}
	年	卖	的	不	见

第九节	^{2}Boa-^{2}shi	^{1}dü	^{2}nnü	^{1}dtü
	bə^{33}ʂʅ^{33}	dy^{21}	nɯ^{33}	tɯ^{21}
	白沙	地	他	启程

第十节	^{1}Ngu-^{2}bä	^{1}dü	^{1}lä	^{2}t'u,	^{1}Ngu-^{2}bä
	ŋgu^{21}be^{33}	dy^{21}	le^{21}	thu^{33}	ŋgu^{21}be^{33}
	古柏	地	又	到	古柏

^{1}dü	^{2}nnü	^{1}dtü
dy^{21}	nɯ^{33}	tɯ^{21}
地	他	启程

第十一节	^{1}Ngu-^{2}bä	^{2}dzhi	^{2}lä	^{2}t'u
	ŋgu^{21}be^{33}	dʐʅ^{33}	le^{33}	thu^{33}
	古柏	集市	又	到

二、句译

第一节：到章章坡，那里他又启程。

第二节：到白沙，

第三节：在白沙，他绕着集市转了三圈。

第四节：看见卖柴和草的，

第五节：但是没有看见卖寿岁的。

第六节：在集市的尾部，绕了三圈。

第七节：看见了买酒和食物的，

第八节：但是没有看见卖寿岁的。

第九节：又从白沙启程，

第十节：然后又到了古柏，从那里又启程。

第十一节：他到古柏的集市。

三、字词详解

第一节：这里我最关注的是第一个字，这是一个字组，但是不能拆开，它像一个布满疏松岩石的山坡，代表一个地名，叫^{1}Dz'a-^{2}dz'a-^{1}mbu。这个字专门用来表示这个地名，这个字组的下半部分读作^{1}mbu，意为“山坡”，通常跟在山坡或者山脉名的后面。这个字组的上半部分像一堆石头或者疏松的岩石。该地位于丽江峡谷的北边，满地都是锋利的石灰岩，对面就是玉龙雪山的最高峰，山坡上长满了矮栎。（参见《中国西南古纳西王国》第1卷，第220页，图77和78）这个山坡的名字也可以读作^{1}Dza-^{2}dza-^{1}mbu。

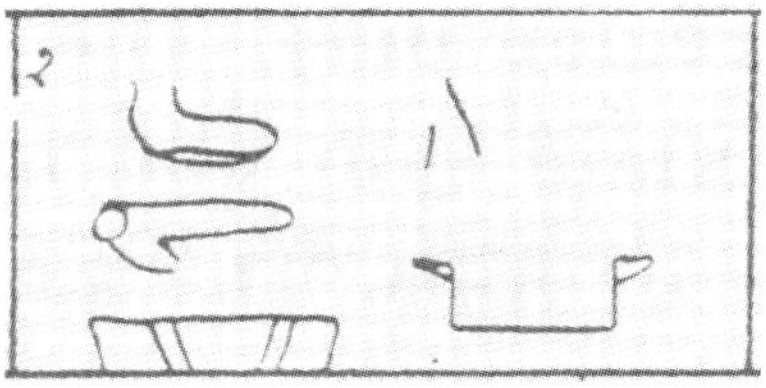

第二节：前两个字常用来表示地名“白沙乡或者县”①，位于丽江的北边，在去玉龙雪山的半路上。第一个字像脚底或者靴子的底部，因此，该字读作^{2}boa，意为“脚底”。下面那个字读作^{2}shi，意为“肉”。（参见《中国西南古纳西王国》第1卷，第173页，图52、54和56）

^{1}dü这个字一般用在地名之后，不读音，指示地名。

①译者按，现在的丽江市玉龙纳西族自治县白沙镇。

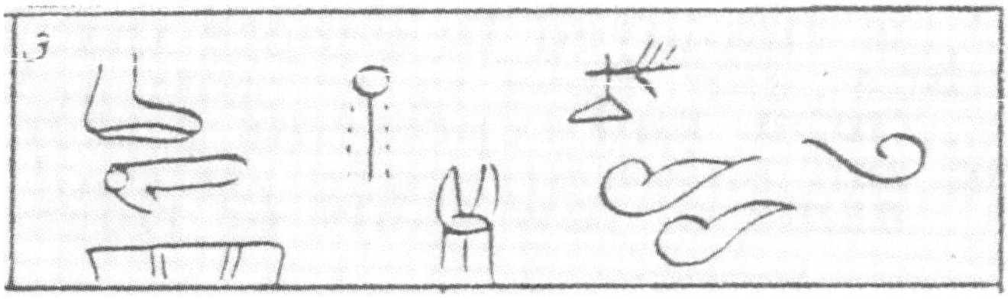

第三节：前三个字在本页第二节已经解释过了。第四个字读作^{2}dzhi，意为“集市”。两边的点表示集市的摊位。“集市”右边那个字读作^{2}gkv，意为“头”，这是表示集市的头部。本书第三页的第四节已经解释过^{1}sso 这个词了，这里表示三，实际上纳西语“三”读作^{3}ssu，它是从藏语的 gsum（三）借过来的。下面两个是相同的字，都读作^{2}ḳhü，两个字连读作^{3}ḳhü-^{2}ḳhü，意为“环绕”，最后一个字没有读，但是表示“环绕”的意思。

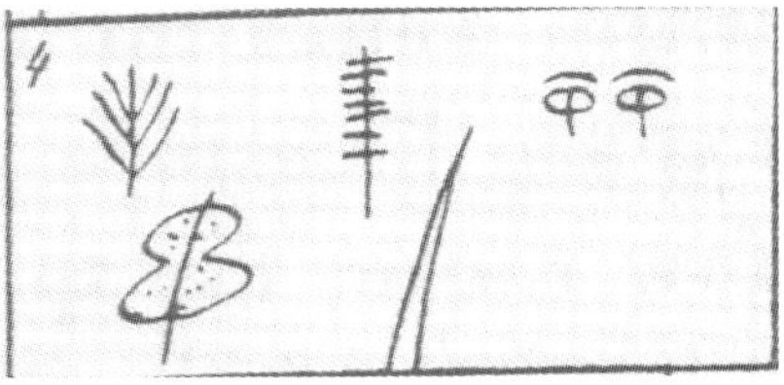

第四节：第一个字像一棵松树，读作^{2}ťo“松树”，也可以读作^{1}ndzěr（树）或^{2}ss（木），这里作^{2}ss（木）。^{1}nä 这个词已经解释过了；^{2}szǐ是“青草”。像刺之形的那个字读作^{2}ťkhi，本义是“刺”，这里借音作“卖”。最后一个字像一双眼睛，眼睛里伸出的两条线代表目光，该字读作^{1}ddo，意为“看见”。该句对译为“柴/和/草/卖/看”。

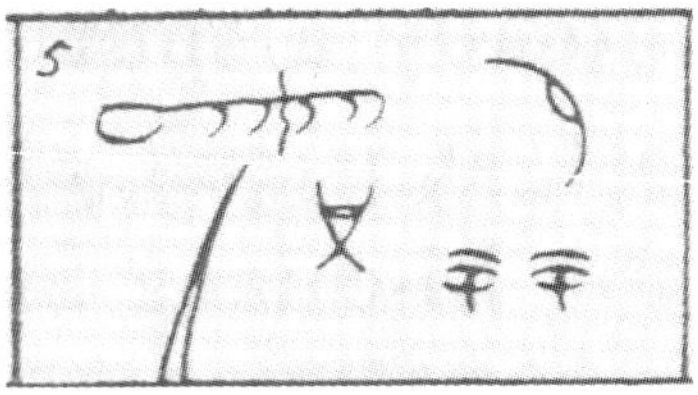

第五节：^{3}k'v 是“年”，（参见本书的第四页第六节的字词详解）^{2}ťkhi 是“卖”，^{2}muàn̠ 是“不”，^{1}ddo 是“看见”。

第六节：第二个字读作^{2}man̠，本义为“尾巴”，这里指集市的尽头，意思与^{2}gkv 相对。

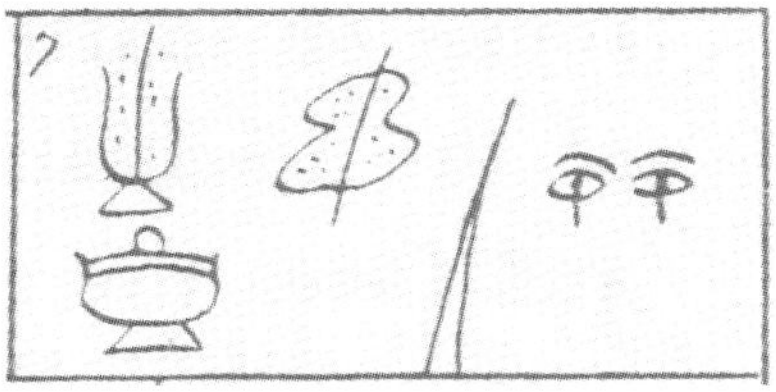

第七节：第一个字读作²zhi，意思是“酒”。这个字告诉我们纳西人的饮酒习惯。这个字像一个大的酒罐，里装满烈酒，然后在酒罐里面插着一根竹管，人们围坐在酒罐周围轮流用竹管喝酒。一边喝一边往酒罐里掺水。等酒喝完只剩下水的时候，这个聚会就结束了，这样不会有人喝醉。“酒”下面那个字读作²haw，意为“食物”。其余的字都已经解释过了。

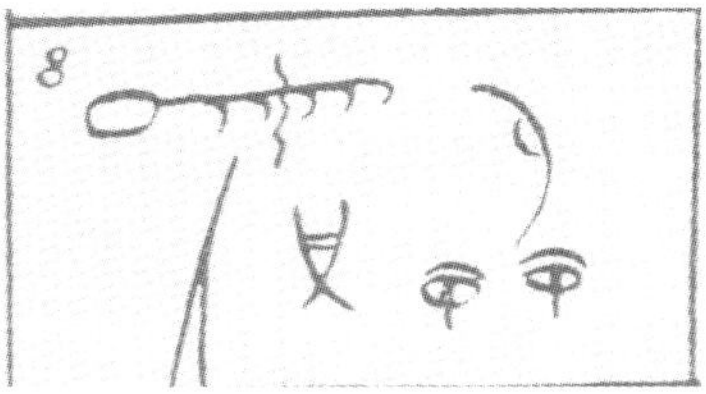

第八节：这一节的所有字在本页第五节已经都解释过了。只有第三个字需要再解释一下，它读作²mä，像女性生殖器，代表母亲，这里借音作“确实”。

第九节：这些字都已经解释过了。

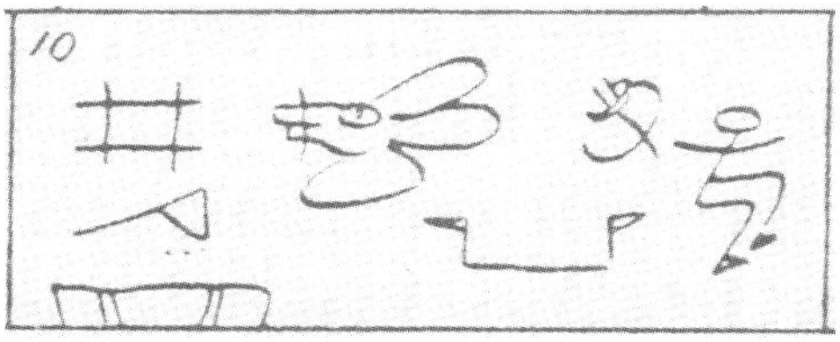

第十节：前两个字中第一个读作¹ngu，本义为“纳西人的粮仓”。（参见本书的第四页第五节的字词详解）第二个字读作²bä，意为“做”，像一把带着泥土的锄头。这两个字借音作纳西地名¹ngu-²bä。（参见《中国西南古纳西王国》

第 1 卷，第 175 页）[1]dü意为“地”，像一块土地，这里指一个地名。其他字已经解释过了。

第十一节：这些字之前已经解释过了。

经卷第七页释义

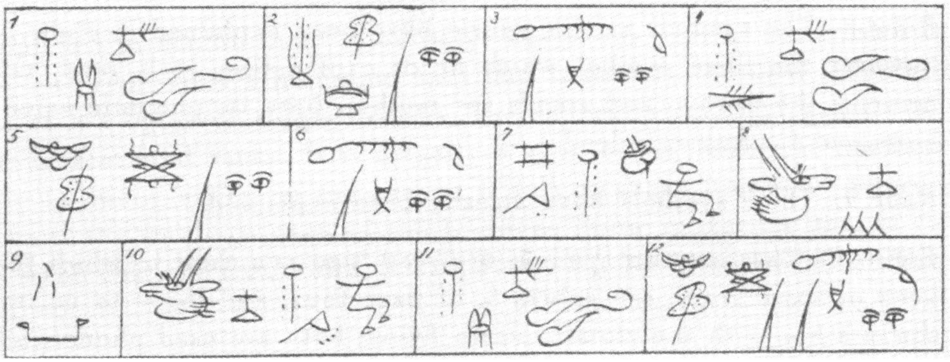

一、全页标音及直译

第一节

^{2}Dzhi	^{2}gkv	^{1}sso	^{3}ḳhü-^{2}ḳhü
dzʅ^{33}	kv^{33}	so^{21}	hɯ^{55}hɯ^{33}
集市	头	三	围绕

第二节

^{2}Zhi	^{1}nä	^{2}haw	^{2}t'khi	^{1}ddo
zʅ^{33}	ne^{21}	hɑ^{33}	tɕhi^{33}	do^{21}
酒	和	饭	卖	见

第三节

^{3}K'v	^{2}t'khi	^{2}mä	^{2}muàṉ	^{1}ddo
khv^{55}	tɕhi^{33}	me^{33}	mə^{33}	do^{21}
年	卖	的	不	见

第四节

^{2}dzhi	^{2}maṉ	^{1}sso	^{3}ḳhü-^{2}ḳhü
dzʅ^{33}	mæ^{33}	so^{21}	hɯ^{55}hɯ^{33}
集市	尾部	三	围绕

第五节

^{1}Nv	^{1}nä	^{1}ha	^{2}t'khi	^{1}ddo
ŋv^{21}	ne^{21}	hæ^{21}	tɕhi^{33}	do^{21}
雪	和	金	卖	见

第六节

^{3}K'v	^{2}t'khi	^{2}mä	^{2}muàṉ	^{1}ddo
khv^{55}	tɕhi^{33}	me^{33}	mə^{33}	do^{21}
年	卖	的	不	见

第七节

^{1}Ngu-^{2}bä	^{2}dzhi	^{2}nnü	^{1}dtü
ŋgu^{21}be^{33}	dzʅ^{33}	nɯ^{33}	tɯ^{21}
古百	集市	他	启程

第八节

^{2}Yi-^{2}ch'i-^{1}mùeṉ
i^{33}tʂhʅ^{33}mɯ^{21}
押赤

第九节	^{1}lä	^{2}t'u,
	le^{21}	thu^{33}
	又	到

第十节	^{2}Yi-^{2}ch'i	^{2}dzhi	^{2}bä	^{1}dtü
	i^{33} tʂhʅ^{33}	dʐʅ^{33}	be^{33}	tɯ^{21}
	押赤	集市	做	启程

第十一节	^{2}Dzhi	^{2}gkv	^{1}sso	^{3}ḳhü-^{2}ḳhü
	dʐʅ^{33}	kv^{33}	so^{21}	hɯ^{55} hɯ^{33}
	集市	头	三	围绕

第十二节	^{1}Nv	^{1}nä	^{1}ha	^{2}t'khi	^{1}ddo,	^{3}k'v	^{2}t'khi
	ŋv^{21}	ne^{21}	hæ^{21}	tɕhi^{33}	do^{21}	khv^{55}	tɕhi^{33}
	银	和	金	卖	见	年	卖

^{2}mä	^{2}muàn̠	^{1}ddo.
me^{33}	mə^{33}	do^{21}
的	不	见

二、句译

第一节：他到集市前绕了三圈，

第二节：他看见卖酒和食物的。

第三节：但是没有看见卖寿岁的。

第四节：到集市尾绕了三圈，

第五节：看见卖金和银的。

第六节：但是没有看见卖寿岁的。

第七节：从古柏集市又启程，

第八、九节：到押赤，

第十节：然后从押赤启程。

第十一节：到集市前绕了三圈，

第十二节：他看见卖金和银的，但是没有看见卖寿岁的。

三、字词详解

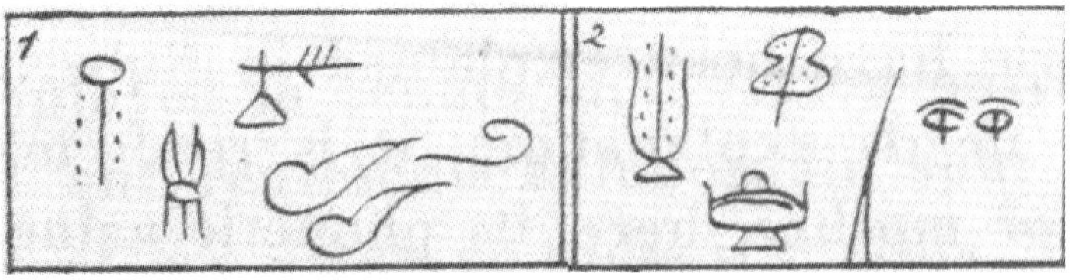

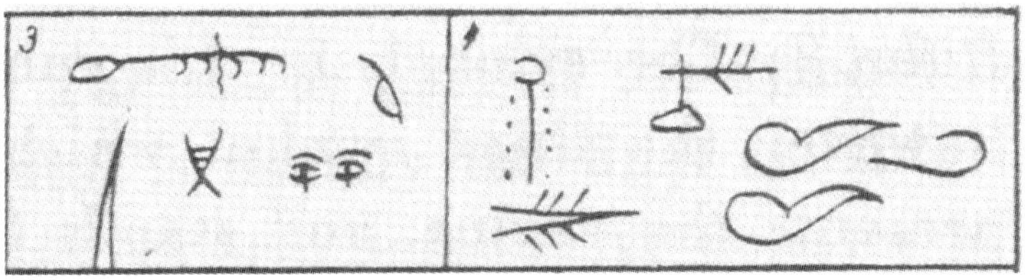

第一至七节：这些字在之前的段落中已经解释过了。

第八节：这一节的三个字代表“昆明”纳西语名。昆明是云南省的省会，“昆明”的纳西语名作 ^{2}Yi-^{2}ch'i-^{1}mùeṉ。^{2}Yi-^{2}ch'i 汉语译作“押赤”，乌蛮的首府。乌蛮是黑蛮人或罗罗部落，是古代爨部落。与之相对的，纳西人是白蛮或羌。第一个字像山羊头，读作 ^{2}yi，意为“山羊”；第二个字读作 ^{2}ch'i，意为“秤”，像汉人使用的秤，秤砣用绳子吊着，可以在秤杆上来回移动。第三个字读作[1]mùeṉ，意为“下面”，即昆明在纳西人居住地的南边。

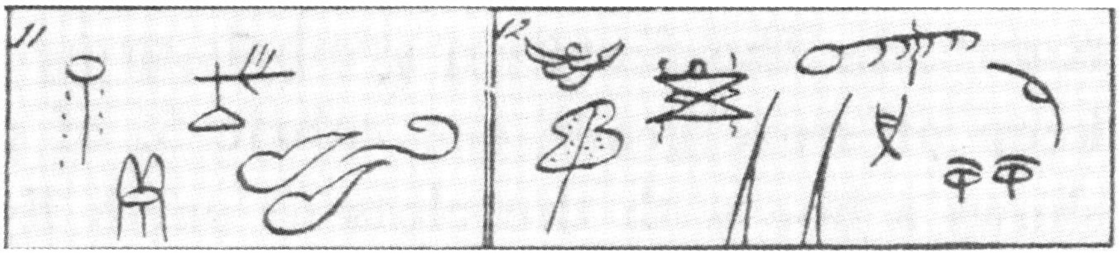

第九至十二节：这些字在之前的段落中都已经解释过了。

经卷第八页释义

一、全页标音及直译

第一节	^{2}Dzhi	^{2}man̠	^{1}sso	^{3}ḳhü-^{2}ḳhü	
	dʐʅ^{33}	mæ^{33}	so^{21}	hɯ^{55} hɯ^{33}	
	集市	尾	三	围绕	
第二节	^{2}T’o-^{3}bpŭ	^{1}ssaw-^{2}sso	^{2}t’khi		
	tho^{33} pv^{55}	sɑ^{21}so^{33}	tɕhi^{33}		
	布	各种	卖		
第三节	^{1}Yi-^{2}bbū	^{2}khi-^{2}bbū	^{2}t’khi	^{1}nä	^{1}ddo
	i^{21}pu^{33}	ɕi^{33}pu^{33}	tɕhi^{33}	ne^{21}	do^{21}
	绸缎	锦缎	卖	正	见
第四节	^{3}K’v	^{2}t’khi	^{2}mä	^{2}muàn̠	^{1}ddo
	khv^{55}	tɕhi^{33}	me^{33}	mə^{33}	do^{21}
	岁	卖	的	不	见
第五节	^{2}Szĭ	^{2}t’khi	^{2}mä	^{2}muàn̠	^{1}ddo
	zʅ^{33}	tɕhi^{33}	me^{33}	mə^{33}	do^{21}
	寿	卖	的	不	见
第六节	^{1}Ng‘a	^{2}mä	^{1}nv	^{2}nnü	^{1}nv
	ŋgæ^{21}	me^{33}	ŋv^{21}	nɯ^{33}	ŋv^{21}
	剑	的	银	它	镶
第七节	^{1}Nv	^{2}lä	^{2}lä	^{1}dgyu	^{1}ds’i
	ŋv^{21}	le^{33}	le^{33}	dʑy^{21}	tshʅ^{21}
	哭	又	又	有	来
第八节	^{2}Yi-^{2}ch’i	^{2}dzhi	^{1}ddü	^{2}lä	
	i^{33} tʂhʅ^{33}	dʐʅ^{33}	dɯ^{21}	le^{33}	
	押赤	集市	大	特别	

第九节	^{2}Muàṉ	^{2}lü	^{2}Muàṉ	^{3}t'a	^{2}t'a
	mə^{33}	ly^{33}	mə^{33}	tha^{55}	tha^{33}
	不	看	不	能	能

第十节	^{2}Lä	^{1}dgyu	^{2}ddü	^{1}lü	^{1}nä
	le^{33}	dʑy^{21}	dɯ^{33}	ly^{21}	ne^{21}
	又	回来	一	看	着

第十一节	^{2}Yi-^{2}ch'i	^{2}dzhi	^{2}t'ü	^{2}dzhi
	i^{33} tʂhʅ^{33}	dzʅ^{33}	thɯ^{33}	dzʅ^{33}
	押赤	集市	那	集市

二、句译

第一节：他到集市尾绕了三圈。

第二节：看见有人在卖各种材质的布。

第三节：包括绸缎和锦缎。

第四节：但是没有看见卖年岁的。

第五节：也没有看见卖寿岁的。

第六节：有一把镶银的剑，

第七节：他又哭起来。

第八节：押赤的集市非常大。

第九节：不再看看也不行。

第十节：他又回头看一眼

第十一节：押赤的那个集市。

三、字词详解

第一节：这些字已经解释过了。

第二节：从上到下，前两个字读作^{2}T'o-^{3}bpŭ，意为“棉布”。第一个字像盾牌或者剑柄，它最初的意义已经消失了，现在只作一个标音符使用。第二个字像滤网，读作^{3}bpŭ。这两个字都用作标音符。接下来两个字读作^{1}ssaw-^{2}sso，第一个字像呼出来的空气，已经解释过了。第二个字也解释过了。这两个音节表示“各种各样的”，表示各种各样材质的布料。^{2}t'khi 是“卖”。

第三节：第一个字是哥巴文，读作^{1}yi。下面一个字像一个人拿着一样东西，读作^{2}bbū“拿”，这里借音作^{1}bbū，“送、提供”。两字连读作^{1}yi-^{2}bbū，意为“绸缎”。下两个字读作^{2}khi-^{2}bbū，“锦缎”。其中第一个字读作^{2}khi，本义为“稻谷”；第二个字本义为“拿”；它们在这里都用作标音符。

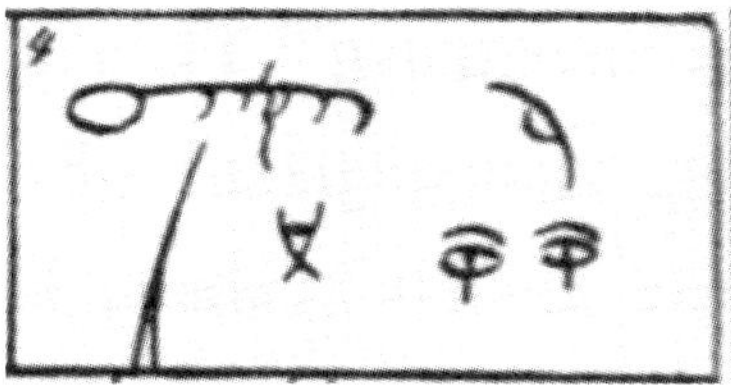

第四、五节：这些字已经解释过了。

第六节：第一个字像一把古代纳西（或摩梭）人使用的宝剑，可能在南诏①时代。宝剑被狭长的皮制剑鞘包裹，剑鞘的外边用珍珠装饰。剑鞘很长，把它背在身后，高度会超过肩膀。这是纳西（或摩梭）人特有的一种宝剑，可能很早之前就在使用了。一些宝剑现在还能看到，我个人收藏了两把，还带全套的铠甲和铁的头盔。（参见《中国西南的古纳西王国》第1卷，图82）在永宁地区的吕西（²lü-²khi）人十年前还在使用这种剑。吕西人自称Hli-khin，但是汉人都叫他们么些。永宁的土司有三或四副铠甲，还有剑和头盔。这些都用在土司的葬礼中。在葬礼上，三或四名男子穿上铠甲，戴上头盔，手执宝剑，随着音乐起舞，为死者开路。这把剑被称为¹Ng'a，这个符号在经书中与《中国西南的古纳西王国》图82中的剑是一样的。

²mä是一个表示肯定的词，意为“有，是”。¹nv 是“银”，²nnü是“它”¹nv也是“银”，实际上是镶银，不是纯银。这一句话已经解释过了。¹nv 在这里作“银”，下一节里作“哭”，这是一个文字游戏②。这些都是纳西人在放牧的时候即兴创作的。

第七节：第一个是复合字，像一个走路的人，眼睛被放大，眼中延伸出两条曲线。这里读作¹nv，意为“哭泣”。²lä这个音节需要读两次，但是只写出一个字。下面一个字读作¹dgyu，这里作标音符。¹dgyu-¹ds'i 意为“回来”，¹ds'i 这个词已经

①译者按，即公元738—740年。
②译者按，文字游戏即增苴。

解释过了。（参见本书第四页第七节的字词详解）

第八节：需要解释的是第四个字，读作^{1}ddü，据说像一种树的果实，这种树的纳西语名叫^{1}Ddü-^{1}ndzěr，拉丁学名作 *Machilus nournei*，这里借用它的读音。^{2}lä是一个后缀，不能翻译。我将它译为“特别”，^{1}ddü ^{2}lä即特别大。

第九节：第一个字读作^{2}lü，字形像一根长矛，长矛上部有一个圆圈。下一个字读作^{2}muàn̠，意为“不，没有”，“不”字写了两次，第二个字用在后半句。最后两个字像佛塔，汉语叫“塔”，这个词明显是个汉语借词，纳西语读作^{3}t'a，意为“塔”。^{2}muàn̠ ^{3}t'a ^{2}t'a 意为“不能”。本节经文的意思是“必须看”。

第十节：^{2}lä ^{1}dgyu 是“（他）又回来，再看一次”，^{2}ddü是“一次”，^{1}lü是“看”，^{1}nä是一个后缀。

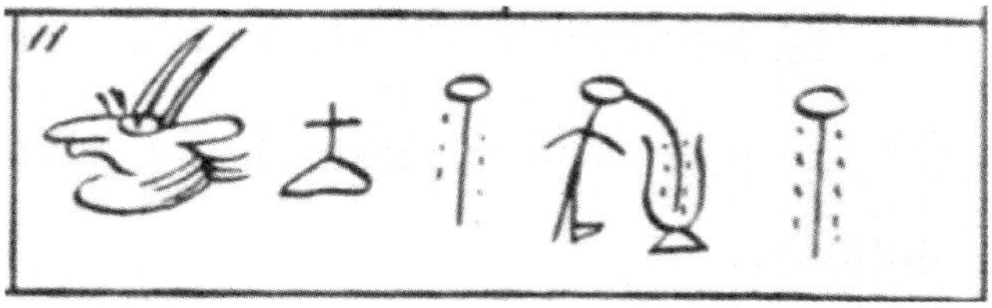

第十一节：除了第四个字之外都解释过了。这个字像一个人在喝酒，这种喝酒的方式，我在本书第七页的第二节已经解释过了。这个字读作^{1}t'ü，意为“喝”，这里借音作“那个”，也表示第三人称代词，读第二声。

经卷第九页释义

一、全页标音及直译

第一节	^{2}Dzhi	^{2}llü	^{1}ng‘a	^{1}ssä	^{2}yu
	dʐʅ^{33}	lɯ^{33}	ŋgæ^{21}	se^{21}	iə^{33}
	集市	（虚）	消失	了	呀

第二节	^{2}Yi-^{2}ch’i	^{3}ḳhü	^{2}t’ü	^{3}ḳhü
	i^{33} tʂhʅ^{33}	hɯ^{55}	thɯ^{33}	hɯ^{55}
	押赤	湖	那	湖

第三节	^{3}Ḳhü	^{2}llü	^{3}gko	^{1}ssä	^{2}yu
	hɯ^{55}	lɯ^{33}	ko^{55}	se^{21}	iə^{33}
	湖	（虚）	干	了	呀

第四节	^{2}Yi-^{2}ch’i	^{2}Lv-^{2}mä-^{1}na
	i^{33} tʂhʅ^{33}	lv^{33}me^{33} na^{21}
	押赤	石头　黑

第五节	^{2}lv	^{2}llü	^{2}nggü	^{1}ssä	^{2}yu
	lv^{33}	lɯ^{33}	ŋgɯ^{33}	se^{21}	iə^{33}
	石	（虚）	裂开	了	呀

第六节	^{2}Yi-^{2}ch’i	^{3}mùeṉ-^{3}llü-^{1}ndzĕr
	i^{33} tʂhʅ^{33}	mɯ^{55}lɯ^{55}ndʑər^{21}
	押赤	竹子　树

第七节	^{3}K’ö	^{1}dgyu	^{1}hăr	^{2}lĕr-^{1}lĕr
	kɯ^{55}	dʑy^{21}	hər^{21}	lər^{33}lər^{21}
	去	有	绿	茵茵

第八节	^{2}Lä	^{1}ts’i	^{1}shi	^{3}p’u-^{2}p’u
	le^{33}	tshɿ^{21}	ʂʅ^{21}	phu^{55}phu^{33}
	又	来	黄	澄澄

第九节

^{1}Ndzěr	^{2}llü	^{3}mun̲	^{2}ndu	^{2}yu
ndzər^{21}	lɯ^{33}	mu^{55}	ndu^{33}	iə^{33}
树	（虚）	死	习俗	呀

第十节

^{3}Gko	^{2}llü	^{1}lä	^{2}ndu	^{2}yu
ko^{55}	lɯ^{33}	le^{21}	ndu^{33}	iə^{33}
树枝	（虚）	变黄	习俗	呀

第十一节

^{3}Mun̲	^{2}mä	^{2}dgyu	^{2}yu	^{1}shu
mu^{55}	me^{33}	ʥy^{33}	iə^{33}	ʂu^{21}
老	的	有	呀	真的

二、句译

第一节：集市上的人都走光了。

第二节：昆明湖的

第三节：湖水都干了。

第四节：昆明湖的黑石头

第五节：已经裂开

第六节：昆明的竹子

第七节：第一次来的时候，竹叶还绿油油的。

第八节：要离开的时候，竹叶已经是黄焦焦的了。

第九节：所以树木也会死，这是规律。

第十节：树枝也变会黄。

第十一节：万物都会死，是吗？

三、字词详解

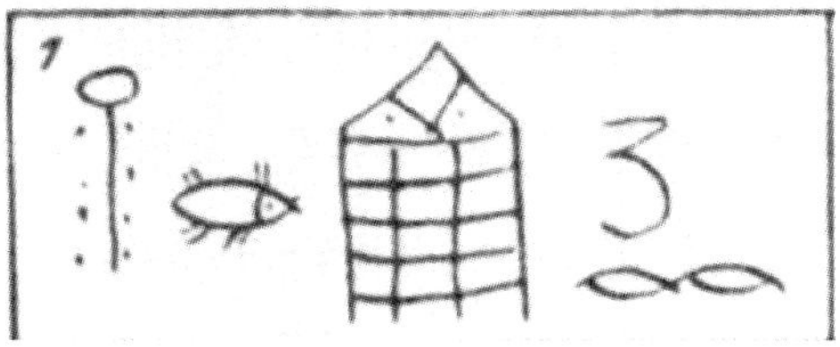

第一节：第一个字已经解释过了，第二个字读作^{3}llü，本义为“虱子”，这里读作^{2}llü，作后缀，很难解释，表示惊奇，相当于汉语的小品词，或者所谓的虚词，不能翻译。第三个字读作^{1}ng‘a，像一副铠甲（参见图 2），这里借音作“消失，分散”，也读作^{1}ng‘a。^{1}ng‘a 这个词实际上不是指穿在外边的铠甲，而是一种穿在里面保护身体的坎肩（带袖子的铠甲见图 2），叫作^{1}ng‘a-^{2}gyi，也叫作^{3}k’wua。铠甲后面的那个哥巴文读作^{1}ssä，表示过去时。这里增加了助动词^{2}yu，译作“是”。因此，^{1}ng‘a ^{1}ssä ^{2}yu 意为“已经消失了”。第一个字读作^{2}dzhi，意为“集市”。“集市”后面那个字读作^{2}llü，也有另外的意思，可以表示“人们”，这些人是洪水之后的人类始祖崇则利恩的后代。

第二节：第一个字读作^{2}yi，是一个哥巴文。下面一个字读作^{2}ch’i，这两个字已经解释过了。^{2}yi-^{2}ch’i 是“昆明”。接下来一个字读作^{3}ḳhü，本义为“湖”，即昆明湖，也就是汉语所谓的“滇池、昆明池或昆明湖”。（参见《中国西南古纳西王国》第 1 卷，图 1 和 2）最后一个字像一个人在喝酒，这个习俗在之前已经解释过，“喝”读作^{1}t’ü，这里读^{2}t’ü，作指示代词“那”。最后一个字又是^{3}ḳhü“湖”。

第三节：我们又看到“湖”这个字，^{2}llü这个词在第一节也已经解释过了。第三个字像一根针，针的顶部有一个眼儿，该字读作^{1}gko，这里借音作^{3}gko，意为“干涸”。^{1}ssä ^{2}yu 这两个词之前已经解释过了。

第四节：关于^{2}yi-^{2}ch'i 这个词的解释，参见本页的第二节的字词详解，第三个字读作^{2}lv，像石头之形，三块石头里分别有一个黑点，表示“黑”，读作^{1}na。“大石头”读作^{2}lv-^{2}mä。整个字读作^{2}lv-^{2}mä-^{1}na。^{1}na借自藏文ནག，读作 nag，意为“黑”。

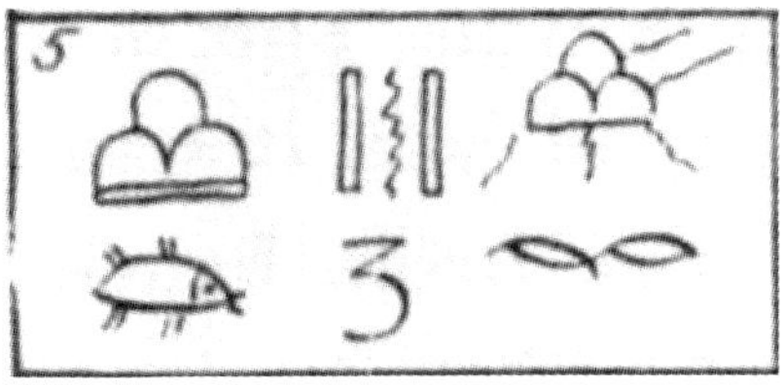

第五节：第一个字像石头，读作^{2}lv。这里的石头里面没有黑点。在第一节中，^{2}llü已经解释过了。第三个字是一个象形字，读作^{2}nggü，本义为“裂开”，像一块板子从中间裂成两块。这一节的右上方的角落有一个石头形状的字，不读出来，这里示意石头裂开。^{1}ssä ^{2}yu 这两个词表示过去时。

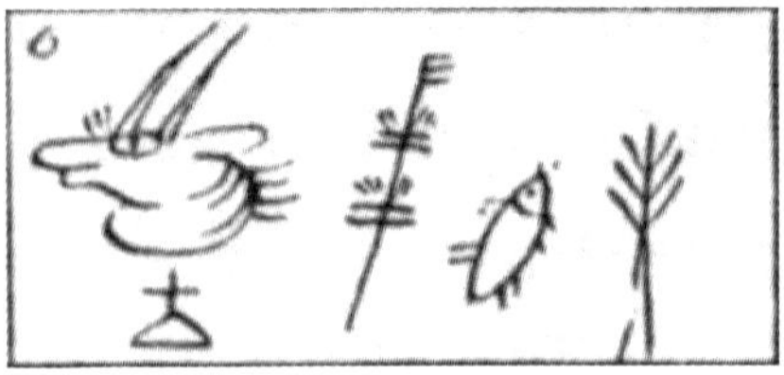

第六节：^{2}yi-^{2}ch'i 这个词的第一个音节用一只羱羚的头部来表示。“羱羚”的读音为^{2}yi，用它代替之前使用的哥巴文。接下来三个字标示生长在昆明高山之中的竹子的名字。^{3}mùeṉ是“竹子”，字形像一根竹子，字中的竹节和叶子用短线表示。下一个字本义是“虱子”，读作^{2}llü，这里作标音符。下一个字读作^{1}ndzěr，意为“树”，它实际上像一棵松树。它可能用来说明竹子很高大，像一棵大树一样，或者这里的^{1}ndzěr 根本没有用。

第七节：第一个字像狗之形，读作^{2}k'ö，这里借音作汉语的“去”，云南话读作 k'ö或k'e，意思是“走或离开”。^{1}dgyu 是“有”。^{2}ō-^{1}hăr 意为“绿松石”，这里读作^{1}hăr，意为“绿色”。下面两个男人的形象，都读作^{1}lĕr，意为“呼喊”，两个字读作^{2}lĕr-^{1}lĕr，表示“很深的颜色”，跟^{1}hăr 连在一起，表示“深绿色”。这里用^{2}k'ö并不是一个最好的选择，因为下一节用^{1}ts'i 这个词，这里才用^{2}k'ö。①

第八节：前两个字已经解释过了。第三个字读作^{2}shi，本义为“肉”，这里借音作^{1}shi，意为“黄色”。^{3}p'u-^{2}p'u表示“深色”。^{2}p'u 字像泡沫之形，之前已经解释过了。因此，当他来到昆明时，树叶是深绿色的；当他离开的时候，树叶已经变成了深黄。

第九节：这一节只有^{2}ndu 这个词需要解释。^{2}ndu 相当于汉语的“阳”。纳西语将之人格化了。（参见《纳西族

①译者按，为了避免重复。

的纳迦崇拜及其相关仪式》第 1 卷，第 158 页，注释 211）这里借音作^{2}ndu，意为“习俗”。因此，^{2}ndu ^{2}yu 意为“有这个习俗？”^{2}llü表示惊奇，在第一节已经解释过了。

第十节：第一个字像鹰，读作^{3}gko，这里借音作“树枝”，^{3}llü这个词跟之前一样，用作^{2}llü。第三个字像獐子的头，读作^{2}lä，意为“獐子”，这里读作^{1}lä，表示“枯萎”。纳西人是在中国西部唯一使用这个词的民族。^{2}ndu ^{2}yu 意为“有这个习俗？”跟上一节相同。

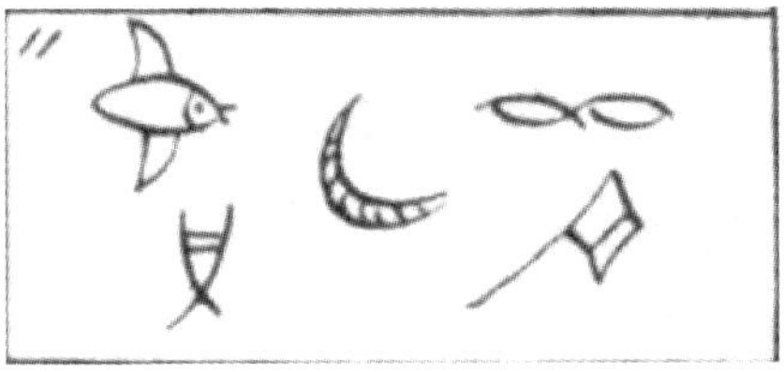

第十一节：这些字将在本书的第十页第一节解释。除了将^{2}llü换成了^{2}mä之外，其余相同。^{2}mä作一个表示肯定的小品词，译作“是，有”。

经卷第十页释义

一、全页标音及直译

第一节

^{3}Mun̲	^{2}llü	^{2}dgyu	^{2}yu	^{1}shu
mu^{55}	lɯ^{33}	ʥy^{33}	iə^{33}	ʂu^{21}
老	了	是	衰老	真的

第二节

^{1}Ng‘a	^{2}mä	^{1}ha	^{2}nnü	^{2}z‘a
ŋgæ^{21}	me^{33}	hæ^{21}	nɯ^{33}	zæ^{33}
剑	的	金	它	镶

第三节

^{1}Z‘a	^{2}lä	^{2}lä	^{1}dgyu	^{1}ts’i
zæ^{21}	le^{33}	le^{33}	ʥy^{21}	tshʅ^{21}
笑	又	又	返回	来

第四节

^{1}Ggŏ	^{1}yü	^{3}Dto-^{2}k’ö-^{1}pĕr	^{2}Gv-^{1}dzu
go^{21}	y^{21}	to^{55}khɯ^{33}phər^{21}	gv^{33}ʥu^{21}
上	生	多可盘	古宗

^{1}ä-^{1}ssĭ	^{3}mun̲
ə^{21}sʅ^{21}	mu^{55}
父亲	死

第五节

^{1}Bpŭ-^{1}shwua	^{1}bbŭ	^{2}nnü	^{3}mun̲
pv^{21}ʂua^{21}	bv^{21}	nɯ^{33}	mu^{55}
平顶房	下	他	老

第六节

^{2}Dzhu	^{2}ggŏ	^{2}zo	^{1}ddü-^{3}hoa
dẓu^{33}	go^{33}	zo^{33}	dɯ^{21} hua^{55}
悲伤	的	儿子	所有

第七节

^{1}Bpŭ-^{1}shwua	^{1}bbŭ	^{2}nnü	^{2}dzhu
pv^{21}ʂua^{21}	bv^{21}	nɯ^{33}	dẓu^{33}
平顶房	下	他	治丧

第八节	^{2}Bbǔ-^{3}lv-^{2}zhi-^{1}zaw-^{2}maṉ	^{2}Lä-^{1}bbǔ	^{1}ä-^{1}ssǐ	^{3}muṉ,
	bv^{33}lv^{55}ʐʅ^{33}zɑ^{21}mæ^{33}	le^{33}bv^{21}	ə^{21}sʅ^{21}	mu^{55}
	牧羊路之尾	勒布	父亲	死

^{2}wuà-^{1}gyi	^{1}bbǔ	^{2}nnü	^{3}muṉ.
ua^{33}dʑi^{21}	bv^{21}	nɯ^{33}	mu^{55}
瓦房	下	他	死

二、句译

第一节：老和死是不会改变的。

第二节：剑是镶金的。

第三节：他笑着又回来了。

第四节：住在上面多可盘的藏人的父亲死了，

第五节：他死在土夯实的平顶房下面。

第六节：所有的孝子

第七节：在土夯实的平顶房下面办丧事。

第八节：住在牧羊路之尾的勒布人①的父亲死了，他死在石瓦房下面。

三、字词详解

第一节：第一个字读作^{3}muṉ，意为“老”，它下面那个字像虱子之形，读作^{3}llü，这里读第二声，表示疑问，大致相当于汉语的“夫”，是一个表示时间变化的虚词，指“现在，然后”。^{2}dgyu 的意思是“是，有”，已经解释过了。第四个字读作^{1}yu，像枯

①译者按，勒布人，又称民家人，都是白族的旧称。

叶之形，意为“腐烂、衰退”，这里读第二声，也有“衰老”的意思。最后一个字读作[1]shu，像一把斧头，因此还可以表示“铁”，这里借音表示“真实的、正确的”。铁是不变的。[1]shu-[1]mun̲意为“习俗”。

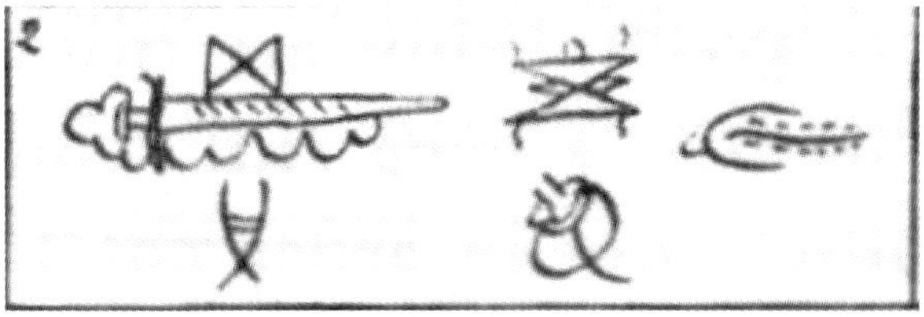

第二节：[1]ng‘a [2]mä这个词在本书的第八页第六节已经解释过了。接下来两个字读作[1]ha [2]nnü，第一个字像金子；第二个字像心脏，在这里作第三人称的“他、她或它”。最后一个字读作[2]z‘a，本义为“笑”，动词，这里作“闪亮”，用来修饰“金”。这句话跟本书的第八页第六节类似，[2]z‘a 与下一节的[1]z‘a 相对。这是一个文字游戏，两个音节读音相同，但是意思不同。①

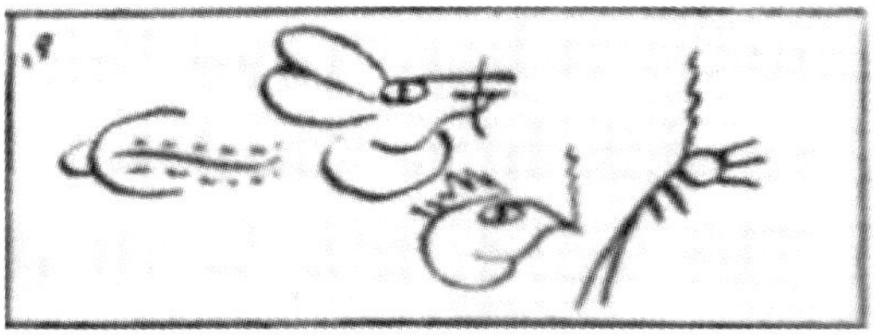

第三节：第一个字在上一节也出现了，读第一声，作[1]z‘a，本义为“笑”。[2]lä 已经解释过了。[1]dgyu 意为“开始，第一”，因为公鸡是所有动物中起得最早的，它负责打鸣，所以用公鸡表示“开始、第一”，这里借音作“返回”。最后一个字读[2]ts’u，字形像一个上吊的人，这里读作[1]ts’i，“返回”，因此，[1]dgyu [1]ts’i 意为“返回”。

第四节：前两个字已经解释过了，读作[1]ggŏ [1]yü。第三个字像

①译者按，相当于顶针的修辞手法。

一座山之形（“山”读作^{1}ngyu），山的里面有一个木板形状的符号，读作^{1}dto，它意为“山丘”，这里借音作山名的一个音节。“山”不读出来，这里只示意。因为如果没有山这个字，就不知道这里表示的是一座山的名字。山名作^{3}dto-^{2}k’ö-^{1}pĕr。在其他经书中，^{3}dto-^{2}k’ö-^{1}pĕr 前还要加上^{2}la-^{1}ssaw，表示拉萨，西藏的首府。山旁边的字读作^{2}k’ö，字形像人的脚。“脚”下面的字读作^{1}p’ĕr，它们都记录山名的一个音节。下一个字像一个戴着毡帽、长着长头发的藏人，这是黄河西岸，靠近阿尼玛卿山的游牧部落的装扮。纳西语叫藏人作^{2}gv-^{1}dzu，在云南，汉语中藏人作 Ku-tsung“古宗”，纳西语^{2}gv-^{1}dzu 可能是从这里借过来的。其他字已经解释过了。

第五节：第一个字像一座房子，读作^{1}gyi，但是没读出来。如果没有后面两个字，很难理解第一个字的意思。第二个字读作^{1}bpŭ，本义为“滤网”；第三个字读作^{1}shwua，本义是“高”，两字连读作^{1}bpŭ-^{1}shwua，意为“平顶”。大多数藏人的房子都是平顶房，他们先从灌木丛中砍来杜鹃花的树枝，加上更细的柳树枝，把它们与泥土混合，然后再加细土。在夏天和秋天，再加入石块搅拌，否则会漏水。这种房顶叫作^{1}bpŭ-^{1}shwua。^{1}bpŭ意为“夯实的土墙”，需要先竖一个木框，再往木框里面填充干土，然后夯实。做屋顶也是相同的步骤。^{1}shwua 是加上去的，因为房顶在一座房子的最高处。其他字已经解释过了。

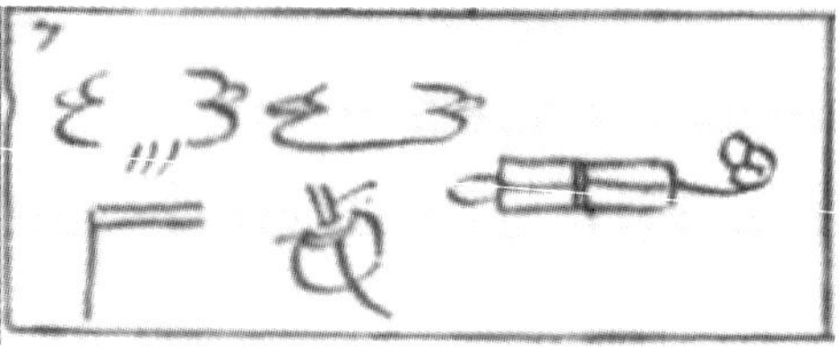

第六、七节：这两节的字已经解释过了。

第八节：这里用六个字记录了五个音节。一个手拿棍子的人通常读作^{3}nddü，意为“驱赶”，但是这里不读音。前面四个字实际上读两个音节，即^{2}bbŭ-^{3}lv。“羊”字也没有读出来，它们表示驱赶羊群的动作。为准确理解“羊”字的意思，这里又加了“石头”这个字。“石头”读作^{2}lv，字形像三块石头叠加在一起，借音作“放牧”。^{2}zhi 是“路”，字没有写出来。第五个字读作^{1}zaw，本义为“行星”，第六个字读作^{2}man̲，本义为“尾巴”，它们都作标音符。整句话的意思是“牧羊之路”。^{1}zaw 这里是“下降”，^{2}man̲是“末尾”。牧羊路之尾，从丽江南部民家人的居住地开始。民家居住地在丽江南部 40 里（大约 12 英里）的地方。纳西人称之为^{2}bbŭ-^{3}lv-^{2}zhi-^{1}zaw-^{2}man̲。一个半倒人的字形表示民家。附加在民家头上的木头符号读作^{2}ss，这里作标音符，读作^{1}ä-^{1}ssĭ，意为“父亲”。之前已经解释过了。剩余的字除了^{2}wuà-^{1}gyi“瓦房”都已经解释过了。房子里面有一个数字五，用五条短线表示。^{2}wuà这个词是从汉语“瓦”借过来的。^{1}gyi 是“房子”。^{1}bbŭ ^{2}nnü ^{3}mun̲意为“死在下面”。

经卷第十一页释义

一、全页标音及直译

第一节	^{2}Dzhu	^{2}zo	^{2}ch’i-^{1}ddü-^{3}hoa
	dzʯ^{33}	zo^{33}	tʂhʅ^{33}dɯ^{21}hua^{55}
	悲伤	儿子	所有

第二节	^{2}Wuà-^{1}gyi	^{1}bbŭ	^{2}nnü	^{2}dzhu
	ua^{33}ʥi^{21}	bv^{21}	nɯ^{33}	dzʯ^{33}
	瓦房	下	他	治丧

第三节	^{2}Dzī	^{1}yü	^{3}lü-^{2}gv	^{1}ō
	dzi^{33}	y^{21}	ly^{55}gv^{33}	o^{21}
	人	生	中间	那里

第四节	^{1}Na-^{2}khi	^{1}ä-^{1}ssĭ	^{3}mun̠
	na^{21}ɕi^{33}	ə^{21}sɿ^{21}	mu^{55}
	纳西	父亲	死

第五节	^{1}Nggü-^{1}gyi	^{1}bbŭ	^{2}nnü	^{3}mun̠
	ŋgɯ^{21}ʥi^{21}	bv^{21}	nɯ^{33}	mu^{55}
	木瓦房	下	他	死

第六节	^{2}Dzhu	^{2}zo	^{2}ch’i-^{1}ddü-^{3}hoa
	dzʯ^{33}	zo^{33}	tʂhʅ^{33}dɯ^{21}hua^{55}
	悲伤	儿子	这一群

第七节	^{1}Nggü-^{1}gyi	^{1}bbŭ	^{2}nnü	^{2}dzhu
	ŋgɯ^{21}ʥi^{21}	bv^{21}	nɯ^{33}	dzʯ^{33}
	木瓦房	下	他	治丧

第八节	^{2}Muàn̠	^{3}mun̠	^{2}mùan̠	^{3}mun̠
	mɯ^{33}	mu^{55}	mə^{33}	mu^{55}
	天	死	不	死

第九节	^{2}Muàn̠	^{3}llü	^{1}ä-^{1}ssĭ	^{3}mun̠
	mɯ^{33}	lɯ^{55}	ə^{21}sɿ^{21}	mu^{55}
	天	（虚）	父亲	死

第十节	^{2}Muàn̠	^{1}tgkye	^{1}ssu-^{2}ndzĕr	^{3}mun̠
	mɯ^{33}	tɕə^{21}	su^{21}ndzər^{33}	mu^{55}
	天	上	三神	死

第十一节	^{2}K’wua-^{1}dtv-^{1}mbĕr-^{2}ddv	^{3}mun̠，	^{2}dzī-^{1}la-^{1}ä-^{2}p’u
	kua^{33}tv^{21}mbər^{21}dv^{33}	mu^{55}	dzi^{33}la^{21}ə^{21}phu^{33}
	夸都盘都	死	精拉阿普

^{3}mun̠，	^{2}Mùan̠-^{2}zo-^{3}bpä-^{2}dsä	^{3}mun̠.
mu^{55}	mə^{33}zo^{33}pe^{55}tse^{33}	mu^{55}
死	末若配者	死

二、句译

第一节：所有的孝子

第二节：在木瓦房下办丧事。

第三节：生活在中间的纳西人

第四节：他的父亲死了。

第五节：死在木瓦房下面。

第六节：所有的孝子

第七节：在木瓦房下面办丧事

第八节：谁没有死？天没有死。

第九节：天的父亲不死。

第十节：天上死了三个尊者。

第十一节：夸都盘都死了，精拉阿普死了，末若配者死了。

三、字词详解

第一节：第一个字读作²dzhu，意为“悲伤”，在解释本书书名时已经解释过了。下一个字读作²zo，意为“男孩，男人，儿子”。²ch'i-¹ddü-³hoa 意为“所有，每个”。²ch'i 在本书的第七页第八节已经解释过了。¹ddü在本书的第八页第八节也解释过了。最后一个字读作³hoa-¹p'ěr，像藏耳雉（拉丁学名作*Corssoptlion*），它是一种生活在海拔 13000—14000 英尺高原灌木丛中的大鸟。头顶和腿是红色的，身体和和羽毛是灰白色的，尾巴是黑色的。鸟头上的三条曲线表示大尾羽。（参见《东巴教的教主东巴什罗的诞生》，图 12）²ch'i-¹ddü-³hoa 意为“所有”，²ch'i 的字面意思是“这”。¹ddü是“大”，³hoa 是“群”，因此合起来有“所有”的意思。“所有”的另一个表达是²ch'i-¹wuà。

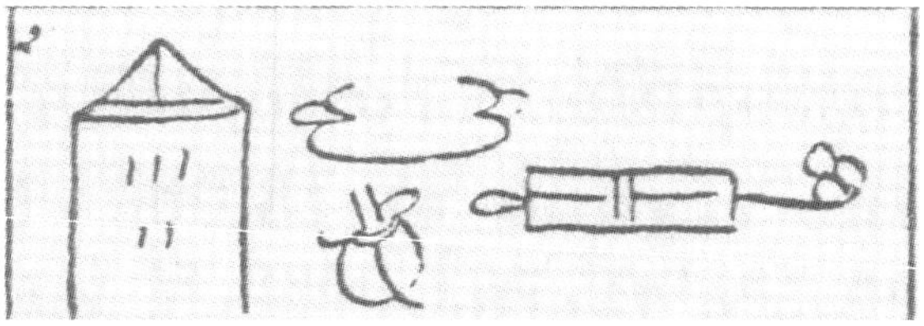

第二节：这一节的所有字已经解释过了。

第三节：第一个字像一只豺的头，读作²dzī，口语叫作¹p'a。²dzī表示“人们，人类”，在²dzī ¹nä ¹ts'o 中，指²dzī-¹la-¹ä-²p'u 和¹ts'o-²zä-³llü-

²ghügh 的后代。（参见《纳西族祭天仪式》，第 71—88 页）也可能¹ts'o 是指洪水之前纳西人的祖先²dzī-²zä-¹ts'o-²zä或者¹Dgyu-²zä ²Dzī-²zä，古代纳西人父子连名，父亲的名字一般放在儿子名字的前面。（参见《中国西南古纳西王国》第 1 卷，第 82 页）¹yü这个字，意为“出生”，已经解释过了。下一个是字组，包括天（读作²mùaṉ）、长矛（读作³lü）和地（读作¹dü）三个字，四个圆圈表示罗盘的四个方位。这个字读作²mùaṉ ¹nä ¹dü ³lü ²gv，意为“天和地的中间”。因此这个中心就在天和地之间，但是这里只读作³lü ²gv，纳西人住在藏人居住地和民家人居住地之间的地方。最后一个字像用绿松石镶嵌的盒子，因此读作¹ō-¹hăr，意为“绿松石”，又读作¹ō，意为“蓝色或绿色”，这里读作¹ō，意为“那里”。

第四节：第一个字读作¹na，这是藏文元音字母的第十二个字母，意为“黑色”。第二个字读作²khi，字形像小麦。这两个字这里用作标音符，意为“纳西人”，不是指黑人，如果要表示黑人，应该说成²khi-¹na。跟藏语一样，形容词修饰名词需要放在名词后边。下一个字读作¹ä-¹ssĭ，意为“父亲”。³muṉ是“死”，之前已经解释过。

第五节：第一个字像一所房子，读作¹gyi。屋顶上有两块板子（实际是木瓦）和一块石头。¹nggü意为“木瓦”，因此，¹nggü-¹gyi 意为“木瓦房”。与之形成对比的是藏人居住的平顶房，还有民家人居住的砖瓦房。（参见《中国西南古纳西王国》第 1 卷，图 132）³muṉ是“死”，该字写在房字里面。其他字已经解释过了。

第六、七节：这两节的字已经解释过了。

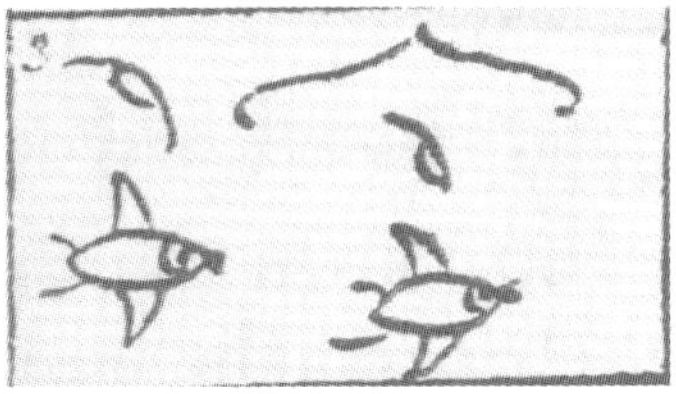

第八节：这一节只需要提示一下语法。这是一个疑问句，疑问词“谁”没有写出来，但是必须补出来。“谁不死？天不死。”注意“不”字（读作^{2}Muàṉ）与“天”字（读作^{2}mùaṉ）读音的区别，前面的重音符号在是a，后面在u，都读第二声。

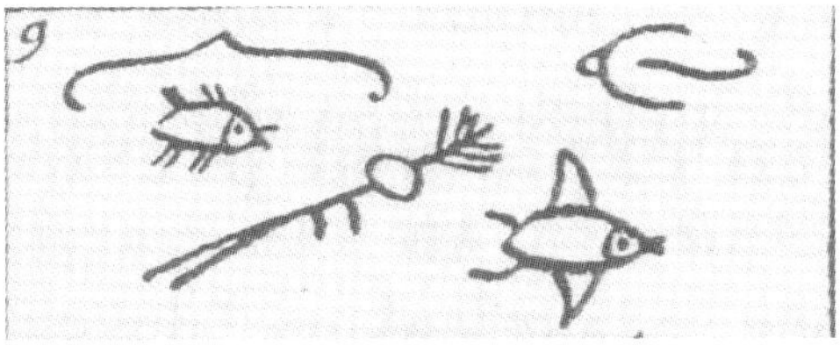

第九节：这一节的所有字都解释过了。

第十节：第一个字是“天”，读作^{2}mùaṉ。“天”下面那个字像一盏油灯，读作^{2}tgkye，这里借音作^{1}tgkye，意为“上”。下一个字是数字三，读作^{1}ssu，跟在“三”后面的字，读作^{2}ndzĕr，意为“树木”，这里用作敬语，可能译作“令人尊重”。

第十一节：我们看到三个身体有点儿倾斜的人，其中两个人是动物头，第一个是牦牛（“牦牛”读作^{1}mběr），第二个是虎（“虎”读作^{2}la）。在第二个人头上的那个字读作^{2}p'u。第三个像带着头盔的人。“牦牛”“虎”和^{1}Dsä鬼都作标音符，并不是说这三个人分别长了牦牛头、虎头和^{1}Dsä鬼头。前两个人的名字没写出来，但是第三个人名的四个音节完全写出来了。后面三个字为第三个人名标音，第一个字读作^{2}mùaṉ，本义是“天”，“天”下面那个字读作^{3}bpä，本义是“酒糟或烘干的麦芽糖”。“酒糟”下面那个字读作^{2}zo，本义是“陶罐”。人身^{1}Dsä鬼头那个字读作^{2}dsä。在第二个人上方的^{2}p'u 字作人名^{2} dzī-^{1}la-^{1}ä-^{2}p'u 的最后一音节。这三个人被认为是最先死在天上的人。与他们相关的事迹见于东巴经书^{2}Ts'u ^{1}yi①，这本书在我个人藏书中编号1078，属于日美仪式。

①译者按，意为荐祖经。

经卷第十二页释义

一、全页标音及直译

第一节	^{2}Mùan̠	^{2}ggŏ	^{1}t'o	^{2}nnü	^{3}mun̠
	mɯ^{33}	go^{33}	tho^{21}	nɯ^{33}	mu^{55}
	天	的	后	他	死

第二节	^{2}Mùan̠	^{2}zo	^{2}ngv	^{2}bä-^{2}gu
	mɯ^{33}	zo^{33}	ŋgv^{33}	be^{33}gu^{33}
	天	儿子	九	弟兄

第三节	^{2}Mùan̠	^{2}ggŏ	^{1}t'o	^{2}nnü	^{2}dzhu
	mɯ^{33}	go^{33}	tho^{21}	nɯ^{33}	dzu̜^{33}
	天	的	后	他	治丧

第四节	^{2}Mùan̠	^{3}mun̠	^{1}dü	^{2}muàn̠	^{3}mun̠
	mɯ^{33}	mu^{55}	dy^{21}	mə^{33}	mu^{55}
	天	死	地	不	死

第五节	^{1}Dü	^{3}llü	^{1}ä-^{2}mä	^{3}mun̠
	dy^{21}	lɯ^{55}	ə^{21}me^{33}	mu^{55}
	地	（虚）	母亲	死

第六节	^{1}Dü	^{1}tgkye	^{1}ssu-^{2}ndzĕr	^{3}mun̠
	dy^{21}	tɕə^{21}	su^{21}nʥər^{33}	mu^{55}
	地	上	三神	死

第七节	^{2}La-^{2}lĕr-^{1}dü-^{2}ndzĭ	^{3}mun̠,	^{1}Dü-^{3}mi-^{3}ts'ä-^{1}ts'u
	la^{33}lər^{33}dy^{21}ndzɿ^{33}	mu^{55}	dy^{21}mi^{55}tshe^{55}tshu^{21}
	拉勒都支	死	地米衬楚

^{3}mun̠,	^{1}dü-^{3}mi-^{2}yu-^{1}lu	^{3}mun̠.
mu^{55}	dy^{21}mi^{55}iə^{33}lu^{21}	mu^{55}
死	地米余露	死

第八节	^{1}Dü	^{2}ggŏ	^{1}ťo	^{2}nnü	^{3}muṉ
	dy^{21}	go^{33}	tho^{21}	nɯ^{33}	mu^{55}
	地	的	后	他	死

第九节	^{1}Dü	^{2}zo	^{2}shĕr	^{2}bä-^{2}gu
	dy^{21}	zo^{33}	ʂər^{33}	be^{33}gu^{33}
	地	儿	七	弟兄

第十节	^{1}Dü	^{2}ggŏ	^{1}ťo	^{2}nnü	^{2}dzhu.
	dy^{21}	go^{33}	tho^{21}	nɯ^{33}	dʐu^{33}
	地	的	后	他	治丧

二、句译

第一节：他们死在天的后面。

第二节：这九个上天的儿子，

第三节：他们在天上办丧事。

第四节：谁没有死？大地没有死。

第五节：但是大地的母亲死了。

第六节：地上死了三位尊者，

第七节：拉勒都支死了，地米衬楚死了，地米余露死了。

第八节：他们死在地的后面，

第九节：这七个大地的儿子，

第十节：他们在地的后面办了丧事。

三、字词详解

第一节：第一个字读作^{2}mùaṉ，意为“天”，第二个字读作^{2}ggŏ，意为“……的”，表示属格。下面这些字已经解释过了。第三个字读作^{1}t'o，在本书的第八页第二节已经解释过了，这里借音作副词“后面”，因此，整句话的意思是“天的后面”。^{2}nnü ^{3}muṉ是“他们死了”，已经解释过了。

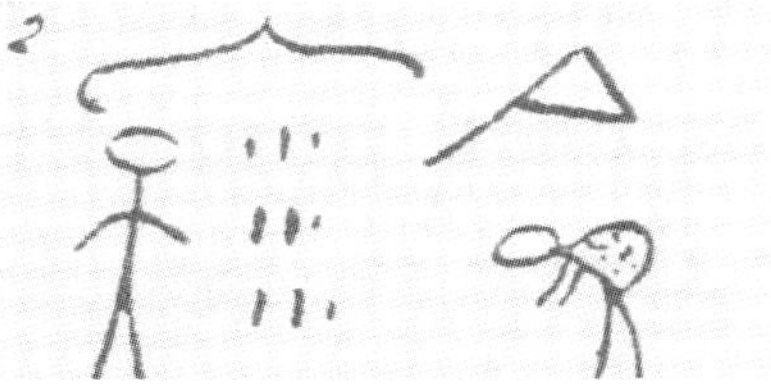

第二节：^{2}Mùaṉ ^{2}zo 是“天的儿子”。^{2}ngv 是“九”。^{2}bä-^{2}gu 实际上是“兄弟”的意思。这里^{2}bä本义是“做”，^{2}gu 本义是“背、扛”。^{2}bä-^{2}gu 这个词中^{2}bä是指怀孕，这里指孩子出生之后，父母把他背在背上。哥哥需要背弟弟，大人需要背小孩。数字九由九条短线组成，每三条为一组。

第三节：^{1}t'o 是“后面”的意思，与第一节中的用字不同，这里用“松树”这个字。其他字已经解释过了。

第四节：这一节与本书的第十一页第八节相同，这里把“天”字换成“地”字。

第五节：这一节跟本书第十一页第九节相似，只是将^{1}ä-^{1}ssĭ（父亲）换成了^{1}ä-^{2}mä（母亲）。天被看作是男性，地（^{1}dü）被看作是女性。第二个字读作^{1}dü，第三、四个字读作^{1}ä-^{2}mä。^{1}ä像张开的大嘴，好像在说“啊”。^{2}mä像女性生殖器。

第六节：这一节跟本书第十一页第十节相似，这里把“天”字换成“地”字。

第七节：这一节有三个女人，她们是第一批在地上去世的人，她们是第一批在天上去世的三个男人的妻子。第一个人的头部是一个虎头的形象，并不是说这个女人真的长着一个虎头，而是因为她名字中的第一个音节是^{2}la，“虎”也读作^{2}la。纳西人在记录鬼名、纳迦名、神名等的时候，习惯用动物的头来作标音符。如果要说某个人长了一个动物的头，经常加上^{2}gkv ^{1}dzu（长着）两个音节。她站在长满青草的地上，这个字读作^{2}Dzī-^{1}gyu-^{2}la-^{2}lĕr-^{1}dü，意为“人类世界”，字面意思是“人类活动的广阔土地”。这个虎头女人经常读作^{2}la-^{2}lĕr-^{1}dü-^{2}ndzĭ ^{3}mi（女），只用这一个符号表示。^{3}mu̱n这个音节是“死”，也可以表示“老”，之前已经解释过了。

第二个女人站在地（“地”读作^{1}dü）上，她戴着典型纳西妇女的头饰，在她的脚边有一个字形像火焰的字①，读作^{2}mi，本义为“火”，这里作标音符，读作^{3}mi，意为“女”。^{1}dü-^{3}mi 意为“地上的女人”，她实际的名字叫^{3}ts'ä-^{3}ts'u。字形像一件东西，一个长方形里面有两条交叉线，这个字读作^{3}ts'ä，本义是“盐”②。“盐”下面是一个哥巴文，读作^{3}ts'u，意为“鬼”，这里不是画一个鬼的形象。这个哥巴文经常代表鬼。第三个女人的名字叫^{2}yu-^{1}lu，剩下两个字都作标音符③，像腐烂树叶的那个字已经解释过了，第二个字是哥巴文。最后一个字读作^{3}muṉ，意为“死”。像本书的十一页第十一节的天上男人一样，这一节与之相对。他们也出现在日美仪式中的^{2}Ts'u ^{1}yi 这本书中。（参见本书的第十一页十一节的字词详解）

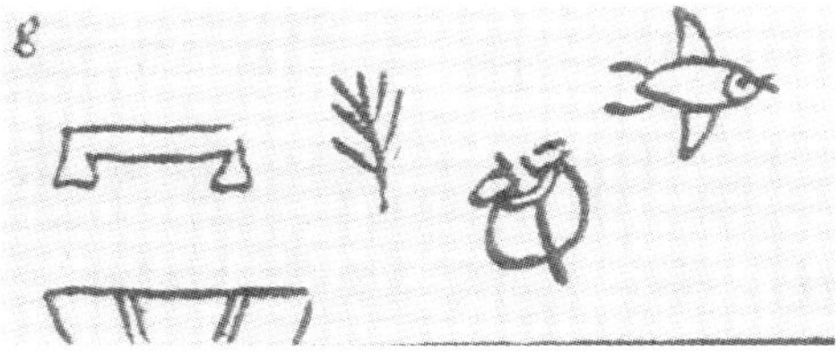

第八节：这一节与这一页的第一和第二节相同，这里只是把“天”字换成“地”字。

第九节：这一节我们看到一个男人站在地上，下一个字是数字七，由七条短线组成。剩下的字与这一页的第二节相同。^{1}dü ^{2}zo ^{2}shĕr ^{2}bä-^{2}gu 不应该译作“地的七个儿子”，因为“地”和数字“七”经常跟“女”一

①译者按，洛克这里的解释与经书原文不符。
②译者按，像盐块之形。
③译者按，即倒数第二和第三个字。

起，不跟“男”放在一起说。在父母的葬礼上，女人不能当孝子，因为女人嫁人后就被当作别人家的人。

婚后的女人回到娘家会被认为是客人。如果她生了病，又不能回到丈夫家，会被安排住在父母家的门外，让她在粮架下死去。父母家已经不再是她的家了，因此不能死在这里。

第十节：本节的解释参见这一页的第三节的字词详解，这里只是把“天”换成“地”。

《挽歌》经文十二页之后的要换另外一个曲调，具体参见《中国西南纳西族的日美丧仪》导论。

经卷第十三页释义

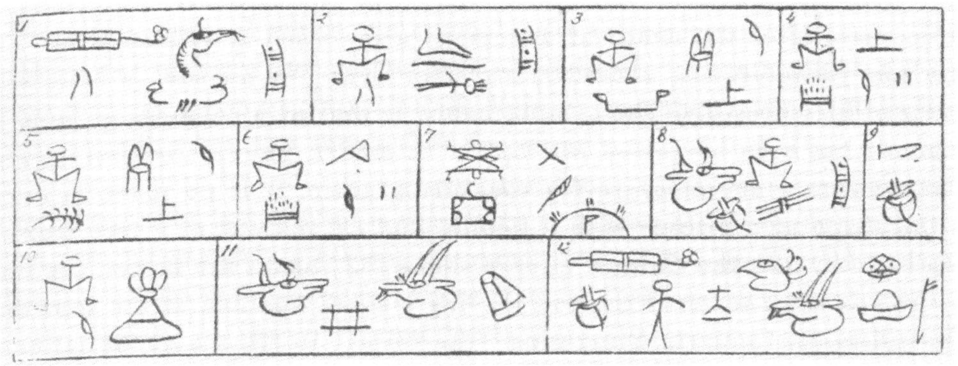

一、全页标音及直译

第一节	^{2}Dzhu	^{2}lä	^{1}zhi	^{3}bpŭ	^{2}bbŭe
	dʐu^{33}	le^{33}	zʅ^{21}	pv^{55}	bɯ^{33}
	治丧	又	死者	送	去

第二节	^{2}Ts'o	^{2}lä	^{1}ts'u	^{1}szĕr	^{2}bbŭe
	tsho^{33}	le^{33}	tshu^{21}	zər^{21}	bɯ^{33}
	跳舞	又	鬼	压	去

第三节	^{2}Ts'o	^{2}t'u	^{2}gkv	^{2}muàn	^{3}shou
	tsho^{33}	thu^{33}	kv^{33}	mə^{33}	ʂou^{55}
	跳舞	出现	处	不	说

第四节	^{2}Ts'o	^{1}dzo	^{3}shou	^{2}muàn̠	^{2}nyi
	tsho^{33}	dʑo^{21}	ʂə^{55}	mə^{33}	ȵi^{33}
	跳舞	关于	说	不	要

第五节	^{2}Ts'o	^{2}bbŭe	^{2}gkv	^{2}muàn̠	^{3}shou
	tsho^{33}	pɯ^{33}	kv^{33}	mə^{33}	ʂə^{55}
	跳舞	来历	处	不	说

第六节	^{2}Ts'o	^{1}dzo	^{2}bä	^{2}muàn̠	^{2}nyi
	tsho^{33}	dʑo^{21}	be^{33}	mə^{33}	ȵi^{33}
	跳舞	关于	做	不	要

第七节	^{1}Ha-^{2}gyu-^{2}la-^{3}ts'ü	^{1}gko
	ha^{21}dʑə^{33}la^{33}tshy^{55}	ko^{21}
	哈居拉趣	高原

第八节	^{1}Mbĕr	^{2}nnü	^{2}ts'o	^{2}bbŭe	^{3}dzĭ
	mbər^{21}	nɯ^{33}	tsho^{33}	bɯ^{33}	dʑʅ^{55}
	牦牛	它	跳舞	去	呀

第九节	^{1}mběr	^{2}nnü			
	mbər^{21}	nɯ^{33}			
	牦牛	它			

第十节	^{2}Ts'o	^{2}muàn̠	^{2}ndu		
	tsho^{33}	mə^{33}	ndu^{33}		
	跳舞	不	兴		

第十一节	^{1}Mběr	^{1}ngu	^{3}ds'ĭ	^{1}ds'ĭ	^{3}ds'ĭ
	mbər^{21}	ŋgu^{21}	tshɿ^{55}	tshɿ^{21}	tshɿ^{55}
	牦牛	后	山羊	来	来

第十二节	^{2}Dzhu	^{2}nnü	^{2}zo	^{2}ch'i-^{3}hoa,	
	dzʮ^{33}	nɯ^{33}	zo^{33}	tʂhʅ^{33}hua^{55}	
	悲伤	（助）	儿子	所有	

^{3}Ds'ĭ-^{2}bpa	^{2}gu-^{1}mun̠	^{2}t'an̠
tshɿ^{55}pa^{33}	gu^{33}mu^{21}	thæ^{33}
支帕	帽子	戴

二、句译

第一节：现在我们要办丧事送别死者。

第二节：我们会再次跳舞和镇压魔鬼。

第三节：如果不知道舞蹈的出处，

第四节：就不要谈论它，

第五节：如果不知道舞蹈的来历。

第六节：不能做跳舞的动作，

第七节：在哈居拉趣高原，

第八节：牦牛说他喜欢跳舞。

第九、十节：对于牦牛，没有跳舞的习俗。

第十一节：牦牛之后，山羊又来了。

第十二节：所有的孝子，他们戴着牦牛尾做的支帕帽子。

三、字词详解

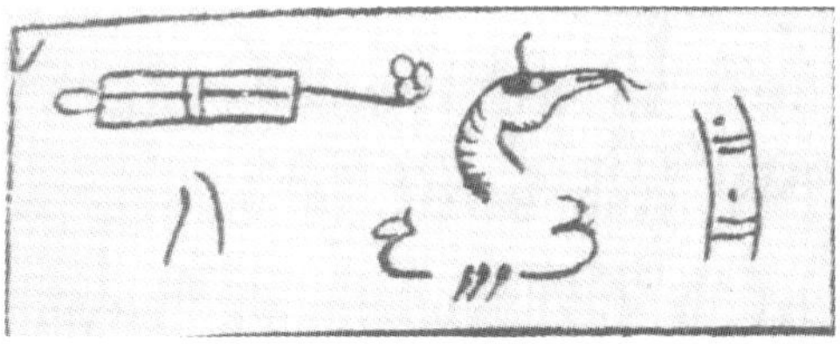

第一节：前两个字已经解释过了，^{2}dzhu ^{2}lä表示“又经历悲伤”。第三个字像一条蛇，读作^{1}zhi。据说，人死后会变成一条蛇，他被称为^{1}Zhi-^{3}mun̠-^{2}llü-^{2}ssĭ。举行^{2}Khi ^{3}Nv 仪式之后（在死者死后三年内举行），死者被称为^{1}Yü-^{3}mun-^{2}llü-^{2}ssĭ。^{1}yü是“祖先”。^{2}Khi ^{3}Nv 仪式之后，死者的灵魂就会被送到祖先居住地去。蛇下面那个字像滤网，读作^{3}bpŭ，这里借音作“送”。最后一个字读作^{2}bbŭe，像一个专门测量粮食的量斗，现在已经不再用了。它像一个带柄的罐子，由一根树干雕刻而成。相当于汉人还在使用的“升”，升的底小口大。^{2}bbŭe在木里、永宁（之前属于西康，现在属于云南）和甘肃的西部（二十五年前，我曾经到那里考察过）还在使用。这里读作^{1}bbŭe，意为“去，实际是将要去”，它放在动词后面表示将来时。

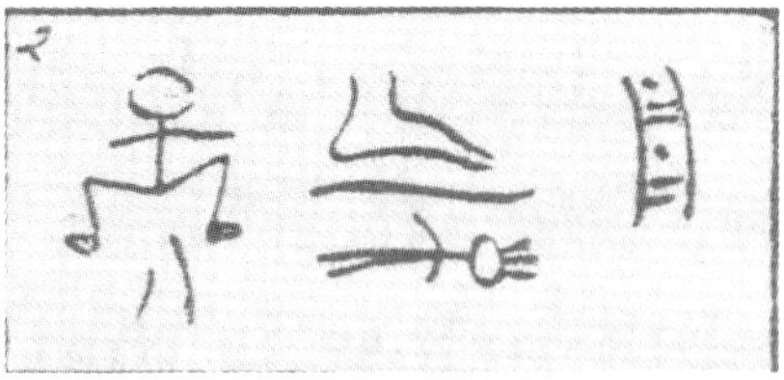

第二节：第一个字读^{2}ts’o，意为“跳舞”，字形像一个人在跳舞。下面又是一个哥巴文，读作^{2}lä，这里作“又”。下一个是字组，该字展示的是一只脚踩在一个鬼（读作^{1}ts’u）身上。该字读作^{1}ts’u ^{1}szĕr，意为“压鬼”。

^{2}bbǔe 表示将来时，表示将要做。

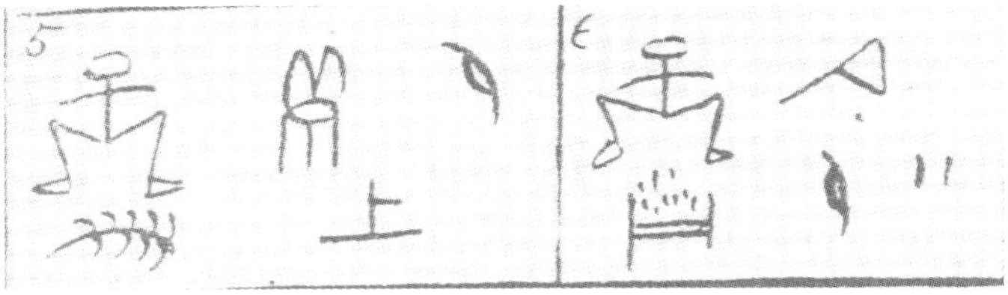

第三至六节：这几节里的所有字在第一页的三到五节都已经解释过了。只是这里将^{2}ts'o 替换成了^{2}dzhu。

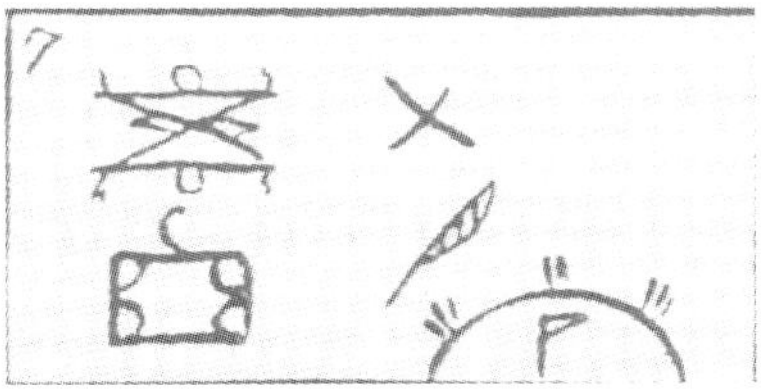

第七节：^{1}ha-^{2}gyu-^{2}la-^{3}ts'ü是高原的名字，高原读作^{1}gko。这一节的所有字都作标音符，在之前的段落中已经解释过了。只有倒数第二个字需要解释，它像粟之形，读作^{3}ts'ü。

第八节：第一个字像牦牛头，读作^{1}mběr。^{2}nnü是“你”，^{2}ts'o 是“跳舞”，^{2}bbǔe ^{3}dzǐ是“要去”。^{2}dzǐ这个字本义为“结”，像一个绳结的形状，这里读作^{3}dzǐ，它作为疑问词，意思是“是这样吗？”

第九节：第一个是哥巴文，读作^{1}mběr，像牦牛。^{2}nnü是“他”，两个字对译为“牦牛/他”。

第十节：^{2}ts'o 是“跳舞”，^{2}muàn̲是“不”，^{2}ndu是“习俗”，这几个字已经解释过了。

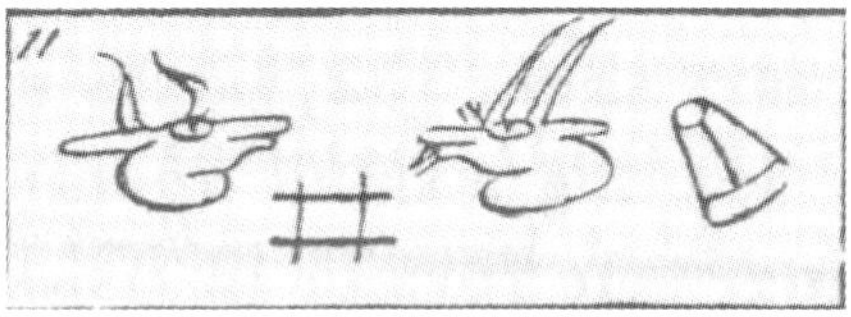

第十一节：我们又一次看到这个象形字^{1}mbĕr，意为“牦牛”。下一个字读作^{1}ngu，像粮仓之形，这里借音作“后面”。像山羊头那个字读作^{3}ds'ĭ字，意为“山羊”，这里借音作^{1}ds'ĭ是，意为“来”。像肩胛骨之形那个字有两读，即^{1}p'i 和^{1}ds'ĭ，这里读作^{1}ds'ĭ。由于这首歌要求每句五个音节，因此，重复一个^{1}ds'ĭ。

第十二节：前五个字已经在第十一页的第六节解释过了。^{2}nnü是“他们”，字没有写出来。这句经文把^{1}ddü这个音节漏掉了①。接下来两个字读作^{3}ds'ĭ-^{2}bpa，其中第一个字像山羊，第二个字像青蛙，它们在这里用作一顶帽子的名字。“帽子”在这里读作^{2}gu-^{1}mun̲。“帽子”实际读作^{3}ds'ĭ-^{2}bpa-^{1}na，因为帽子是用黑山羊的毛做的，被称作^{1}Mbĕr-^{2}ssu（牦牛毛）^{3}ds'ĭ-^{2}bpa-^{1}na，这顶帽子的实际名字是^{3}ds'ĭ-^{2}bpa。孝子在葬礼跳舞的时候戴这种帽子，现在这种帽子已经失传了。最后一个字读作^{2}ť'an，像树枝之形，这种多刺的树枝经常用来做成篱笆，这里借音作“戴”。（参见《纳西文献研究》图 25，第 80 页）这根棍子经常用栎树枝制作而成，口语称为^{3}gku-^{2}ť'an̲。

---

①译者按，第十一页第六节作^{2}ch'i-^{1}ddü-^{3}hoa，这里作^{2}ch'i-^{3}hoa。

经卷第十四页释义

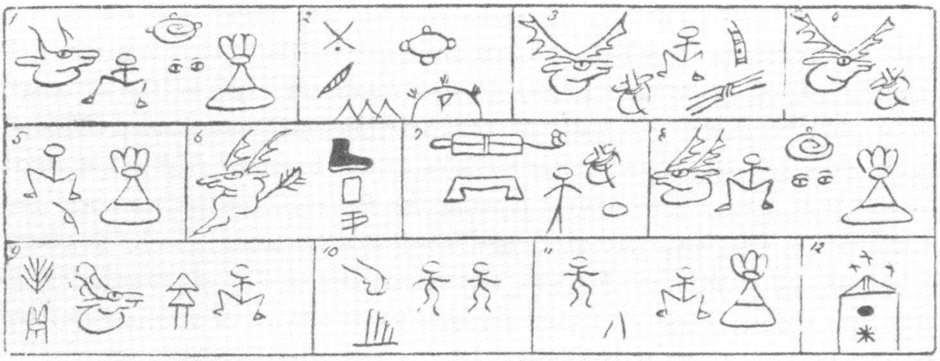

一、全页标音及直译

第一节

^{1}Mbĕr	^{2}ts'o	^{3}ch'ou-^{1}nyu	^{2}ndu
mbər^{21}	tsho^{33}	tʂhə^{55}ȵy^{21}	ndu^{33}
牦牛	跳	这里	兴

第二节

^{2}La-^{3}ts'ü-^{1}hö-^{1}ddü	^{1}gko
la^{33}tshy^{55}hy^{21}dɯ^{21}	ko^{21}
拉趣序得	高原

第三节

^{3}Ch'wua	^{2}nnü	^{2}ts'o	^{2}bbŭe	^{3}dzĭ
tʂhua^{55}	nɯ^{33}	tsho^{33}	bɯ^{33}	ʥʅ^{55}
雄鹿	它	跳	去	呀

第四节

^{3}Ch'wua	^{2}nnü
tʂhua^{55}	nɯ^{33}
雄鹿	它

第五节

^{2}Ts'o	^{2}muàṉ	^{2}ndu
tsho^{33}	mə^{33}	ndu^{33}
跳舞	不	兴

第六节

^{3}Ch'wua	^{2}khi	^{2}zaw	^{3}dto	^{1}p'ĕr
tʂhua^{55}	ɕi^{33}	zɑ^{33}	to^{55}	phər^{21}
雄鹿	皮	鞋子	前面	白色

第七节

^{2}Dzhu	^{2}ggŏ	^{2}zo	^{2}nnü	^{3}gkü
dʐu^{33}	go^{33}	zo^{33}	nɯ^{33}	kɯ^{55}
悲伤	的	儿子	他	穿

第八节

^{3}Ch'wua	^{2}ts'o	^{3}ch'ou-^{1}nyu	^{2}ndu
tʂhua^{55}	tsho^{33}	tʂhə^{55}ȵy^{21}	ndu^{33}
雄鹿	跳	这里	兴

第九节	^{2}T'o	^{2}gkv	^{1}t'khi	^{3}t'a	^{2}ts'o
	tho^{33}	kv^{33}	tɕhi^{21}	tha^{55}	tsho^{33}
	松树	处	鹿	小	跳舞

第十节	^{2}K'wua	^{1}dzu	^{2}k'wua	^{3}nyu-^{2}nyu
	kua^{33}	dʑu^{21}	khua^{33}	ȵy^{55} ȵy^{33}
	蹄子	生	蹄子	摇摆

第十一节	^{3}Nyu	^{2}lä	^{2}ddü	^{2}ts'o	^{2}ndu
	ȵy^{55}	le^{33}	dɯ^{33}	tsho^{33}	ndu^{33}
	摇摆	又	一	跳舞	兴

第十二节　^{1}Na-^{2}mu̠n-^{2}mbe-^{3}dtv-^{2}ddü.
na^{21}mu^{33}mbe^{33}tv^{55}dɯ^{33}
纳西村子　千　一

二、句译

第一节：这里有牦牛跳舞的习俗。

第二节：在拉趣序得高原。

第三节：雄鹿说它喜欢跳舞，

第四节：对于雄鹿，

第五节：没有跳舞的习俗。

第六节：前面是白色的鹿皮鞋子。

第七节：这是孝子穿的鞋。

第八节：这里有雄鹿跳舞的习俗。

第九节：小鹿想去松树林里跳舞，

第十节：偶蹄动物跟着小鹿有节奏地摇摆。

第十一节：他们有跳舞的习俗

第十二节：所有的纳西村里的人。

三、字词详解

第一节：前两个字已经解释过了。第三个字读作^{3}ch’ou，意为“难闻的，恶臭，不洁的”，像人粪便的形状，其他东巴说，它像人的胎盘，因此表示不洁的。下面一个字像两只眼睛，读作^{1}miu，又读作^{1}nyu。前两个字读作^{3}ch’ou-^{1}nyu，意为“这里”，^{2}ndu 是“习俗”。这句话的意思是孝子们戴着用山羊和牦牛尾巴做的帽子，其实不是山羊和牦牛在跳舞，而是戴着山羊和牦牛尾巴帽子的人跳舞，因此，山羊和牦牛是间接在跳舞。

第二节：这一节五个字中的四个字之前都已经解释过了。第三个字在其他地方解释过了，这里意思不同，字形像火焰，读作^{2}mi，这里读作^{1}hö，意为“红色”。前四个字都是标音符，标示高原的名字。

第三节：这一节的字都已经解释过了。第一个字形像雄鹿，读作^{3}ch’wua，它是想去跳舞的雄鹿。

第四、五节：这两节的字已经解释过了。

第六节：第一个是字组，一个雄鹿头加一条前腿。字组后面那个字读作²khi，像稻子之形。这里意为“加工过的皮肤”①，因此整个字表示一个被扒皮的雄鹿。没有被晒黑的皮肤叫²ghügh。下一个字读作²zaw，意为“鞋”，³dto 字本义是“木板”，这里借音作“前面”，¹p’ĕr是“白”的意思。一双鹿皮做的鞋，足尖是白色的。②

第七节：这一节对译作“悲伤的/儿子/他/穿”。这一节的最后一个字像星星之形，读作¹gkü，借音作³gkü，意为“穿”。

第八节：这一节已经解释过了，参见这一页的第一节的字词详解。只是把雄鹿换成了牦牛。

①译者按，指被扒下来的鹿皮。
②译者按，从文字上来看，鞋底是白色的。

第九节：第一个字读作^{2}t'o，字形像一棵松树。下一个字读作^{2}gkv，意为“头”，这里作“那里”，指示代词，指一个地方。因此，那里的松树林中有^{1}t'khi ^{3}t'a（小鹿）想去跳舞。在“鹿”和“跳舞”中间的那个字是“佛塔”（读作^{3}t'a），这里读作^{3}t'a-（^{2}mä），意为“一只两三岁的小鹿”。这里指代年轻人，他的朋友和同伴在下一页会提到。

第十节：第一个字像偶蹄动物的前腿。下面那个字读作^{1}dzu，像一堵墙，这里读作^{2}dzu，意为“出生”。因此，这句话的意思是这些长着偶蹄的动物。最后两个字读作^{3}nyu-^{2}nyu，意为“摇摆”，随着音乐摇摆。

第十一节：^{3}nyu 是“摇摆”，^{2}lä是“又”，^{2}ts'o 是“跳舞”，^{2}ndu 是“习俗”。

第十二节：这一节的所有音节表示纳西人的一个村庄名，主体像一间房子，上面是一个“雪”的符号，读作^{2}mbe。房子里面有一个黑点，读作^{1}na，意为“黑”，这里表示纳西人家。^{3}dtv 是“千”，作标音符。它意味着所有村民，也表示所有的村民和邻居，这句话不能逐字解释。

经卷第十五页释义

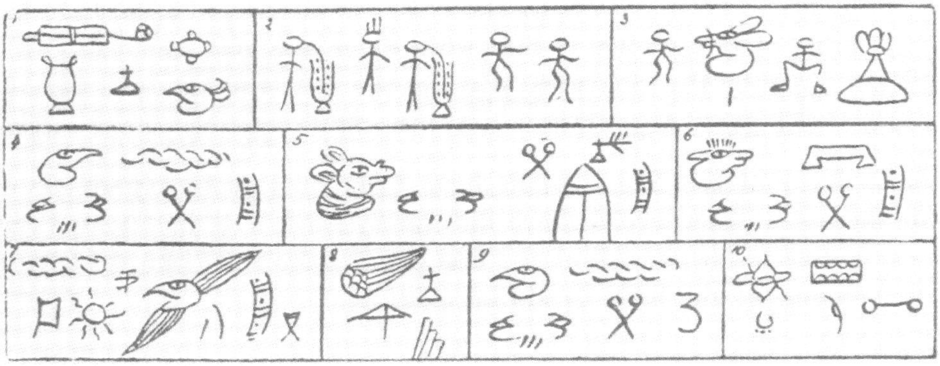

一、全页标音及直译

第一节	^{2}Dzhu	^{2}zo	^{2}ch'i-^{1}ddü-^{3}hoa		
	dʐhu^{33}	zo^{33}	tʂhʅ^{33}dɯ^{21}hua^{55}		
	悲伤	儿子	所有		

第二节	^{3}T'ü-^{1}ts'u	^{2}t'ü	^{3}nyu-^{2}nyu		
	thɯ^{55}tshu^{21}	thɯ^{33}	ȵy^{55} ȵy^{33}		
	细腰	他们	摇摆		

第三节	^{3}Nyu	^{1}lä	^{2}ddü	^{2}ts'o	^{2}ndu
	ȵy^{33}	le^{21}	dɯ^{33}	tsho^{33}	ndu^{33}
	摇	又	一	跳舞	兴

第四节	^{2}Gko	^{3}bpŭ	^{1}gkyi	^{2}gkyi	^{2}bbŭe
	ko^{33}	pv^{55}	tɕi^{21}	tɕi^{33}	bɯ^{33}
	鹤	送	云	放	去

第五节	^{2}La	^{3}bpŭ	^{2}sso	^{2}gkyi	^{2}bbŭe
	la^{33}	pv^{55}	so^{33}	tɕi^{33}	bɯ^{33}
	虎	送	山巅	放	去

第六节	^{1}Yü	^{3}bpŭ	^{1}ggŏ	^{2}gkyi	^{2}bbŭe
	y^{21}	pv^{55}	go^{21}	tɕi^{33}	bɯ^{33}
	祖先	送	高	放	去

第七节	^{1}Gkyi	^{2}k'u	^{1}p'ĕr	^{3}lv-^{1}la,	
	tɕi^{21}	khu^{33}	phər^{21}	lv^{55}la^{21}	
	云	门	白	闪亮	

^{2}gko	^{1}ndzī	^{2}lä	^{2}bbŭe	^{2}mä
ko^{33}	ndzi	le^{33}	bɯ^{33}	me^{33}
鹤	飞	又	去	的

第八节	^{1}Ndǔ	^{2}mun̲	^{2}ndǔ	^{2}ch'i	^{1}dzu
	ndv^{21}	mu^{33}	ndv^{33}	tʂhʅ^{33}	dzu^{21}
	翅膀	动物	翅膀	所有	生

第九节	^{2}Gko	^{3}bpǔ	^{1}gkyi	^{2}gkyi	^{1}ssä
	ko^{33}	pv^{55}	tɕi^{21}	tɕi^{33}	se^{21}
	鹤	送	云	放	了

第十节	^{2}Non̲-^{1}ō	^{2}ḳhü	^{2}muàn̲	^{1}chěr
	no^{33}o^{21}	hɯ^{33}	mə^{33}	tʂər^{21}
	遗福	过	不	允许

二、句译

第一节：所有孝子，

第二节：他们的细腰在有节奏地摇摆。

第三节：摇摆和跳舞是他们的习俗。

第四节：我们将要送仙鹤去云端。

第五节：将要送老虎去高山。

第六节：我们将要送祖先到高处。

第七节：到云端闪亮的白门处，仙鹤想飞。

第八节：他们都有翅膀，

第九节：已经送仙鹤倒云端，

第十节：但是他的遗福不允许带走。

三、字词详解

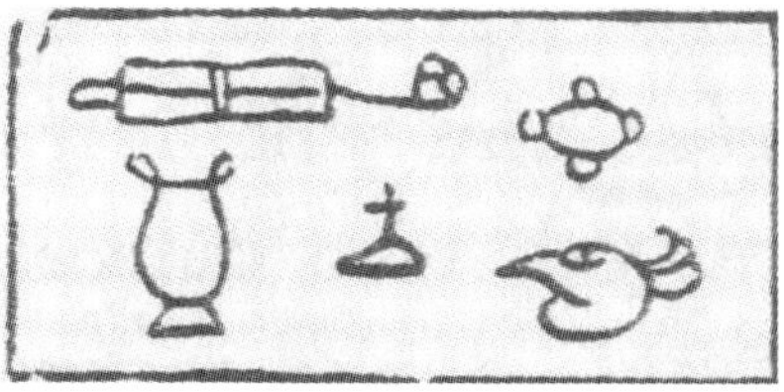

第一节：这一节的所有字都已经解释过了。

第二节：前两个字中，第一个读作^{1}t'ü，意为“喝”，第二个读作^{1}ts'u，意为“鬼”。它们在这里作标音符，^{3}t'ü-^{1}ts'u意为“腰细”。第三个字读作^{2}t'ü，作人称代词“它们”。最后两个字读作^{3}nyu-^{2}nyu，意为“摇摆”，就像字形所表现的那样。

第三节：这一节跟本书的第十四页第十一节相同。

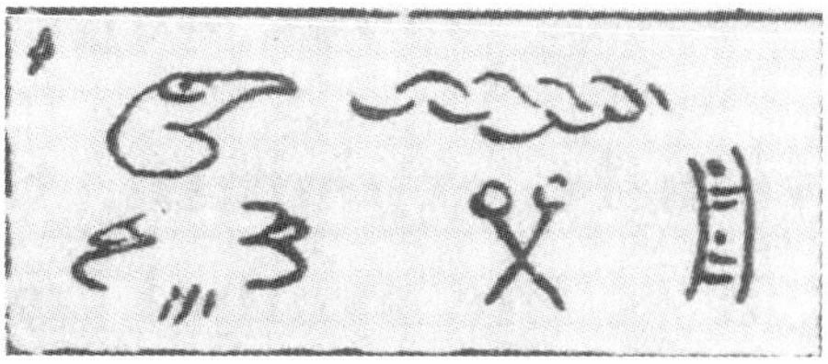

第四节：^{2}gko是“鹤”，^{3}bpŭ是“送”，第三个字读作^{1}gkyi，意为“云”，字形像云之形。“云”下面那个字像一把羊毛剪，读作^{2}gkyi，这里借音作“放置”，最后一个字读作^{2}bbŭe，表示将来时。

第五节：^{2}la ^{3}bpŭ是“送老虎”，剩余的字已经解释过了。^{2}sso是“高山”。（参见本书的第三页第四节的字词详解）老虎经常与高山联系在一起。^{2}gkyi 是“放”。整句话的意思是：送老虎到它要到的地方，即直到它被安置在属于它的地方。

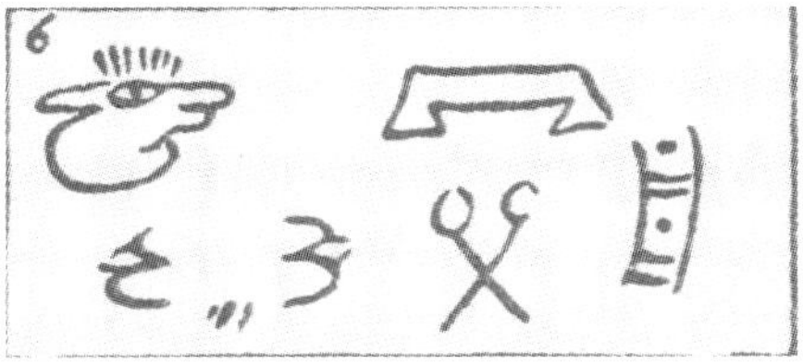

第六节：唯一需要解释的是第一个字，像猴子，读作^{1}yü，这里借音作“祖先”。有意思的是藏族相信他们的祖先是猴子，纳西人并不这样认为。他们用猴子来表示祖先，可能只是因为“猴子”的读音与“祖先”的读音相近而已。在崇则利恩的故事中讲到，他的部落中有一个人和魔鬼生了一只猴子，然后被这个人被赶了出去。

^{1}ggŏ字的本义是“凳子”，但是这里借音作属格，意为“……的”，也有“上或北方”的意思，这里作“在高处”。他被送往高处神的王国。

第七节：这一节第四和第五两个字是之前没有出现过的。^{1}gkyi ^{2}k’u是“云的门”。“云”旁边的那个字读作^{1}p’ĕr，意为“白色”。下面一个字是一个圆圈，四周附加了一些曲线的字形，读作^{3}lv-^{1}la，意为“光辉、闪光的东西”。下一个字像一只飞鸟，鸟头上有一个^{1}p’ĕr（白）字，但是这里“白”字不读出来，示意这只鸟是“白鹤”，应该读作 gko ^{1}p’ĕr。^{1}ndzī意为“飞”。这里白鹤展翅表示要起飞，因此，^{2}gko-^{1}ndzī意为“鹤飞”。^{2}mä是虚词，放在句末表示肯定。

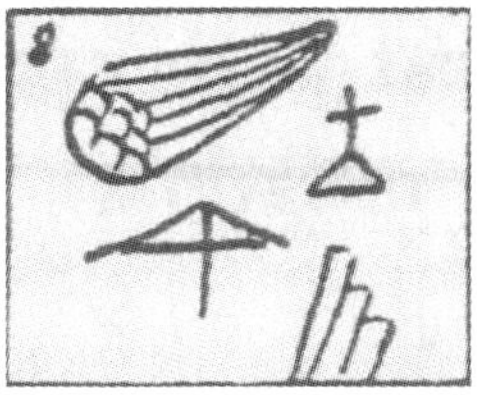

第八节：我们看到的两个字之前已经解释过了。第一个字读作^{2}ndŭ，字形像翅膀。下面一个字读作^{2}muṉ。另外一个字读作^{2}mùaṉ，意为“天”，这里读作^{2}muṉ，意为“动物”。^{1}ndŭ这个词需要读两次。^{2}ch’i 是^{2}ch’i-^{1}wuà的省略形式。最后一字读作^{1}dzu，意为“生”。本节经文对译作“翅膀/动物，翅膀/所有/生”。句子剩下部分的解释见本页第九节。

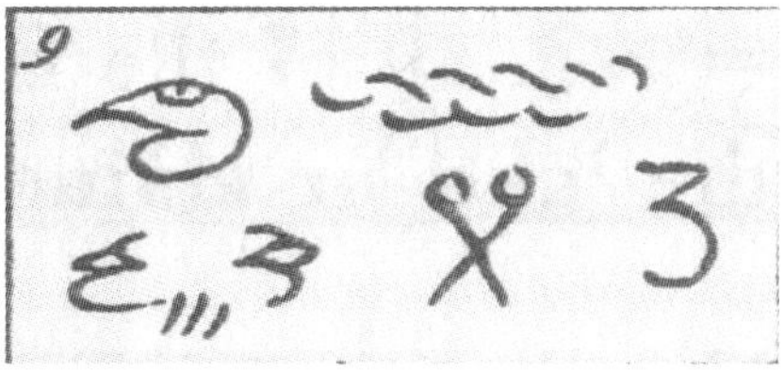

第九节：^{2}gko ^{3}bpŭ是“送鹤”，^{1}gkyi 是“云”，^{2}gkyi 是“放置”，^{1}ssä是哥巴文，表示过去时。

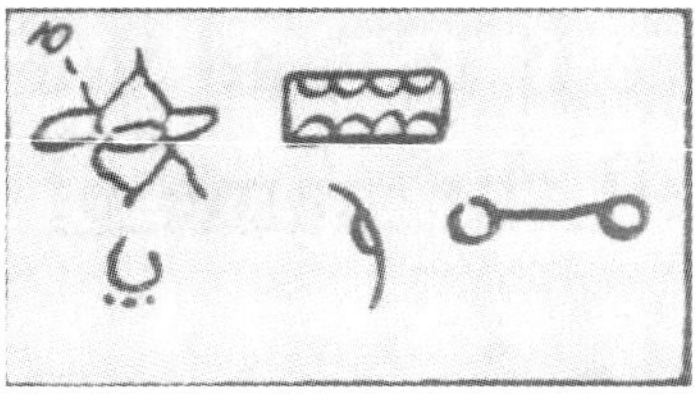

第十节：第一个是字组，上面一个字读作^{1}ō，下面一个字读作^{2}noṉ，像牛奶之形。第一个字不同于字形像绿松石的^{1}ō。上面的曲线表示这个字是“灵魂”的意思。实际上读作^{2}noṉ-^{1}ō，不能按照文字书写顺序来读，必须反过来读。表示“成就、能力、品质等”，这些意思包含在^{2}noṉ-^{1}ō①这个词里。^{2}noṉ是“牛奶”，从一个动物身上生出来的，用以表达

①译者按，我们将之译作“遗物或遗福”。

这个意思，这只是一种猜测。所有死者留下来的好东西，也就是他的遗物。被死者汗水浸透的衣物也叫^{2}non̠-^{1}ō。葬礼结束后，死者留下的东西会被亲属分掉。有一本名叫^{2}non̠-^{1}ō ^{3}ssaw[no^{33}o^{21}sɑ^{55}]（请死者的^{2}non̠-^{1}ō）的经书。这本经书是东巴祭司在葬礼上吟诵的。吟诵这本书的时候，主持仪式的东巴把^{2}ds-^{1}lĕr①，五佛冠、剑等法器交给死者的儿子。下一个字像嘴里有牙，读作^{2}ḳhü，意为“牙”，这里表示动词“度过、去”。下一个字读作^{2}muàn̠，意为“不”。最后一个字读作^{1}chĕr，字形像关节。它也读作^{2}ō，意为“骨头”，这里读作^{1}chĕr，意为“允许”，因此，不允许带走遗福（^{2}non̠-^{1}ō）。

①译者按，板铃。

经卷第十六页释义

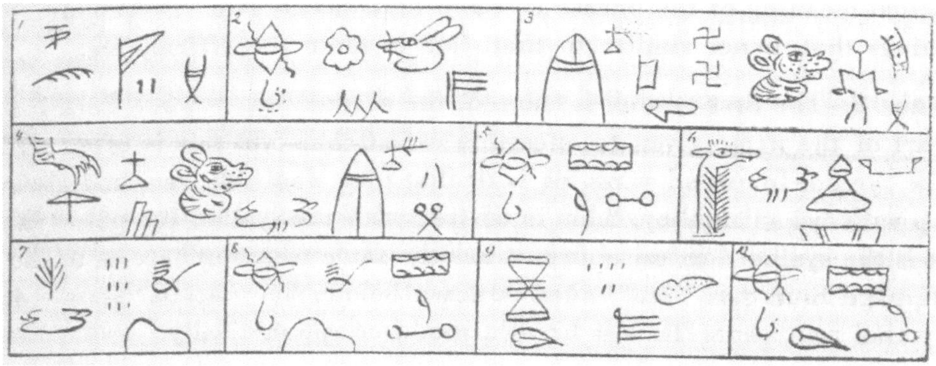

一、全页标音及直译

第一节				
	^{1}Non̠	^{1}p'ĕr	^{2}t'ä^{2}nyi	^{2}mä
	no^{21}	phər^{21}	the^{33}ȵi^{33}	me^{33}
	羽毛	白	像	的

第二节					
	^{2}Non-^{1}ō	^{2}ssu	^{1}mùen̠	^{2}lä	^{3}ssaw
	no^{33} o^{21}	su^{33}	mɯ^{21}	le^{33}	sɑ^{55}
	遗福	祖先	下	又	请

第三节						
	^{2}Sso	^{2}k'u	^{1}shi	^{3}ghügh-^{2}ghügh	^{2}la	^{2}ts'o
	so^{33}	khu^{33}	ʂʅ^{21}	ɯ^{55}ɯ^{33}	la^{33}	tsho^{33}
	山巅	门	黄	闪耀	虎	跳

^{2}lä	^{2}bbŭe	^{2}mä
le^{33}	bɯ^{33}	me^{33}
又	去	的

第四节							
	^{1}Dshi	^{2}mun̠	^{2}ch'i	^{1}dzu	^{2}la	^{3}bpŭ	^{2}sso
	tʂʅ^{21}	mu^{33}	tʂhʅ^{33}	dzu^{21}	la^{33}	pv^{55}	so^{33}
	爪	动物	所有	生	虎	送	山巅

^{2}lä	^{2}gkyi
le^{33}	tɕi^{33}
又	放

第五节				
	^{2}Non̠-^{1}ō	^{2}ḳhü	^{2}muàn̠	^{1}chĕr
	no^{33}o^{21}	hɯ^{33}	mə^{33}	tʂər^{21}
	遗福	去	不	允许

第六节					
	^{1}Yü	^{3}bpŭ	^{1}hä	^{1}dü	^{2}t'u
	y^{21}	pv^{55}	he^{21}	dy^{21}	thu^{33}
	祖先	送	神	地	到

第七节	^{2}Ssu-^{2}bbǔ	^{2}ngv	^{1}mbu			
	su^{33}bv^{33}	ŋgv^{33}	mbu^{21}			
	祖先	九	坡			

第八节	^{2}Non̠-^{1}ō	^{1}mbu	^{3}lo	^{2}k̥hü	^{2}muàn̠	^{1}chĕr
	no^{33}o^{21}	mbu^{21}	lo^{55}	hɯ^{33}	mə^{33}	tʂ̥ər^{21}
	遗福	坡	里	去	不	允许

第九节	^{1}P'ä-^{1}gyi	^{2}shĕr	^{1}ho	^{2}ndĕr
	phe^{21}ʥi^{21}	ʂ̥ər^{33}	ho^{21}	ndər^{33}
	潘水	七	条	应该

第十节	^{2}Non̠-^{1}ō	^{1}gyi	^{2}ndĕr	^{2}k̥hü	^{2}muàn̠	^{1}chĕr.
	no^{33}o^{21}	ʥi^{21}	ndər^{33}	hɯ^{33}	mə^{33}	tʂ̥ər^{21}
	遗福	水	应该	去	不	允许

二、句译

第一节：像一只白色羽毛的鹤，

第二节：请回祖先的遗福。

第三节：去高山的耀眼的黄色大门口，老虎想去跳舞。

第四节：所有有爪子的动物送老虎去高山。

第五节：但是不让他的遗福离开他。

第六节：但是让我们送祖先离开，他们可能到神之地。

第七节：祖先必须越过九座山坡。

第八节：但是不要让他的遗福越过九座山坡。

第九节：他必须渡过七条河，

第十节：但不要让他的遗福跟他一起过河。

三、字词详解

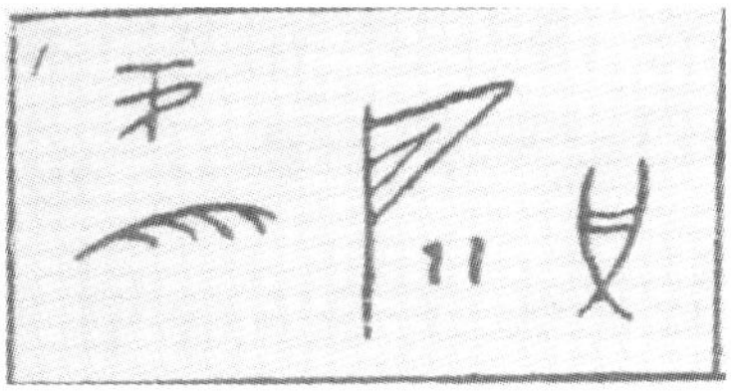

第一节：第一个字读作^{1}p'ĕr，意为“白色”，第二个字读作^{1}non̠，像羽毛之形，鹤的白色羽毛被称作它的^{1}non-^{1}ō，这里玩了一个文字游戏，“羽毛”^{1}non̠与^{1}non-^{1}ō的第一个音节相同。第三个字读作^{2}t'ä，像一面旗帜。第四个字是“二”，读作^{2}nyi。^{2}t'ä-^{2}nyi 意为“像（羽毛）”。^{2}t'ä-^{2}nyi ^{2}gv 这个短语在东巴经书中经常遇到，实际意思^{2}t'ä是“那”，^{2}nyi 是“二”，^{2}gv 是“身体”。即两件东西很像。^{2}Mä表示肯定。

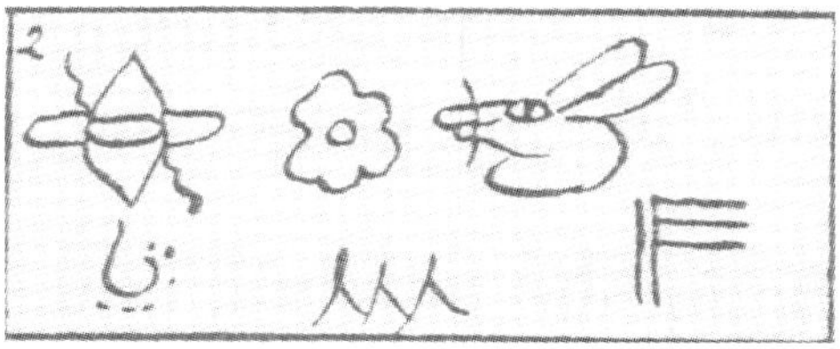

第二节：第一个字组读作^{2}non̠-^{1}ō，第二个字读作^{2}ssu，这里借音作祖先名^{2}ssu-^{2}bbŭ-^{1}yü的第一个音节，这个词经常用字形像木头（“木头”读作^{2}ss）的字表示，或者用字形像羊毛毡（“羊毛毡”读作^{2}ssu）的那个字表示。^{1}yü经常用字形像猴子（“猴子”读作^{1}yü）的字表示。^{2}bbŭ经常用字形像罐子（“罐子”读作^{2}bbŭ）的字表示。接下来一个字像火焰，读作^{2}mi。在本书第四页的第七节也有“火”这个字，这里读作^{1}mùen̠，意为“低”。^{2}lä 是“又”，^{3}ssaw 是“请”，该字像呼出的空气，这里用作标音符。

第三节：^{2}Sso 意为“高山”。（参见本书第十五页第五节的字词详解）^{2}k'u 是“门”，^{2}shi 是“肉”，

这里借音作^{1}shi，意为“黄色”。三个字合起来意为，黄色的高山之门。后面是一个本教的梵文字符，读作^{2}ghügh，这里读作^{3}ghügh-^{2}ghügh，“明亮的”。剩下的字已经解释过了。

第四节：

第一个字像捕食性动物的前爪，读作^{1}dshi。下面一个字读作^{2}muṉ。^{1}Dshi ^{2}muṉ意为“生爪的动物”。下两个字读作^{2}ch'i ^{1}dzu，意为“所有生爪的动物”，^{2}la ^{3}bpŭ 是“送虎”，^{2}sso 是“高山”，^{2}lä是“又”， ^{2}gkyi 是“放置”。

第五节：参见本书的第十五页第十节的字词详解。

第六节：第一个字这里读作^{1}yü，意为“祖先”，实际上该字应该读作^{1}Yü-^{3}muṉ-^{2}llü-^{2}ssĭ，意为：“死者变成祖先”，以此与^{1}Zhi-^{3}muṉ-^{2}llü-^{2}ssĭ“死者变成蛇”相区别。猴头下面的横线代表松树枝。^{2}Khi ^{3}nv 丧葬仪式在死者死后三年内的农历十一月举行。全村要为所有死去的男子举行这个仪式。每一个参加的家庭都要准备一只羊作祭品。这个仪式在高原上举行，需要为每一个死者做一座小的纸房子，这些纸房子两两相对，排成两排。每一座纸房子里面都有一根松枝代表死者，我们把它叫^{2}nv。在^{2}Khi ^{3}nv 仪式上需要吟诵一本名叫^{2}Nv ^{3}hăr（砍^{2}nv）的经书。东巴一边吟诵经书，一边拿起一根带杈的松枝，树杈代表手臂，上面的叶子代表头发，用小刀刻上眼睛、耳朵、嘴、鼻子等。这个松枝就变成了一个^{2}nv，用它代替或者想象成死者。当山羊被杀了作祭品以后，每家都要拿着特制的^{2}nv 放在一个白色的羊毛毡上。主祭家的纸房子放在最前面，位于这两排纸房子中间。主祭家的儿子在队伍的最前面，把所有的^{2}nv 都被卷在白毛毡里，然后骑上一匹马，脸朝后，去举行丧礼的山洞。这个山洞叫^{2}Nv-^{1}t'khi-^{2}k'o-^{1}ndv，又叫^{2}Nv-^{1}gkyi-^{2}k'o-^{1}ndv 和^{2}Nv-^{1}gkyi-^{1}'a-^{2}k'o。在古代洞口有一个看门人，但是自从丽江地区不举行^{2}khi ^{3}nv 仪式以后，山洞就没有看门人了。^{2}nv 也不再放置在山洞里了，它们被放在石灰岩上，面朝东，位于丽江山谷平原的最后一个村子和地势较低的^{2}nga-^{1}ba 之间。（参见《中国西南纳西族的日美丧仪》的附图 4）

首领叫^{2}Ts'u-^{1}bpö-^{2}swue-^{2}p'ä-^{3}haw，其中^{2}swue-^{2}p'ä是“首领”，^{2}ts'u 是“鬼”，^{1}bpö是“仪式”，^{3}haw 是“睡觉”。在举行^{2}Khi ^{3}nv 仪式之前，死者被认为是鬼，首领指的是举行这个仪式的首领。这些祭品会被当作仪式参加者的食物。他们也睡在这个房子里，所以要加上^{3}haw。举行^{2}Khi ^{3}nv 仪式的地方被称作^{2}Ts'u-^{1}bpö-^{2}lü-^{2}k'u-^{2}dtü，一般叫^{2}Khi ^{3}nv ^{1}d'a，就是举行^{2}Khi ^{3}nv 仪式的地方。主持仪式的东巴被称为^{2}Lo-^{1}ch'ung-^{2}ndaw-^{1}khü，他戴一顶黑色的毡帽，手里拿着^{3}Mùeṉ-^{1}t'u（丧棒）。^{3}Bpŭ是“送”，下一个字像神之形，读作^{1}hä，意为“神”。下面那个字读作^{1}dü，意为“地”，最后一个字读作^{2}t'u，意为“到”。

第七节：前两个字读作²ssu-²bbŭ，表示²ssu-²bbŭ（祖先）。下一个字是数字九，读作²ngv。下一个字像山坡，读作¹mbu。上面的那个哥巴文读作²lo，意为“过”。

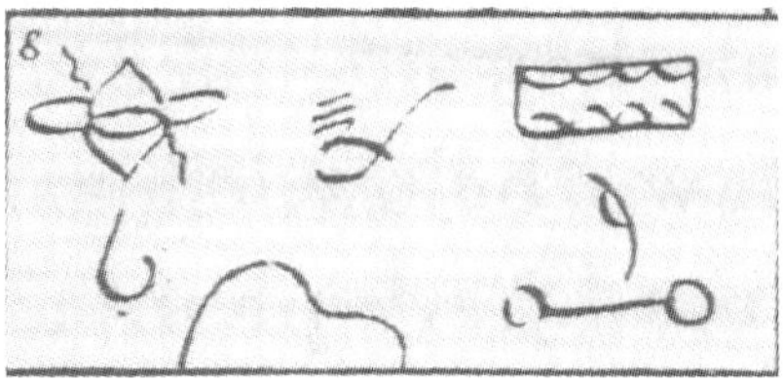

第八节：不允许²non̲-¹ō 越过山坡。（参见本页第五节和第十五页第十节的字词详解）“九坡”被读作¹p'ä-¹mbu ²ngv-¹mbu。

第九节：第一个通常读作¹ddaw，意为“织布机”，它还可以读作¹p'ä，意为“头盔”。这里读作¹p'ä，下一个字读作¹gyi，意为“水”。¹p'ä ¹gyi 中¹p'ä相关的地名是¹P'ä-¹mbe-³lo-¹nddü。第三个字是“七”，读作²shĕr。下一个字像肋骨，读作¹ho，这里借音作¹ho，意为“渡（河）”。¹P'ä-¹gyi ²shĕr ¹ho 意为“过七条潘河”，¹ho 的实际意思是“人骑着会游泳的动物过河”。最后一个字像一个快要干涸的池塘，下面的点代表沙子，表示水清澈见底。该字读作²ndĕr，这里借音作“应该”。

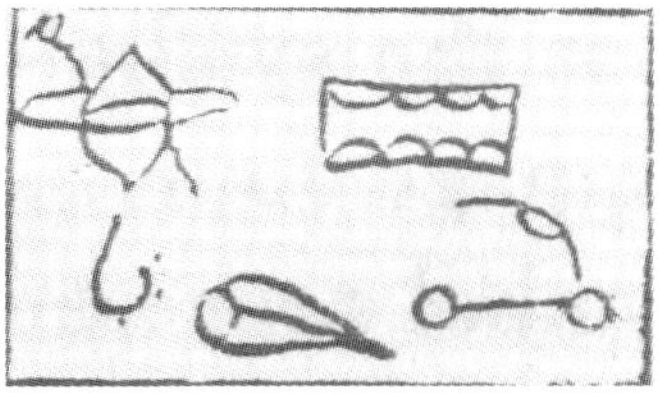

第十节：这一节的字都已经解释过了。不允许²non̲-¹ō渡河。

经卷第十七页释义

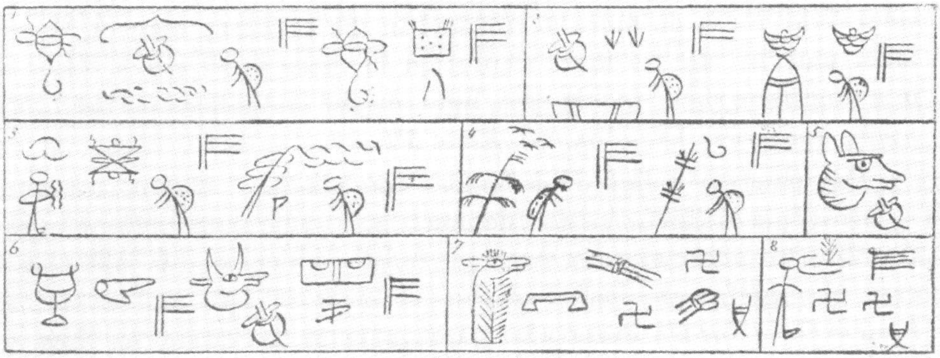

一、全页标音及直译

第一节	^{2}Non̠-^{1}ō	^{2}muàn̠	^{2}nnü	^{1}gkyi	^{2}gu	^{3}ssaw,
	no^{33}o^{21}	mɯ^{33}	nɯ^{33}	tɕi^{21}	gu^{33}	sɑ^{55}
	遗福	天	的	云	像	请

^{2}non̠-^{1}ō	^{3}ssu	^{2}lä	^{3}ssaw
no^{33}o^{21}	su^{55}	le^{33}	sɑ^{55}
遗福	收集	又	请

第二节	^{1}Dü	^{2}nnü	^{1}zhou	^{2}gu	^{3}ssaw,	^{2}Nv-^{2}lv
	dy^{21}	nɯ^{33}	z̧ə^{21}	gu^{33}	sɑ^{55}	ŋv^{33}lv^{33}
	地	的	草	像	请	雪山

^{1}nv	^{1}gu	^{3}ssaw
ŋv^{21}	gu^{21}	sɑ^{55}
银	像	请

第三节	^{2}Yi-^{1}bi	^{1}ha	^{2}gu	^{3}ssaw,	^{3}khyü	^{3}gko
	i^{33}bi^{21}	hæ^{21}	gu^{33}	sɑ^{55}	ɕy^{55}	ko^{55}
	江	金	像	请	松柏	枝

^{1}gkyi	^{1}gu	^{3}ssaw
tɕi^{21}	gu^{21}	sa^{55}
云	像	请

第四节	^{2}Llü	^{3}gko	^{2}mbe	^{1}gu	^{3}ssaw,	^{3}mùen̠-^{2}ts'ä
	lɯ^{33}	ko^{55}	mbe^{33}	gu^{21}	sɑ^{55}	mɯ^{55}tshe^{33}
	杉树	枝	雪	像	请	竹子

^{2}ndzhĕr	^{1}gu	^{3}ssaw
ndz̧ər^{33}	gu^{21}	sɑ^{55}
露水	像	请

第五节	^{1}Ngu	^{2}nnü
	ŋgu^{21}	nɯ^{33}
	马	的

第六节	^{3}gkyi	^{1}shi	^{3}ssaw,	^{1}mun̠	^{2}nnü	^{1}lo
	tɕhi^{55}	ʂʅ^{21}	sɑ^{55}	mu^{21}	nɯ^{33}	lo^{21}
	马鞍	黄	请	死者	的	车轭

^{1}p'ĕr	^{3}ssaw
phər^{21}	sɑ^{55}
白	请

第七节	^{1}Yü-^{3}mun̠-^{2}llü-^{2}ssĭ	^{2}ggŏ	^{1}dzĭ	^{2}ghügh
	y^{21}mu^{55}lɯ^{33}sʅ^{33}	go^{33}	ʥʅ^{21}	ɯ^{33}
	祖先	的	数	好

^{3}gku	^{2}ghügh	^{2}mä
ku^{55}	ɯ^{33}	me^{33}
记录	好	的

第八节	^{2}Ndzĕr	^{2}ghügh	^{1}ho	^{2}ghügh	^{2}mä.
	ndzər^{33}	ɯ^{33}	ho^{21}	ɯ^{33}	me^{33}
	唱	好	吟诵	好	的

二、句译

第一节：遗福像天上众多的云彩，让我们把它请回来，让它重新护佑着我们。

第二节：（遗福）像草地上茂盛的青草，像雪山上的银子，让我们把它请回来。

第三节：（遗福）像从扬子江中淘来的金子，让我们把它请回来。

第四节：（遗福）像落在杉树枝上的雪，像留在竹子上的露水，让我们把它请回来。

第五节：（遗福）像马的

第六节：黄色马鞍，像公牛的白色车轭，让我们把死者的遗福请回来。

第七节：让我们请回死者所有的遗福，像他一样有计算和书写的能力。

第八节：他有唱歌的能力，大家也跟着一起唱。

三、字词详解

第一节：实际上这一节的所有字都已经解释过了。第一个字组读作²noṉ-¹ō，意为“死者的精神、力量、能力等”。接下来一个字读作²muàṉ，本义为“天”，“天”下面那个字读作²nnü，本义为“心”。两个字合起来读作²muàṉ ²nnü，这是一种所有格的形式，即“天的”。“心”下面那个字读作¹gkyi，意为“云”。下一个字读作¹gu，意为“背、扛”，像一个人背着包袱，因此表示背（东西）。这里既作“背”（读作¹gu）又作“像”（读作²gu）①。³ssaw 是“请”。这个句子很简洁，动词都是现在时，也没有体现单复数。²noṉ-¹ō ³ssu 是“带来或收集遗福”，²lä 是“又”，³ssaw 是“请”。

①译者按，此处存疑，不解其意。

第二节：句子结构跟上一句是一样的。^{1}dü 是“地”。像心之形的那个字读作^{2}nnü，用在这里相当于英语的所有格。“心”旁边那两个比较小的符号读作^{1}zhou，意为“草”，像地上的草。^{1}gu 这里的意思是“背（像）请”。^{2}Nv-^{2}lv 是“雪山”，“山”实际上读作^{1}ngyu。^{1}nv 是“叠在一起的银子”，表示丽江的雪山。^{1}gu 是“背”，^{3}ssaw 是“请”。

第三节：前两个字是假借字，相当于哥巴文，读作^{2}yi-^{1}bi，^{1}bi 字像一个人在搓麻绳，都用作标音符，^{2}yi-^{1}bi 是指“长江或扬子江”，长江绕丽江地区而行，西部海拔 6000 英尺，东部海拔 5000 英尺，富含金子。因此，纳西语叫^{2}la-^{2}lĕr-^{1}ha-^{2}yi-^{1}bi，广阔的金江，汉语叫“金沙江”。下一个字是^{1}ha“金”，^{2}gu 是“背”，^{3}ssaw 是“请”。后半句第一个字读作^{3}khyü，意为“柏树”，最上面那个字读作^{1}gkyi，意为“云”。“柏树”下面那个字读作^{3}gko，字形像针，本义为“针”，这里借音作“树枝”；^{1}gu 是“背”，^{3}ssaw 是“请”。

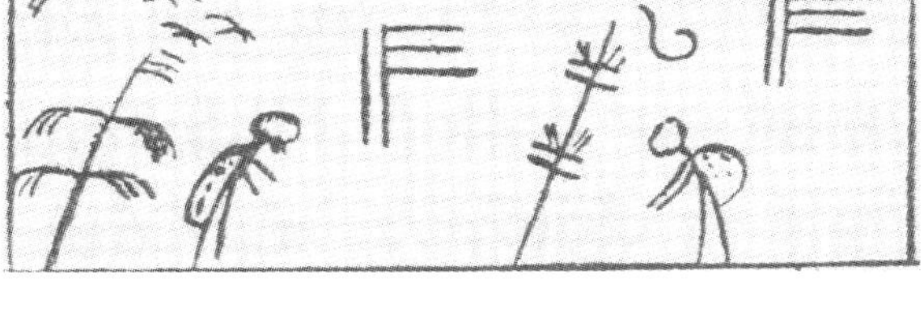

第四节：第一个字读作^{2}llü，意为“杉树”，它在村庄（读作^{2}mbe）这个字的上面。^{3}gko 是“树枝”，字没写出来，但是要读出来。^{1}gu 是“块、片”，^{3}ssaw 是“请”。后半句中，^{3}mùen̲-^{2}ts'ä是一种竹子，生长在海拔 11 000—12 000 英尺的杉树林中，拉丁学名作 *Arundinaria Faberi*，这里只写出一个音节^{3}mùeṉ（竹），^{2}ts'ä这个音节没写出来。顶部的那条曲线表示“露水”，读作^{2}ndzěr。^{1}gu 是“背”，^{3}ssaw 是“请”。

第五节：这一节只有两个字，^{1}ngu 是“马”，^{2}nnü是“心”这里也读^{2}nnü，意为“它的”，表示属格。在纳西语中，马有还几个词，书面语作^{1}ngu，口语作^{2}zhwua；经常在东巴经中出现的有一个借词^{2}dta，借自藏语的 rta。

第六节：第一个字读作^{3}gkyi，意为“马鞍”。它也可以表示马背上驮的东西，这里作马鞍。下一个字读^{1}shi，意为“黄色”，已经解释过了。^{3}ssaw 是“请”。后半句读作^{2}ghügh，意为“牛”，还有另一个词^{1}muṉ，意为“公牛”。经文中不经常读作^{2}ghügh，^{2}ghügh 是口语。^{2}nnü是“它的”，表示属格。下一个字读作^{1}lo，字形像牛轭。^{1}p'ěr 是“白”，^{3}ssaw 是“请”。

经文的意思是：请回死者的马鞍。第一个字读作^{1}shi，字形像肉。该字也可以读作^{1}shi，意为“黄色”，又可以读作^{2}shi，意为“死者”。它跟在名词^{3}gkyi“马鞍”的后面，作形容词，修饰名词。我把它译作“黄色”。在第二个分句中，^{1}p'ěr“白色”这个词跟在名词^{1}lo“车轭”后面，它们是并列关系。因此，^{1}shi 这里不是指“死者”而是“黄色”。东巴解释为死者遗留下来的精神、力量、能力，像一个人脱下一匹死马的马鞍一样。在本书中，^{1}muṉ意为“死牛或进献给神的牛”。

一般的“牛”读第二声，表示“祭祀用的牺牲”的时候读第一声。可能东巴说的是对的。（参见本书的第十五页第八节，那里的表示动物）

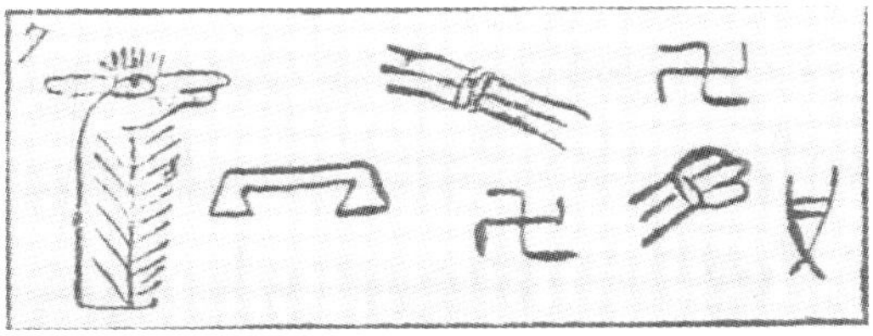

第七节：第一个字应该是蛇头，这里换成了猴头，读作[1]yü，意为“祖先”。只有在[2]Khi [3]nv 仪式之后，死者才能被称作[1]Yü-[3]mun̠-[2]llü-[2]ssĭ。这是在葬礼上吟唱的。第二个字读作[2]ggŏ，表示“……的”，表示属格。[1]dzĭ是“计算”，字形像绳结，它表示在文字产生之前，人类用结绳记事。这个梵文符号读作[2]ghügh，意为“好”。两个梵文符号中间的那个字读作[3]gku，字形像姜的根，所以本义是“姜”，这里借音作“书写、记录”。[2]mä表示肯定的语气。

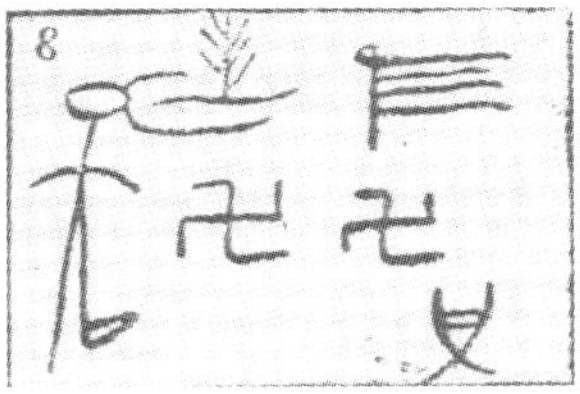

第八节：第一个字像一个男子边走边唱。（歌曲的内容详见《中国西南纳西族的日美丧仪》前言部分对《挽歌》的介绍）这个字读作[1]ho，本义为“肋骨”，这里借音作“吟诵（用很低沉的声音）”，它也有“跟着唱”的意思。[2]ghügh 作“好”，它的字形像纳西一个神的心脏，因此，意思是“好、品质好”。[2]mä是虚词，表示肯定的语气。

经卷第十八页释义

一、全页标音及直译

第一节	^{1}Gkwua	^{2}ghügh	^{3}t'khi	^{2}ghügh	^{2}mä	^{3}gkv	^{2}ssĭ
	kua^{21}	ɯ^{33}	tɕhi^{55}	ɯ^{33}	me^{33}	kv^{55}	sɿ^{33}
	呱	好	齐	好	的	能力	智慧

^{2}ndzĭ	^{1}nddü	^{2}mä
ndzɿ^{33}	ndɯ^{21}	me^{33}
首领	村长	的

第二节	^{2}Gkv	^{1}p'ĕr	^{1}nds'a	^{1}shĕr	^{2}mä
	kv^{33}	phər^{21}	ndʑæ^{21}	ʂər^{21}	me^{33}
	头	白	獠牙	长	的

第三节	^{2}P'u	^{1}ddo	^{3}llü	^{1}ddo	^{2}mä
	phu^{33}	do^{21}	lɯ^{55}	do^{21}	me^{33}
	祖父	见	孙子	见	的

第四节	^{2}T'ä-^{2}nyi	^{2}non̲-^{1}ō	^{2}ssu	^{3}yu	^{1}mùen̲
	the^{33}ȵi^{33}	no^{33}o^{21}	su^{33}	iə^{55}	mɯ^{21}
	像	遗福	祖先	给	下

^{2}lä	^{3}ssaw
le^{33}	sɑ^{55}
又	请

第五节	^{2}Non̲-^{1}ō	^{1}ssĭ	^{2}nnü	^{2}zo	^{1}nyu	^{3}ssaw
	no^{33}o^{21}	sɿ^{21}	nɯ^{33}	zo^{33}	ȵy^{21}	sɑ^{55}
	遗福	父亲	和	儿子	传递	请

第六节	^{1}Ssĭ	^{2}dto	^{2}zo	^{2}dto	^{3}ddü-^{2}ddü	^{3}hu
	sɿ^{21}	to^{33}	zo^{33}	to^{33}	dɯ^{55}dɯ^{33}	hu^{55}
	父亲	在	儿子	在	同样	愿

第七节	^{2}Mä					
	me^{33}					
	母亲					
第八节	^{2}nnü	^{3}mi	^{1}nyu	^{3}ssaw		
	nɯ^{33}	mi^{55}	ȵy^{21}	sɑ^{55}		
	和	女儿	传递	请		
第九节	^{2}Mä	^{1}hö	^{1}mi	^{1}hö	^{2}shwua-^{2}shwua	^{3}hu
	me^{33}	hy^{21}	mi^{21}	hy^{21}	ṣua^{33} ṣua^{33}	hu^{55}
	母亲	站立	女儿	站立	高高的	愿
第十节	^{2}Non̲-^{1}ō	^{3}bpŭ	^{2}nnü	^{2}mbe	^{1}nyu	^{3}ssaw
	no^{33}o^{21}	pv^{55}	nɯ^{33}	mbe^{33}	ȵy^{21}	sɑ^{55}
	遗福	邻居	和	村庄	上	请
第十一节	^{3}Bpŭ	^{1}ddü	^{2}mbe	^{1}la	^{3}hu.	
	pv^{55}	dɯ^{21}	mbe^{33}	la^{21}	hu^{55}	
	邻居	大	村庄	厚	愿	

二、句译

第一节：他会唱喜歌和悲歌一样的歌曲，有像首领的能力和智慧。

第二节：让我们像死者一样头白牙长、

第三节：祖孙同堂。

第四节：像请回祖先的遗福一样。

第五节：让我们把父亲的遗福传给儿子，

第六节：把父亲的才能和力量传给儿子。

第七节：母亲（的遗福），

第八节：传给女儿，

第九节：愿母亲与女儿一样有才能。

第十节：愿遗福传给邻居和村庄，

第十一节：愿村庄和邻居①增加。

三、字词详解

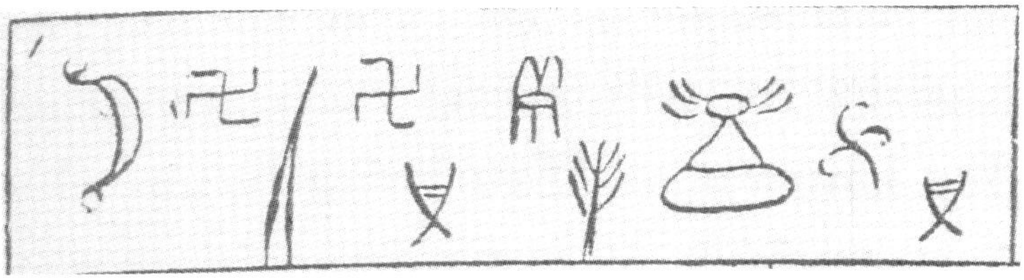

第一节：第一个字读作^{1}gkwua，像木匠使用的工具，它可以把木料弄成条状，它实际上像一个弯曲的刀片，两边有把手，过去它用于制作木盆（“木盆”读作^{2}lo-^{1}bpä）。在工匠用的刨子没有传到纳西地区之前，主要用这种工具。这里的^{1}gkwua 代表一种类型的音乐，是老人在婚礼上演唱的，即喜歌。这种歌曲口语作^{3}Ssu-^{3}wùa-^{1}wùa-^{1}gkwua，^{3}Ssu 是生命之神（参见《纳西族的纳迦崇拜及其相关仪式》，第 250 页，注释 527）。歌词中讲述了纳西人的历史。^{2}ghügh 是“好”，第三个字像一根刺，读作^{3}t'khi，在这里借音作“疼痛”，读第一声。^{2}t'khi 是“卖”，^{3}t'khi 是“冷”，^{1}t'khi 是“甜”。所有这些义项都借“刺（^{2}t'khi）”这个字形表示。这里^{3}t'khi 表示一种类型的歌曲，是在山上放牧或者男子唱的。以 Eh eh eh eh 开头，直到男子力竭为止。这种歌曲一般在高山上演唱，讲述悲伤的故事，即悲歌。因此，^{3}t'khi 这里有“冷”的意思。男孩和女孩开始唱这些歌曲的时候，结尾都是即兴的。这些歌曲会变成性暗示。这句话的前半句的其他字已经解释过了。后

①译者按，这里将“邻居”译作“邻村”比较合适。最后一句经文的意思是邻村和本村的人口兴旺。

半句的^{3}gkv 的本义是“头”，这里借音作“能够”。下一个字像松树，可以读三个音：^{1}ndzĕr 是“树”，^{2}t’o 是“松树”，^{2}ss 是“木”，这里读作^{2}ss，借音作“智慧，知识”。下一个字读作^{2}ndzĭ，意为“首领”。

这个字的本义已经迷失了。该字的下半部分跟神字①的下本部分是一样的，把首领写成神的样子是对首领的敬仰。首领的发型是卷发。下一个字读作^{1}ndi，意为“蕨类植物的叶子”。实际指嫩的老鹰之箭或者巴拉根蕨（拉丁学名作*Pteridium aquilinum*），这里借音作^{1}ndü或者^{1}nddü，意为“村长”，这个字也写作，读作^{1}ndü。^{2}mä是虚词，表示肯定语气，作用相当于冒号。

第二节：这一节写出来的字没有作动词的。^{1}gv ^{2}bä ^{3}hu 是动词而不是一个句子，意为“让我们有”。这一节只写出下面几个字，即^{1}p’ĕr 是“白色”，^{2}gkv 是“头”，^{1}nds‘a 是“獠牙”。^{1}shĕr 本义是“七”，这里借音作“长”。所以，整句话的意思是：白头长牙，意思是一个老人应该有“白头长牙”。白发和快要脱落的牙齿是人年老的标志。

第三节：第一个字读作^{2}P’u，意为“长发的祖父”。^{3}p’u-^{2}p’u 是曾祖父。下一个字读作^{1}ddo，意为“看见”。下面一个字像一个小男孩。“男孩”下面那个字像虱子之形，读作^{3}llü，这是一个合体字，“虱子”作声符，该字意为“孙子”。因此，整句话对译为：祖父/见/孙子/见，意思是“祖孙同堂”。纳西语口语中，“孙子”读作^{2}lv-^{2}bbŭ，“曾孙”读作^{3}lv-^{2}bbŭ，两者只是在声调上有区别。

①译者按，“神”一般作。

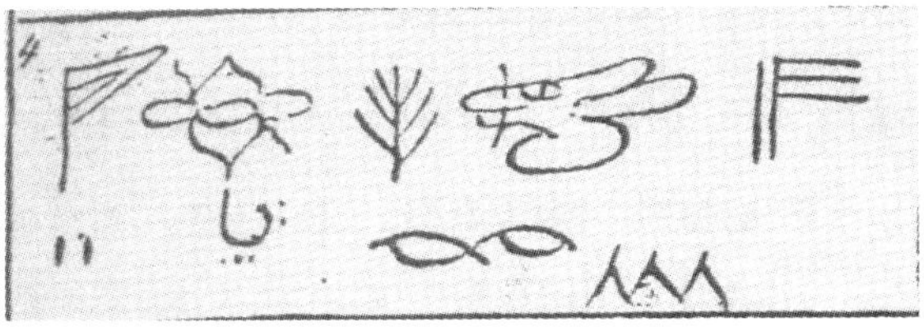

第四节：前两个字在前面已经解释过了。“松树”这个字又出现一次，这里读作^{2}ssu，意为“祖先”。“松树”下面那个字读作^{1}yu，意为“给”，这里读作^{3}yu。下面三个词^{1}mùen̲ ^{2}lä ^{3}ssaw，意为“下又请”。

第五节：这三个字已经解释过了。^{2}non̲-^{1}ō是“能力”等。^{1}ä ^{1}ssǐ是“父亲”，^{2}nnü是“他的”，^{2}zo 是“儿子”，^{1}nyu 是“在”，^{3}ssaw 是“请”。像眼睛那个字读作^{1}miu 或者^{1}nyu，这里读^{1}nyu，表示“在……上”。

第六节：^{1}ä ^{1}ssǐ是“父亲”，^{2}dto 是“在……里面”，^{2}zo 是“儿子”，^{2}dto 是“在……里面”，^{3}ddü-^{2}ddü是“相等”。最后一个字像一扇门，“门”读作^{2}k'u，这里读作^{3}hu，它作^{2}gv ^{2}bä ^{3}hu“就那样吧”这句话的第三个音节。这句话一般出现在经书的末尾。

第七节：^{2}Mä是“母亲”。

第八节：^{2}Nnü 是“她的”，^{3}mi 是“女儿”，^{1}nyu 是“在”，^{3}ssaw 是“请”，即请回她的精神、能力等。（参见本页第五节的字词详解）

第九节：^{2}Mä是“母亲”。下一个字读作^{1}mi，本义为“火”，这里读作^{1}hö，意为“站”。实际上应该读作^{3}hö，但是为了押韵读作^{1}hö。“站”字像一个人岔开腿站着，即

，读作^{3}hö。这里想体现高度的概念，因此母亲和女儿的身高是一样的。^{2}shwua-^{2}shwua 是“身高一样的、整齐的”。^{3}hu 意思是“就这样吧”。

第十节：^{2}Non-^{1}ō是“精神、能力、力量等”，^{3}bpŭ 是“邻居”，由一座房子和一个滤网表示，“滤网”读作^{3}bpŭ，在这里作标音符。nnü 作连词，^{2}mbe 是“村庄”，跟“房子”是同形字。里面是“雪”，读作^{2}mbe，作声符。最后一个字读作^{1}nyu，意为“在，致，传递”，^{3}ssaw 是“请”。有时候^{2}mbe 和^{3}bpŭ两个字会同时写在“房子”里面，读作^{3}bpŭ和^{2}mbe，意为“邻居和村庄”。

第十一节：^{3}bpŭ 是“邻居”，^{1}ddü是“大”，^{2}mbe 是“村庄”。^{1}la 是“厚的、粗的”，^{3}hu 是“就这样吧”。意思是“邻居增加和村庄繁荣”。

歌曲结束后，孝子们跪在东巴的面前，东巴把一碗糖水递给死者的儿子，死者的儿子将糖水喝下，这象征着儿子请回了父亲的遗福（^{2}Non-^{1}ō）。

校勘记

英文原版 p63（本书 39 页）倒数第 5 行，ellucidate，应为 elucidate。

英文原版 p99（本书 75 页）第 3 行，ters，应为 terse。

后　记

2008年，我有幸考入西南大学汉语言文献研究所，师从喻遂生先生学习纳西东巴文和甲金文字。入学后就对美国学者洛克及其纳西学研究产生了浓厚的兴趣，洛克关于纳西学的最重要的著作是《纳西语英语百科辞典》，它被称为洛克纳西学研究的集大成之作。于是跟喻老师商量以后，我将硕士论文题目定在《纳西语英语百科辞典》的研究上，此时和匠宇先生翻译的《纳西语英语百科辞典》[1]也已经出版，这对于我的研究帮助很大。尤其值得称道的是该书保留了英文原文，可以让读者相互参照。2011年，我的硕士论文《洛克〈纳西语英语百科辞典〉研究》顺利通过答辩，该论文分别获得西南大学和重庆市优秀硕士论文。硕士毕业后，我继续跟随喻遂生先生研习纳西东巴文。西方学者对于纳西学的产生和发展起了重要的作用，当时国内只有白庚胜先生和杨福泉先生编的《国际东巴文化研究集萃》一书介绍西方纳西学研究的相关情况，对于西方早期的纳西学研究更是语焉不详。主要原因在于这些文献比较分散，难于搜集，再加上这些文献用英文、法文和德文等西文撰写，阅读难度大。因此，我把博士论文的选题定为《西方纳西学史研究》，希望可以梳理百余年来西方学者的纳西学研究史。要想完成这篇博士论文，必须首先阅读大量的外文文献，对于一些重要的西方纳西学论著，我边读边译。2014年，我通过博士论文答辩，我的论文获西南大学优秀博士论文。在答辩会上，我发愿要将西方纳西学的主

①《纳西语英语百科辞典》中文版更名为《纳西语英语汉语语汇》，云南教育出版社，2004年版。

要论著译成中文出版。博士毕业后，留校任教。此后一直致力于西方纳西学史的研究和西方纳西学论著的译介。2015 年，我在赵心愚先生、和继全先生主编的《纳西学研究》上发表洛克的《纳西族日喜人及其宗教文献》的汉语译文，但是除此之外，很少有机会将我翻译的其他纳西学论著的汉语译文发表。

2017 年，我受国家留学基金委的资助赴美访学，期间多次到哈佛大学燕京图书馆、怀德纳图书馆、阿诺德植物园档案馆查阅洛克的相关资料，并采访了哈佛燕京学社的副社长李若虹女士和哈佛燕京图书馆中文部主任马小鹤先生。2018 年 9 月，云南大学出版社段然女士突然找到我，希望我可以参加“境外东巴经释义”项目，翻译海外所藏东巴经。目前海外所藏的东巴经大多数是洛克收集的，洛克不仅是经书的收集者，还是研究者，他翻译了大量的东巴经，有很多在西方已经出版，但是洛克翻译的东巴经大多数只有每一页经文的大意，并没有做太多的解释。在洛克已经出版的论著中，我挑选了《大鹏与署争斗的故事》《挽歌》《鲁般鲁饶》（上、下）和《手执油灯》四种作为“境外东巴经释义”项目的第一辑。这四本经书之间本来没有什么联系，只是因为洛克不仅记录了这四种东巴经的经文大意，而且记录了经文的读音和东巴对字词的详细解说。这些东巴经的译本都是洛克在二十世纪二三十年代记录的，当时东巴文化十分兴盛，大东巴迭出，因此，这些资料都弥足珍贵。于是我想将它们首先翻译出版，让更多的国内学者看到。我的这个想法得到段然女士的支持，于是开始着手开展这个项目，经过两年多的艰苦努力，书稿终于付梓。以前认为翻译不是一件难事，只需要将一种文字转换为另一种文字即可，但是翻译了这套书之后才知道翻译之难。这套书不仅涉及英语、汉语、法语、德语、纳西语、藏语等多种语言和东巴文、哥巴文、汉字、藏文、梵文等多种文字，还需要用到语言学、文字学、历史学、地理学、人类学、博物学等多学科的知识。其间数易其稿，甘苦自知，但是为了能让国内学界看到这些珍贵资料，从而推动纳西学的研究，我想所付出的一切都是值得的。

首先要感谢我的导师喻遂生先生，他是我学术的领路人，自从2008年拜入门下，一直追随先生，先生为人高洁，学问精深，平时对我耳提面命，使我受益匪浅。

还要感谢云南大学出版社的段然女士和石可先生，没有他们的努力就没有这套书的出版。

我的爱人李真真女士，她不仅要照顾家庭，还协助我翻译了整部书稿，在这里对她的默默支持与付出表示感谢。

2020年8月18日于西南大学文化村2舍